'Wh_at _____ _____?' Alexei taunted, the most fiendish smile curling the corners of his beautiful mouth. 'Not enjoying this? It's no fun having to beg, is it? No fun having to crawl to someone you'd much rather die than even talk to.'

Once more that searing gaze raked over her, from the top of Ria's uncharacteristically controlled hair down to the neat, highly polished black shoes. It was a look that took her back ten years, forced her to remember how coldly he had regarded her before he had walked away and out of her life. For good, she had thought then.

'And I should know, angel—I've been there, remember? I've been exactly where you are now—begged, pleaded—and walked away with nothing. Tell me, what is the price of betrayal these days? Is it still thirty pieces of silver? Of course you could try asking…'

A THRONE
FOR THE TAKING

BY
KATE WALKER

First published in Great Britain 2013
by Mills & Boon, an imprint of Harlequin (UK) Limited.
Harlequin (UK) Limited, Eton House, 18-24 Paradise Road,
Richmond, Surrey TW9 1SR

© Kate Walker 2013

ISBN: 978 0 263 90015 6

Harlequin (UK) policy is to use papers that are natural, renewable and recyclable products and made from wood grown in sustainable forests. The logging and manufacturing process conform to the legal environmental regulations of the country of origin.

Printed and bound in Spain
by Blackprint CPI, Barcelona

Kate Walker was born in Nottinghamshire, but as she grew up in Yorkshire she has always felt that her roots are there. She met her husband at university, and originally worked as a children's librarian, but after the birth of her son she returned to her old childhood love of writing. When she's not working she divides her time between her family, their three cats, and her interests of embroidery, antiques, film and theatre—and, of course, reading.

You can visit Kate at www.kate-walker.com

Recent titles by the same author:

THE DEVIL AND MISS JONES
THE RETURN OF THE STRANGER
   (The Powerful and the Pure)
THE PROUD WIFE
THE GOOD GREEK WIFE?

**Did you know these are also available as eBooks?
Visit www.millsandboon.co.uk**

For the class of Fishghuard, February 2012.
Thanks for such a fun and inspiring weekend.

CHAPTER ONE

HE WAS COMING. The sound of footsteps in the corridor outside told her that. Brisk, heavy footsteps, the sound of expensive leather soles on the marble floor.

A big man, moving fast and impatiently towards the room where she had been told to wait for him. A room that was not as she had expected, but then nothing had been as she had expected since she had started out on this campaign, least of all this man she hadn't seen in so long. It had been more than ten years since she had spoken to him, but they would now be coming face to face in less than thirty seconds.

How was she going to handle this?

Ria adjusted her position in the smart leather chair, crossing one leg over the other then, rethinking, moving it back again so that her feet were neatly on the floor, placed precisely together in their elegant black courts, knees closed tight, her blue and green flowered dress stretched sleekly over them. Lifting her hand, she made to smooth back a non-existent wandering strand of dark auburn hair. Her style would be immaculate, she knew. She'd pulled her hair back tightly from her face so that there was nothing loose to get in a mess or distract her. Nothing to look frivolous or even carefree. That was not the image she'd aimed for.

She'd even fretted at the thought that her dress might be a little too casual and relaxed when she'd put it on, but the below knee length of the swirling skirt covered her almost as much as the tailored trousers she'd considered wearing, and the lightweight black linen jacket she'd pulled on over the top added a needed touch of formality that made her feel better.

The room she sat in was sleek and sophisticated with pale wood furniture. Far sleeker and much more luxurious than she had ever anticipated. One of the soft grey walls displayed a set of dramatic photographs, sharply framed. In black and white only, they were the sort of images that had made Alexei Sarova his reputation and his fortune. They were superb, stunning but— Ria frowned as she looked at them. They were bleak and somehow lonely. Photographs of landscapes, places, no people in them at all. He did sometimes photograph people—she knew that from the magazines she had read and the stunning images that had appeared in the articles—but none of those commissions were displayed here.

Outside the door, those determined, heavy footsteps slowed, then halted and she heard the murmur of voices through the thick wood, the deep, gravelly tones making it plain that the speaker was a man.

The man. The one she had come here to meet, to give him the message that might save her country from all-out civil war, and she had vowed that she was not leaving until she had done so. Even if the nerves in her stomach tied themselves into tight, painful knots at the thought and her restless fingers had started to beat an unsettled tattoo on the wooden arm of the chair.

'No!' Ria reproved herself aloud. 'Stop it! Now!'

She brought her nervous hand together with the other one, to clasp them both demurely in her lap, forcing herself to wait with every semblance of control and composure, even if the churning of her stomach told her that this was very far from the case. Too much rested on this meeting and she wasn't really sure that she could handle it.

Oh, this was ridiculous! Ria drew in a deep, ragged sigh as she put back her head and stared fixedly at the white-painted ceiling, fighting for control of her breathing. She should be well able to cope with this. She'd been trained practically from birth to meet strangers, talk with them, making polite social chit-chat at court events. It was what she could do as naturally as breathing while all the time keeping her head up high, her spine straight so that she looked as good as possible, with first her nanny's then her father's voice in her ear, telling her that the reputation of the Escalona family—an offshoot of the *royal* family—should be the first and foremost thing in her mind.

She could talk to presidents' wives about their trips round the glass-making factories, discuss the agricultural output of the vineyards, the farms. She could even, if she was allowed, converse intelligently on the vital role of exports, or the mining of eruminum, the new miracle mineral that had just been discovered in the Trilesian mountains. Not that she was often asked to do any such thing. Those important details were usually left to her grandfather or, until recently, to her second cousin Felix, the Crown Prince of Mecjoria.

But she had never before had to deal with any mission that meant so much in the way of freedom, both to her country and herself. That restless hand threatened to escape her careful control and start its nervous tattoo all over again at just the thought.

'Do it, then.'

The voice from the corridor sounded sharp and clear

this time, bringing her head up in a rush as she straightened once again in her chair. *Shoulders back, head up...*
She could almost hear her father's strict commands as
she drew in a long, deep breath to calm herself as she had
done on so many other previous occasions.

But this wasn't one of those events. This man wasn't
exactly a stranger and polite chit-chat was the last thing
she expected to be exchanging with him.

The handle turned as someone grasped it from the
other side. Ria tensed, shifted in her chair, half-looked
over her shoulder then rethought and turned back again.
She didn't want him to think that she was nervous. She
had to appear calm, collected, in command of the situation.

Command. The word rang hollowly inside her head.
Once she had only to command something and it would be
hers. In just a few short months her life had been turned
upside down, and in ways that made her status in society
the least of her concerns, so that now nothing was as it
had ever been before, and the future loomed ahead, dark
and dangerous.

But perhaps if she could manage this meeting with
some degree of success she could claw back something
from the disaster that had overtaken her country—and
family. She could hope to put right the wrongs of the past
and, on a personal level, save her mother's happiness, her
sanity, possibly. And for her father... No, she couldn't go
there, not yet. Thoughts of her father would weaken her,
drain away the strength she needed to see this through.

'I'll expect a report on my desk by the end of the day.'

The door was opening, swinging wide. The man she
had come to see was here, and she had no more time to
think.

As he entered the doorway her heart jerked sharply

under her ribcage, taking her breath with it. For the first time she felt suddenly lost, vulnerable without the ever-present security man at her back. All her life he had been there, just waiting and watching in case he was needed. And she had come to rely on him to deal with any awkward situation.

The *once* ever-present security man, she reminded herself. The protection that was no longer there, no longer part of her life or her status here or in her homeland of Mecjoria. She was no longer entitled to such protection. It was the first thing that had been stripped from her and the rest of her family in the upheaval that had followed Felix's unexpected death, and the shocking discovery of her father's scheming in the past. After that, things had changed so fast that she had never had time even to think about the possible repercussions of the changes and to consider them now, with the possible consequences for her own future, made her stomach twist painfully.

'No delays… Good afternoon.'

The abrupt change of subject caught Ria on the hop. She hadn't quite realised that his companion had been dismissed and that he was now in the room, long strides covering the ground so fast that he was halfway towards her before she realised it.

'Good afternoon.'

It was stronger, harsher, much more pointed, and she almost felt as if the words were hitting her in the small of her back. She should turn round, she knew. She needed to face him. But the enormity of the reason why she was here, and the thought of his reaction when she did, made it difficult to move.

'Miss…'

The warning in his tone now kicked her into action, fast. Her head jerked round, the suddenness and abruptness of the movement jolting her up and out of her seat so that she came to her feet even as she swung round to face him. And was glad that she had done so when she saw the size and the strength of his powerful form. She had seen pictures of him in the papers, knew that he was tall, dark and devastating, but in the 3D reality of living, breathing golden-toned flesh, deep ebony eyes and crisp black hair, he was so much more than she had ever imagined. His steel-grey suit hugged his impressive form lovingly, the broad, straight shoulders needing no extra padding to enhance them. A crisp white shirt, silver and black tie, turned him into the sleek, sophisticated businessman who was light-years away from the Alexei she remembered, the wiry boy with the unkempt mane of hair who had once been her friend buried under the expensive tailoring. Snatching in a deep, shocked breath, she could inhale the tang of some citrus soap or shampoo, the scent of clean male skin.

'Good afternoon,' she managed and was relieved to hear that her control over her voice was as strong as she could have wanted. Perhaps it made it sound a little too tight, too stiff, but that was surely better than letting the tremor she knew was just at the bottom of her thoughts actually affect her tongue. 'Alexei Sarova, I assume.'

He had been moving towards her but her response had a shocking effect on him.

'You!' he said, the single word thick and dark with hostility

He stopped dead, then swung round back towards the door, grabbing at the handle to stop it slotting into the frame. This was worse than she had expected. She had known that she would have to work hard to get him to give her any sort of a hearing, but she hadn't expected this total rejection.

'Oh—please,' Ria managed. 'Please don't walk out.'

That brought his head round, the black, glittering eyes looking straight into hers, not a flicker of emotion in their polished depths.

'Walk out?'

He shook his dark head and there was actually the faintest hint of a smile on those beautifully sensual lips. But a shiver ran down Ria's spine as she saw the way that that smile was not reflected in his eyes at all. They remained as cold and emotionless as black glass.

'I'm not walking out. You are.'

It was far worse than she had expected. She hadn't really believed that he would recognise her that fast and that easily. Ten years was a long time and they had been little more than children when they had last had any close contact. She knew she was no longer the chubby, awkward girl he had once known. She was inches taller, slimmer, and her hair had darkened so that it was now a rich auburn instead of the nondescript brown of her childhood. So she had expected to have to explain herself to him. But she had thought that he would wait to hear that explanation, had hoped, at least, that he would want to know just why she was here.

'No...' She shook her head. 'No, I'm not.'

Dark eyes flashed in sudden anger and she barely controlled her instinctive shrinking away with an effort. Royal duchesses didn't shrink. Not even ex-royal duchesses.

'No?'

How did he manage to put such cynicism, such hostility into one word?

'I should point out to you that I own this building. I am the one who says who can stay and who should go. And you are going.'

'Don't you want to know why I'm here?'

If she had thrown something into the face of a marble statue, it couldn't have had less effect. Perhaps his stunning features became a little more unyielding, those brilliant eyes even colder, but it was hard to say for sure.

'Not really. In fact, not at all. What I want is you out of here and not coming back.'

No, what he really wanted was for her never to have come here at all, Alexei told himself, coming to a halt in the middle of his office, restless as a caged tiger that had reached the metal bars that held him imprisoned. But the truth was that it wasn't anything physical that kept him captive. It was the memories of the past that now reached out to ensnare him, fastening shackles around his ankles to keep him from getting away.

He had never expected to see her or anyone from Mecjoria ever again. He thought he had moved on; he'd turned his life around, made a new existence for himself and his mother. It had taken years, sadly too many to give his mother the life she deserved as she'd aged, but he'd got there. And now he was wealthier than he'd ever been as a…as a prince, his mind finished for him, even though it was the last thing he wanted. He had no wish to remember anything about his connection to the Mecjorian royal family—or the country itself. He had severed all links with the place—had them severed for him—and he was determined that was the way it was going to stay. He would never have looked back at all if it hadn't been for the sudden and shockingly unexpected appearance of Ria here in this room.

He waited a moment and then pulled the door open again. 'Or do I have to call security?'

Ria's eyebrows rose sharply until they disappeared under her fringe as she turned a cool, green gaze on him.

Suddenly she had become the Grand Duchess she was right before his eyes and he loathed the way that made him feel.

'You'd resort to the heavy gang? That wouldn't look good in the gossip columns. "International playboy needs help to deal with one small female intruder".'

'Small? I would hardly call you small,' he drawled coolly. 'You must have grown—what?—six inches since I saw you last?'

She had grown in other ways too, he acknowledged, admitting to himself the instant and very basic male re-action that had taken him by storm in the first moments he had seen her. Before he had realised just who she was.

He hadn't seen such a stunning woman in years—in his life. Everything that was male in him had responded to the sight of her tall, slender figure, the burnished hair, porcelain skin, long, long legs...

And then he had realised that it was Ria. She had grown up, grown taller, slimmed down. Her face had de-veloped planes and angles where there had once been just firm, round, apple-rosy cheeks. He had loved those cheeks, he admitted to himself. They had been soft and curved, so smooth, that he had loved to pinch them softly, pretending he was teasing but knowing that what he ac-tually wanted was to feel the satin of her skin, stroke it with his fingertips. These days, Ria had cheekbones that looked as if they would slice open any stroking finger, and the rosy cheeks were carefully toned down with skil-ful make-up. The slant of those cheekbones emphasised the jade green of her eyes, and the soft pink curve of her mouth, but it was obvious that any softness in her ap-pearance was turned into a lie by the way she behaved.

In a series of pulsing jolts, like the effect of an electric current pounding into him, he had known stunning attraction and the rush of desire that heated his entire body, the shock of recognition, of disbelief, of frank confusion as to just why she should be here at all. And then, just as the memory of how they had once been together had slid into his mind, she had destroyed it totally, shattering the memory as effectively as if she had taken a heavy metal hammer to it.

That had been when she had looked down her aristocratic nose at him, her expression obviously meant to make him feel less than the dirt beneath her neatly-shod feet. And Ria, who had once been his friend and confidant, Ria who he had just recognised as a sweet girl who had grown into a stunningly sensual woman, had become once more the Ria who together with her father and her family had stuck a knife in his back, ruined his mother's life and cast them out into the wilderness.

'And, as to the gossip columns, I'm sure they'd be much more interested in the scoop of seeing the Grand Duchess Honoria Maria Escalona being forcibly ejected from the offices of Sarova International—and I can just imagine some of the stories they might come up with to explain your expulsion.'

'Not so much of a Grand Duchess any more,' Ria admitted without thinking. 'Not so much of a duchess of any sort.'

'What?'

That brought him up sharp. Just for a second or two blank confusion clouded those amazing eyes and he tilted his head slightly to one side as a puzzled frown drew his brows together. The small, revealing moment caught on something in her heart and twisted painfully.

He had always done that when she had known him before. When they had been children together—well, she had been the child and he a lordly six years older. If he was confused or uncertain that frown had creased the space between his dark brows and his head would angle to the side…

'Lexei—please.' The name slipped from her before she could think. The familiar, affectionate name that she had once been able to use.

But she'd made a fatal mistake. She knew that as soon as the words had left her mouth and his reaction left her in no doubt at all that the one slip of her lips, in the hope of getting a tiny bit closer to him, had had the opposite effect.

His long body stiffened in rejection, that slight tilt of his head turned into a stiff-necked gesture of antagonism as his chin came up, angry, rejecting. His eyes flashed and his mouth tightened, pulling the muscles in his jaw into an uncompromising line.

'No,' he said, hard and rough. 'No. I will not listen to a word you say. Why should I when you and yours turned your back on my mother—on me—and left us to exile and disgrace? My mother *died* in that disgrace. It's not as if anything you have to say is a matter of life or death.'

'Oh, but…'

It could be… The words died on her tongue, burned away in the flare of fury he turned on her, seeming to scorch her skin so painfully.

This was not how she had planned it, but it was obvious that he wasn't prepared to let her lead up to things with a carefully prepared conversation. Hastily she grabbed at her handbag, snapping it open with hands made clumsy by nerves.

'This is for you…' she managed, holding out the sheet of paper she had folded so carefully at the start of her journey. The document she had checked was still there at least once every few minutes on her way here.

His eyes dropped to what she held, expression freezing

into marble stillness as he took in the crest at the head of the sheet of paper, the seal that marked it out for the important document it was.

'You know that your mother needed proof of the legality of her marriage,' she tried and got the briefest, most curt nod possible as his only response, his gaze still fixed on the document she held out.

It was like talking to a statue, he was so stiff, so unmoving, and she found that her tongue was stumbling over itself as she tried to get the words out. If only someone else could have been given this vital duty to carry out. But she had volunteered herself in spite of the fact that the ministers had viewed her with suspicion. A suspicion that was natural, after the way her father had behaved. But they didn't know the half of it. She had only just discovered the truth for herself and hadn't dared to reveal any of it to anyone else. Luckily, the ministers had been convinced that she was the most likely to be successful. Alexei would listen to her, they had said. And besides, with success meaning so much to her personally, to her family, she would be the strongest advocate at this time.

It was a strong irony that all the discipline, the training her father had imposed on her for his own ends, was now to be put to use to try to thwart those ends if she possibly could.

'And for that she needed evidence of the fact that the old king had given his permission for your father—as a member of the royal family—to marry all those years ago, when they first met.'

Why was she repeating all this? He knew every detail as much as she did. After all, it had been his life that had been blasted apart by the scandal that had resulted when it had seemed that his parents' marriage had been declared illegal. Alexei's father and mother had been separated, with him living with his mother in England until he was sixteen, and the fact that her husband was ill—dying of cancer—had brought his mother to Mecjoria in hope of a reconciliation. They hadn't had long and, during what time they had had, Alexei had found the old-fashioned and snobbish aristocracy difficult to deal with, particularly when they had regarded him and his mother as nothing more than commoners who didn't belong at court. His rebellious behaviour had created disapproval, brought him under the disapproving gaze of so many. And too soon, with his father dead, there had been no one to support his mother, or her son, when court conspiracy—a conspiracy Ria had just discovered to her horror of which her father had been an important part—had had her expelled, exiled from the country, taking her son with her.

Then there was her own part in all of it—her own guilty conscience, Ria acknowledged. That was an important part of why she had volunteered to come here today, to bring the news of the discovery of the document…and the rest.

'This is the evidence.'

At last he moved, reached out a hand and took the paper from her. But to her shock he simply glanced swiftly over the text then tossed it aside, dropping it on to his desk without a second glance.

'So?'

The single word seemed to strip all the moisture from her mouth, making her voice cracked and raw as she tried to answer him.

'Don't you see…?' Silly question. Of course he saw, he just wasn't reacting at all as she had expected, as she had been led to believe he would inevitably react. 'This is what you needed back then, this changes everything.

It means that your parents were legally married even in Mecjoria. It makes you legitimate.'

'And that makes me fit to have you come and visit me? Speak to me after all these years?'

The bitterness in his tone made her flinch. Even more so because she knew she deserved it. She'd flung that illegitimacy—that supposed illegitimacy—at him when he had asked for her help. She hadn't known the truth then, but she knew now that she'd done it partly out of hurt and anger too. Hurt and anger that he had turned away from her to become involved in a romantic entanglement with another girl.

A woman, Ria. She could hear his voice through the years. *She's a woman.*

And the implication was that *she* was still a child. Hurt and feeling rejected, she had been the perfect target for her father's story—what she knew now were her father's lies.

'It's not that…' Struggling with her memories, she had to force the words out. 'It's what's *right.*'

She knew how much he'd loathed the label 'bastard'. But more so how he'd hated the way that his mother had been treated because her marriage hadn't been considered legal. So much so that Ria had believed—hoped— that the news she had brought would change everything. She couldn't have been more wrong.

'Right?' he questioned cynically. 'From where I stand it's too little too late. The truth can't help my mother now. And personally I couldn't give a damn what they think of me in Mecjoria any more. But thank you for bringing it to me.'

His tone took the words to a meaning at the far opposite of genuine thankfulness.

There was much more to it than this. The proof of his legitimacy came with so many repercussions, but she had never expected this reaction. Or, rather, this lack of reaction.

'I'm sorry for the way I behaved…' she began, trying a different tack. One that earned her nothing but a cold stare.

'It was ten years ago.' He shrugged powerful shoulders in dismissal of her stumbling apology. 'A lot of water has passed under a lot of bridges since then. And none of it matters any more. I have made my own life and I want nothing more to do with a country that thought my mother and I were not good enough to live there.'

'But…'

There were so many details, so many facts, buzzing inside Ria's head but she didn't dare to let any of them out. Not yet. There was too much riding on them and this man was not prepared to listen to a word she said. If she put one foot wrong he would reject her—and her mission— completely. And she would never get a second chance.

'So now I'd appreciate it if you'd leave. Or I will call security and have you thrown out, and to hell with the paparazzi or the gossip columnists. In fact, perhaps it would be better that way. They could have a field day with what I could tell them.'

Was it a real or an empty threat? And did she dare take the risk of finding out? Not with things the way they were back home, with the country in turmoil, hopes for security and peace depending on her. On a personal level, she feared her mother would break down completely if anything more happened, and she would be back under her father's control herself if she failed. One whiff of scandal in the papers could be so terribly damaging that she shivered just to think of it. The only way she could achieve everything she'd set out to do was to get Alexei on her side— but that was beginning to look increasingly impossible.

'Honoria,' Alexei said dangerously and she didn't need the warning in his tone to have her looking nervously towards the door he still held wide open. The simple fact that he had used her full name was enough on its own. 'Duchess,' he added with a coldly mocking bow.

But she couldn't make her feet move. She couldn't leave. Not with so much unsaid.

CHAPTER TWO

It's not as if it's a matter of life or death, Alexei had declared, the scorn in his voice lashing at her cruelly. But it would be if the situation in Mecjoria wasn't resolved soon; if Ivan took over. The late King Felix might have been petty and mean but he was as nothing when compared to the tyrant who might inherit the throne from him. With a violent effort, Ria controlled the shiver of reaction that threatened her composure.

She hadn't seen Alexei for ten years, but she had had close contact with his distant cousin Ivan in that time. And hadn't enjoyed a moment of it. She'd watched Ivan grow from the sort of small boy who pulled wings off butterflies and kicked cats into a man whose volatile, mean-minded temper was usually only barely under control. He was aggressive, greedy, dangerous for the country—and now, she had learned to her horror, a danger to her personally as a result of her father's machinations. And the only man between them and that possibility was Alexei.

But she knew how much she was asking of him. Especially now, when she knew how he still felt about Mecjoria.

'Please listen!'

But his face was armoured against her, his eyes hooded, and she felt that every look she turned on him, every word she spoke, simply bounced off his thick skin like a pebble off an elephant's hide.

'Please?' he echoed sardonically, his mouth twisting on the word as he turned it into a cruelly derisory echoing of her tone. 'I didn't even realise that you knew that word. Please *what*, Sweetheart?'

'You don't want to know.'

Bleak honesty made her admit it. She could read it in his face, in the cruel opacity of those coal-black eyes. There wasn't the faintest sign of softening in his expression or any of the lines around his nose and mouth. How could he take a gentle word like *'sweetheart'* and turn it into something hateful and vile with just his tone?

'Oh, but I do,' Alexei drawled, folding his arms across his broad chest and lounging back against the wall, one foot hooked round the base of the door so as to keep it open and so making it plain that he was still waiting— expecting her to leave. 'I'd love to know just what you've come looking for.'

'Really?'

Unexpected hope kicked hard in her heart. Had she got this all wrong, read him completely the wrong way round?

'Really,' he echoed sardonically. 'It's fascinating to see the tables turned. Remember how I once asked you for just one thing?'

He'd asked her to help him, and his mother. Asked her to talk to her father, plead with him to at least let them have something to live on, some part of his father's vast fortune that the state had confiscated, leaving Alexei and his mother penniless as well as homeless. And not knowing the truth, not understanding the machinations of the plotters, or how sick his mother actually was, she had seen him as a threat and sided with her father.

'I made a mistake...' she managed. She'd known that

her father was ruthless, ambitious, but she had never really believed that he would lie through his teeth, that he would manipulate an innocent woman and her son.

For the good of the country, Honoria, he had said. And, seeing the outrage Alexei's wayward behaviour had created, she had believed him. Because she had trusted her father. Trusted him and believed in the values of upright behaviour, of loyalty to the crown that he'd insisted on. So she'd believed him when he'd told her how the scandal of Alexei's mother's 'affair' with one of the younger royal sons was creating problems of state. It was only now, years later, that she'd discovered how much further his deception had gone, and how it had involved her.

'What is it, *darling?*' Alexei taunted. 'Not enjoying this?'

She saw the gleam of cruel amusement in his eyes, the fiendish smile curling the corners of the beautiful mouth. Each of them spoke of cold contempt, but together they spelled a callous triumph at the thought of getting her exactly where he wanted her. She knew now that this man would delight in rejecting anything she said, if only to have his revenge on the family that he saw as the ringleaders of his downfall. And who could blame him?

But would he do the same for his country?

'It's no fun having to beg, is it? No fun having to crawl to someone you'd much rather die than even talk to.'

Once more that searing gaze raked over her from the top of her uncharacteristically controlled hair down to the neat, highly polished black shoes. It was a look that took her back ten years, forced her to remember how coldly he had regarded her before he had walked away and out of her life. For good, she had thought then.

'And I should know, angel—I've been there, remember? I've been exactly where you are now—begged, pleaded—and walked away with nothing.'

He might look indolently relaxed and at his ease as he lounged back against the wall, still with those strong arms crossed over the width of his chest, but in reality his position was the taut, expectant posture of a wily, knowing hunter, a predator that was poised, watching and waiting. He only needed his prey—her—to make one move and then he would pounce, hard and fast.

But still she had to try.

'You are wanted back in Mecjoria,' she blurted out in an uneven rush.

She could tell his response even before he opened his mouth. The way that long straight spine stiffened, the tightening of the beautiful lips, the way a muscle in his jaw jerked just once.

'You couldn't have said anything less likely to make me want to know more,' he drawled, dark and slow. 'But you could try to persuade me...'

She could try, but it would have no effect, his tone, his stony expression told her. And she didn't like the thought of just what sort of 'persuasion' could be in his mind. She wasn't prepared to give him that satisfaction.

Calling on every ounce of strength she possessed, stiffening her back, straightening her shoulders, she managed to lift her head high, force her green eyes to meet those icy black ones head-on.

'No thank you,' she managed, her tone pure ice.

Her father would have been proud of her for this at least. She was the Grand Duchess Honoria Maria at her very best. The only daughter of the Chancellor, faced by a troublesome member of the public. The trouble was that after all she had learned about her father's schemes, the way that he had seen her as a way to further his own power, she didn't want to be that woman any more. She had actually hoped that by coming here today she could free herself from the toxic inheritance that came with that title.

'You might get off on that sort of thing, but it certainly does nothing for me.'

If she had hoped that he would look at least a little crestfallen, a touch deflated, then she was doomed to disappointment. There might have been a tiny acknowledgement of her response in his eyes, a gleam that could have been a touch of admiration—or a hint of dark satisfaction from a man who had known all along just how she would respond.

She'd dug herself a hole without him needing to push her into it. But, for now, was discretion the better part of valour? She could let Alexei think that he had won this round at least but it was only one battle, not the whole war. There was too much at stake for that.

'Thank you for your time.'

She couldn't so much as turn a glance in his direction, even though she caught another wave of that citrus scent as he came closer, with the undertones of clean male skin that almost destroyed her hard-won courage. But even as she fought with her reactions he fired another comment at her. One that tightened a slackening resolve, and reminded her just how much the boy she had once known had changed.

'I wish that I could say it had been a pleasure,' he drawled cynically. 'But we both know that that would be a lie.'

'We certainly do,' Ria managed from between lips that felt as if they had turned to wood, they were so stiff and tight.

'So now you'll leave. Give my regards to your father,' Alexei tossed after her.

He couldn't have said anything that was more guaranteed to force her to stay. A battle, not the war, she reminded herself. She wasn't going to let this be the last of it. She couldn't.

He was going to let her go, Alexei told himself. In fact he would be glad to do so even if the thundering response that she had so unexpectedly woken in his body demanded otherwise. He wanted her to walk away, to take with her the remembrance of the family he had hoped to find, a life he had once tried to live, a girl he had once cared for.

'Lexei... Please...'

The echo of her voice, soft and shaken—or so he would have sworn—swirled in his thoughts in spite of his determination to clamp down on the memory, to refuse to let it take root there. Violently he shook his head to try and drive away the sound but it seemed to cling like dark smoke around his thoughts, bringing with it too many memories that he had thought he'd driven far away.

At first she had knocked him mentally off-balance with the news she had brought. The news he had been waiting to hear for so long—half a lifetime, it seemed. The document she had held out to him now lay on his desk, giving him the legitimacy, the position in Mecjoria he had wanted—that he had thought he wanted—but he didn't even spare it a second glance. It was too late. Far, far too late. His mother, to whom this had mattered so much, was dead, and he no longer gave a damn.

But something tugging at the back of his thoughts, an itch of something uncomfortable and unexpected, told him that that wasn't the real truth. There was more to this than just the delivery of that document.

'Not so much of Grand Duchess any more,' Ria had

said to him unexpectedly. *'Not so much of a duchess of any sort.'*

And that was when it struck him. There was something missing. *Someone* missing. Someone he should have noticed was not there from the first moment in the room but he had been so knocked off-balance that he hadn't registered anything beyond the fact that *Ria* was there in his office, waiting for him.

Where was the dark-suited bodyguard? The man who had the knack of blending into the background when necessary but who was alert and ready to move forward at any moment if their patron appeared to be in any difficulty?

There was no one with her now. There had been no one when he had arrived in this room to find her waiting for him. And there should have been.

What the hell was going on?

He couldn't be unaware of the present political situation in Mecjoria. There had been so many reports of marches on the streets, of protest meetings in the square of the capital. Ria's father, the Grand Duke Escalona, High Chancellor of the country, had been seen making impassioned speeches, ardent broadcasts, calling for calm—ordering the people to stay indoors, keep off the streets. But that had been before first the King and then the new heir to the throne had died so unexpectedly. Before the whole question of the succession had come under scrutiny with meetings and conferences and legal debates to call into question just what would happen next. He had paid it as little attention as it deserved in his own mind, but it had been impossible to ignore some of the headlines—like the ones that declared the country was on the brink of revolution.

It was his father's country after all. The place he should have called his home if he hadn't been forced out before he came to settle in any way. Without ever having a chance to get to know the father who had been missing from his life.

'Lexei... Please...'

He would have been all right if she hadn't used that name. If she hadn't—deliberately he was sure—turned on him the once warm, affectionate name she had used back in the gentler, more innocent days when he had thought that they were friends. And so whirled him back into memories of a past he'd wanted to forget.

'All right, I'm intrigued.' And that was nothing less than the truth. 'You clearly have something more to say. So—you have ten minutes. Ten minutes in which to tell me the truth about why you're here. What had you appearing in my office unannounced, declaring you were no longer a grand duchess. Is that the truth?'

It seemed it had to be—or at least that something in what he had said had really got to her. She had reacted to his words as if she had been stung violently. Her head had gone back, her green eyes widening in reaction at something. Her soft rose-tinted mouth had opened slightly on a gasp of shock.

A shock that ricocheted through his own frame as a hard kick of some totally primitive sexual hunger hit home low down in his body. Those widened eyes looked stunning and dark against the translucent delicacy of her skin, and that mouth was pure temptation in its half-open state.

His little friend Ria had grown up into a beautiful woman and that unthinkingly primitive reaction to the fact jolted him out of any hope of seeing her just as the girl she had once been. Suddenly he was unable to look at her in any way other than as a man looks at a woman he desires. His own mouth hungered to take those softly parted lips, to taste her, feel her yield to him, surrendering, opening... His heart thudded hard and deep in his chest, making him need to catch his breath as his body tightened in pagan hunger.

'You don't believe me?' she questioned and the uncharacteristic hesitation on the word twisted something deep inside him, something he no longer thought existed. Something that it seemed that only this woman could drag up from deep inside him. A woman who had once been the only friend he thought he had and who now had been reincarnated as a woman who heated his blood and turned him on more than he could recall anyone doing in the past months—the past years.

It was like coming awake again after being dead to his senses for years—and it hurt.

'It's not that I don't believe you.'

The fight he was having to control the sensual impulses of his body showed in his voice and he saw the worried, apprehensive look she shot him sideways from under the long, lush lashes. She clearly didn't know which way to take him, a thought that sent a heated rush of satisfaction through his blood. He wanted her off-balance, on edge. That way she might let slip more than her carefully cultivated, court training would allow her.

'Merely that I see no reason why you or any member of your family would renounce the royal title that has meant so much to you.'

'We didn't renounce it. It was renounced for us.'

A frown snapped Alexei's black brows together sharply as he focussed even more intently on her face, trying to read what was there.

'And just what does that mean? I've heard nothing of this.'

How had he missed such an important event? The people he had employed to watch what was happening in

Mecjoria should have been aware of it. They should have investigated and reported back to him.

'It's been kept very quiet—at the moment my father is officially "resting" to recover from illness.'

'When the reality is?'

'That he's under arrest.'

Her voice caught on the word, a soft little hiccup that did disturbing things to the tension at his groin, tightening it a notch or two uncomfortably.

'And is now in the state prison.'

That was the last thing he'd expected and it shocked some of the desire from him, making his head swim slightly at the rush of blood from one part of his body to his head.

'On what charge?' he demanded sharply.

'No charge.' She shook her head, sending her dark hair flying. 'Not as yet—that—that all depends on how things work out.'

'So what the hell did he do wrong?' Gregor had always seemed such a canny player. Someone who knew how best to feather his own nest. So had he got too greedy, made some mistake?

'He—chose the wrong side in the recent inheritance battle. For the throne.'

So that was what was behind this. Alexei might never want to set foot in Mecjoria ever again, but he couldn't be unaware—no one could be unaware—of the struggle that had gone on over the inheritance of the throne once old King Leopold had died. First Leopold's son Marcus had inherited, but only briefly. A savage heart attack had killed him barely months into his reign. Because he had died childless, his nephew Felix should have inherited the crown, but his wild way of life had been his undoing, so that he had died in a high-speed car crash before he had even ascended to the throne. Now there were several factions warring over just who was the legal heir to follow Felix.

'And then when Felix died... My father is currently seen as an enemy—as a threat to the throne.'

She wasn't telling the full truth, Alexei realised. There was something she was holding back, he was sure of it. Something that clouded those amazing eyes, tightened the muscles around her delicate jawline, pulling the pretty mouth tight, though there was no mistaking the quiver of those softly sensual lips.

Lips that he wished to hell he could taste, feel that trembling softness under his own mouth, plunder the moist interior...

'It will all work out in the end.'

Once again his own burning inner feelings made the words sound abrupt, dismissive, and he saw her blink slowly, withdrawing from him. Her head came up, that smooth chin lifting in defiance as she met his stare face-on.

'You can promise that, can you?' Ria asked, her tone appallingly cynical.

And where her unexpected weakness hadn't beaten him now, shockingly, her boldness did. There was a new spark in her eyes, fresh colour in her cheeks. She was once more the proud Grand Duchess Honoria and not the strangely defeated girl who had reached out to something he had thought was long dead inside him. *This* Ria was a challenge; a challenge he welcomed. The sound of his blood was like a roar inside his head, the heated race of his pulse burning along every vein. He had never wanted a woman so much as he wanted her now, and the need was like an ache in every nerve.

'How would you know? You were the one who turned

your back on Mecjoria—haven't even been back once in ten years.'

'Not turned my back,' Alexei growled. 'We weren't given a chance to stay. In fact it was made plain that we were not wanted.'

And who had been behind that? Her father—the very same man who was now, according to her story, locked in a prison cell. Did she expect him to feel sorry for him? To give a damn what might happen to the monster who hadn't even waited to allow him and his mother time to mourn their loss, or even to attend the state funeral, before he had had them escorted to the airport and put on the first plane out of the country?

First making sure that every penny of his father's fortune, every jewel, every tiny personal inheritance, had been taken from them, leaving them with little but the clothes they stood up in, not even the most basic allowance to see them into their new life in exile. Worst of all, Gregor had taken their name from them. The name his mother had been entitled to, and with it her honour, the legality of her marriage into the royal house of Mecjoria. He must have done it deliberately, hiding away the document that showed the old king's permission. The document that Ria had been commissioned to bring here so unexpectedly—because it now suited her father. Was it any wonder that he loathed the man—that he would do anything to bring him down?

But it seemed that Gregor had managed that all on his own.

'And I don't have to be in the country to know what is going on.'

'The papers don't report everything. And certainly not always accurately.'

Something new had clouded those clear eyes and

turned her expression into an intriguing mixture of defiance and uncertainty. There was just the tiniest sheen of moisture under one eye, where a trace of an unexpected tear had escaped the determined control she had been trying to impose on it and slipped out on to her lashes.

Unable to resist the impulse, he reached out and touched her face, letting his fingers rest lightly on the fine skin along the high, slanting cheekbone, wiping away that touch of moisture. The warmth and softness of the contact made his nerves burn, sending stinging arrows of response down into his body. He wanted so much more and yet he wanted to keep things just as they were—for now. It was a struggle not to do more, not to curve his hand around her cheek, cup that defiant little chin against his palm, lift her face towards his so that he could capture her mouth…

And that would ruin things completely. She would react like a scalded cat, he had no doubt. All that silent defiance would return in full force, and she'd swing away from him, repulsing the gesture with a rough shake of her head. She was still too tense, too on edge. But like any nervous cat, with a few moments' careful attention—perhaps a soothing stroke or two—she would soon settle down.

So for now it was enough to watch the storm of emotions that swept over her face. The response that turned those citrine eyes smoky, that darkened and deepened the black of her pupils, making them spread like the flow of ink until they covered almost all of her irises. The way that her mouth opened again to show the tips of small white teeth was a temptation that kicked at his libido, making it hungrier than ever. The clamour in his body urged him to act, to make his move now, when she was at her weakest, but for a little while at least he was enjoying imposing restraint on himself, letting the sensual hunger build—anticipating what might come later—and watching the effect his behaviour had on her.

'So tell me the rest.'

She didn't know if she could go through with this. Ria struggled to find some of the certainty, the conviction of doing the right thing, that had buoyed her up on her journey here, held her in the room in spite of the frantic thudding of her heart. So much depended on what she said now and the possible repercussions of her failure, personal and political, were almost impossible to imagine. The image of her mother, too pale, far too thin, drifting through life like a wraith, with no appetite, no interest in anything slid into her mind. Her days were haunted by fears, her nights plagued by terrifying nightmares.

Her father was the cause of those nightmares. Since the night that the state police had come to arrest him, taking him away in handcuffs, they had never seen him for a moment. But they knew where he was. The state prison doors had slammed closed on him and, unless Ria could find some way of helping him, then behind those locked doors was where he was going to stay. She had wanted to help him—wanted to return him to her mother—and it had been because she had been looking for some way to do that that she had found the hidden documents, the ones that proved Alexei's legitimacy and the others that had revealed the whole truth about what had been going on.

The full, appalling truth.

CHAPTER THREE

IT WAS WHAT she had come here for, Ria reminded herself. To tell him the story that had not yet leaked into the papers. The full details of the archaic inheritance laws that had come into play in the country since the unexpected death of the man they had believed to be the heir to the throne. But that would also mean telling him how those laws involved him, and his reaction just a moment before had made it plain that he harboured no warmth towards the country that had once been his home.

But when he had touched her—the way he still touched her—just that one tiny contact seemed to have broken through the careful, deliberate barriers she had built around herself. It was so long since she had felt that someone sympathised; that someone might be on her side. And the fact that it was someone as strong and forceful—and devastating—as this particular man, the man who had once been a special friend to her, stripped away several much-needed protective layers of skin, leaving her raw and disturbingly vulnerable.

He was so close she couldn't actually judge his expression without lifting her head, tilting it back just a little. And that movement brought her eyes up to clash with his. Suddenly even breathing naturally was impossible as their

gazes locked, the darkness and intensity of his stare closing her throat in the space of a single uneven heartbeat.

In that moment everything that had happened in the
past months rushed up to swamp her mind, taking with
it any hope of rational thought. Except that right now she
needed him. Needed the friend he had once been. So much
about him might have changed: that hard-boned face had
thinned, toughened into that of a stunningly mature male
in his sexual prime; those eyes might now be five inches
above hers where once they had been so much closer to
her own... But they were still the eyes of the friend she
had known. Still the eyes of the one person she had felt
she could confide in and get a sympathetic hearing.

They were the eyes she had once let herself dream of
seeing warm with more than just the easy light of friendship. And the memory of how in the past she had fallen
asleep and into dreams of them being so much more than
friends twisted in her heart with the bitterness of loss.

'Tell me everything.'

'You don't really want that,' she flung at him, gulping
in air so that she could loosen her throat.

'No? Try me.'

Challenge blended with something else in his tone.
And it was that something else that made her heart jerk,
her breath catch.

Was it possible that he really did want to know? That
he might help her? Memories of their past friendship surfaced once again, tugging at her feelings. She was so
lonely, so dragged down by it all, so tired of coping with
everything on her own. So wretched at the thought of
what the future might bring. And here was this man who
had once been the boy she adored, the friend who had let
her offload her troubles on to his shoulders—shoulders

that even then had seemed broad enough to take on the world. They were so much broader, so much stronger now.

Tell me everything, he'd said, and as he spoke the hand that rested against her face moved slightly, the pressure of his fingers softening, his palm curving so that it lay over her cheek, warm and hard and yet gentle all at the same time.

'*The truth,* Ria,' he said and the sound of her name on his lips was her weakness, her undoing.

Unable to stop herself, she turned her face into his hold, inhaling the scent of his skin, pursing her lips to press a small, soft kiss against the warmth of his palm.

Instantly everything changed. Her heart seemed to stop, her breathing stilled. The clean, musky aroma of his body was all around her, the taste of his flesh tangy on her tongue. It was like taking a sip of a fine, smoky brandy, one that intoxicated in a moment, sending fizzing bubbles of electricity along every nerve.

She wanted more. Needed to deepen the contact. Needed it like never before.

The boy who had been her friend had never made her feel like this; never made her pulse race so fast and heavy, her head spin so wildly. In all her adolescent dreams she had never known this feeling of awareness, of hunger. A pulsing, heated adult hunger that grew and sharpened as he moved his hold on her, taking her chin and lifting it so that their eyes clashed and scorched. Something blazed in these black depths, creating a golden glow that had more heat than an inferno and yet was almost—*almost*—under control.

'Ria…' he said again, his tone very different this time, his voice roughening at the edges. He had moved closer somehow, without her noticing, and the warmth of his breath on her skin as he spoke her name sent heated shivers running down her spine, making her toes curl inside her neat, polished shoes.

'Alex…'

But speaking had been a mistake. It made her mouth move against his skin, brought that powerfully sensual taste onto her tongue once again, so that she swallowed convulsively, taking the essence of him into herself in an echo of a much more intimate blending. Immediately it was as if a lighted match had been set to desert-dry brush-wood. As if the tiny flicker that had been smouldering deep inside from the moment that she had come face to face with him again in his office had suddenly burst into wild and uncontrollable flame, the force of it moving her forward sharply, close up against him.

She heard his breath hiss in between his teeth in an uncontrolled response that both shocked and thrilled her. The thought that he felt as she did, so much that he was unable to hide his response from her, made her head spin. She could hardly believe that it could be possible, but there was no denying the evidence of the way that his grip tightened on her chin, hard fingers digging into her skin as he lifted her face towards his with a roughness that betrayed the urgency of his feelings.

'Alex…' she tried again, trying to follow the safe, the sensible path and persuade him to stop, but realising as she heard her own voice that she was doing exactly the opposite. The quaver on his name sounded so much more like shaken encouragement.

But a moment later it didn't matter what she said or how she said it. The truth was that she was incapable of any further speech as Alexei's dark head swooped down, his mouth capturing hers in a savage kiss. Hard lips crushed hers, bringing them open to the invasion of his tongue in an intimate dance that made her knees weaken so that she swayed against him, her body melting soft and yielding against the hardness of his.

She heard him mutter something dark and deep in his throat and the next moment she was swung round and up into his arms. Half-walked, half-carried across the room, his mouth never leaving hers, until she was hard up against the wall, its support cold and hard against her back. Both thrilled and shocked by his unexpected response, she shivered under the impact of his powerful form on her, the heat and hardness of him crushed against the cradle of her pelvis. If she had needed any further evidence of the fact that his blood was burning as hot as hers, then it was there in the swollen, powerful erection that was crushed between them.

His mouth was plundering hers, his tongue sweeping into the innermost corners, tasting her, tormenting her. The heated pressure of his hands matched the intimate invasion of his mouth, hot, hard palms skimming over her body, burning through the flowered cotton of her dress, curving over the swell of her hips, cupping her buttocks to pull her closer to him. Ria's blood pounded at her temples, along every nerve. Her breasts prickled and tightened in stinging response, nipples pressing against the soft lace of her bra, hungry for the feel of those wickedly enticing fingers against her flesh.

Unable to stop herself, she nipped sharply at his lower lip, catching it between her teeth and taking his gasp of response into her mouth with the taste of him clear and wild against her lips. Pushed into penitence by his reaction, she let her tongue slide over the damaged skin, soothing the small pressure wounds her teeth had inflicted and sucking the fullness of it to ease away any soreness. But the low growl she heard deep in his throat told her that his reaction had not been one of discomfort. Instead he was encouraging her to take further liberties, crushing her hard against him and letting his hands wander freely over her yearning body.

'Hell, but you're beautiful…'

He muttered the words against her arching throat, his breath warm against her flesh, and she could hardly believe that she was hearing them. Had he truly said beautiful? Was it possible that the man the gossip columns labelled the playboy prince, who had his pick of the sexiest women in the world—socialites, models, actresses—could think her so attractive? Memories of the adolescent dreams she had once indulged in, the yearning crush she had felt for this man surfaced all over again, reminding her of how much she would have given to hear those words back then, years ago. Then all he had ever shown her was a kind, but rather offhand friendship that was light-years away from this carnal hunger that seemed to grip them now.

'Who would have thought that you would grow up like this?'

'It—it's been a long time,' Ria managed to choke out, her throat dry with tension and need. 'I missed…'

But a sudden rush of self-preservation had her catching up the words in shock, clamping her mouth tight shut against what she had almost revealed. The heady rush of sensuality had driven common sense so far from her mind but she needed to grab it back now—and quickly. Alexei was no longer even her friend. He was the man who held her future and that of her country in his hands, even if he didn't know it yet.

In the strong, sensual hands that had been creating such electric pulses of pleasure in her body only a moment before. Pulses she wanted to feel more of. That made her whole body ache with need. But she must deny herself such caresses even though her whole body screamed in protest at the thought of stopping now, here, like this, when every nerve had suddenly come alive and awake in a whole new way. She had to remember why she was here.

'You—you've been missed,' she managed, though her voice shook on the words, betraying the effort she was making to get them out. And then, suddenly aware of how that might sound—that he could interpret it as meaning she was telling him just how much *she* had missed him— she rushed on. 'You've been missed in Mecjoria.'

The sound of that name brought exactly the reaction she feared. She felt the new tension in the long body pressed against hers as he stilled, withdrawing from her immediately, his hands freezing, denying her the shivers of pleasure that had radiated out from his touch.

'I doubt that very much,' he muttered, his voice rough and harsh so that it scraped over her rawly exposed nerves. 'I don't think that could ever be true.'

'Oh, but it is!' Ria protested, forcing herself to go on because this was what she had come here for after all. 'You're missed in Mecjoria—and wanted and needed there.'

'Needed?'

Her heart sank as he pushed himself away from her to stand looking down into her face with icy onyx eyes, all fire, all warmth fading from them in the space of a heartbeat. She had done what she needed to do, turned things back on to the real reason why she was here, so that at last she could tell him just why she had come to find him. But she felt lost and alone, her body suddenly cold and bereft without the heat and power of his surrounding it; her skin, her breasts, her lips cooling sharply as the imprint of his whipcord strength evaporated into the cool of the afternoon air.

She'd lost him again. That much was obvious from one swift glance at his face, seeing the way it had closed off against her, black eyes opaque and expressionless, revealing nothing. His only movement was when his hand went to his throat, tugging at the tie around his neck as if it was choking him. He pulled it loose, flicked open the top button on his shirt, then another, as if just one was not enough. And the restless movement was enough to draw her eyes, make her watch in stunned fascination.

No, that was a mistake—a major mistake. Looking into those deep-set black eyes, she suddenly saw a new light, a darkly burning, disturbing light in their depths, and it warned that there was more to this than anything she might have anticipated already. Memory swung her back to the scene of just moments before. Then, pinned up against the wall with his hands hot on her, she had known exactly what he wanted. And she had been dangerously close to giving it to him, with no thought of her own sanity or safety. Her body still tingled with the aftershocks of that encounter, the taste of him still lingered on her mouth. If she licked her lips she revived the sensation, almost as if he had just kissed her again. And oh, dear heaven, but she wanted him to kiss her again.

'There is no one there who would miss me and as for anyone who might *want* me for any reason whatsoever...'

'Oh, but you're wrong there. You really are.'

But how did she convince him of that? If there was anything that brought home to her how difficult her task was then this office, this building, was it. She didn't need to be told how much Alexei had made his new life here in England. More than a new life, his fortune, his *home*. And it was plain from the way he spoke of Mecjoria that his father's country meant nothing to him. Did she even have the right to ask him to give this up?

She didn't know. But the one thing she was sure of was that she didn't have the right to keep it from him. The decision, whatever it was, had to be his.

'I'll make it easy for you, shall I?' Alexei drawled cynically. 'Twice now you have told me that I am wanted—and needed—in Mecjoria. You have to be lying.'

'No lie. Really.'

'You expect me to believe that I am needed in the country that rejected me as not fit to be even the smallest part of the royal family? Needed by the place that has disowned and ignored me for the past ten years?'

The only response Ria could manage was a sharp, swift nod of her head. She couldn't persuade her voice to work on anything else.

'Then you'll have to explain. Needed as what?'

'As…'

Twice Ria opened her mouth to try to get the words out. Twice she failed, and it was only when Alexei turned his narrow-eyed glare on her and muttered her name as if in threat that she forced herself to speak, bringing it out in a rush.

'As—as their king. You're needed to take the throne of Mecjoria now that Felix is dead.'

CHAPTER FOUR

AS THEIR KING.

The words hit like a blow to the head, making Alexei's thoughts reel. Had he heard right?

You're needed to take the throne of Mecjoria now that Felix is dead.

Whatever else he had expected, it had not been that. She had made it plain that she and her family had suffered some strong reversal of their fortunes in the upheaval that had followed the struggles over the inheritance of the Mecjorian crown. She had come here to ask for help, that much was obvious. Softening him up by producing the proof of his legitimacy first. Perhaps to play on the fact that they had once been friends in order to get him to use his fortune to help, rescue her family. Why else would she be here?

Why else would she have responded to his kisses as she had?

Because even as he had felt her mouth opening under his, the soft curves of her body melting against him, he had known that she was only doing this for her own private reasons.

Known it and hadn't cared. He had let her lead him on in that way because he'd wanted it. No woman had excited him, aroused him so much with a single kiss. And there had been plenty of women. His reputation as a playboy had been well earned, and he had had a lot of fun earning it. At least at the beginning. It was only after Mariette—and Belle—that everything had changed. His mind flinched away from the memory but there was no getting away from the after-effects of that terrible day. His appetites had become jaded; his senses numbed. Nothing seemed to touch him like before. There was no longer the thrill of the chase.

Not that he had to do any chasing. Women practically threw themselves at him and he could have his pick of any of them simply by saying the right word, turning a practised smile in their direction. He was under no illusions; he knew it was his position and wealth that was such a strong part of the attraction. That and the bad-boy reputation that haunted him like a dark shadow. So many women wanted to be the one who tamed him. But not one of them had ever stood a chance. He had enjoyed them, shared their beds, sometimes finding the oblivion he sought in their arms. But not one of them had ever heated his blood, set his pulse racing in burning hunger as this one kiss from the former friend he had once known as a young girl, but who had grown into a stunningly sexual woman.

A woman who, like so many others, had been prepared to use that sexuality to persuade him to give her what she wanted.

But this…

'That's one hell of a bad joke!' He tossed the words at her, saw her flinch from the harshness of his tone and didn't care.

But then something about the way she looked, a widening of those amazing eyes, the sight of white, sharp teeth digging into the rose-tinted softness of her lower lip caught him up short and made him look again, more closely this time. There was more to this than he believed.

'It was a joke, wasn't it?'

A bad, black-humorous joke. One meant to stick a knife in between his ribs with the reminder of just how his father's homeland could never, ever be home to him again. Even if he was the legitimate son of one of their royal family. Disbelief was like an itch in his blood, making him want to pace around the room. Only the determination not to show the way she had rocked his sense of reality kept him still, one hand on the big, carved mantelpiece, the other tightly clenched into a fist inside the pocket of his trousers.

'A very bad joke...*no*...?'

She had shaken her head as he spoke, sending the auburn mane of her hair flying around her face. But it still couldn't conceal the way she had lost even more colour, her skin looking like putty, shocking in contrast to the wide darkness of her eyes and the way that the blush of colour flooded to where she had bitten into her lip again.

'No joke—' she stammered, low and uneven. 'It's not something I'd ever joke about.'

How she wished he would show some sort of reaction, Ria told herself. His stillness and the intent, fixed glare were becoming seriously oppressive.

'But there's no way you can be telling the truth. How would your father benefit from this?'

'My—my father?'

It would have the opposite effect, if only he knew. Her father wouldn't benefit from this, rather he would gain so much more from the back-up plan that would fall into place if Alexei refused the request she had come to him with. But she had promised herself that she would not tell Alexei that; that she would never use the dark reality of her own situation to try to persuade him into the decision she wanted—needed. Her family had committed enough crimes against his in the past. It was going to stop here, no matter what the result.

But she had hesitated too long. That, and her stammering response, had given her away.

'Your father must hope to get exactly what he wants from this.' It was a flat, cruel statement. 'Why else would he send you here?'

How did he manage to stay so still, so stiff, his eyes dark gleaming pools of contempt? He looked like a jewel-eyed cobra, silent, unmoving, just waiting for the moment to strike.

'My father wasn't the one who sent me, but obviously whatever you decide will affect him. And everyone in Mecjoria.'

'And I should care about that because…?'

'Because if you don't then the whole country will fall into chaos. There will be civil unrest, perhaps even revolution. People will be hurt—killed—they'll lose everything.'

The desperation she felt now sounded in her voice but it was clear that it had no effect on that flinty-eyed stare, the cold set of his hard jaw.

'And if you don't take the throne, the only other person who can is Ivan.'

That hit home to him.

She saw his head go back, eyes narrowing sharply at that, and knew the impact her words had had. Only very distantly related, Alexei and Ivan Kolosky had always detested each other. In fact Ivan had once been one of the ringleaders in making Alexei's life hell as he tried to adjust to life at the Mecjorian court, and they had once bonded together against this cousin several times removed who now was the only other possible heir to the Mecjo-rian throne.

With one proviso. One that affected her personally in a way that made her stomach curdle just to think of it. And she certainly didn't want Alexei to know of it or she would be putting extra power into his hands. Power she had no idea just how he would use.

'How would he be next in line to the succession?'

'There are ancient laws about the possible heirs. With both the old king and Felix gone, they have to look fur-ther afield. And with no one who's a direct descendant left then the net spreads wider—to you.'

'And to Ivan.'

It was throwaway, totally dismissive, and it warned her of just what was coming. The indifferent shrug of his shoulders only confirmed it.

'So, problem solved. You already have an heir—one who will want the throne much more than I ever would. You wouldn't even need to prove his legitimacy.'

The bitterness that twisted on his tongue made her wince in discomfort.

'But Ivan isn't the first in line. It's only if you refuse the crown that he has a claim.' Or if she played her own part in his succession as her father wanted. The knots in her stomach tightened painfully at the thought. 'And we can't let him take the crown!'

That had him turning a narrow-eyed stare on her shocked and worried face. It was so coldly, bleakly as-sessing that it made her shift uncomfortably where she stood. She was afraid that he would see her own fears in her expression and know that that gave him an advantage to hold over her.

'We?' he queried cynically. 'Since when was there any "we" involved in this?'

'You have to consider Mecjoria.'

'I do? I think you'll find that I don't have to do any-thing—or have anything to do with a country that was never a home to me.'

'But you must know all about the eruminium…the min-eral that has been discovered in the mountains,' she ex-plained when he made no response other than a sardonic lift of one black brow that cynically questioned her as-sertion. 'You'll know that it's being mined…'

'An excellent source of wealth for my cousin,' Alexei drawled, lounging back indolently against the wall in a way that expressed his total indifference to everything she said.

'But it's what it could be used for—eruminium can be used to make weapons almost as dangerous as an atomic bomb. Ivan won't care what it's used for—he'll sell the mining rights to anyone for the highest offer.'

Something flickered in the depths of those stunning eyes. But she couldn't be sure whether it was the sort of reaction that might help her or one that displayed exactly the opposite.

'And you actually concede that I might not do just the same?'

'I have to hope that you wouldn't.'

Ria no longer cared if her near-panic showed in her voice. Nothing about this meeting was going as she had thought—as she had hoped. Everyone had told her that all she had to do was to talk with Alexei, get him to lis-ten to reason. He would grab at the position, the crown, they had assured her. How could he not when it offered him the wealth and power he must want?

Anyone who thought that had never seen the man Alexei had become, she told herself, looking at the el-egantly lean and dangerous figure opposite her. It was obvious that Alexei Sarova had everything he wanted right here.

And, worst of all, was any suggestion that his taking the crown would do anything to help her, as her father's daughter, would just provide the death blow to any hope of persuading him to do so. The hatred that burned bone-deep was not going to be easily tossed aside.

'Only hope?' His question seemed to chip away layers of her protective shell, leaving gaping holes where she most needed a shield. 'Well, what else should I have expected?'

There was something that burned in those deep, black eyes that challenged and scoured across her nerves all in the same moment. But there was something else mixed in there too, something she couldn't begin to interpret.

'I can't say for sure, can I? After all, I don't know you.'

'No,' Alexei drawled, another challenge, darker than ever. 'You don't.'

'But I do know that if the problem of the succession isn't solved soon then the whole country will fall into chaos—possibly even revolution. You have to see that.'

'And I see that your father will find it very uncomfortable if that happens. But I don't understand why I need to have any part in helping to deal with it. Your father betrayed mine—his memory—by claiming that his marriage to my mother had never been legal. That was when he wanted someone else to be on the throne—and for himself to have the strongest influence possible.'

The words seemed to strip away a much-needed protective layer of skin, leaving Ria feeling raw and painfully exposed. Deep inside she knew she couldn't defend her father from Alexei's accusations, and the truth was that she didn't want to. In fact, she could add more to the list if she had the chance.

'He destroyed my mother, took everything she had and threw her out of her home, the country.'

And her son with her, Ria acknowledged to herself, wincing inwardly at the cruelly sharp twist at her heart that the memory brought with it. Like everyone else, she'd believed her father's claims. She'd believed that he was loyal to the crown and to the country. She'd trusted him on that, only to find that all the time he had just been feathering his own nest, and planning on using her as his ace card if he could. But that had been before she had discovered that Gregor had held the document of permission all the time. That he had hidden it in order to get Alexei and his mother away from the court. Only now did she realise exactly why.

'But you've done fine for yourself since then.'

'Fine?'

One dark brow lifted in cynical mockery as he echoed her tone with deliberate accuracy.

'If you mean working every hour God sends to earn enough to support my mother and keep her in the way that she needed, give her some comfort and enjoyment when she was desperately ill, then yes, we've done "fine". But that in no way excuses your father for what he has done or puts me under any obligation at all to help him with anything.'

'No—no you're not,' she admitted. 'But don't you think that you might have played some part in what had driven him to push you into exile and kept you there afterwards?'

'And what exactly do you mean by that?'

The silence that greeted her question was appalling, dark and dangerous, bringing her up sharp against what she had said. What she had risked.

Oh, dear heaven, she had really opened her mouth and put both feet right in it there! All she had meant was that it had been his own irresponsible behaviour, the wildness of his ways, that had contributed to her father's reaction against him and his family. But now she had opened a very ugly can of worms, one she could never put the lid back on ever again. Alexei's behaviour at court had been one thing. There had been another, darker scandal that had cast a black shadow over his existence once he had settled in England.

'No—I'm sorry. Obviously…'

'Obviously?' Alexei echoed cynically. 'Obviously you think you know the answer to your question so why ask it?'

'I didn't mean to rake over the past.'

'You would be wise not to—not if you want me to do anything to help your father, because I'll see him in hell first.'

And that cold-blooded declaration was just too much. It wrenched the top off her control, taking her temper with it.

'Well, you'll be right there with him—won't you?' she flung at him. 'After all, what has my father done that compares with letting his baby die?'

It was as if the whole room had frozen over. As if the air had turned to ice, burning in her lungs and making it impossible to breathe. The cold was like a mist before her eyes but even with the swirling haze she could still see the blaze of his eyes, searing through the blurring clouds and scouring over her skin like some brutal laser.

'What indeed?'

She'd gone too far, said too much, and put herself in danger by doing so. Not physical danger because, no matter how darkly furious she knew that Alexei was, she also had a fiercely stubborn conviction that there was no way he would hurt her.

But mentally…that was another matter entirely. And

just the thought of it had her taking several hurried and shaken steps backwards, away from him, putting the width of the polished wooden desk between them for her own safety.

'I wouldn't be too sure of that.' The image of the jewel-eyed serpent was back in Ria's mind as she heard the vicious hiss of his words, felt the flicking sting of their poison. 'There are more ways than one to destroy a child's life.'

That brought her up sharply, blinking in shock and incomprehension as she stared into his dark shuttered face, trying to work out just what he meant. Had he known—or at the very least suspected—just what her father had planned? Was that why he had always been so aggressively hostile to the older man back in Mecjoria, so defiant, rejecting everything the Chancellor had tried to teach him? It was nothing but oppression, bullying, he had declared, and she had always come back with the belief that her father was doing it for their own good, and for the image of the country. At least that was how she had seen it at the time. Now, recognising the side of her father that had shown itself more recently, she was forced to see it in such a very different light, and the sense of betrayal was like acid in her mouth. But had Alexei, with the advantage of extra years, been able to interpret things much more accurately?

Because how could she deny the relevance his words had for her now, coming so close to the secret she had vowed she would keep from him at all costs?

'I didn't mean to rake over the past,' she said hesitantly, trying for appeasement.

'But nevertheless you have done just that.'

Black eyes blazed against skin drawn white across his slashing cheekbones and he slung the words at her like pellets of ice, each one seeming to hit hard and cold on her unprotected skin so that she flinched back, away from them.

'I'm sorry,' she tried but the icy flash of his eyes shrivelled the words on her tongue.

'Why apologise? Doesn't everyone know that I was once a useless, irresponsible drunk? The type of man who left my child alone while I went on a bender? Who drank myself into a stupor so that I didn't even know that my baby daughter had died in her cot?'

'Oh, don't!'

Her hands came up before her sharply in a gesture of defence. She didn't understand why it hurt so much just to hear the words. She'd known about it after all—everyone had. The scandal had exploded into the papers like an atom bomb, shattering lives, destroying what little reputation Alexei might still have had. Most of all it had ripped apart any hope she had clung on to that he might still be the boy she had loved so much—the friend who had once been her support and strength through a difficult, lonely childhood. It had certainly kept her from trying to contact him again when she had been tempted to do just that.

'Don't what?' he parried harshly. 'Don't acknowledge the truth?'

CHAPTER FIVE

HE'D BEEN HOLDING it together until she'd said that, Alexei acknowledged. Until she'd ripped away the protective wall he had built between himself and the dark remembrance of the past. And now the red mist of aching memory had seeped out and flooded his brain, making it impossible to think or to speak rationally.

Belle. One tiny little girl had changed his life and made him pull himself up, haul himself back from the edge of the precipice he had been rushing towards. But not soon enough. He had failed Belle, failed his daughter, and her death would always be on his conscience.

Looking into Ria's face, he could almost swear that he could see the sheen of moisture on those beautiful eyes and found that some inner of stab of jealousy actually twisted deep in his guts. He had never been able to weep for Belle, never been able to fully mourn her loss. He had been too busy trying to deal with the fallout from that tragedy.

But Ria... How could she have tears for a child she had never known, for a baby she had no connection to? He envied her her ease of response, the uncomplicated emotion.

'Why should I deny the facts when the world and his wife know what happened?' he demanded. 'And no one would believe a word that's different.'

'What possible different interpretation could there be?'

Was that what she was looking for? Hoping for? The questions thundered inside Ria's head, shocking her with their force, the bruising power of the need it startled into wakefulness. Was this what she wanted? That he could provide a different explanation for the terrible events of three years before? That he could explain it all away, say it had never happened—or at least that it had never been the way it had been reported? Was this why it tore at her so much, pulling a need she hadn't realised existed out of her heart and forcing her to face it head-on?

If that was it, then she was doomed to disappointment. She knew it as soon as she saw the way his face changed again, the bitter sneer that twisted his beautiful mouth, distorting its sensual softness.

'None, of course,' he drawled so softly that she almost missed it. 'That is unless you can tell me that you believe it could have been any other way. Can you do that, hmm, sweetheart?'

He went even more on to the attack, driving the savage stiletto blade of his cruelty deeper into her heart. And it was all the more devastating because it was still spoken in that dangerously gentle tone.

'Can you find a way to change the past so that the devil is transformed into an angel? A fallen angel, granted, but not the fiend incarnate that the world sees?'

Could she? Her mouth opened but no sound came out because there was no thought inside her head she could voice but the knowledge that what he spoke was the bitter, black truth.

'No...'

'No.'

The corners of his mouth curled up into a smile that

ripped into her heart, it was so strangely gentle and yet so at odds with the fiendish darkness of his eyes.

'Of course. I thought not.'

'If there is any explanation…'

For the sake of their past, the sake of the friend he had once been, she had to try just once more, though without any real hope.

'No. There is no explanation that I want to give you.'

It was a brutal, crushing dismissal, accompanied by a slashing gesture of one hand, cutting her off before she could complete the sentence.

'Nothing that would change a thing. So why don't we accept that as fact and move on?'

'Do we have anywhere to move on to?'

Where could they go from here? He had declared that everything she had heard about him was the truth. He had taken the weak, idealistic image she had once had of him and dashed it viciously to the ground, letting it splinter into tiny, irreparable shards that would never again let her form the picture of a wild but generous-spirited boy who had once been her rock, someone she could turn to when things got too bad to bear.

'I know my father's no saint, but you—you're hateful.'

She was past thinking now, past caring about what she said. Deep inside, where she prayed he would never be able to find it, she knew she was having to face up to the painful bitter truth. And that truth was that when she had found out the reality of what her father had been up to, what he had planned, then she had come running to find Alexei, to find her friend, hoping, believing that he of all people would be there for her, that he would help her. But the reality was that her friend Alexei no longer existed and this cold-eyed monster could be an even more deadly enemy than the cousin she feared so much.

'Not so hateful a moment ago,' Alexei tossed at her. 'Not when you were hungry for my kisses, my touch— for anything I would give you.'

'You took me by surprise!' Ria broke in sharply, knowing she was trying to avoid the image of herself he was showing her.

'And it was only the *surprise* that made you react as you did.'

'What else could there be?' Ria challenged, bringing up her chin as she glared her defiance at him, wanting to deny the cynicism that burned in his words. 'You're not so damn irresistible as you think...'

'Except when I have something that you want. So if I were to kiss you again...'

'No!'

It made her jump, taking a hasty step backwards, banging into the chair and almost sending it flying. The bruise stung sharply but nothing like the feeling inside as she faced the dark mockery in his face and knew that her reaction had only confirmed his worst suspicions.

'You wouldn't...' she tried again.

Her wary protest had his mouth curling at the corners, the sardonic humour more shocking than the cold anger of just moments before. She should have taken that anger as a warning, Ria acknowledged to herself. If anything, that should give her her cue to get out of here—fast. She had tried to persuade him to come back to Mecjoria. Tried to make him see that he was the best—the only—man who could take the throne. Tried and failed. And the worst realisation was the fact that she had miscalculated this so totally. She had thought that she was the best person for this task, but the truth was that she had really been the worst possible one. She had blundered in where she should have feared to tread, raising all the hatred and the anger he had been letting fester for ten long, bitter years and the only thing she could do was to walk out now while she could still hold her head high.

'Oh, but I would.' That dark mockery curled through his words like smoke around a newly extinguished candle, sending shivers of uncomfortable response sliding down her spine. 'And so would you, if you were prepared to be honest and admit it.'

'I wouldn't.'

She was shaking her head desperately even though she knew the vehemence of her response only betrayed her more, dug in deeper into the hole that was opening up around her feet. Impossibly she was actually wishing for the cold-eyed serpent back in place of that wicked smile, the calculated mockery.

'Liar.'

It was soft and deadly, terrifyingly so as he emphasised it with a couple of slow, deliberate steps towards her, and she could feel the colour coming and going in her cheeks as she tried to get a grip on the seesaw of emotions that swung sickeningly up and down inside her. It would be so much easier if her senses weren't on red alert in response to the potently masculine impact of his powerful form, the lean, lithe frame, the powerful chest and arms in contrast to the fine linen of his shirt. Her eyes were fixed on the bronzed skin of his throat and the dark curls of hair exposed by the open neckline. He was so close that she could see the faint shadow on his jaw where the dark growth of stubble was already beginning to appear, and the clean musky aroma of his skin, topped with the tang of some bergamot scent, was tantalising her nostrils.

The memory of that kiss was so sharp in her mind, the scent of his body bringing back to her how it had felt to be enclosed in his arms, feel the strength of muscle, the heat of his skin surrounding her. The trouble was that she did want him to kiss her—that was something she couldn't deny. It was there in the dryness of her mouth, the tightness of her throat so that she could barely breathe, let alone swallow. The heavy thuds of her heart against her ribs were a blend of excited anticipation and a shocking sense of dread. She wanted his kiss, wanted his touch—but she knew just what she would be unleashing if she allowed anything to happen. And she already had far too much to lose to take any extra risks.

'No lie,' she flung at him. 'Not then and not now. I can see I'm wasting my time here.'

'That's one thing we can agree on.'

It was when he swung away from her that she knew every last chance of being heard, or even getting him to give her a single moment's consideration, was over. The hard, straight line of his back was turned to her, taut and powerful as a stone wall against any appeal she might direct towards him. And the way his hands were pushed deep into the pockets of his trousers showed the fierce control he was imposing on himself and the volatile temper she sensed was almost slipping away from him.

'It seems that you're not going to be any use to me so I might as well call it a day.'

'Please do.'

If he stayed turned away, Alexei told himself, then he might just keep his wayward senses under control until she had left. It was shocking to find the way that cold fury warred with an aching burn of lust that held him in its grip, unable to move, unable to think straight.

In the moment that she had stood up and faced him he had known that the rush of hard, hot sensuality of a few moments before had not been a one-off. And that it was not something that was going to go away any time soon.

Something about the woman that Ria had become reached out and caught him in a net of sexual hunger, one that thudded heavily through his body, centring on the hardness between his legs. The fall of the shining darkness of her hair, the gleam of her beautiful almond-shaped eyes, the rose-tinted curve of her lips, shockingly touched with a sexual gleam of moisture where she had slicked her small pink tongue along them, had all woven a sensual spell around him, one he was struggling to free himself from. He could still taste her if he let his tongue touch his own lips, the scent of her skin was on his clothes, topped by that slight spicy floral scent she wore that made him want to press his lips; to her soft flesh, inhale the essence of her as he kissed her all over.

He still did. He still wanted to reach out and haul her into his arms, kiss her, touch her. She was the last person in the world he should feel this way about, the worst person in the world to have any sort of association with, let alone the hot passionate sex his body hungered for. She came with far too much baggage, not the least of which was the connection with Mecjoria, the country that had once been so much a part of his past and had almost destroyed him as a result. Everything about her threatened to drag him back into that past, to enclose him in the memories he hated, imprison him again in all that he had escaped from. Ria might tempt him—hell, the temptation she offered was so strong that he could feel it twining round him, tightening, like great coils of rope, almost impossible to resist—but he was not going to give in to it. It would only drag him back into the past he had barely walked away from, reduce him all over again to the boy he had once been, lonely, needy, and that was not going to happen.

And then she had done it again. She had turned that

look on him. The Grand Duchess Honoria look. It had hit him hard. It was the same look that she'd turned on him ten years before. He didn't know which was the worst, the fact that she still thought she could look at him in that way or the fact that it could still get to him. That she could still make him feel that way. As if all he had done and achieved had never been. As if he was still the Alexei who had hungered for approval and friendship, especially from her. From Ria. His friend.

No longer a friend. That was too innocent a word, and what he felt now was definitely not innocent. Hearing her voice and the way that something—pride? Anger? Defiance?—had hardened it, he knew what he was going to do, even if the roar of heat in his blood made it a struggle to make his body behave as his mind told him he should. Hungry sensuality and coldly rational thought fought an ugly little battle that tightened every muscle, twisted every nerve.

But it was a battle he was determined to win.

'I would appreciate it if you left now.'

It was something of a shock to find that echoes of the training his father had given him before the cancer had stolen even his voice had surfaced from his past to make him impose the sort of control over his tone that turned the formal politeness into an icy-cold distance. She would have had something of the same training so he didn't doubt that she knew exactly what that tone meant.

'But I can't…'

'But you can. You can accept that this is never going to happen—that you have failed. Whoever advised you to come here you should let them know that they sent quite the wrong person to plead their case. They would have done better to send your father—I might actually have listened to him more than I would to you.'

He heard her sharply indrawn breath and almost turned to see the reaction stamped on her face.

Almost. But he caught himself in time. He was not going to subject himself to that sort of temptation ever again.

'So now just go. I have nothing more to say to you, and I never want to see you in my life again.'

Would she fight him on this? Would she try once more to persuade him? Dear God, was he almost tempted by the thought that she might? Fiercely he fixed his gaze on the darkness beyond the window. A darkness in which he could see the faint reflection of her shape, the pale gleam of her skin, the dark pools of her eyes. The silence that followed his words was total, and it dragged on and on, it seemed, stretching over the space of too many heartbeats.

But then at last he saw her head drop slightly, acknowledging defeat. She turned one last look on him, but clearly thought better of even trying to speak as she twisted on her heel and headed for the door, slender back straight, auburn head held high.

It was only as the door swung to behind her, the wood thudding into the frame, that he realised how unconsciously he had used exactly the words that she had thrown at him in their last meeting in Mecjoria ten years before. She had been the one to turn and walk away then too, marching away from him without a backward glance, taking with her the last hope he had had.

Recalling how it had felt then, it was impossible not to remember all he had ever wanted and now could never have—all over again. He had wanted to belong, damn it, he'd tried. He'd thought that when his parents had reconciled that at last he'd found the father, the family, he'd always wanted. But his father's illness had meant that he had never had the time to make a reality out of that dream. It had all crumbled around him.

But this time it had been his own decision to throw it all away. He had had his revenge for the way she and her family had treated him, turning the tables on her completely and reversing the roles they had once had. It should have been what he wanted. It should have provided him with the sort of dark satisfaction that would have made these last ten years of exile and of struggle finally worthwhile. But the troubling thing was the uncomfortable sensation in the pit of his stomach that told him that satisfaction was the furthest thing from what he was feeling. If anything, he felt emptier and hungrier than ever before.

The royal document still lay on his desk where he had dropped it, and for a moment he let himself touch it, resting his fingers on the ornate signature next to the dark-red seal. The signature of his grandfather. King of Mecjoria.

King.

Just four letters of a word but it seemed to explode inside his head. Ria had offered him the chance to return to Mecjoria, not just as himself—but as its king.

It was ironic that Ria claimed to have come here today to ask him to take the crown—to be King of Mecjoria when all that her appearance had done was to bring home to him how totally unsuited he was for any such role. He had failed as a prince, but that had been as nothing when compared to his failure as a father. But she thought that she could persuade him that he was needed in her homeland.

Her homeland. Not his.

But then she had said that the only alternative was for Ivan to be king. What a choice. Poor Mecjoria. To be torn between a bully boy and a man who knew nothing at all about being a royal—let alone running a country. His father's country.

His father must be spinning in his grave at just the thought.

And yet his father had had Ivan sussed even all those years ago. From the corners of his memory came the recollection of a conversation—one of the very rare conversations—he had had with his dying father. Weak, barely able to open his eyes, let alone move, his father had known of the stand-up argument, almost a fight, Alexei had had with Ivan the previous day.

'That boy is trouble,' he had whispered. 'He's dangerous. Watch him—and watch your back when you're with him. Never let him win.'

And this was the man who could take over the throne—unless he stopped him.

Moving to the window, he looked down into the street to see Ria's tall, slim figure emerge from the front of the Sarova building and start to walk away down the street, pausing to cross at the traffic lights. He had wanted her to leave, so why did he now feel as if she was taking with her some essential part of him, something that made him whole?

The part he had once thought that Belle would fill.

'Hell, no.'

He turned away fiercely as the scene before him blurred disturbingly.

Did he really think that Ria would fill that hole in his life? It was just sex. Nothing but the reawakening of his senses that had started from the moment he had walked into the room and set eyes on her. And he had the disturbing feeling that there was only one way to erase the yearning sensations that tormented his body.

The only real satisfaction he could find would be to

have Ria—the Grand Duchess Honoria—in his bed so that he could sate himself in her body and so hope, at last, to erase the bitterness of memories that had been festering for far too long. But he had just destroyed his chances of ever having that happen. He had driven her away, and in that moment he had believed that that was the wisest, the only rational course.

Except of course that rationality had nothing to do with the burning sensuality of his reaction to her, the carnal storm that still pounded through him, even after she had left the room.

Rationality might tell him that walking away from her was the sanest path to take but the bruise of sexual hunger that made his body ache still left no room for sanity or rational thought. This restless, nagging feeling was so much like the way he had felt when he had first come to England, into exile with his mother, a feeling that he had thought he had subdued, even erased completely. One brief meeting with Ria had revived everything he had never wanted to feel ever again, but in the past those feelings had been those of a youth who had not long left boyhood behind. Now he was a grown man, with an experience of life, and Ria was a full-grown woman. He *wanted* Ria as he had never wanted another woman in his life, craved her like a yearning addict needing a fix, and he knew that these feelings would take far more than ten years longer to bury all over again—if, in fact, they could ever be truly buried at all.

He had vowed to himself that he would throw her out of his life and forget about her. Already he was regretting and rethinking that vow, knowing that forgetting her was going to be impossible. He was going to have her—but it had to be on his own terms.

CHAPTER SIX

'You must have this wrong.'

Coming to a dead halt, Ria stood in the doorway, staring out across the airport tarmac, shaking her head in disbelief. The sleek, elegant jet that stood gleaming in the sunshine was not at all what she had been anticipating and she couldn't imagine why anyone should think that it was there for her.

When she had arrived at the airport for her flight home, she had been feeling more raw and vulnerable than she had ever been in her life. With her one hope gone, the future now stretched ahead of her and her country, dark and oppressive, with no way of rescue or escape unless she took the way her father had planned.

She certainly hadn't expected to be greeted by a man in uniform, swept through the briefest of security checks and delivered out here where the luxurious private jets of the rich, famous and powerful waited for permission to take off to whatever private island or sophisticated resort might be their ultimate destination.

'There really has to be some mistake...' she tried again, coming to an abrupt halt at the foot of the steps up to the plane, as he stood back to let her precede him.

'No mistake.'

The words came from above her, at the top of the steps,

and in spite of the noise of the wind blowing across the tarmac she knew immediately who had spoken.

The open door at the head of the steps was now filled with the tall, powerful figure of Alexei Sarova, the man she had believed she had left behind in London and would never, ever see again. Casually dressed in a loose white shirt and worn denim jeans, his hair blown about in the breeze, his powerful frame still had a heart-stopping impact, an effect that was multiplied a hundred times by his dominant position so high up above her.

'No mistake at all,' he said now, dark eyes locking with hers. 'I asked for you to be brought here.'

'You did? But why?'

'It seemed ridiculous to let you fly cattle class when we are both going to the same place.'

'We are?'

Had she heard right? Was he actually saying that he was flying to Mecjoria? Could he be thinking of agreeing to her request that he claim the throne? The man who had turned his back on her both physically and emotionally.

'We are. So are you going to stand there dithering for much longer or are you going to come up here and take your seat? Everything is ready for take-off but if we don't leave soon we will miss our allocated slot.'

'I'm not going anywhere with you.'

He couldn't have reversed that brutally unyielding decision in the space of less than twenty-four hours, could he? And yet if not then why was he here?

The slightest of adjustments in the way that he stood gave away the hint of a change in his mood—for the worse.

'So it really isn't a matter of life or death that I go to Mecjoria and look into the situation for the accession after all?'

As he echoed the description she'd given him, he managed to put a sardonic note on the words that twisted a knife even more disturbingly in her nerves. She didn't know why this was happening, she only knew that suddenly, for some reason, he seemed prepared to toss her a lifeline, one that she would be the greatest fool in the world to ignore.

'All right!'

Not giving herself any more time to think, Ria pushed herself into action, flinging one foot on to the steps and then the other, grabbing at the rail for support, almost tumbling to the ground at Alexei's feet as she reached the top.

What else could she do? She had spent last night wide awake and restless, going over the scene in his house again and again, berating herself for failing so badly, for driving him further away rather than persuading him round to her side. She had cursed herself for bringing her father into the discussion, seeing the black rage and hatred simply thinking of him had brought into his eyes. She had even reached for her phone a couple of times, wondering if she rang him that he might actually listen, and each time she had dropped it back down again, knowing that the man who had turned his back on her and told her to leave so brutally had no room in his mind or his heart for second thoughts or second chances. Today she'd faced the prospect of going back home knowing that everything was lost, and with no idea how she was going to face the future.

And then suddenly this...

'I don't understand.'

She was gasping as if she'd run a mile rather than just up a short flight of steps, but it was tension and not lack of fitness that caught her round her throat, making it impossible to breathe.

But Alexei was clearly in no mood to offer any explanations. Instead with a bruising grip on her arm he steered her out of the sunlight and into the plane where she blinked hard as her eyes adjusted to the change in light.

Once she would have been the one with access to a private plane. Not for her sole use, or even that of her family, but she had sometimes travelled with a member of the royal family, or accompanying her father in his official role. But it had never been like this. The Mecjorian royal plane had been as old-fashioned and stiffly formal as the regime itself, reflecting the views of the old king. This one was a symphony of cool calm, with pale bronze carpets, wide, soft seats just waiting for someone to sink into their creamy leather cushions. Everything was light and space, and spoke of luxury beyond price; and the impact of it hit like a blow, making her head spin.

Once again that unanswerable question pounded at her thoughts. Just why—*why*—would Alexei want Mecjoria, a small, insignificant, run-down Eastern European country, when he had all this? Why would he even spare a thought for the place or the chaos that would swamp the inhabitants if he refused the throne and let it pass to Ivan?

With his hand still on her arm, the heat of his palm burning through the soft pink cotton of her top and into her skin, the power and strength of his body so close beside her was overwhelming and almost shocking. In spite of the fact that he was so casually dressed, he carried himself with the sort of power that few men could show, making her heart kick hard against her ribs in a lethal combination of physical response and apprehension.

'Take a seat.'

Ria was grateful to sink down into the enveloping comfort of the nearest seat, her legs disturbingly unsteady beneath her. The air seemed suddenly too thick to breathe, the roar of the engines as the pilot prepared the plane for flight too loud in her ears so that she couldn't think straight or do anything other than obey him. She was on her way to Mecjoria and, for his own private reasons, Alexei was with her. That and the powerful thrust of the plane as it set off down the runway was more than enough to cope with at the moment.

'Fasten your seatbelt.'

Alexei was clearly not going to take the trouble to enlighten her on anything—not yet anyway, as he took the seat opposite her, long legs stretched out, crossed at the ankles—and settled himself, ready for take-off.

She was dismissed from his thoughts as he turned his head, focussing his attention through the window to where the green of the grass on the side of the runway was now flashing past at an incredible speed as the plane raced towards take-off. Another couple of minutes and the wheels had left the ground, the jet soaring away from the ground and up into the sky. The impact pushed Ria back into her seat, her head against the rest, her hands clutching the arms of her chair. Unexpectedly, unbelievably, she had another chance and she was going to take it if she possibly could.

But that added a whole new burden of worry to the nervousness she was already feeling. Just for a moment her thoughts reeled. Had she done the right thing coming here? Was she justified in putting her own family, her own personal needs, first like this? It was true that she feared the consequences if Ivan took the crown. She dreaded the thought of what it meant for her personally if she had to follow her father's plans for that event, but how did she know if Alexei would be any better? The memory of the stories of his life in London that had been reported in the papers back home came back to haunt her. There had been one where he had been caught unaware, his hand half-lifted to his face to escape the flash of the camera. But he hadn't been quick enough to conceal the fact that he had obviously been in a fight; that his eye was blackened, his nose bloodied.

And of course there had been his neglect of his poor little daughter. A neglect that he hadn't even tried to deny. Was she right in bringing such a man back to Mecjoria— as its king?

But he was the rightful king. That was the one argument she was totally sure of.

The plane had reached its cruising height and had straightened out of the steep climb but Ria's stomach was still knotted in that unnerving tension that the fast ascent, combined with her own inner turmoil, had created. She had a dreadful feeling of no going back, knowing that she could only go forward—though she had no idea where that might lead.

'Would you like a drink? Something to eat?'

It was perfectly polite, the calm enquiry of a courteous host as a slightly raised hand summoned an attendant who jumped to attention as if she had just been waiting for the signal.

'Some coffee would be nice.' She hadn't been able to eat any breakfast before she left for the airport. 'We do have almost five hours to fill.'

'I don't think you need to worry about filling time on this flight,' Alexei told her. 'We'll have plenty to keep us occupied.'

'We will?' It was sharp and tight with a new rush of nerves.

In contrast, Alexei looked supremely relaxed, lounging back in his seat opposite her as he nodded.

'You have…' he checked the workmanlike heavy watch on his wrist '…four hours to convince me that I should even consider taking up the crown of Mecjoria and allowing myself to be declared king.'

'But I thought—I mean—you're here now. And we're heading for…'

The words shrivelled on her tongue as she looked into the cold darkness of his face and saw that there was nothing there to give her confidence that this was all going to work out right.

'I'm here now,' he agreed soberly, dark eyes hooded and shadowed. 'And we are on a flight path for Mecjoria—for the capital. This plane will land there, if only to let you off so you can go and talk to the courtiers who sent you. But that does not mean that I will disembark as well.'

His tone was flat, emotionless, unyielding, and looking into his eyes was like staring into the icy depth of a deep, deep lake, frozen over with a coating of thick black ice, bleak and impenetrable. He had made one tiny concession and that was all he was going to let her have—unless she could convince him otherwise.

'Our estimated time of arrival is five in the afternoon, Mecjorian time. You have until then to persuade me that I should not just turn round and head home as soon as we have let you disembark.'

He meant it, she had no doubt about that, and a sensation like cold slimy footsteps crept down her back. The thought of being so near yet so far curdled in her stomach. The attendant appeared with her coffee and she took refuge in huddling over the cup as if the warmth from the hot liquid might melt the ice that seemed to have frozen right through to her bones. Just when she had thought she could relax, that Alexei was heading for Mecjoria, and taking her with him to return home—if not in triumph then at least with some hope of success and a more positive future for the country—suddenly he had shown that he had been working on a totally different plan.

It didn't help at all that she was sitting opposite the most devastatingly attractive man she had ever seen in her whole life. Her schoolgirl crush on the adolescent Alexei seemed like froth and bubble compared to the raw, gut-deep sensual impact of his adult self on all that was female inside her. If he so much as moved, her senses sprang to life, heat and moisture pooling between her thighs so that she shifted uncomfortably in her seat, crossing and uncrossing her legs restlessly.

'I told you...'

Another smile was a swift flash on and off, one that put no light in his eyes.

'Tell me again.' It was a command, not a suggestion. 'We have plenty of time.'

It was going to be interesting to see if she came up with exactly the same arguments as she had given him yesterday, Alexei reflected. Arguments that would change his way of life; hell, his whole future if the decision he had come to in the middle of the night was anything to go by. He hadn't been able to sleep and had spent long hours surfing the Internet, researching the situation in Mecjoria even more intensely than usual, finding out as much as he possibly could. There was plenty he already knew. In spite of the mask of indifference he had hidden behind when Ria had confronted him, he had kept a careful eye on all that was happening in his father's homeland ever since he and his mother had been exiled from the place. His research had told him that everything she had said was true, but this time, driven to dig more deeply, he had

found there was more to it than that. That there was one
vital element to this whole succession business that he had
never suspected, and that she had not revealed.

And that was something that changed everything.

Why had she not told him the full truth? What did she
have to gain from keeping it from him?

In the seat opposite, Ria stirred slightly, the soft sound
of her denim-clad legs sliding across each other setting
his senses on red alert in a heartbeat. It was hell to sit here
with his body hardening in response to just the thought of
her being there, so close and yet so far away. He should
never have touched her, never have let the feel of the warm
velvet of her skin, the scent of her hair, start off the heavy
pulse of hunger that was like a thickness in his blood. It
stopped him thinking straight and made him *want*. And
wanting was going to have to be put aside for now, for a
time at least. He had her just where he wanted her, and he
wasn't going to let her get away. But first he was going to
make her acknowledge that this was the only way that it
could be. The sensual pleasure he anticipated would be
one thing. Bringing her to admit that she had nowhere
else to go would add a whole new dimension of satisfaction to his revenge on the family that had been responsible for his and his mother's exile from the country where
they belonged.

'Persuade me.'

With no other alternative, Ria had to go over it all
again. The one thing she didn't do was to mention anything about personal involvement. Deep down inside she
knew instinctively that that could only act against her. She
knew now how much he hated her family, how he would
do anything rather than help them in any way. It was perhaps an hour and a half later that she stopped, drawing
in a much-needed breath, reaching for the glass of water

that had replaced the coffee of earlier. Gulping down the drink she had left ignored as she focussed totally on the man opposite her, she struggled to ease the discomfort of her parched throat as she waited for his response.

It was a long time coming. A long, uncomfortable time as he subjected her to a burning scrutiny. Like her he reached for his crystal tumbler of iced water but the swallow he took was long, slow and indolently relaxed.

'Very interesting,' he drawled, leaning back in his seat, never taking his eyes off her for a moment. 'But you neglected to explain that the situation is not quite as simple as you made out. There's one more thing I want to know.'

'Anything.' She didn't care if she sounded close to desperate. That was how she felt, so why try to hide it at this delicate stage?

'Anything?' There was a definite challenge in the dark-eyed look he slanted in her direction. 'Then tell me about the marriage.'

'The—the marriage...'

Ria's stomach twisted painfully, her discomfort made all the worse by the way that the plane had suddenly hit a patch of turbulence and lurched violently, dropping frighteningly, down and then back up again.

'Yes, the marriage your father has arranged for you. I am the heir to the throne if the individual positions in the hierarchy—the direct line—are considered. On my own, I have the stronger claim—if I want it.'

There it was again, that note of threat that he might refuse the crown, and leave her stranded without a hope of finding any other way out—as she now suspected he had known all along. How he must have enjoyed watching her perform all over again, knowing all the while that he understood the real truth of her position, the cleft stick she was caught in with little hope of escape.

'But you omitted to point out that it is not just Ivan who also has a distant potential claim to the throne.'

The glass he held was placed on the table with deliberate care. The same control showed as he stood up, big and dark and lean, towering over her and making even the space of the luxurious jet feel confined and restricted in a sudden and shocking way. Forced to raise her head to look up at him, she found that the air in the cabin seemed to have thickened and grown heavier.

'You forgot to say…' His tone made it plain that he didn't think for a moment she had forgotten anything. 'that you and Ivan have a unique connection where the crown is concerned. Individually his claim is so much weaker, but *together* you would be almost unassailable.'

Ria could almost feel the blood draining from her face. She must look like a ghost, and that would show him how perfectly he had hit the mark.

'There is no together!'

His gesture might have been flicking away a fly, it was so scornfully dismissive of her protest.

'Are you saying that none of this is true? That Ivan's claim to the throne is clear and open, with no other help needed—and you won't need him to free your father, restore your family fortunes to the way they used to be?'

He made it sound so mercenary. But then what had she expected from a man who so blatantly despised her and every member of her family?

'No—'

There was no togetherness between Ivan and her. Nothing except the one that had been forced on her, that she would have to accept if Alexei didn't listen to her pleas. The prospect of freedom from the future she dreaded that had seemed to open up before her now seemed to be moving further away with every breath she took. Ria pushed herself to her feet, needing the greater strength of a position facing him on a much better level, her green eyes meeting his head-on.

'I mean, yes, it's true that if I marry him his right to the throne is strengthened...'

'Isn't it *when* you marry him?' Alexei slipped in, cold and deadly. 'I understand that the contract has already been signed.'

By her father. Without any consultation or even her knowledge. She had been used as a pawn in the political bargaining.

'I— How did you find out that?' How could he know about the contract her father had made with Ivan, when she had only become aware of it herself just days before?

'I have my sources.'

He'd been up all night, and he'd called in all his contacts, investigating exactly what was behind this sudden desire of hers to have him as king in Mecjoria. All the time she had been talking yesterday—and again just now—he had sensed she was holding something back, keeping something hidden. He had never expected that it would be this.

Once he had found the real explanation he had been unable to think of anything else. Because this turned everything upside down from the way he'd seen everything at first. He'd been convinced that Ria had brought him the document that proved his parents' marriage valid, and that he was the rightful king, because that would give her—and her family—an advantage if he came to the throne. She was softening him up so that he would release her father, restore the family fortunes...

The discovery of the proposed marriage to Ivan Kolosky made a nonsense out of all that. Even more so because she had never said a word about it.

That marriage would give her everything she wanted—
and more. It would make her Queen of Mecjoria and he
knew that had always been Gregor Escalona's deepest
ambition. The reason why he had insisted on his daughter's immaculate behaviour, training her to be the perfect
young royal, controlling every move, every decision she
made. It was the reason why Gregor had betrayed his father's memory by bringing the legitimacy of his marriage
into question. So why had she even brought the marriage
certificate to him in the first place? And why had she
never mentioned the proposed marriage to Ivan?

Last night he had thought he had decided on a way to
play this that would give him retribution for all that had
happened to him and his mother when they had been
exiled from their home, losing every last penny of the
fortune that should have been theirs, his mother's good
name along with it, but at last it seemed that payback was
within his grasp.

But one more discovery and everything had changed.
There was more on offer now. More than he could ever
have dreamed of. He wanted more. And there was one
way he was sure of getting it.

'So now how about you tell me the real truth?'

He saw the wariness in her eyes, the shadow that
crossed her face, and it made him all the more determined to get to the bottom of all of this.

He'd planned on giving her another chance to give him
the real facts this morning, but the truth was that as soon
as she'd started to speak his concentration had been shot
to pieces. All he could focus on was the way she looked,
with that dark auburn hair pulled back into a pony tail so
that it exposed the fine bone structure of her features, the
brilliance of her eyes. Tiny silver earrings sparkled in her
lobes, seeming to catch the flash of her eyes as she leaned

towards him, elegant hands coming up to emphasise her points. The movement of her mouth fascinated him, the soft rose-tinted curve of her lips moving to emphasise what she had to say, the faint sheen of moisture on them making him want to lean forward and kiss her hard and fierce, plunge his tongue into her open mouth and taste her again as he had done the night before.

She hadn't said anything about Ivan and that made him grit his teeth tight against the questions that needed answers. Now he couldn't look at her without thinking about Ivan—and about her with Ivan. Acid rose in his throat at just the thought of it and the blood heated in his veins, making his heart punch harshly, a pulse throbbing near his temple. The thought of her with anyone else—anyone but him—was too much to take. But with *Ivan*...

And that feeling—that fury of jealousy, the hunger, that sensation of being alive that had been missing in his life for so long—told him so much. It erased the numbness he had been living—existing—with, the deadness that had invaded his world since the loss of first his father, and later the baby daughter he had barely started to get to know. He hadn't felt this way in years and he wanted it back. And he wanted Ria, as the woman who had given sensation back to him.

'That if you can't persuade me to take the throne, then you are tied into a contract to marry Ivan, and so strengthen his claim to the inheritance. Tell me—why not just go with the marriage to Ivan? After all it would make you Queen of Mecjoria.'

'My father might want that, perhaps, but not me!'

But this was what her father had been training her for, the summit of her family's ambitions. And if being queen had been her ambition too then all she had had to do was to leave the marriage document where it was.

'You don't want to be queen?'

'And you want to be king?' she tossed back, earning herself a faint, twisted smile and an ironical inclination of his head in acknowledgement of the hit. But she hadn't spent the past ten years exiled from the country he was now supposed to rule.

'Where was the marriage certificate found?' he demanded now, wanting to get at the truth.

It was a question she didn't want to answer, that much was obvious, and yet he didn't think she was trying to deceive him. Sharp white teeth dug into the softness of her lower lip, and he was suddenly assailed by the impulse to protest at the damage she was doing to the delicate skin. Instead he made himself repeat the question in order to divert his thoughts.

'Where?'

Her delicate chin came up defiantly, gold-green eyes blazing into his.

'My father had it all the time. It was in his safe when I checked in there after he was arrested. My mother begged me to look for something that might help.' Once more her teeth worried at her lip as she obviously had to push herself to go on. 'I also found the contract between him and Ivan then.'

'You hadn't known before?'

He could well believe that of Gregor, conspiring with anyone he could in secret. But would he really sign his daughter's life away without her knowing?

'I knew nothing about it!' There was the tremor of real horror in her voice.

'Your father can't force you into this.'

Her soft mouth twisted into an expression of resignation—or was it bitterness?

'In Mecjoria, royalty—even unimportant royalty like

me—don't expect to marry for love. Dynastic contracts matter so much more than personal feelings. And right now peace is what matters. I meant everything I said about the possible consequences if the succession isn't easy and smooth. If not you, then Ivan is the only logical candidate.'

'But neither of us wants Ivan to take the throne.'

'No, we both know what a disaster that would be.'

The way she rushed to agree with him, the tone in which she did it, scraped roughly across his exposed skin. The mood of calm and control that had come from feeling that he had her just where he wanted her was starting to fray at the edges, coming unravelled with every breath he drew in. Last night she had claimed she'd given him every argument she possessed but she'd kept this vital point carefully back. And hiding that point showed him just how much she had wanted to influence him into agreeing to her plans without ever knowing the full story.

She had only forced herself to come to him because she had no possible alternative. Because her country needed it now that she had proof that he wasn't illegitimate, that he was truly as royal as she was—more. But because she needed it too. Would she have told him about the document if she hadn't also been able to use it to her own advantage? Because she wasn't prepared to sacrifice her own freedom in order to rescue the place herself. She hadn't reckoned on him ever finding out about the proposed union between her family and Ivan's—at least not until it was too late.

'So you will do as I ask? You will take the throne?'

There was a very different mood in the words, with a whole new sparkle in those eyes, a lift to the warm curve of her mouth. She thought she had got what she wanted from him—that she had worked out a way of ensuring an heir to the throne but without her having to tie herself into marriage with the only other candidate for the crown. So that he could live the restricted, controlled life of a royal while she kept her freedom and could live as she pleased.

He felt used, manipulated. But it didn't stop him wanting her.

And wanting her didn't stop him recognising that her father had done a good job in training her up to be a queen—whoever's wife she might be. From acknowledging what an asset she would be as anyone's consort—and it didn't have to be Ivan's. He didn't want her to be Ivan's any more than she did.

'I could be persuaded,' he said slowly.

The light that her smile brought to her eyes almost made him lose his grip on his temper as icy rage swamped him. She thought she was winning and that pushed him dangerously close to the edge. All he wanted was to pull the rug out from under her, let her know that he already had all her secrets and he fully intended to use them to his own advantage.

But there was more pleasure in letting things out bit by bit than in dumping everything on her all at once.

'I will do as you ask,' he said slowly, keeping his eyes locked on her face to enjoy watching her reaction. 'But there are terms.'

CHAPTER SEVEN

'TERMS?' RIA ECHOED the word on a note of pure horror. 'What sort of terms?'

'Terms that you and I need to agree between us. We need to plan the future.'

'But we have no future…'

She looked so appalled at the thought of any more time spent with him. She would even refute the flames that burned between them if she could. It was there in the darkness that clouded her eyes, the way she was fighting to deny there was anything between them.

'You think?'

Their eyes clashed, held for a moment. Hers were the first to drop as she recognised the unyielding challenge in his.

'What terms?' she asked.

So much of the attack had gone out of her voice, leaving it weakened and deflated. Was it possible that she suspected what was coming? A dark wave of satisfaction flooded through his veins.

'I will be king—on the same conditions as it would have been for Ivan to take the throne.'

It took a moment for her to register just what he had said, several more to have the words sink in and the meaning behind the flat statement become real. He watched every change of emotion spill across her face, the way that it tightened the muscles around her mouth and jaw, made her elegant throat contract on a hard swallow. One that he felt echo in his own throat as he fought the urge to press his lips to the pale skin of her neck and follow the movement down.

'But those conditions were only for Ivan…' Ria stammered.

She still hadn't quite realised just what he was talking about. Either that or she didn't want to accept that he could actually mean it.

'It's that or nothing. And I wish you joy being Ivan's wife.'

'And the country?' She'd found some new strength from somewhere, enough to challenge him. 'Are you prepared for the civil unrest that will follow if you walk away now?'

That caught him up sharp. Took him back to the darkness of the night where his memories of his father's dying words had forced him to face the prospect of a future in which the repercussions of his decisions, his actions, reverberated out into the coming days and years with the possibility of guilt and the dreadful responsibility of the wrong choices made in anger. He'd been there once before and it was a hell he had no wish to return to. He'd let someone—not just anyone, he'd let *Belle*—down because of that anger once and even after years the stab of memory, of guilt, was brutal. Was he going to do it again? Let down a whole nation? Thousands of families—hundreds of Belles?

He'd be letting down his father too if he let Ivan take over the throne, ignoring the warning Mikail had given him.

If he stayed angry, that was always the risk. But this,

this was a decision he had made in cold blood. To defeat Ivan. And her father. And to have Ria at his side as his queen and in his bed.

'There is one way to ensure that doesn't happen. And to keep Ivan from the crown at the same time. Believe me, I feel the same as you do at the thought of him ruling Mecjoria.'

She should have expected this, Ria told herself. She knew how much he and Ivan had loathed each other back in the days when they had all lived at the court when the old king had been alive. She should have remembered how the other man had sneered at everything Alexei did, and had made appallingly insulting remarks about his mother—the commoner who had dared to think that she could become a member of the royal family.

A few moments before she had been afraid of the direction in which his thoughts seemed to be heading, but this… Was it possible that he meant that they could work together on this? The thought of doing something with Alexei rather than fighting him for everything made her heart twist on a little judder of excitement. She had hoped to have her friend Alexei back in her life. She had never dreamed it might actually happen.

But did her friend Alexei still exist? Did she want him to? That friend had never made her feel this way. This very adult, very female, very sexual way.

'Exactly what terms are you talking about?' Deep down, she feared she knew but she couldn't believe it.

'I told you. I will accept the throne on the same conditions as would have applied if Ivan was to inherit. The ones your father agreed—and it seems you were prepared to go along with.'

Ria's head went back, her eyes widening. The ice-blooded statement slammed into her mind with the force of a lightning bolt, making her head spin sickeningly. It was like reliving the moment she had found the signed agreement amongst her father's papers, but somehow worse. She had always known her father was an arch manipulator—but Alexei? She'd gone to him with such hope, but now it seemed that she was trapped even more than before. And her own impulsive declaration of just moments before had just entangled her further in this dark spider's web.

'Marriage.' It was dull and flat, the death knell to the hopes she had only just allowed to creep into her mind. 'The terms of that agreement were marriage.'

He didn't respond; didn't even incline his head in any indication of agreement. Just blinked hard, once, and then those black, black eyes were fixed on her face, as unmoving and unyielding as the rest of him.

'You want me to *marry* you?' The words tasted like poison on her tongue. 'Just like that? I won't—I can't!'

'Not what you'd hoped for?' he enquired sardonically, the corners of his mouth curling into a cynical trace of a smile. 'The prospect doesn't appeal as much as being married to Ivan?'

'It doesn't appeal at all.'

The truth was that it was far worse.

She had never had any feeling except of fear and dislike for Ivan. Hadn't once loved him. Had never dreamed of the prospect of a future with him. Hadn't let herself imagine the possibility of loving and being loved by him as she had once dreamed of happening with Alexei.

So now to be proposed to… No, not proposed to—*propositioned*—so coldly, so heartlessly by him tore at her heart until she thought it must be bleeding to death inside.

She didn't want to look at him, couldn't bear to look into his face, and yet she found that she could look nowhere else. Those deep, dark eyes seemed to draw her in; the sculpted beauty of his mouth was a sensual temptation that she fought to resist. Once she'd dreamed of being kissed by those lips. Lying awake in her adolescent bed, she had imagined how it would feel, longed for it to be reality. Last night that dream had come true. She knew now how that mouth kissed, knew how it tasted, and the reality had been as sensually wonderful as she had hoped. It had left her with a hunger to feel those sensual lips on all the other, more intimate parts of her body. But all the time it had been tainted with a poison that threatened to destroy her emotionally.

And once she had dreamed of a marriage proposal from those lips too. But not like this.

'You can't really believe this is possible.'

'Why not? You've already admitted that neither of us wants Ivan on the throne—but if we made a pact to work together we could ensure that never happens, ensure peace for Mecjoria. You say I am the rightful king—you would make a good queen. After all, that was what your father trained you for.'

'I brought you that document because you are the rightful king!'

'And because you didn't want to marry Ivan.'

How could she deny that when it was nothing but the truth?

'My father had delusions of grandeur.' She tried to focus on his face but his powerful features blurred before her eyes. 'That's not the same as tying myself to someone I barely know.'

'You would have agreed to just this with Ivan.' Alexei pushed the point home. 'You said yourself that the royal family doesn't expect to marry for love.'

No, but they could dream of it—and she had dreamed…
Dreams that were now crashing in pieces around her.

'You'd simply be exchanging one political marriage
for another. What if I promise your father's freedom too?'

'You'd do that?' It was something she'd thought she'd
have to give up on, no matter how much her mother had
begged her to plead for Gregor's release.

'For you as my queen—yes, I'd do it. Oh, I don't expect a wedding right here and now—or even one as soon
as we land. I have the proclamation—the accession—to
deal with first.'

He actually sounded as if he thought that he was making some huge concession. The truth was that in his mind,
he *was* making that concession, obviously. He would give
her a breathing space—a short, barely tolerable breathing
space. But the ruthless, cold determination stamped on his
face told her that was all she would get. And it would be
only the barest minimum of time that he would allow her.

'Well, that's a relief!' Shock and horror made her voice
rigid and cold as she fought against showing the real depth
of her feelings. Her shoulders were so tight that they hurt
and her mouth ached with the control she was imposing
on it. 'Do you expect me to thank you?'

'No more than you should expect me to thank you for
cooperating in this.'

'I haven't said yet that I will cooperate!'

'But you will.' It was coldly, cruelly confident. No
room for argument or doubt. 'And you have to admit that
we have far more between us than you would ever have
had with Ivan.'

'I— No!'

She didn't know how she had managed to sit still so
long. She only knew that she couldn't do it now. She
pushed herself to her feet, up and away from him. From

his oppressive closeness, the dangerous warmth of his hard, lean frame, the disturbing scent of his skin that tantalised her senses. She wanted to go further—so much further—but in the cabin there wasn't enough space to run and hide. And at the same time her need to get away warred with a sensual compulsion to turn back into his atmosphere, to throw herself close against him and recapture that wild enticement that had swamped her totally on the previous night.

'Sit down!'

It was pure command, harsh and autocratic, flung at her so hard that she almost felt the words hit her in the back.

It took all her control to turn and face him, bringing her chin up in defiance so as not to let him see the turmoil she was feeling.

'What's this then, Alexei? Practising for when you're king?'

His scowl was dark and dangerous, making her shift uncomfortably where she stood, the movement aggravated by the lurch of the aircraft so that she almost lost her footing. Stubbornly she refused to reach out and grab the back of the nearest seat for support, however much she needed it.

'According to you, I will need all the practice I can get,' he shot back, the ice in his tone taking the temperature in the cabin down ten degrees or more. 'A commoner jumped up from the gutter, with no true nobility to speak of.'

'That was Ivan, not me!' Ria protested.

'Ivan—your prospective husband.'

She knew he was watching for her instinctive shudder but all the same she couldn't hold it back in spite of knowing how much she was giving away.

'But there is some truth in there—so there's another

reason why this marriage will work out,' Alexei continued coldly. 'I can give you the status and the fortune you want…'

Ria opened her mouth in a rush, needing to tell him that she didn't want either. But a swift, brutal glare stopped her mid-breath.

'And you—well you can be the civilising influence I need. You can teach me how to handle the court procedures—the etiquette I'll need to function as king.'

He almost sounded as if he meant it. Was it possible? Could he really be feeling a touch of insecurity here— and being prepared to admit to it? There was no way it seemed possible. But that twist to his mouth tugged on something deep inside her.

'But you grew up at court—for some years at least. You must have learned…'

'The basics, perhaps. But most of it I have forgotten. I didn't exactly see any use for it in the life I'm living now. And, as your father was so determined to point out, I was never really civilised.' The bite of acid in the words seemed to sear into Ria's skin, making her rub her hands down her arms to ease the burning sensation. 'Not quite blue-blooded enough.'

'Well, I'm sure you'll remember it quickly—without any help from me.'

'Ah, but I'm sure I'll pick it up faster with you at my side—as my partner and consort. My wife.'

'I won't do it.' She shook her head violently, sending her hair flying around her face.

Another lurch of the plane, more violent this time, made her stumble. She almost expected to hear the sound of shattering dreams falling to the floor as the movement coincided with the loss of all those hopes she had once had for the word 'wife' coming from this man.

'You can't make me.'

'I won't have to. You've done it to yourself already.'

As Ria watched in stunned disbelief, Alexei seemed to change mood completely, subsiding into his seat again and relaxing back against the soft, buttery leather.

'Let's see now—where shall I begin? Ah yes—the er-uminium mines.'

She knew then what was coming, acknowledging an aching sense of despair as she watched him lift one long-fingered hand and tick off his points across it one by one. All the arguments she had ever brought to bear on the subject of his possible accession to the throne, all the reasons she had given why he had to take the crown, to prevent Ivan doing so, to protect the country and to avoid civil unrest. They were now all repeated but turned upside down, twisted back against her, landing sharp as poisoned darts in her bruised soul. Alexei used them to provide evidence of the fact that she had no choice. That she had to do as he demanded or prove herself a liar and a traitor to everything she had held dear.

And break her mother's heart and health—possibly her mind too—if she left her father mouldering in his prison cell, as she had feared she was going to do when she had failed to bring Alexei back with her.

She had no choice. Or, rather, she did have a choice but it was between being trapped into this marriage and honouring the contract her father had made with Ivan. An arranged marriage to a man she loathed and feared. A man who made her skin crawl. Or a cold-blooded union to Alexei who would give her a marriage without love. A marriage with no heart. A marriage of shattered dreams.

'Do I have to go on?' Alexei enquired.

'Don't trouble yourself.' She dripped the sarcasm so

strongly that she fully expected it to form a pool at her feet. 'I think I can guess the rest.'

She couldn't see any way out of it. He had tied her up with her own arguments, left her without a leg to stand on. Looking at him now—at the ice that glazed his eyes, the cold, hard set of his face—the momentary hesitation, if that was what she had seen earlier, now seemed positively laughable. She had to have been imagining things.

'Good, so now we understand each other. I said *sit down,* Ria.' One lean hand pointed to the seat she had vacated.

Fury spiked, making her see sparks before her eyes.

'Don't order me around, Alexei! You don't have the right.'

'Oh, but I do,' he inserted smoothly. 'That is, I do if I am to do as you want. As king I can command and you...'

'You're not king yet.'

'Perhaps not, but we are approaching Mecjoria.' A nod towards the window indicated the way that the deep blue of the sea over which they had been flying had now given way to a wild coastline, a range of mountains. 'Any moment now we will be coming in to land. You should sit down and fasten your seatbelt.'

Was that the quirk of a smile at the corners of his mouth? Knowing she was beaten, Ria forced herself forward, dumping down into the seat with her teeth digging hard into her tongue to hold back the wave of anger that almost escaped her. Focussing her attention on snapping on her seatbelt, she addressed the man opposite with her head still bent.

'I had it wrong earlier, Alexei. You don't need any practice, you have the autocratic tyrant down pat—absolutely perfect. No need for anyone at your side to support you or to instruct you in any of the etiquette needed.'

'Perhaps so.'

His tone was infuriatingly relaxed, disturbingly assured.

'But you know as well as I do that the one way to settle this accession situation once and for all and to bring peace to the country for the future is to have someone with an unassailable right on the throne. Mecjoria rejected me once—what's to stop them doing it again? But you as queen will bring that unassailable right along with you. You can choose to give it to me—or to Ivan.'

Choose. There was the word that hit home, sticking in her throat like a piece of broken glass.

She didn't *have* a choice. She had set out on this mission to make sure that Ivan didn't become king—and that she didn't have to marry him. She'd achieved one aim but only by painting herself into a corner to do it. Alexei would be king, if she married him. She could escape the loveless arranged marriage to Ivan only if she agreed to a different one with Alexei.

Out of the frying pan and into the fire.

The way that the plane swayed and jumped, turning into a new course, and the change in the sound of its engines brought home to her the fact that they were circling, ready to approach the airport and the runway on which the jet would land very soon.

This plane will land there, if only to let you off... Alexei's words came back to haunt her. *But that does not mean that I will disembark as well.*

Marriage to Ivan or marriage to Alexei? She knew which one was better for the country—but right now she was thinking on a very personal level and that made everything so very different. The thought of both marriages made her shudder inside, but with very different responses.

One was a sense of cold horror of being tied to a bully like Ivan. For the other, the instinctive fear she was a prey to blended with a shiver of dangerous, treacherous excitement. The memory of last night and the rush of raw, carnal response that had flooded through her when Alexei had taken her in his arms, when he had kissed her, made it impossible to think beyond how it might feel to know that again.

The marriage would be a pretence but that would be real. She wouldn't be able to hide the hunger she felt or even attempt to disguise it.

'You call that a choice? You know I can't let Ivan take the crown. The results for the country would be so appalling.'

'And how do you know that I will not be as bad?'

She could only stare at him, asking herself the same question and finding no answer for it. She knew about Ivan's alliances with dangerous governments, his profligate habits, his cold nature, but the reality was that she knew nothing about Alexei other than the reports in the papers she had read. But she did know that like her he wanted to make sure Ivan didn't inherit.

'For me or for the country?'

'I thought we had agreed that we were largely irrelevant in this. It is the future of Mecjoria and her people that matters. It isn't personal.'

But he had made it personal with this cold-blooded proposition.

'It certainly isn't personal. It's dynastic necessity, pure and simple.

'You don't need to look as if you're facing imminent execution, Ria,' Alexei continued dryly. 'I'm not a monster. I don't expect you to take your marriage vows as soon as we land. For now all that I ask of you is that you

take your place as my promised bride. My devoted fiancée,' he added pointedly. 'No one must doubt that this is
a real relationship. A whirlwind romance perhaps, but
very definitely real.'

Could the atmosphere in the luxurious cabin get any
colder? Ria asked herself as she swallowed down his statement. Could there be any less emotion in his tone?

A sudden violent jolt, the screech of brakes, the rumble
of tyres on the runway brought her to the realisation that
they were down, had landed and the plane was now taxi-
ing towards the airport building. They had arrived; they
were on Mecjorian soil.

Peering out of the window, she saw the sun-baked
countryside that was familiar, the range of mountains
over in the distance, their tops covered in a coating of
snow. It should have felt like coming home. It was home.
She had only been away for less than a week, one hundred and twenty hours at the most, but it seemed that everything had changed totally. Her life was no longer her
own; her future had taken a totally different path from
the one she had believed it would follow. She had thought
that she would persuade Alexei to take the throne and then
she could quietly retreat into the background, live her life
in private. Now it seemed that instead she was going to
have to be up front and centre.

With Alexei.

Awkwardly she fumbled with her seatbelt, feeling imprisoned, tied down and needing desperately to be free.
But the way her future was going it seemed she would
never be free. She had gone to Alexei in the hope of being
freed from the future that her father had planned for her
but instead she had come up against a man who was even
more ruthless and controlling than Gregor had ever been.

As a result she had jumped out of the frying pan and right into the fire. And she faced the prospect of being burned alive as a result.

CHAPTER EIGHT

'LET ME...'

Alexei had already dispensed with his seatbelt with clinical efficiency and he was standing beside her, his hand reaching out for the awkward buckle on hers. When he bent his head to deal with it the softness of his dark hair brushed against her cheek, caressing her skin and sending shivers of response down her spine. She could smell the citrus shampoo on his hair, the clean scent of his skin, and up this close she could see how already, even at this stage of the day, the dark shadow of the growth of beard marked his cheeks.

Her heart thudded in her throat and she had to sit back and clench her hands into tight fists down at her sides to stop herself from giving in to the urge to reach out and stroke his cheek, feel the contrast between warm satin skin and the rough scrape of hair against her fingertips. Heat flooded every part of her, pooling at the spot just between her legs, so close to where those strong, square-tipped fingers had just completed their task.

Would this instant, shockingly primitive reaction to his nearness make the future he had dictated to her so much easier or so very much harder? She didn't know and with sparks of response flaring in her brain, spots rising in front of her eyes, she couldn't even begin to think of finding a way to answer her own question. She didn't even know if she could get to her feet, the muscles in her legs, even her bones, seeming to have melted in the burn of response that possessed her.

'I can't...' she began but then, afraid of what she might be revealing, swallowed down the admission and changed it to, 'I don't think I can do this. How does a devoted fiancée—your devoted fiancée—behave?'

'You need to ask that? Here...'

Those strong hands came down again, clamping over hers as he straightened up. He hauled her upwards, lifting her to her feet, so fast so roughly that she fell against him, her breasts thrust into the hard, muscled planes of his chest, her face pressed to the lean column of his throat, her senses swimming from immediate sensual overload.

'Of course I need to ask!' Her physical response thickened her tone, making it husky and raw, alien in her own ears. 'I'm not your fiancée—nor am I devoted to you. We have nothing between us.'

'Nothing?' His laughter made it only too plain what he thought of that. 'Lady, if this is nothing...'

His dark head came down fast and hard, those beautiful lips finding hers and clamping tight against her mouth, crushing hers back against her teeth so that she could only gasp in shocked response.

As a kiss it was cold and cruel, more like a punishment than a caress, but appallingly it didn't matter. She didn't care, couldn't think, could only feel. And the feeling that was uppermost in her thoughts, pounding through her body, was a raw hunger, a desperate need for this—and so much more. She would have flung her hands up around his neck, bringing his head down even closer, to deepen and prolong that burning pressure, but the way he still held her prevented that. She couldn't hold back and she crushed her mouth against his, strained her body closer, feeling the heat and hardness of his erection that pushed against the cradle of her pelvis, telling her of his desire and feeding her own until she was swimming on a heated tide of longing, losing herself in him.

The moment when he broke off the kiss, snatched his mouth from hers, dropped her back down on to her feet—feet that she hadn't even been aware had left the floor—was like a brutal slap to her face. His name almost escaped her in a cry of shocked distress but she dragged her hands from his and flung them up and over her mouth to hold back the revealing sound.

'I think that showed you—showed both of us—how this will work. You say you don't know how to do this but it's so easy. I want you…'

Reaching out, he stroked a finger down the side of her cheek, watching intently as in spite of herself she shivered, her eyes closing in instinctive response.

'And I can have you if I want.'

That brought her eyes flying open again to stare, shocked, into his.

'No!'

He ignored her furious protest. 'Because you want me just as much. You responded. More than responded. You know as I do that if we'd been somewhere more private then things would have gone so much further.'

Breathing unevenly, he smoothed a hand over his face, brushed the other down his body to straighten the shirt her actions had creased, pulling it from his trousers at his waist.

'Perhaps it's best that things can't go any further now—before I do something that we'll both regret.'

'You've already done something I regret—something I wish had never happened!'

Was it the fact that it was a lie that made her voice so shrill? Or the way that her body was still struggling with the aftershocks of the reaction his kiss had sparked off in her, sparks fizzing along every nerve, burning up in her blood?

'Really? Then if that's the case, you'll not want this, either.'

She knew what was coming, and the tiny part of her mind that was still rational told her to step back, move away. Fast. But that tiny part was totally submerged in the burning flood of sensual need that swamped common sense, drowning it in the heat of the hunger that still throbbed deep inside. She saw the change in his eyes, the switch from ice to smoky shadows that matched her own mood, and her breath caught in her throat, her lips parting, ready for the very different kiss she knew he planned.

And the kiss she really wanted.

This time it was warm and gentle. It gave instead of taking. His mouth caressed hers, teased, tantalised, tempting it further open to allow the intimate invasion of his tongue. The cool, fresh taste of him was like a powerful aphrodisiac exploding against her lips, totally intoxicating, instantly addictive.

She melted into that kiss, almost swooning against him as the throb of desire took all the strength from her legs, made them feel like damp cotton wool beneath her. And when Alexei's arms came round her it only added to the sensual overload that had her at its mercy. The heat and scent of his body was like the burn of incense in her nostrils making her head swim.

This was the kiss she had always dreamed of, the kiss she had been waiting for all her life. The kiss she had once lain awake imagining long into the night as she felt the awakening of her female sexuality It was a kiss that made her know what it felt like to be a woman.

A woman who had found the man she wanted most in all of the world.

A woman who had discovered the man she...

Oh no! *No, no, no!*

Panic-stricken she froze, jerked back, tore herself away from him. What was she thinking? Where had that come from? How had she let that thought—that terrible, foolish, dangerous thought—creep into her mind?

Was she really so weak that she was allowing her adolescent self to resurface with all her foolish, gullible dreams, the fantasies she had indulged in when she couldn't face reality? The fictions she had created for herself when she had let herself pretend that perhaps one day, Alexei, the boy she had had such a heavyweight crush on, would turn to her and want her as a man would want a woman.

Well, yes, he wanted her now, there was no denying that. And she wanted him. He was right, he could have her if he wanted her. There was no way she was going to be able to resist him if he turned on the true high-octane power of his sensuality, the enticement of the seduction she knew he could channel without trying. But was she going to mistake the white-hot burn of adult sexuality for anything more?

This was the first real experience of true lust she had ever known and it seemed it had the power to burn away some much-needed brain cells, foolishly allowing her to confuse it with real feelings—emotions that her younger, naïve sense had once dreamed of knowing.

'No.'

Alexei had felt her withdrawal and his voice seemed to echo her thoughts, but so much more assuredly, calm and controlled—disturbingly so, considering the fires that had just blazed between them, the sparks that still seemed to sizzle in the air.

'No—we can't take this any further now.'

Shockingly he dropped another kiss on her upturned face. A brief, casual, almost affectionate kiss on her cheek. And the easiness of his response, the light-heartedness of his touch, rocked her even more than her own shattered thoughts of a moment before. They were kisses of certainty, relaxed, almost careless. The kisses of a man who knew that he could get exactly what he wanted—whenever he wanted—so that he didn't have to take too much trouble now.

'Too much to do. A reception committee outside.'

'Really?'

Knocked even more off-balance, Ria twisted on her heel, still within the confines of his arms, and bent slightly to look out the window.

Someone must have radioed ahead, informing the airport authorities—and more—of their planned arrival. And that someone must have announced not just that Alexei's private jet requested permission to land—but that Alexei Joachim Sarova, Crown Prince and future King of Mecjoria, was arriving back in his country, ready to take possession of the throne. There was a fleet of sleek black cars drawn up at the far side of the tarmac, smoked glass, bullet-proof windows, black bodyworks gleaming in the sun. A small Mecjorian flag fluttered on the bonnet of the lead vehicle and someone had rolled out a red carpet across the runway, leading to the bottom of the flight of steps that had now been brought to the door of the plane. A door that a member of the flight crew was hurrying to unlock, to let them out.

'We're here,' Alexei said. 'I'm here. This is what you wanted.'

What she wanted. He was going to make his claim for the throne; and that could only mean that he believed she had agreed to his conditions.

But why shouldn't he think that? Hadn't she given him every indication that she had accepted his terms—welcomed them if her response to his kiss was anything to go by?

After all, what other choice did she have? If she wanted Alexei to take the throne instead of Ivan then she had to go along with what he demanded of her. She had to marry him, become his queen. It was either that or marry Ivan, and the way that her blood ran cold at just the thought was enough to tell her that somewhere along the line she had decided to go along with Alexei's proposal even though she had no recollection of ever rationally doing so. She had no other possible alternative.

Turning back from the window, Alexei looked down into her face, dark eyes probing hers.

'We can make this work, Ria,' he said sombrely. 'Together we can do what's best for Mecjoria.'

Did he read anything else in her face? She would never know, but something made him pause, then go on to add, 'You're right that the royal family doesn't expect to marry for love—and I'm not offering that. I can't love you. I loved once—adored her... Lost her.'

Something darkened his face, his eyes. Something reaching out from the past and coiling round his memory, Ria realised as he went on.

Mariette. He meant Mariette, the dark-haired beauty who had been the mother of his child, who had had a total breakdown when the baby died and had ended up in a psychiatric hospital. Refusing ever to see him again.

'I'll never feel like that again. But as my queen you would be my equal. My consort. And I know you'll be a fine queen. How can you not when your father has trained you for this almost from the moment you were born?'

He must have known how the mention of her father would make her react because he waited as she tried to look away, to look anywhere but into his stunning face. Once again he touched her cheek very softly.

'We'll finish this later.'

It was his total assurance that terrified her. Particularly when she knew she had only herself to blame. Hadn't she practically flung herself into his arms like a sex-starved adolescent who had only been kissed for the very first time?

Well, yes, she wasn't going to deny the desire—the hunger—she felt when he kissed her. But knowing she wanted him was one thing, tying herself to him in the sort of cold-blooded dynastic marriage she had hoped to escape from totally another.

'Later...'

It was all that she could manage as someone knocked on the cabin door and she found herself released so swiftly that she stumbled backwards and away from him. The speed with which he discarded her and turned his attention to other matters, reaching for his jacket, shrugging it on, smoothing a hand over his hair, made her feel like some dirty little secret to be kept hidden away until he had time for her again. He had her cooperation in the bag, he believed, and now he wanted to focus on the reason why he was—why they were both—here.

Reaction setting in made her vision blur, her hands shake, as she collected her own coat and her bag. She couldn't look at Alexei, couldn't bear to see the dark certainty, the satisfaction that she knew must show on his face. She wanted to get out of here, get her feet back down on the ground in more ways than one.

As she reached the door of the plane she was ahead of him. Just a couple of steps but enough. In the doorway at the top of the steps she suddenly realised, all her training kicking in, so that she hesitated, stopped. Reality hit home with the truth of who he now was. Carefully she took that couple of steps back and out of the way.

'Sir,' she said, resisting the urge to drop a curtsey even if only to defy him, to prove that he might have her in a cleft stick, but she wasn't going down without a fight. She was still her own woman and she would hang on to that for as long as she could.

She saw that elegant mouth twitch slightly, curling at the corners in a way that told her he knew only too well what was in her mind and a brief inclination of his head acknowledged everything unspoken that had passed between them. A moment later he was past her, standing in the doorway, looking down at the reception committee waiting for him, before stepping out into the warmth of the evening air.

As he went down the steps to the tarmac with cameras flashing like wild lightning in the distance, warning them of what was to come, what was inevitable now that the prodigal prince had come home, she spotted one moment when he paused, just for the space of a heartbeat, and squared his shoulders like a man accepting his destiny and going to meet his future. He hadn't wanted this, she recalled. He had practically thrown her out of his house when she had first put the proposition to him. Whatever else she might think of him, she could see that unlike Ivan, who wanted the crown for the prestige, the power, and of course the huge wealth that came with it,

Alexei appeared to have totally different reasons for going ahead with this.

Together we can do what's best for Mecjoria.

Whatever else was between them was personal—*this* was for the country's future. And at least on that she and Alexei were in agreement. But it—with her involvement—had taken away his freedom, the life he had lived up to now. His existence would never be the same again, and knowing the position she was in now, with her own freedom given up to secure peace for the country, Ria felt she understood that on a much deeper level than when she had got on a plane here at this same airport to go and try to persuade him to do just this.

So when he paused at the foot of the step, stopping before he actually set foot on Mecjorian land—his country—she spotted it at once. She was there so close behind him that they were almost touching, his sudden hesitation making her almost slam into him from behind. And when he half-turned, dark eyes meeting hers just for a moment, and he held out his hand to her, she moved forward quickly, putting her fingers into his without hesitation or uncertainty. She felt the power of his touch close round her, holding firm and strong, and welcomed it as she walked down beside him, stepping onto Mecjorian soil together.

It was only when she looked back at that moment later, when it was played over and over on national TV, seeing it from the view of the reception committee of government ministers and army top brass lined up beside the red carpet waiting to greet Alexei, that she saw it properly. Saw how clearly it demonstrated that she had made her choice even before she had actually done so rationally within her own thoughts. That she had cast in her lot with Alexei, and without ever saying so had agreed to the future that he had decreed for both of them.

CHAPTER NINE

TOGETHER.

The word seemed to have taken up permanent residence inside Ria's head, mocking her with the memories of the day they had arrived in Mecjoria and the thoughts she had let herself consider then.

Together. She had let herself believe that Alexei had meant that there was a together in all this. That she and Alexei were working to the same ends. That her role as his fiancée might mean that she would actually be by his side, that they could be partners in this.

That he might actually need her just a little bit.

But it seemed that, having announced their engagement and presented her to the court, to the country, as his prospective bride, he had lost interest. There had been the moment when they had set foot on the red carpet, when the army officers, the dignitaries, had moved forward, bowed, saluted, address him as 'Your Majesty' and she had known that this was after all coming true.

Then Alexei had acknowledged their greetings, shaken hands, all the time holding on to hers so tightly that his grip felt like a manacle around her wrist. She had had to move with him; it was either that or create an ugly little scene as she tried to break away. She had to endure the fusillade of camera flashes, the frankly curious and assessing stares of everyone who was there—the ones who knew of her father's fall from grace, his imprisonment, her own loss of any title and status at the court as a result.

And then, at last, just before they headed for the waiting cars, Alexei had finally announced the reason why she was there.

'Gentlemen,' he had said in a voice that carried clear and strong in spite of the wicked breeze that was swirling round them now. 'Let me present to you my fiancée—and future queen—the Grand Duchess Honoria Maria Escalona…'

And with that her place in all this was fixed, settled once and for all. Her title it seemed was restored to her, her place in society reinstated. But she was trapped even more tightly in the web of intrigue and plotting that had created this situation in the first place. The speed and conviction with which it had happened made her head spin.

But once they were back in Mecjoria it seemed that everything she had been anticipating hadn't happened. Nothing might have changed for all the difference it made in her relationship with Alexei. He didn't even seem to want her sexually any more. She had been convinced that he would press home the advantage he'd made it clear he knew he had while they were on the plane. But it appeared that as soon as he had her on his side for the future of Mecjoria and had introduced her as his fiancée, so putting her firmly in the limelight and in the place he wanted her at his side, he seemed to have lost interest.

She had been settled in a beautiful suite in the huge, golden-stoned palace high on the hill above the capital. A far more beautiful and luxurious suite than she had ever enjoyed on her rare visits there in the past. Her clothes, her personal belongings, had been brought from her home and delivered to her room, and she had been left to settle in.

Alone.

Later she had been sent a series of instructions—details of where she was expected to be and when. There were dinners, receptions, public appearances. There had been a whole new wardrobe provided for these events too with visits from top couturiers, fittings for every sort of dress, shoes, jewellery imaginable. She was now dressed more glamorously than ever in life before. But then she was used to this. It was how it had always been with her father. What was different was the way that, once he had let her know where she was to be, Alexei left everything else up to her. Her father had wanted more control than that. For each event she had been given a series of commands disguised as strict guidelines, as to what she was to do, when she was to appear, what she was to wear, the subjects she should read up on in order to be able to talk about. Alexei made no such demands; and she valued the confidence, the trust, he put in her that way.

She had performed her duty at Alexei's side, smiled when she needed to, made polite, careful conversation with everyone she was introduced to, walked with her hand on his arm, eaten the meals put in front of her. She had executed her role of the apparently devoted fiancée to perfection, and then returned to her room.

Alone.

But there had been one special duty that he had entrusted to her. One that he felt that she was the best person in the country to carry out.

'We need to broadcast the story of the discovery of the proof of my parents' marriage,' he told her. 'Everyone is asking questions, making up the most impossible stories.'

Between them, they had come up with a version that came close enough to the truth. A story that involved the missing document being discovered in some long-unopened files. There was no need to detail Ria's father's involvement in it, Alexei had conceded, obviously not wanting his new fiancée's name blackened by any connection with Gregor's plotting.

'You'll be able to get close enough to the truth when you say how you discovered it, and it will explain why you came to England to contact me,' he told her as he escorted her to the TV studios from which she was to broadcast the details the press wanted.

She knew it was all show, just part of the masquerade they were putting on, but all the same she hugged to herself a feeling of delight at the way that Alexei left her to herself to decide what to say and how to say it. She knew he was watching in the background, scrutinising every move she made, but he had trusted her and that was what mattered. And at the end of the interview, when all the cameras were turned off, he had put his hand on her shoulder, drawing her close to drop a kiss on to her cheek.

'Thank you,' he had said quietly, his breath warm on her skin. 'The mention of the way that your visit to London meant we had the chance to renew our friendship from when we were here in Mecjoria all those years ago was inspired. It was just what was needed.'

Ria nodded agreement, swallowing down the way that 'friendship' covered such a multitude of sins. 'And with any luck the romance story will grab the headlines more.'

Her instincts proved right. The 'fairy-tale romance' between the new king and the daughter of one of the oldest families in Mecjoria was what caught the headlines. For every appearance Alexei made on his own, the interest was trebled if the two of them were seen together. The flash and crash of cameras on every occasion was like an assault, and the coverage in every newspaper made it seem as if there was no other subject under the sun.

Alexei hadn't allowed her to make any contact with her family. Her mother might have packed up her clothes for delivery to the castle, and she had included a brief note, just a card, to thank Ria for her success in bringing Alexei to Mecjoria, but that was all. And nothing more was allowed, it seemed. There might be murmurs of curiosity as to where Ria's father could be, but as her mother was known to be ill and had retired to the family's country house to recover it was rarely taken any further than a comment. And when it was, then the next walkabout by the 'fairy tale' couple pushed the query well away from the front page. Her family would be in touch, there would be news about her father, when the time was right, Ria was told.

But when would the time be right?

She had never managed to snatch more than a few moments' conversation with the man she was engaged to and even those were necessarily casual and uncontroversial because of their public setting, with hundreds of listeners in to every word they said, a phalanx of photographers lined up to record their every move. At the end of the day Alexei would smile, give her a kiss on both cheeks, one more on her mouth that their audience was waiting for, and walk away, back to the council rooms or his office, to discuss the next steps in the preparation for the coronation, leaving her alone.

And wanting more.

He might be able to switch off so completely, to concentrate on what mattered most to him—but she couldn't. She spent long, sleepless nights alone in the huge soft bed in the luxurious gold and white room, unable to settle. She was lonely, side-lined—frustrated. It was too painful a reminder of how she had once felt, all those years before, when she had been just an adolescent and she hadn't truly understood what these feelings were, where they came from. Now she was a grown woman, experiencing adult feelings for an adult male, and she knew exactly what they meant.

She wanted him. In every way that a woman wanted a man. She wanted him in her life, in her bed…inside her body. So much so that she ached now just thinking of it. Sighing, Ria tossed and turned, hunger buzzing along her nerves. She had never thought when she had agreed to go and find Alexei, talk to him, that she would open this whole Pandora's Box of memories. She had thought that she could face him as an adult, face down the hurt of past times. That she could persuade him to set her country free from the threats that surrounded it, and put herself on to a new path into the future as a result.

Instead she had thrown herself into a whole new volcano of sensual reaction, taken the lid off a set of feelings that, developed and matured by time, were now too big, too powerful to ever go quietly back into the box no matter how hard she tried.

But had she got it so terribly wrong? Was the truth that he was using her, using the desire she had been unable to hide, to make her do as he said, act in the way that benefitted him most? She had been manoeuvred into this position, playing the role of his fiancée, only to be frozen out on any more personal level. So was she really just a pawn in the game of dynastic chess he had set out to play with the country's future—and with hers? Just a way to cement his position as king or did he want something more from her?

'Oh why do I have to feel this way? Still!'

Turning restlessly on fine linen sheets that suddenly seemed as rough as cheap polyester against her sensitised skin, Ria pummelled her pillow, desperately trying to find a comfortable spot that might help her relax. Outside, the dark of the night was filled with a heavy, oppressive warmth, the low, rumble of thunder circling against the mountains and across the valley towards the castle. The long voile curtains waved in the breeze, as restless and unsettled as her thoughts. But it wasn't the heat outside that made her body burn but the flare of feelings deep inside.

Alexei had declared openly that he would never love her, but she had thought that he had responded to her at least as a woman. That he had wanted her as much as she did him. She had told herself that she wouldn't ask for more. She hadn't thought that she might have to settle for so much less.

Knowing that sleep was impossible, Ria tossed back the bedclothes, swinging her feet to the floor and reaching for the pale blue robe that lay at the foot of the bed, a match for the beautiful silk nightdress she was wearing.

When it had been delivered, along with the other new outfits she was expected to wear for her official duties, she had thought that there was perhaps a secret message in the garments. That they were meant for the time when she and Alexei would get together and finish what they had started in London and later on the plane journey here. She had waited six long nights, the pretty blue nightgown had become crumpled with wear. But not any more.

'Six nights is long enough!'

She wasn't going to sit here any longer like some unwanted spare part. She wasn't thirteen any more, trained to be compliant, doing as her father said.

She didn't even have to do as Alexei said; not unless she wanted to.

Tightening the belt of the blue robe around her waist and pushing her feet into soft white slippers, she marched towards the door and flung it open.

'Madame?'

The instant response, in a quiet, respectful male voice, startled her. She had forgotten that Alexei had warned her of the need for security following the unrest that had resulted from the problems over the accession to the throne. Drawing herself up hastily, she directed a cool gaze at the security officer.

'His Majesty asked to see me.'

'Of course, madame. If you'll just follow me...'

The problem was, Ria acknowledged to herself as he led her down long high-ceilinged corridors, that now she was committed. How would this man react if she suddenly declared that she wasn't going to obey the summons she had claimed after all?

But they had reached their destination before she had time to think things through, her guide stopping by another huge carved wooden door, rapping lightly on it and then standing back with a swift, neat bow.

'Yes?'

The door was yanked open and Alexei stood in the doorway, tall and devastating, more imposing than ever.

He had discarded the dinner jacket he'd had on earlier that evening but he still wore the immaculate white shirt, now pulled open at the throat with his black bow tie, tugged loose and left dangling around his neck. His hair was in ruffled disarray, as if he had been running his hands through it again and again, and he held a crystal tumbler with some clear liquid swirling about at the bottom of it.

'Madame Duchess...'

His voice was dark with cynicism, no warmth of welcome in it.

Without thinking, Ria reverted to the formality of etiquette she had been trained in and dipped into a neat curtsey, holding the blue skirts of her robe out around her as if they were some formal ball gown.

'You asked to see me, sir.'

I did? She could see the question in his eyes, the way the straight black brows snapped together in astonishment, but luckily his sharp jet gaze went to the man behind her and obviously caught on. He nodded and stepped back, opening the door even wider.

'I did, duchess,' he responded with a grave formality that was at odds with the twitch of the corners of his mouth. 'Come in.'

It took all Ria's control to move forward, walk past the security guard and into the room. Just at the last moment she recovered enough composure to turn and switch on a swift, controlled smile.

'Thank you,' she murmured.

Then she was inside and the door was closed behind her, leaving her alone with Alexei.

This suite was larger even than the one she had spent the last week in. Huge rooms, vast windows, decorated in shades of dark green. But now, seeing it with him standing beside her, she couldn't help recalling the building she had seen him in in London. Here, the stiff formality of the décor, the furnishings in the dark heavy wood, made it look as if it had been decorated twenty years or more before. There were no photographs here, she noticed, recalling how those elegant but somehow cold, isolated—lonely—images had hit home the first time she had seen them. In fact there was nothing personal here, nothing of Alexei. Only the new king.

Ria managed another couple of steps into the room, then slowed, stopped, as the full force of the scene outside the door hit home.

'Oh dear heaven...' Even she couldn't tell if her voice

shook with laughter or embarrassment. 'Henri. What he must have thought!'

'And what was that?' Alexei drawled, taking a sip of his drink.

'That you— He must have thought that you had summoned me to your room...'

She couldn't complete the sentence but the dark gleam in Alexei's eyes told her that he had followed her thought processes exactly.

'And would it have been so very terrible if I had? Why should you not be in my room? We are engaged to be married, after all. And from the stories of our romance in the press, everyone will be expecting that we are already lovers.'

The last of his drink was tossed to the back of his throat, swallowed hard. Ria watched every last inch of its progress down the lean bronzed length of his throat, almost to the point where the first evidence of crisp, dark body hair showed at the neck of his white shirt. Compulsively she found herself matching the movement, though her own gulping swallow did nothing to ease the heated dryness of her mouth.

'That being so, they probably wondered why you haven't been here before. So tell me—to what do I owe the honour of this visit?'

What had seemed so totally right when she had been tossing and turning in her bed, her body on fire with longing, now seemed impossible. The restless hunger hadn't eased—if anything, standing here like this so close to the living, breathing reality of her dreams, able to see the gleam of health on the golden skin, the lustre of his black hair, smell the personal scent of his body, made it all so much worse, much more visceral and primitive. But how could she come right out and *say* it?

'Perhaps I feel the way the paparazzi feel…'

His frown revealed his confusion and perhaps a touch of disbelief.

'I want to know more than just what event I'm attending, what dress I'll be wearing. I'm wondering just what I'm doing here—why you have me imprisoned.'

It was the first thing that came to her mind—and the worst, it seemed. Danger flared in his eyes, and the glass he held slammed down on a nearby table.

'Not imprisoned! You are free to come and go as you please.'

'Oh perhaps not like my father, I agree. I'm your fiancée—we're supposed to be getting married but that's almost as much as I know. I need to know just what I'm doing here.'

I need to know what we can do to make this work, she added in her own thoughts but totally lost the nerve to actually say the words aloud.

CHAPTER TEN

'Oh come now, Ria,' Alexei mocked. 'You know only too well why you are here. I want you—and you want me. We have only to look at each other and we go up in flames.'

Right now she felt that that was exactly the truth. The moment of cold had vanished and now the surface of her skin seemed to be burning up. When he prowled nearer she had to clench her hands in the skirts of her nightdress and robe, keeping them prisoner and away from the dangerous impulse to reach out and touch him.

'So much so that you haven't even been near me!' she scorned. 'You've sent me jewels—flowers.'

'I thought women liked flowers—and jewellery.'

Ria batted the interruption aside with a wave of her fingers then snatched her hand back again as if stung as skin met skin where it had accidentally brushed his cheek. She could feel the wave of colour rising in her cheeks as she saw the way his eyes darkened in instant response, sending her body temperature rocketing skywards.

'And you look beautiful in that nightdress,' he continued, unrepressed.

'So beautiful that ever since we came back to Mecjoria you have barely spent a day in my company.'

'Are you saying that you've been missing me?' Alexei questioned with sudden softness.

Missing you so badly that it's eating me up inside.

'I am supposed to be your fiancée!' she flung back.

Alexei's slow smile mocked the vehemence of her response.

'And right now you are doing a wonderful job of sounding exactly like the jealous fiancée I would like you to be.'

'Jealous of what—who?'

'Of the time I spend with my new mistresses.'

It took her several moments to realise exactly what he meant. Not real women but the demands of the kingdom, the affairs of state.

'It was inevitable that you would be so occupied in these first days,' she acknowledged. 'You have so much to do. But you were wrong, you know, you didn't need any help.'

She had been impressed at the way he had taken charge since they had returned to Mecjoria. She'd watched him go through all the ceremony, the diplomatic meetings, seen the calm dignity and strength with which he'd conducted himself. He'd handled everyone, from the highest nobility to the ordinary commoner, with grace and ease.

'You've done wonderfully well—never put a foot wrong.'

A slight inclination of his head acknowledged the compliment which had been nothing less than the truth.

'I had a good teacher.'

Now it was her turn to frown. But then her expression changed abruptly as she met his eyes.

'I've done nothing,' she protested.

'The people want to see you,' Alexei countered. 'They love you and so do the press.'

'It's the Romeo and Juliet element—our "romance"—' She broke off abruptly as he shook his head almost savagely.

'You've been at my side every day. You're a link to the old monarchy and you've lived in Mecjoria all your life. People value that.'

Was he saying that he valued it too? Her heart ached to know the answer to that question.

'Who else could I ask this of other than someone like you?' His hand cupped her cheek, dark eyes looking down into hers in a way that somehow made this so personal between the two of them, not just a matter of state. 'Someone who loves Mecjoria, who belongs here.'

'You belong here now!'

Too late she heard that 'now' fall into a dangerous silence. One that came with too many memories, too much darkness attached to it. And she knew that he felt that way too when his hand fell away, breaking the fragile contact between them.

'I know you never wanted to come back to Mecjoria.'

'Ah, but there you couldn't be more wrong,' Alexei put in sharply. 'Why do you think I was so furious when we got thrown out? Why I hated what had happened to us? This was my father's homeland. I wanted to be accepted here. To belong here. And I grew to love the countryside—the lakes, the mountains.'

His eyes went to the windows where in the daylight those mountains could be seen, rising majestically against the horizon, so high that they were always capped with a layer of snow, even in the summer.

'That was what got me hooked on photography. I wanted to capture the stunning beauty of Alabria. The wildlife in the forests. It was my father who gave me my first camera. That was the one thing I managed to take with me into exile.'

Exile. That single word spoke of so much more. Of love and loss and loneliness. Particularly when she was remembering those photographs on the walls of his office. The ones that had made him his fortune, built his reputation. Their stylised bleakness could not have been in starker contrast to the gentle beauty of the forests and lakes, the animals that had first made him want to capture their images.

'Do you still have that camera?'

He didn't use words to answer her. Instead he gestured to a heavy wooden chest of drawers that stood against the wall. Only now did Ria see the well-worn leather camera case that stood on top of it, its plain and battered appearance at odds with the old-fashioned ornate décor of the rest of the room. Her heart clenched, making her catch her breath.

'Your father would have been proud of you.'

Something in what she had said made his mouth, which had relaxed for a moment, twist tightly, cynically.

'Now,' he said roughly. 'He would have felt very differently about the son he had while he was still alive.'

'You didn't exactly get a chance.' Honesty forced her to say it. 'The court is hidebound by archaic rules and protocols. They can take years to learn if you haven't grown up getting used to them. And it was so much worse ten years ago. Even now it's bad enough.'

Alexei's smile was wry, almost boyish, reminding her sharply of so many occasions from the past. 'And have you any idea how many times I've checked you out at some moment this week when I've needed to know exactly what the protocol was?'

'You have?' She had never noticed that. And the fact that he would admit to it stunned her.

'Like I said—I've had a good teacher.'

'I wish I'd done more in the past. I could have helped you then.'

'Your father made sure you had no opportunity for that,' he commented cynically. 'He had his plans for you even then and nothing was going to get in the way. Particularly not some jumped-up commoner from an inconvenient marriage he had thought was long forgotten.'

'You think that even then…?'

She fought against the nausea rising in her throat. It was worse than she thought.

'I know.'

Alexei's nod was like a hammer blow on any hopes that things were not as bad as she had feared. A death blow to the dream that Alexei would not want to take the revenge that he was justified in seeking.

'If it had not been Ivan, it would have been someone else. Whoever offered him the greatest chance at being the power behind the throne.'

'Anyone but you.' It was just a whisper.

'Anyone but me.'

And there it was. The real reason why she was here. What was it people said—don't ask the question if you can't take the answer? She'd asked and so she had only herself to blame if the answer was not what she wanted to hear. And how could she want to hear that her place at Alexei's side, the link to the old monarchy she brought with her, provided the perfect revenge for all that Gregor had ever done to this man, the inheritance he had deprived him of? The father. The homeland.

'Tell me.' Alexei's voice seemed to come from a long way away. 'Could you really have married Ivan?'

Even for the country? She had once thought that she could but now, in the darkness of the night, she couldn't suppress the shudder that shook her at just the thought.

That was why her father was still in jail, Alexei acknowledged privately as he watched the colour drain from her face. All the investigations he had carried out since returning to Mecjoria had only proved even further just what sort of a slippery, devious cold fish Gregor Escalona still was. The man who had plotted his downfall and his mother's ruin would sell his soul to the devil if the price was right. He was not about to let the bastard out of jail until he was sure that he had control of him in other ways. And that control came through Escalona's daughter. With Ria at his side, as his wife, he had an unassailable claim to the throne. Surely even Gregor would think twice about staging a palace revolution when it would harm his daughter?

Though even that was something he still couldn't be sure of. Gregor had always been a cold and neglectful father. That was one of the reasons why Ria had sought out his friendship back in the past. They had been—he'd thought—two lost and lonely youngsters caught in the heartless world of power struggles and conspiracies. The sort of conspiracy in which Gregor had shown himself to be quite prepared to use his daughter to his own advantage. Signing the treaty with Ivan was evidence of that.

Which was why he had to marry Ria—*another* reason why he had to marry her, he admitted. He wasn't going to let Escalona near her until she was truly his wife. Only then could he protect her from being forced to marry Ivan in any counter-revolution to gain the crown. It was the thought of her married to Ivan that had pushed him into the proposal from the start—but now the thought that she might have been pressured into marrying a man she so obviously feared reinforced that already steel-hard resolve to make her his queen.

Whatever else Gregor had done wrong, the way he had raised his daughter had prepared her so well for the role she would fulfil. He had been sure she would be an asset to his claim to the throne and she had proved herself in so many ways.

But of course they weren't married yet. And until they were he wasn't going to let Escalona anywhere near his daughter.

But when an ugly little question was raised inside his head, demanding to know just what made him any different from the bullying father who would have pushed her into a forced marriage without considering her feelings, he was uncomfortably aware of the fact that he didn't have an answer to give, not one that would satisfy even himself.

'And marrying me?' he demanded roughly.

A small flick of her head might have been an answer. It might just as well have been a dismissal of the question as one she refused to answer. Her lips were pressed tight against each other, as if refusing to let any real response out. The problem was the deep gut-instinct that wrenched at him, seeing that. He wanted to lean forward, to stroke his thumb along the line of her mouth, ease those rose-tinted lips apart, cover her mouth with his, taste her, invade the moist warmth.

His heart thudded so hard against his rib cage that he felt sure she must hear it and his body hardened in hunger that made him want to groan aloud. When he had chosen that blue nightdress and robe he had imagined how she might look in it, the pale silk and darker blue lace contrasting with the creamy softness of her skin; the deep vee neckline plunging over the smooth curves of her breasts, the rich tumble of her hair along her shoulders. The reality far overshadowed his imaginings and his senses were even further besieged by the perfume of some floral shampoo as she moved her head, the scent of her skin driving him half-crazy with sexual need.

'That's a *fait accompli*.' Ria's cool voice sliced into his heated imaginings, making him fight to pay attention to what she was actually saying. 'But don't you think our "romance" will be more convincing if we spend more time together—as a man and a woman, not just as king and queen? I appreciate that you have many commitments—duties. Though I would have thought that when those duties were done…'

'You'd have liked me to come to your room, to snatch an hour—maybe less?' he challenged. 'You would have thought that was worth it?'

If he'd gone to her room then he wouldn't have stayed just for an hour, that was the truth. If he'd visited her there once, they would never have emerged until both of them were sated and exhausted. And he would have been totally in her power, sexually enslaved as never before in his life. He wasn't ready to risk that yet. He had the disturbing feeling that it would not be enough. That he would never be free again.

'I would have liked some attention—other than these *gifts!*'

'You don't like presents?'

'Presents are not…'

Ria almost choked on the realisation of what she had been about to say. Presents are not feelings. Presents are not *love.* Just where had that word come from?

Love. She didn't want to think that. She most definitely didn't want to feel that. But, now that the word had slipped into her thoughts, there was no way she was going to get it back into its box.

'Presents are not…?' Alexei prompted when she found her tongue frozen, unable to continue.

'Not important.' She bit the words out.

'A pity.' It actually sounded genuine. 'I had hoped you

would enjoy them. So perhaps I should cancel tomorrow's sessions with the couturier?'

'What would I need *more* dresses for? I have more than—'

'For the Black and White Ball,' Alexei inserted smoothly, cutting her off. There was a new glint in his eyes and his mouth seemed to have softened unexpectedly. 'You didn't think I would go ahead with that?' he asked as he saw the astonishment she couldn't hide. 'It is tradition. And you always wanted to attend such an event.'

She'd told him that when she was thirteen. Ten years ago. And he'd remembered?

'With the masks and everything?'

She couldn't stop the excitement from creeping into her voice. She had always been fascinated by the black and white masked ball that was traditionally held to mark the start of the coronation celebrations. The last time it had happened she had been too young to attend, and the sudden and unexpected death of the new king had come before there had been time to organise it.

'With the masks,' Alexei confirmed.

'I never expected that you of all people would be interested.'

'Me of all people?'

Another mistake. His mood had changed totally, taking with it the lighter atmosphere that had touched the room.

'And why is that, my dear duchess? Did you think that a commoner like me would not be able to cope with a formal ball?'

'I never…' She had been thinking of his wild past, the stories in the papers of long sessions in nightclubs, the images of him emerging, bleary-eyed and dishevelled, in the early hours of the morning. That terrible photo of him battered and bruised, his face bloody. 'I didn't think it would be your sort of thing.'

'I can dance. My father insisted that I had lessons—it's not something I'm likely to forget.'

There was such a wealth of memory in that statement that it woke echoes in Ria's mind.

'Madame Herone?' she questioned, recalling the hours she had spent being drilled in ballroom dancing by the stern disciplinarian.

Alexei nodded, that gleam deepening in the darkness of his eyes.

'I'm surprised we didn't end up having lessons together.'

No, she'd overstepped some mark there, she realised, feeling a painful twist of regret as the warmth faded like an ebbing tide.

'Your father was determined that we should never spend time together.'

She hadn't known that. Had simply believed that the dance lessons, like so many other things, were something that Alexei had rebelled against. How many other stories had she been told that had been just that—lies told to prevent her getting too close to him, getting to know him properly?

'It might have made everything so much more bearable. Do you remember that cane she had?'

Ria shuddered as she remembered how the dance teacher had wielded the cane like a weapon, rapping it sharply and painfully against her pupils' ankles if they made a mistake.

'I used to come out of lessons with my legs a mass of bruises.'

'No Huh-Honoria...' Alexei's tone mimicked the teacher's delivery perfectly, with a strange half-breath before her name. 'On your toes, if you please... And one, two, three—one, two, three...'

He was holding out his arms to Ria as he spoke and she found herself moving into them, picking up the rhythm.

'*One*, two, three...'

The speed was building. She was being swung around, whirled about the room, faster and faster. And she was being held so close, his arm at her back, clamped against the base of her spine, crushing her against him so that she could feel the heat of his body through the fine silk of her nightdress. Not just the heat; crushed this close, she couldn't be unaware of the hardness and power of his erection that spoke of a deeper, more primitive need than the light-hearted dance he had lead her into. Her feet barely seemed to touch the floor, her toes lifting from the carpet as she was steered across the room.

But it wasn't just the speed of the dance or the whirling turns that made her head spin. It was the sensation of being held in his arms, their strength supporting her, the burn of his palm at her back where the nightgown dipped low over her spine. His heartbeat, heavy, powerful, strong just under her cheek, seemed to take her pulse and lift it, make it throb in an unconscious echo of his, her breathing quickening, become shallow.

'One, two, three...'

She would never know if it was an accident or deliberate but at that moment it seemed that his foot caught on the edge of a rug, throwing them off-balance, stumbling, falling. Somehow Alexei twisted so that she landed safely on to the huge soft bed, crushed a heartbeat later by the heavy weight of Alexei's long body.

'Alex!' His name escaped on a rush of air, gasping in a mix of complicated reactions.

With her face buried against the strong column of his

neck, nose against the warm satin of his skin, she could inhale the personal scent of his body, feel the effect of it slide through her like warm smoke. If she just pushed her lips forward a centimetre or less she would taste him, be able to press her tongue against the lean muscles, the heavy pulse.

Above her Alexei went totally still, freezing into an immobility that caught the breath in her throat and held it there, tightly knotted.

'Ria,' he said, rough and raw as if dragged from a painfully sore throat. 'Ria, look at me…'

Half-fearful, half-excited, she made herself look up at him, meeting the gleaming onyx blaze of his eyes and feeling it burning up inside her. His face was set and raw, skin stretched tight across his broad cheekbones where a flash of red stained them darkly. She knew what that meant, knew her own face must bear a similar mark. Her blood was molten in her veins, her heartbeat thundering at her temples so that she couldn't think straight.

'*This* is why I never came to you before now. I knew that if I came to you it would be like this.'

He moved slightly, stroking a warm palm over her exposed skin, shifting against her so that she felt the heated swell of his erection. The heady mix of excitement and hunger drove her to make a soft mewling sound that had him drawing in a raw, unsteady breath.

'I knew that I would never get away again.'

He shook his dark head roughly, closing his eyes against the admission that had been dragged from him. Pushing both hands into the drift of her hair across the pillows, he held her head just so, dark eyes fixing hers, his mouth just a few centimetres of temptation away from her own.

'I didn't want to want you so much—never did. But

there is little point in denying it any more. So now, my duchess, it is decision time. If you are going to say no then say it now—while I can still act on it.'

Bending his head, he took her lips in a kiss that was pure temptation, sliding into a hungry pressure that told its own story. It was barely there then gone again and the moan of disappointment that rose in her throat, the way that her own mouth followed his, trying to snatch back the caress, made it plain that she wanted more. The hands that had been in her hair now slid down the length of her body, one cupping her bottom and pressing her closer against him, the other slipping under the lace-trimmed edge of the blue silk gown, sliding it from her shoulder, baring the creamy skin to his mouth.

The heat of his kiss made her writhe on the dark green covers, and when his teeth grazed her skin in a tender pain another soft cry of response escaped her.

Six restless nights had brought her to his door. Six nights of wakefulness and frustration, six nights of long-ing and growing need. And every one of those nights was behind her action now. She was hungry, needy, her hands shaking as she pulled at his clothes, wrenching his shirt from the waistband of his trousers, tugging it up so that she had access to the smooth warmth of the skin of his back. With the other hand, she reached up, catching the dangling ends of his unfastened bow tie and holding them together, pulling down on them to draw his head towards her, his mouth imprisoned against her own, his groan es-caping from between their joined lips.

She was lost in those kisses, abandoned to his touch. His hands were even more impatient than her own, dis-pensing with the fine blue silk that covered her with a roughness and a lack of finesse that had the fine ma-terial ripping as he tore it away from her. And then his

mouth was on her breast, hot and hungry, kissing, nip-
ping, suckling in a way that brought a moaning response
from her own throat.

'Lexei…' she sobbed, daring at last to use again the affectionate nickname he had once let her call him. 'Lexei…'

A sudden thought seemed to catch him, making him
pause, lift his head.

'You're not…?'

'What? A virgin?' Ria finished for him, the fight she
was having to cope with this abrupt change making her
tone sharp, the words shake on her tongue. 'What—do
you think I spent all these years just waiting, saving myself for you? Don't be silly.'

She might just as well have done, she added in the
privacy of her own thoughts. She had believed herself
in love with Alexei, had had fantasies, dreams in which
he had been the one—her first. So when he had left and
had made it plain that he had never spared a thought for
the former friend he had left behind, when he had been
seen everywhere with the beautiful, glamorous Mariette,
when he had had a baby with the other woman, she had
later flung herself into a relationship at the age of twenty
that she'd known within days had been a major mistake.
And if she had needed any further proof then it was right
here, right now in the storm of feelings breaking over her.
The sort of tempest that no other person had ever been
able to arouse in her.

The nightdress was gone, ripped away and discarded
on the floor, and somehow he had managed to shed his
own clothes, the heat and hair-roughened texture of his
skin a torment of delight against her own sensitised flesh.
And when he combined it with the stinging delight of
his hot mouth closing over one pouting nipple she could

only throw back her head against the pillows and choke his name out loud.

When he threw a leg over hers, pushing her thighs apart, opening her to him, she went with him willingly, arching up to meet him, to encourage him, to welcome him. With her face muffled against his throat she slid her hands down to his buttocks and pressed hard, urging him on.

'Ria...' Her name was rough and thick on his tongue, revealing that if she was on the brink of losing control then he was right there with her all the way. His mouth was at one breast, his hands teasing the other, tugging at her nipple, drawing it tighter, and she thought that she might lose the little that was left of her consciousness as she felt her head swim with the sensual pleasure that was burning up inside her.

The moment that he eased himself inside her had her holding her breath, abandoning herself, yielding herself up to him. The slow slide of his body into hers was like that teenage dream come true but harder, hotter, so much more than she had ever been able to imagine in her fantasies. It went beyond any experience that she could have ever thought was possible.

She was so close to the edge already that there was barely time to breathe between this moment of intense connection and the pulse of something new, something hot and hungry and demanding as he moved within her, and she lifted herself to meet his thrusts, gasping her delight as they took her higher, higher...soaring into the heavens, it seemed.

A moment later she was lost. Sensations stormed every inch of her body, assaulting every nerve, her mind whirling in the delirium of ecstasy. She froze with her body arched up to his, her internal muscles clamping around him so that she caught his choking cry of release as he too let go and abandoned himself to the tidal wave of pleasure, losing himself in the oblivion of fulfilment.

The storm of sensual ecstasy that had exploded inside Alexei's head took a long time to recede. Even then, it was impossible to move, impossible to think. His heart thundered against his ribs and it seemed his breathing would never get back under control. But at long last the red-hot tide receded, his blood cooled, his mind was his own again. With Ria's soft warmth curled up close beside him, her face buried against his chest, her hair spilling across his arms, he knew a powerful sense of satisfaction, of the closest thing to contentment he had known in a long time.

A contentment that was shattered in the moment that the first rational thought invaded his mind like a shaft of ice.

What the hell had he done?

He had known that he had kept away from Ria for a reason. The reason being that he didn't trust his own control when he was with her. He wanted her but, after the bitter lesson he had learned in the past, he had vowed that never again would he risk sleeping with any woman without contraception. But the moment Ria had been in his arms, the heat of the hunger he had felt as she lay underneath him, open to him, giving to him, had taken all his ability to think and shattered it. He hadn't even had a brain cell working that had thought of protection or consequences or the future. Only here and now and what was happening between them.

In a lifetime of wild, reckless, foolish mistakes, he might just have made the worst possible one ever.

CHAPTER ELEVEN

RIA STARED AT her reflection in the mirror and tried to recognise herself in the woman she saw there. The change wasn't just physical, though the groomed, elegant person who looked back at her was so far from any previous image of herself she had ever seen. There was so much more to it than that. And that meant that she found it hard to look herself in the eye, harder to admit to what she was seeing there.

Her dress was perfection, the sort of dress she might have imagined in her dreams. A narrow, strapless column of white silk, it had tiny crystals stitched into the material so that the effect when she moved was like a fall of stars. Her hair was swept into an elegant half-up, half-down style with the rich glowing strands falling over the creamy skin of her shoulders and partway down her back.

Growing up, she had always dreamed about one day being able to attend the black and white masked ball. She had also dreamed of falling in love, of marrying and living her own happy ever after. And the biggest part of that dream had been loving just one man.

Loving Alexei Sarova.

Well, she had done just that. She'd given him her heart as a child, but now she'd fallen in love with him for real, as an adult woman, and there was no going back. But the dream she had longed for had turned into a total, bitter nightmare as more and more of it came true. Because there was no happy ever after. Now here she was, about to attend the ball that people were calling the event of the decade. She would be expected to put on her public face, stand at Alexei's side, dance with him, smile—always smile!—and never let anyone see just how bruised and crushed her heart actually was.

Least of all Alexei himself.

Alexei, who had made it so plain that he desired her—in a physical sense at least. Who had acknowledged that he wanted her at his side, as his queen, his consort, but only in a dynastic marriage. She would be deceiving herself if she even allowed the hope of anything more to creep into her mind. Nothing had changed since the night she had gone to Alexei's room.

Well, yes, one thing had changed. And that was that she no longer lay awake, alone in her bed, in an agony of sexual hunger and frustration. She shared Alexei's room, Alexei's bed, every night and the passionate fire that had burned through them both that first time showed no signs of dimming. If anything, it had grown wilder, fiercer, stronger, with every night that passed. Though after that one heated coming together Alexei had always been meticulous, even dogmatic, about using the contraception they had both forgotten in the heat of the moment the first time.

But there was more to life than their searing sexual connection. There were the days to get through as well. The rest of the time it was business as usual, the demands of the throne taking so much time, so much energy. She woke every morning to find that the space beside her where Alexei had lain was cold and empty, revealing how he had been up so much earlier and how long he had been gone. Spending time with those 'new mistresses', the affairs of state that absorbed him so completely.

He had nothing else to offer her. No emotion, no caring, no...

Choking up inside on the last word, Ria swung away from the mirror, unable to meet her own eyes.

I can't love you. I loved once—adored her... Lost her.

No love. That was the word she was avoiding. The word she was running away from. The one that had no place in Alexei's life but that had taken over her existence completely.

The acid of unshed tears burned at the back of her eyes as she remembered that morning, when Alexei had been up early and dressing as usual while she still dozed. She had tried to lie still, not speaking a word, but in the end it had proved impossible. He had been heading towards the door when she had been unable to hold back any longer.

'When will you be back?'

She knew the words were a mistake as soon as she let them pass her lips, digging her teeth down painfully into her tongue as if she could hold them back. But too late. The stiffness of that long, straight spine, the set of his shoulders under the impeccably tailored steel-grey silk suit, told its own story without words.

'I have a full day.' It was flat, unemotional. 'But we will be together this evening. For the ball.'

Tonight the Black and White Ball would mark the culmination of all the ceremonial that led up to Alexei's accession to the throne. After tonight there would be the coronation itself.

And then their wedding.

On their wedding day he had said he would release her father. That move would mean that the balance of her mother's mind would be restored, possibly even her life would be saved when she had her husband back at her side. But wouldn't the dark hand of the past still reach out and touch the present, overshadowing it?

'Alexei. Are you sure you should release my father?'

He had started to move away again but that brought him up short, stilling totally.

'I thought that was what you wanted.'

'For my mother, yes. I'd give anything to see her happy and healthy again. And no matter what he is, she loves my father. But won't Gregor still be a threat? To Mecjoria. To you.'

To us, she wanted to add but it was a step too far.

'Why do you think I haven't let your father out already?'

When had he turned, swinging round to face her? She didn't think she had actually seen him move, but suddenly she was looking into his face, drawn into sculpted lines, hard and carved as a marble statue.

'Do you really think I would want him to have any more chances to bully you?'

Bully *her?* It was the last thing she had been expecting. She had thought that Alexei had left her father in prison out of revenge. That he had wanted to show he had control over the other man as Gregor had once had control over his future. She had never dreamed that he might actually be doing this to protect her.

'I'd like to see him try. I came to you because you are the king Mecjoria needs and everything I've seen just proves I was right in that. If he saw you now—saw how you've handled things—even my father would have to think again.'

'He'd have hated the walkabout.'

He was thinking of the events of the day before, when she and Alexei had opened a brand-new children's hospital here in the capital. The official part of the ceremony had been over in less than an hour, but the crush of people waiting to see them had shouted and called their names until Alexei had totally discarded the protocol and planning that had set the timetable for the day and launched into a spontaneous walkabout, shaking hands, talking, smiling. She doubted if she had ever seen him smile so much. He'd even…

A sudden memory of the day came back to haunt her.

A little boy had been pushed to the front of the crowd, a slightly bent and dented bunch of flowers in his hand. He'd tugged on Alexei's trousers, drawing the response he'd needed. And Alexei had turned, crouching down beside him, his attention totally focussed on the one small person. Totally at ease, he had lifted the child up, balancing him against his hip as he'd turned to face Ria.

'You have an admirer,' he'd said. 'And he wants to give his flowers to the princess.'

'Not protocol…' Her voice broke the last word into two disjointed syllables as she struggled with the memory. 'Not at all what I was trained for.' Her smile said how little she cared. 'But it was the right thing for the day.'

'And the future.'

Alexei wished he could express just what that reception had meant to him. Those smiling faces, the cheers, the flowers, the hands thrust forward to take his, the women wanting to press kisses on his cheek. His mouth had ached with smiling, his fingers raw from clasping so many other hands. So many times he had been told he was the image of his father; so many people had said 'welcome back'. If he turned or glanced out of the corner of his eyes, Ria had been at his side as she had been so many times and with her support he had actually felt free…

'It felt like coming home.'

'You are home. This is where you belong.'

But where did she belong? The question hit him like a blow in the face. She had been at his side but had that been from choice? What would she do if she was left free to follow her own destiny, without being trapped into linking it with his? The thought of how he had ensnared her, how he had manipulated her into his life, into his bed, was like the sting of a whip on his soul.

No—he hadn't manipulated her into his bed. She had come to him. When they had reached the palace he had tried to keep his distance from her, wanting to give her time to consider her position, but she had broken through the walls he had built around himself and just appeared at his door. Walking into his room as if she belonged there.

And that was how he wanted it. Wanted her warm and willing as she had been all night and every night since then. So much so that his body still pulsed at the memory, the burn of hunger not subdued even by the ache of appeasement.

But surely something that burned so white hot inevitably risked burning itself out? How long would this last and when it did end what did they have to put in its place? He had told himself that this was the only way to keep her safe. To marry her for now and then later—when it no longer mattered—he would let her go.

When it no longer mattered? How could it no longer matter? He had come alive, had lived in a new degree of intensity in the past weeks. How could something that felt this way ever fade into nothingness?

But would he ever be justified in keeping her here with him like this? He might call her father a bully but wasn't he trapping her into marriage just as much as Gregor had wanted to do? She had never wanted to be queen, just as he had never wanted to be king. Together they had built a way to take Mecjoria into a peaceful and prosperous future. But would that be enough to create their own futures?

If it wasn't then he'd have to set her free. But not yet. He couldn't let her go yet.

'We make a good team. But I'm not a monster—I won't force you to stay in this marriage for ever.'

The abrupt change of subject caught Ria unaware. One moment she had felt that they had moved to a new understanding, then this had come out of nowhere. Just as she had thought they had been celebrating a new beginning, it seemed that Alexei had already been thinking of the prospect of an end. She supposed she should have expected it. But the real horror was in the way he said it, as if he was offering her something worthwhile. Something that he believed she wanted.

'We could set a limit on the time it has to last,' Alexei stated flatly. 'Two years—three.'

Not a life sentence, then. She should feel relieved. Three weeks ago that was what she would have felt. It would have been a relief to her then to know that she hadn't signed her life away in this heartless marriage of convenience. But relief was not the emotion flooding through her now at the thought of a very limited future with this man. The terrible, tearing sense of loss threatened to rip her heart to pieces. She felt the blood drain down from her cheeks and she was sure that she must look as if she had seen a ghost. The ghost of her hopes and dreams. Dreams she had barely yet acknowledged to herself existed.

'I would give you a generous divorce settlement, of course.'

'Of course,' Ria echoed cynically. 'Once you have been king for a decent amount of time.'

'For which I will have you to thank.'

Again there was the sting of knowing that he meant it as a compliment. Because really he hadn't needed her in the end.

'You've won your own place in the hearts of the country. Surely you could see that yesterday?'

'Your help has been invaluable.' He was addressing her like he was at a public meeting. As if she was one of the ministers of state he had been spending so much time with of late. 'I knew you would make a perfect queen.'

'But only for a strictly limited time.' It was impossible to keep the bitterness from her voice. 'So perhaps we'd better really discuss the precise terms of this arrangement before we go any further? I'm to—what…?'

Sitting up in bed pulling the covers up around her because she felt too vulnerable otherwise, she checked off the points on the fingers of one hand.

'To be your fiancée, create the image of that fairy-tale romance, appear at your side in public, warm your bed in private. Marry you—provide you with an heir… No?'

His reaction had startled her. Shocked her. It was as if a sheet of ice had come down into the room, cutting them off from each other and freezing all the air in the room.

An heir. Of course she had known that was a touchy subject. But that had been when she had been concentrating on the future of Mecjoria. Now she had let herself think about his past, about the way he had fathered a child already, only to neglect the tiny girl who had died so tragically. He hadn't even tried to deny it when she had raised the accusation.

Why should I deny the facts when the world and his wife know what happened? And no one would believe a word that's different. The memory of the bitter words made her flinch inside, her stomach lurching nauseously.

An heir. Alexei felt as if someone had reached inside

his heart and ripped away the dressing he had thought he had slapped on there to protect it, revealing a wound that hadn't really healed but was still raw and vulnerable. A wound that he had been trying to ignore ever since that night that Ria had come to his room. The night that he had thoughtlessly made love to her without using a condom, breaking the number-one rule by which he'd lived his life since Belle had died.

And now this. Now with that one short word she had forced him to face what he had been pushing to the back of his mind, focussing his attention on the duties of being a king—the public duties—while ignoring the one private element that would always be there, needing to be considered for the future.

Ria had put her finger unerringly on it, dragged it out of the darkened corner to which he'd confined it, brought it kicking and screaming into the light—and it couldn't have come at a worse time.

He'd slept badly. Dark dreams had plagued his night. And it was with Ria's words that he had understood why. Yesterday had been a triumph. He knew there was no other word for it. But then there had been the small boy who had wanted his attention.

His heart kicked hard as he remembered the tug on his trousers, barely at calf level. He'd looked down into a pair of wide blue eyes, seen the curly fair hair, the gap-toothed grin. The impulse to pick the child up had been instant and spontaneous. The feel of that strong, compact little body in his arms had been nothing at all like the tiny, fragile speck of life that Belle had been but in a way that had been so much worse. It had hit home so hard with all the might-have-beens that he'd struggled with, forced him to look down into the dark chasm that he'd thought he'd put a lid on once and for all. The chasm he knew he was going to have to open up again someday or fail in his duty to Mecjoria.

Because how could he be a true king if he left the country without an heir for the future? That would mean that all this—that Ria's sacrifice—would be for nothing. The country needed an heir. Poor child with him as its father. But with Ria as its mother...

But how could he ever hope to follow through his resolution to let Ria go if he had made her pregnant?

'This will be a real marriage. In all possible ways. Of course.' It was flat and unemotional, the dangerous truth hidden behind blanked-off eyes. 'What else had you expected? That was what would have happened with Ivan. Wasn't it?'

Ria swallowed hard in an attempt to ease her painfully dry throat. Yes, it had been one of the conditions of the arranged marriage, how could it not have been? Which had been exactly why she had been so desperate to get out of that arrangement. To get away from the horror of being tied to a man she didn't love; to keep her freedom. Only, it seemed, to lose it all over again with the terms that Alexei was tossing out to her.

'And we do at least have huge chemistry between us. Come on Ria, admit it...' he added when he saw her eyes widen, heard the swift intake of breath she was unable to hold back. His eyes went to the other side of the bed in which she still lay, drawing attention to the crumpled pillows, the wildly disordered sheets. 'There is a real flame between us. You know, you've felt it.'

It was more than a flame. It was a raging inferno. She didn't need the state of the bed to remind her of how it was. Remembering last night and the way she had gone up in flames in his arms, the wildfire that his kisses had sent raging through her, she had to admit that there was no way she could deny this. Her whole body still throbbed with the aftermath of their shared passion and the heat he had stirred in her blood through the night had burned so hard that she almost imagined that the sheets would scorch where she touched them.

His implication was that this would make it easier to have that 'real marriage'. To create that much-needed heir. It could have done just that. It should have; it really should.

She wanted Alexei so very much. Being with Alexei, making love with him, was her dream come true. The fantasy she had let herself indulge in in her teens, as she fell in love with him with all the strength of her young, foolish, naïve heart.

But that was also what made the thought of this so terrible. To have been tied into an arranged marriage with Ivan would have been bad enough. But then only her body and her mind would have been involved. Not like with Alexei. With Alexei there was the risk to her heart—her soul.

Because she also knew, when she faced the truth, that there was no way she was making love with Alex every night. He was simply having sex, giving in to that flame he had said burned between them. Throw a child—his child—into the mix and she was done for. It would be lethal emotionally, totally destructive.

'It will be a real marriage—with everything that entails. As king, it will be my duty to have an heir, so naturally…'

'Naturally…' Ria choked, earning herself a cold, flashing sideways look from those deep, dark eyes.

Any child they created together would be so much more than that—at least to her. But that thought caught and twisted her nerves at the prospect of exposing a child to the toxic mix of hunger and distrust that their marriage would be. The temporary marriage that he had insisted was all it was going to be. It made her stomach clench in nausea, pushing bitter words from her uncontrolled mouth.

'Another child for you to neglect?'

She flung it at him, hard and sharp, her own bitterly divided feelings tightening her voice and putting into it more venom than she actually felt. The truth was that she didn't even know if she really felt that bitterness or not. She didn't even know what she should be feeling.

'Another child that might...'

She couldn't say the word. It might only have three letters in it, but 'die' had to be one of the most terrible words in the world.

'I would not neglect her.'

Alexei's eyes had turned translucent, like molten steel, and yet cold as frost in the same dark moment. Ria felt a terrible sense of wrong twist deep inside. There was something here that she didn't understand. Something she couldn't put her finger on and the danger in his expression, in his tone, warned her that she was somehow treading on very thin ice.

'This child would not be neglected,' he continued, each word snapped out, cold and brittle. 'It would be too important, too—'

He choked off the word, leaving her wondering just what he had been about to say. Too significant? Too essential to his plans for the future? His role as king?

'He or she would be cared for, treasured, watched over every moment of its days.'

'Because they would be the heir that you need so much.'

'Because I would have you to be its mother—to take care of it.'

How could something so quietly stated have the force of a deadly assault?

'So that is my future role as you see it? As a brood mare first, and then a nursemaid to your *heir*.'

Something new blazed in those molten eyes, colder and harder than she would have believed possible. She couldn't imagine what she had said to put it there. After all she had simply agreed with what he had declared he wanted from her, making it plain that they both knew where they stood.

'You don't value that role?' he demanded, low and harsh. 'You think Ivan would have offered you anything else?'

'I think that you and Ivan are two of a kind. That you would both use me—use anyone without a second thought—to get what you wanted. Well, don't worry—I'll do my duty.' She laced the word with venom and actually saw him wince away from her attack, his eyes hooded and hidden. 'After all, you've probably achieved all you ever wanted already.'

'Achieved what?' His dark brows snapped together in a hard line. 'What the hell are you talking about?'

'Well, we've made lo—had sex—what, a dozen times now? And you have been scrupulous about using contraceptives—each time but one! I could well be pregnant already with the heir you need. Another nine months and the baby will be born—you'll be crowned king, settled on the throne, and have everything you want. And I'll be free to leave.'

She tried to make it sound airy, careless, but the misery she felt only succeeded in making it seem cold and hard, ruinously so. Alexei obviously took her at her word.

'And you could do that, could you? You could leave your child? Hand it over to be brought up as a prince or princess, the heir to the throne?

He sounded harsh, brutally critical. How dared he?

How dared *he* imply that she would abandon her child when he had neglected his baby in that heartless way?

'No, I could never do that—but then you knew that already! You can guarantee that I will never leave, as long as I have a child to care for. That's how you know that you have me trapped so completely.'

She had never seen him look so, white, so totally bloodless, his skin drawn so tight across his cheekbones that she almost felt they might slice it wide open, leaving a gaping wound. His jaw clenched too, a muscle jerking hard against the control he was forcing over it, and for a moment she flinched inside, wondering just what he was going to come back at her with.

But no such retort ever came. Instead, after a moment seeming frozen into ice, Alexei was suddenly jerked into movement, as his phone on the side table buzzed in timed warning of an upcoming event.

'Duty calls,' he said curtly, and that was all.

A moment later he was gone, snatching up his phone on his way out the door. And when that slammed behind him she was left, stark naked and with only a sheet to cover her, unable to run after him for fear of encountering the ever-watchful Henri or someone else who had taken over today's particular shift.

Not that she had the emotional strength to even try. The war of words might have been physical blows for the effect they had had on her. She could only lie back and stare at the ceiling as the words replayed over in her head, burning tears rolling down her cheeks to soak into the pillow behind her head.

CHAPTER TWELVE

FINDING THAT SHE was still staring blankly at her reflection in the mirror, not having moved for who knew how long, Ria blinked hard, trying to clear her thoughts and failing completely. The truth was that she was emotionally involved in this relationship and so she would be emotionally committed to the marriage. And that was why it would hurt so badly to be confined to the sidelines of Alexei's life. She could be his temporary queen of convenience, his bed mate, the mother of his child, but in his heart she would be nothing.

Ria's hand went to the sparkling diamond necklace that encircled her throat, fingering the brilliant gems as she recalled the way that the ornate jewels and the matching earrings had been delivered to her room earlier that evening.

Wear these for me tonight, the note that accompanied them had said in Alexei's firm, slashing handwriting.

Ria's fingers tightened on the necklace so convulsively that the delicate design was in danger of snapping under her grip. Alexei certainly no longer needed help with his position as king. He was issuing orders left, right and centre. She was strongly tempted to take the damn thing off and...

You don't like presents? Alexei's words came back to her, stilling the impulsive gesture. Remembering them from this distance, she couldn't be sure whether she had really heard the trace of—of what? Defensiveness? Uncertainty?—she had thought she had caught behind the mockery the first time. *I thought women liked flowers—and jewellery.*

Well, not this woman! Ria told him in the privacy of her thoughts. Not when she wanted so much more.

But going down that path was a weakness she couldn't afford. It came too close to dreams she could never have. It even, damn it, brought tears to burn at the back of her eyes. Fiercely she blinked them away, knowing she didn't have time to do any repair job on the make-up that a beautician had applied not an hour before. She would have to hope that the ornate silk mask, edged with sparkling crystals and pearls, would conceal the truth of the way she was feeling.

Swinging away from the mirror, Ria paced restlessly about the room, struggling to control her raw and unsettled breathing. She stumbled for a moment awkwardly when her toe caught on something on the floor, almost tripping her up. Glancing down, she saw that what she had trodden on. A man's wallet. Elderly, its worn brown leather partly hidden under a chair, it looked out of place in the elegant cream and gold room.

It must be Alexei's, she realised, recalling how he had visited her here the day before, his tie tugged loose, his shirt sleeves rolled up, his jacket off and slung over his shoulder as soon as he had escaped from his formal duties of the day. He had tossed the jacket on to the chair as he had gathered her to him and kissed her hard and, as always happened, his touch had ignited the flames between them so that in the space of a couple of heartbeats they had fallen on to the bed, oblivious to everything else. The wallet must have slipped from his pocket then.

Picking it up, she couldn't resist the impulse to flick it open, examine the contents. There was nothing unexpected in there—some credit cards, a few banknotes—but then one thing caught her attention, the corner of a photograph tucked into the back section. Curiosity stinging at her, she pulled it out carefully and felt the room swing wildly round her as she took in what it was.

A small print of a photograph. A tiny baby, barely a few weeks old, with dark, dark eyes and a wild fuzz of black hair on her small head. There was only one person it could be. Sweet little Isabelle, Alexei's baby daughter. The child who had been born as a result of such scandal and disgrace and who had only lived for a few short weeks, dying alone and neglected by her drunken father.

But that was where something caught on a raw exposed corner of Ria's nerves, making her heart jerk hard and sharp in reaction, and she had to close her eyes against the sensation. But when she opened them again, the photo in her hand was still there. Still clutched between her fingers.

Still telling the same story.

She had seen enough of Alexei's photographs in the magazines or the press, in his offices and again in his home. She knew the stylised, stark style he favoured, the careful framing, the deliberate focus. And this photograph had none of those. It was a quick, candid snap, snatched in a moment of spontaneity to capture the first flicker of a smile on the tiny girl's face. He had grabbed for his camera, and as a result he had captured something so truly special.

Not just an image of his little girl's first smile. But also a picture of his daughter snapped, with love, by her doting daddy.

Memory rushed over her like a thick black wave. The memory of a small boy held in strong male arms, totally secure, totally confident, a wilting bunch of flowers in one rather grubby hand, the fingers of the other tangling and twisting in Alexei's hair. The image of Alexei's face that morning when she had accused him of neglecting his baby. Even worse, there was the echo of those terrible, harsh words on that day in London.

Why should I deny the facts when the world and his wife know what happened? And no one would believe a word that's different.

How differently she heard those words now, catching the burn of bitterness, something close to despair that, focussed only on her own needs and plans, she had failed to notice that first time. And, knowing that, her stomach quailed and tied itself into knots at the thought of having to face Alexei again tonight.

'Ria…'

As if called up by her thoughts, there was a knock at the door. Alexei? What was he doing here?

He was standing on the landing so tall and elegant in the beautifully tailored evening clothes, the immaculate white shirt, the plain black silk mask across the upper part of his face, polished jet eyes gleaming through the slits in the fine material. This was Alexei the king, no longer her childhood friend but a man grown to full adulthood and ready to accept his destiny. He was the ruler Mecjoria needed, strong, powerful and in control. And he was her lover. Heat pooled low in her body at just the thought. Ria actually felt her legs weaken, her hand going out to his for support.

'You look wonderful.'

Alexei's dark gaze slid over her body, taking in every inch of the dress that the designer had created for her. The white silk clung to the curves of her breasts and hips in a way that dried his throat in sexual need, leaving him hot and hard in the space between one heartbeat and the next. He could never get enough of this woman, and the carnal thoughts she inspired had turned his brain molten, had tormented him through the day so that he barely had the strength to focus on what he was doing. The white mask gave her an other-worldly appearance, like a character at a Venetian carnival, with its ornate design, the eye pieces edged with pearls and sparkling crystals, drawing attention to the mossy green of her eyes fringed by impossibly thick and long dark lashes.

'You don't scrub up so badly yourself. Madame Herone would be proud of you.'

Was that a trace of uncertain laughter in her voice? The eyes that met his looked unusually, almost suspiciously bright. Her hand, impossibly delicate where it was enclosed in his, held on rather too tight.

The strapless design of her dress exposed the long, beautiful line of her throat, the creamy curve of her shoulders. Only hours ago, in the growing light of dawn, he had kissed his way down that smooth skin, lingering at the point where her pulse now beat at the base of her neck, before moving lower, to the delicious temptation of her breasts. He could almost still taste her rose-tinted nipples against his tongue and his lower body was so hard and tight that it was painful.

This was the way he had felt all week. He had resented the official duties, the diplomatic meetings and governmental debates that had taken so much time away from what he really wanted, from this woman who possessed his body, obsessed his mind. When he was with her he could think of nothing else. And when he was away from her all he could think about was getting back to her and being alone with her, of burying himself in the glorious temptation of her body. He knew she felt that way too—

the long hot nights they had spent together had made it plain that she wanted him every bit as much as he lusted after her. She had been as hungry as he had been, taking every kiss, every caress he offered, opening herself to him and welcoming him into her body as often as he could wish—reaching for him in the middle of the night to encourage him into even more sensual possession when he had thought that she was exhausted and could take no more.

But he couldn't think that way any more. He couldn't let himself think at all or he would back out of this right now. He had done all the thinking he needed to do and, with the memory of the scene in his bedroom that morning, had come to his decision. The only decision he believed was possible. He couldn't live with himself if he went any other way.

And now he had to tell Ria what was going to happen.

'We need to talk.'

Could there be any more ominous line in the whole of the English language? Ria questioned as she made herself step backwards to let him into the room.

'But we said we would meet downstairs, in one of the anterooms, ready to go into the ballroom together.'

'I know we did—but this has to be sorted out before we go down. Before anything else.'

Which was guaranteed to make her throat clench tighter, her lungs constrict, making it hard to breathe. Unthinkingly she lifted her hand to wave some air into her face, remembering only what she held when she saw Alexei's eyes focus sharply on the photograph.

'Belle…'

If she had any doubts left then they evaporated in the

burn of his expression, the shadows of pain that darkened his voice. Ria took a slow deep breath. She owed him this.

'The stories they told about that—you didn't do it. You couldn't have done it.'

He'd dropped her hand, reached out and took the small snapshot, holding it carefully as if afraid it might disintegrate.

'Cot death, they called it. But if someone had been there...'

'But wasn't Mariette?'

'Oh, she was there but she wasn't any help to anyone. Mariette had problems. Depression—drink—drugs.' His voice was low and flat, all emotion ironed out. 'We'd had a savage row. She told me to get out. I planned on getting drunk but I couldn't get rid of the fear that there was something wrong. I had to go back—but Mariette's door was locked against me and she wouldn't answer no matter how much I knocked and shouted. Eventually I had to break the door down—and found a scene of horror inside. Mariette was in a drug-fuelled stupor and Belle had died in her cradle.' His breath caught hard in his throat and he had to force the words out.

Ria hadn't been aware of moving forward, coming closer, but now she realised that she was so very close to him and, reaching out, she took his hand again, but the other way round this time, feeling his fingers curl around hers, hold her tightly.

'But everyone thought— You took the blame.' Incredulity made her voice shake.

Alexei's shrug was weary, dismissive.

'Because you loved her?'

'No, not Mariette.' He was shaking his head before her words were out. 'We'd run our course long before, but we stayed together for the baby's sake.'

Reaching up, he pulled the mask away from his face and let it drop, the lines around his nose and eyes seeming to be more dramatically etched as they were exposed to the light.

'My shoulders are broad enough. And Mariette had demons of her own to fight. She never wanted to be pregnant, and when she found she was she wanted to have an abortion. I persuaded her not to. She hated every minute of it, and I think she suffered from post-natal depression after Belle arrived. She ended up having a complete breakdown and had to be hospitalised. The last thing she needed was a horde of paparazzi hounding her, accusing her...'

For a moment he paused, his head going back, dark eyes looking deep into hers.

'She'd already cracked completely and lashed out when I tried to see her.'

His twisted smile tore at her heart. Could it get any worse? In her mind's eye, Ria was seeing the notorious photo of Alexei, bruised and bloodied. She had assumed— everyone had assumed—that he had been in a fight. But now she could see that those scratches had been scored into his skin by long, feminine nails.

'And I had plenty of my own scandals to live down. But...' His eyes went to the photo in his hand. 'I adored that little girl.'

'I know you did.'

'You believe me?'

Ria nodded mutely, tears clogging her throat. 'You're not capable of anything like they accused you of.'

Just for a moment Alexei rested his forehead against hers and closed his eyes.

'Thank you.'

I can't love you. I loved once—adored her... Lost her.

And it was little Belle, the baby daughter, who had

stolen his heart. If she hadn't seen that photograph she would know it now from the rawness in his voice, the darkness of his eyes. Oh dear heaven, if only she could ever hope to see that look when he thought of her. But he had confided the truth to her. Would she be totally blind, totally foolish to allow herself to hope that that meant he felt more for her than just his convenient, dynastic bride-to-be? Ria couldn't suppress the wild, skittering jump of her heart at the thought.

Downstairs, in the main hall of the castle, the huge golden gong sounded to announce the fact that it was almost time for the ball to start. Another few minutes and they would be expected to go down, ready to make their ceremonial entry. As always, the demands of state were intruding into their private moments. Obviously Alexei thought so too because he lifted his head, raked both his hands through the crisp darkness of his hair.

'You said we needed to talk.' She didn't know if she wanted to push him into saying whatever he had come to tell her. Only that right now she couldn't bear to leave it hanging unsaid for a moment longer.

'We do.'

He had always known that this was going to be hard and the conversation they had just had, the trust she had honoured him with, would only make things so much worse. But he also knew that it was the only way he could do things. The way she was looking at him, eyes bright behind that white satin mask, was going to destroy him if he didn't get things out in the open—fast.

But if ever there was a time that he owed someone the truth then it was now.

'This isn't going to work.'

He could see her recoil, eyes closing, the hand she had put on his snatched away abruptly.

'What isn't working?'

'Everything. The engagement—the marriage—you as my queen. Everything.'

'But I don't understand.' He was giving her what he knew she wanted but she wasn't making things easy for him. 'We've already announced the engagement. To-night…'

'I know. Tonight we are supposed to face the court, the nobility and every last one of the foreign diplomats in the country. Tonight is to mark the first step on to the final public stage of this whole damn king business.'

Tonight they would face the world as a royal couple—the future of the country. The potential royal family. And that was where one great big problem lay. A problem that had grown deeper and darker since this morning. Could he and this woman, this gorgeous, sexy woman, ever be more than the passionate lovers they had been in the past weeks? Could they ever become a *family*?

Family. That was the word that showed him what he wanted most and why he could not ever allow himself to think of letting this continue.

He had always wanted a family. The family he'd hoped to find when they had first come to Mecjoria. The one that had been denied him when his father had died and all that had followed. That was why he had begged Mariette not to have the abortion she'd wanted. Why he'd fallen in love with his little daughter from the moment the doctors had first put her in his arms just after the birth. Memories of Belle and all that he'd lost with her were like a dark bruise on his thoughts. The accusations Ria had flung at him this morning had brought those terrible memories rushing back, so that he hadn't been able to stay and face them down. And even now, when he knew she understood—more so *because* she'd understood—he knew he couldn't keep her trapped with him, not like this. She deserved so much better.

The accusation of trapping her that she'd flung at him was so appallingly justified, and the thought stuck in his throat, made acid burn in his stomach. He'd pushed her into a situation that took all her options, any trace of choice away from her. What made him think that she would want marriage to him any more than she would want to become Ivan's bride? It was true that the country benefited from the arranged marriage but, hell and damnation, he could have handled it so much better.

Did he really want a bride who looked so tense whenever they were alone—unless they were in bed together? A queen who held herself so stiffly that she looked as if she might break into a thousand brittle pieces if he touched her? A woman who, like his own mother, had been used as just a pawn in the power games of court? He had forced Mariette into a situation that she didn't want, and the end result had been a total tragedy. He could not do that to Ria.

'Tell me one thing.' He had to hear it from her own lips. 'Would you have agreed to marry me if I hadn't made it a condition of my accepting the throne?'

'I…' She swallowed down the rest of her answer but he didn't need it. Her hesitation, the way her eyes dodged away from his, told their own story. If he followed this path any longer he was no better—in fact, worse—than her father. He would be using her for his own ends, keeping her a prisoner when she wanted so desperately to fly free.

'I can't ask this of you.'

'You didn't ask,' Ria flung at him. 'You commanded.'

Was that weak, shaken voice really her own? Once again she had retreated behind false flippancy to disguise the way she was really feeling. The way that her life, the future she had thought was hers, had crumbled around her, the dreams she had just allowed herself to let into her mind evaporating in the blink of an eye. But she had let them linger for a moment and the bite of loss was all the more agonising because of that.

Reject that! Please. Argue with me, she begged him in her thoughts. But Alexei was nodding his head, taking her word as truth.

'And you had no choice but to agree. Well, I'm giving you that choice now. I never should have asked you to marry me. I don't need you to validate my position as king. The engagement is off—it should never have happened. You're free to go.'

'Free...'

The room swung round her violently, her eyes blurring, her breath escaping in a wild, shaken gasp. If this was freedom then she wanted none of it.

'Tonight? Right here and now?'

How did he manage to make the most appalling things sound as if he was giving her exactly what she wanted? Their eyes came together, burnished black clashing with clouded jade, and the ruthless conviction in his totally defeated her. She was dismissed, discarded, just like that.

'But what about...?'

In the hallway the gong sounded once again, summoning them. The sound made Alexei shake his head, his eyes closing briefly.

'How could I have been so bloody stupid?' He groaned. 'I'm sorry, Ria. I had meant to talk to you after the ball, but...' His eyes dropped to the photograph of Belle he still held in his hand. 'Things knocked me off-balance. Now everyone is here.'

'Why?'

It was the one thing she could hold on to. The one thing

that had registered in the storm of misery that assailed her. Alexei had decided that he didn't need to marry her—that he didn't want to marry her. *He didn't want her.* And there was no way she could fight back against that.

'Sorry for what?' Somehow she forced herself to ask it. 'Why did you plan to tell me *after* the ball?'

His expression was almost gentle and if it hadn't been for the bleakness of his eyes she might almost have believed that he was the Alexei of ten years before. The Alexei she had first fallen in love with.

'Because it was your dream,' he stated flatly. 'You always wanted to attend the Black and White Ball.' Just for a second, shockingly, the corner of his mouth quirked up into something that was almost a smile. 'You even trained for long hours with Madam Herone just for it. I wanted this to be for you.'

'But the engagement?' She didn't know how she had found the strength to speak. She wasn't even sure how she was managing to stay upright, except that she couldn't give in. She couldn't just collapse into the pathetic, despondent little heap that she felt she had become since he had declared he no longer wanted to marry her.

'After the ball, we would announce that you had changed your mind about marrying me.'

That she had changed her mind. He had thought of everything. But at least he would have left her with some pride by making it seem that she was the one who had ended their relationship. Not that she had been jilted, as she had just been. And for years he had remembered how much she had wanted to go to the ball, and had planned to give her that at least.

It wasn't much, not compared with the lifetime, the love, she had dreamed of. But it was all she was going to get. And, weak and foolish as she was, she knew in her heart that she was going to reach for it. For one last evening with Alexei. For one last night, this Cinderella was going to the ball with the man she loved.

Drawing on every ounce of her strength, she straightened her spine.

'You've obviously thought it all through. We'll do that, then.' She hoped she sounded calm, convincing. If he was giving her her freedom, then she could give him his. She wouldn't beg or cling. If her father had ever taught her anything worthwhile then it was dignity, even in defeat.

Below them they heard the third and final sound of the gong that preceded their arrival in the ballroom. It was now or never.

'Let's go.'

The journey down the wide, sweeping stairs seemed to take a lifetime. Alexei had offered her his arm for support and she managed to force herself to take it, knowing that the stinging film of tears she would not allow herself to shed blurred her vision and made her steps uncertain without his support. And if just having this one last chance to touch him, to hold on to his strength, was a personal indulgence, then that was her private business. An indulgence that she was never going to admit to anyone but keep hidden in the secrecy of her thoughts, stored up against the time when this was no longer possible and memories of how it had felt to be so close to him, to look into his beloved face, were all she had left.

At the bottom of the staircase the Lord Chamberlain was waiting, saying nothing, but the look of carefully controlled concern on his face told them that the world of ceremony and court appearances had already been delayed for long enough.

'Sir…'

Alexei's hand came up, commanding silence.

'I know. We're coming.'

Reaching out, he took Ria's fingers again, folding his own around them as he nodded his head in the direction of the huge doors to the ballroom. The glittering chandeliers and gold-decorated walls were hidden behind the huge double doors, but the buzz of a thousand conversations, the sound of so many feet moving on the polished floor, gave away the fact that their arrival was expected and waited for with huge anticipation.

'Duty calls. Are you sure you want to go through with this?' he murmured.

'Do we have any choice? Right now Mecjoria is what matters,' she managed to assure him, keeping her head high, her eyes now wide and dry.

'Then let's do this.'

They took a step forward, another. Two footmen stepped forward to take hold of the large metal handles, one on each side of the door.

And then, totally unexpectedly, Alexei stopped, looked straight into her face.

'You really are a queen,' he told her, low, husky and intent.

It was meant as a compliment, she knew, and her smile in reply was slow and tinged with the regret that was eating her alive.

'Just not your queen,' she managed, wishing that it was not the truth and knowing that all the wishing in the world would never ease away the agony of loss that was tearing her up inside.

As she spoke the big doors swung open and the buzz of talk and noise rose to a crescendo of excitement. Alexei took her hand in his as they walked forward into the ballroom, putting on the act of the fairy-tale couple for one last time.

CHAPTER THIRTEEN

UNDER ANY OTHER circumstances, it would have been a magical night.

Everything that Ria had ever imagined or dreamed about the Black and White Ball had come true, and most of it had been beyond her wildest imaginings. The huge ballroom was beautifully decorated, the lights from a dozen brilliant crystal chandeliers sparkling over the array of elegant men and women, all dressed, as the convention for the night demanded, in the most stylish variations on the purely monochrome theme of dress. They might be confined to black and white but the fabulous couture gowns, the brilliant jewels and, most of all, the stunningly decorated masks meant that everyone looked so different, so amazing, creating a stunning image in the room as a whole. One that was reflected over and over in the huge mirrored walls.

There was food and wine, glorious, delicious food for all she knew. But none of it passed her lips, and she barely drank a thing. She was strung tight as a wire on the atmosphere, the sensations of actually being here, like this. With Alexei. But at the same time those sensations were sharpened devastatingly by the terrible undercurrent of powerful emotion, the icy burn of pain that came from knowing that the man beside her was the love of her life, her reason for breathing, but that when this night was over he was expecting her to go, walk out of his life for ever.

From the moment they had walked into the room, and paused at the top of the short flight of steps that lead down the highly polished floor, all eyes had been on them. Just their appearance had triggered off a blinding fusillade of camera flashes that made her head spin and had her clutching at Alexei's arm for support. For long minutes afterwards she was still blinking to clear away the spots in her vision and bring her gaze back into focus properly. And he was there, at her side, silently supporting her, seeming to know instinctively just when she was able to see again clearly, when she could stand on her own two feet and turn her attention to the crowds of statesmen, dignitaries and nobility who thronged the room.

That was when Alexei carefully eased his way away from her side, resting his hand on hers just once as he turned her towards another group of guests. A faint inclination of his head, the touch of his hand at the base of her spine, spoke volumes without words. For this one night, still his fiancée, officially soon to be his queen, she should mix with their guests, socialise, talk with them. And he knew she could do it. Knew he didn't have to stay with her. Instead he headed off in the opposite direction, working the room. And the bittersweet rush of pride at the thought that he knew she wouldn't let him down helped Ria's feet move, warmed her smile when all the time she was feeling broken and dead inside.

She had no idea how much time had passed when they met up again. Only that he came to find her just at the point she had started to flag. When her mouth was beginning to ache with smiling, when her fund of small talk was beginning to dry up. Just when she felt she'd had enough, suddenly he was there by her side.

'Dance with me,' he said softly, and she turned to him, feeling as she gave him her hand and he lead her out on to the dance floor that, for her, the evening had really just truly begun.

With his arms round her, warm and strong, his strength supporting her, the scent of his skin in her nostrils, she barely felt as if her feet were on the ground any longer. She was all talked out, unable to find any words to say to him. But Alexei didn't appear to need conversation; seemed instead, like her, to be content to remain in their own silent bubble.

She had wanted to be here so much. Had dreamed of being here in so many ways—at the Black and White Ball, at the start of a new reign for the country, with the succession secured, with Mecjoria safe. With Ivan kept from the throne and Alexei, a strong, honest, powerful ruler, in his place. Here with the man she loved.

And that was when her thoughts stumbled to a halt. Where her mind seemed to blow a fuse and she could go no further, could not get past the thought of how much she loved this man. How much she wanted to be in his arms, and stay there for ever. At this moment she felt that she wouldn't even ask for his love in return. Just to stay with him, love him would be enough.

But already the clock was ticking towards the end of the convenient engagement Alexei had decided he no longer needed. Like Cinderella, she had until midnight before all the magic in her life disappeared and she found she was once more back in reality, all her dreams shattered around her. Already, an hour or more of the last remaining precious time she had with Alexei had passed and try as she might she couldn't hold back a single minute of the little that was left.

'Enjoying yourself?'

Alexei asked the question strangely stiffly, his breath warm against her ear, her cheek pressed close to his. She could only nod silently in answer, not daring to look up into his face, meet his eyes through the black silk mask. It would destroy her if she did. She would shatter into tiny pieces right here on the polished floor.

Enjoying yourself! Alexei couldn't believe he had been stupid enough to ask the inane question. The same one that he had asked a dozen, a hundred, times already that evening. It was the sort of polite, formal small talk that he used to put people at their ease, to make them feel that he had noticed them, that he appreciated the fact that they were there. It was for the Mecjorian nobility, the foreign dignitaries, the press even.

It was not for Ria. Not for this woman who he now held in his arms for perhaps the last time and who, at the end of this evening, would walk out of his life and into her own future—totally free for the first time ever.

Because how could he not notice Ria when she looked so stunningly beautiful, when she was all his private sensual fantasies come at once? How could he not appreciate what she was, who she was, when she had been there with him, always at his side, always offering her support through the long weeks since she had come to him with the news that he was king? Because it was right.

That was why he had known tonight that he had only one way forward. That, like Ria, he had to do what was right. Right for her, even if everything that was in him ached in protest at the thought. He had forced her into the marriage that he had believed would bring him the satisfaction he craved. It had brought him all that satisfaction—and more. So much more. But to keep her in such a marriage would be like chaining up some beautiful, exotic wild creature.

She would die in captivity. And he couldn't bear to see that happen to her. So tonight he was setting her free.

But first he would have just a few more hours to dance with her, hold her, maybe even kiss her. In spite of himself, he let his arms tighten round her, drew her soft warmth closer, inhaled the perfume of her skin against his. The bittersweet delight of it made his body burn in a hunger that he knew would have him lying awake through the night, and many more long, empty nights when this was done. He had until midnight. A few more hours to pretend that she was still his.

His! The lie cut terribly deep. The truth was that Ria had never been his. And that was why tonight had been inevitable, right from the start. But everything that was in him rebelled at the thought.

He couldn't do it. He couldn't let her go.

Ria was so lost in her thoughts, in the deep sensual awareness of being held so close to Alexei that at first the flurry of interest was just like a blur at the edge of her consciousness. She heard the buzz of sound as if it was that of a swarm of bees somewhere far distant, on the horizon but coming closer, growing louder, with every second.

Uncharacteristically, Alexei's smooth steps in the waltz stumbled slightly, hesitated, slowed. She heard him mutter a low toned, dark, fierce curse, the furious, 'Too early. Too damn early,' and suddenly the whole dance was stuttering to a halt as the murmur around them grew, as if that swarm of bees was coming closer, dangerously so.

'Escalona…'

On a sense of shock she heard her own name muttered over and over again. But once or twice it came with an addition that startled her, shocked her into stillness, bringing her head up and round.

'It's Gregor Escalona. And his wife.'

Beside her Alexei had stilled, his powerful body freezing in shock and rejection. She could almost feel the pulse of anger along the length of his frame. It was there in the tightening of the hand that held hers, the extra pressure of the one now clamped against her spine, the delicate dancer's hold replaced by something that felt disturbingly like imprisonment, a fierce control that shocked and upset her.

'Alexei…' she began, her use of his name clashing with the way he said hers.

'Ria…'

It shocked her because it sounded so rough, so ominous it made her heart thump nervously. Instinctively she wrenched herself out of his constraining hold, swivelling round against the pressure of his hands. Her vision blurring in disbelief, she could only stand and stare as she tried to take in the impossible reality of what she saw.

'*Mum!* And—and—'

And her father.

Her father who had just made his way into the room and was now standing at the top of the steps, her mother beside him. He looked paler, thinner, diminished somehow, though nothing like as pale and wan as Elizabetta who was holding onto his arm for grim death, and seeming dangerously close to collapsing in a heap on the floor if she loosened her grip. It couldn't be real; it was impossible. Her father was still locked away in the state prison, his freedom dependent on her marriage to Alexei…

But there wasn't going to be a marriage any more.

'Ria.'

Alexei's hands were on her shoulders, straining to turn her round, working against the instinctive resistance she put up. She couldn't believe what was happening. Why this was happening? Why they were there?

'Ria, look at me!'

One hand had come up in a slashing gesture to silence the orchestra and the whole room was suddenly still and frozen. In the quiet, the note of command was enough to take the strength from her. Her shoulders slumped and she found herself swung back again to face him, trapped in the sudden circles of isolation that had formed round them as every one of the other dancers froze, silently watching.

She had only a moment to look up into his dark, shuttered face, see the glare of fury he directed at her father, before he moved again suddenly, stunning her by going down on one knee right there in front of her. In front of the whole crowded ballroom.

Alexei—don't. She tried to open her mouth to say the words but nothing would come out. She knew just what was coming and she couldn't bear it. Couldn't cope with this. Not now; not like this.

Please, not like this...

She wanted to run but Alexei's grip tightened around it, holding her still. But what held her stiller was the deep, dark gaze that clashed with hers from behind the black silk mask.

'Ria, I didn't do this right last time. I want to do it properly now. I want your family—all the country—to know that I want you to be my queen. I don't want to be king without you at my side.'

'No...' She tried again but her voice was only a thin thread of sound, buried under the buzz of curiosity, the murmurs of incredulity and interest that came from their audience who were clearly hanging on to every word.

'Ria—will you marry me?'

Was the room really swinging round her, lurching nauseously, or was that just the rush of shock and panic to her head? She could see that her parents had been prevented from moving forward, the security guard putting a restraining hand on her father's arm, her mother stopping at his side though her eyes were fixed on her daughter's face. She saw the stunned, astonished, the frankly curious expressions on the faces of those around them, expressions that even the concealing masks could not disguise. And there, at her feet, was Alexei...

Alexei, the man she loved and whose proposal she would have so loved to hear—if only he had meant it. But not like this! Only this evening he had told her that he didn't want to marry her, that he was breaking off their engagement, that it was over. So this...

So this could only be some cold-blooded political statement. A statement of power in front of every dignitary, every statesman at the ball.

The conditions were that I would free your father when you became my wife. Call it a wedding day gift from me.

Oh, why did she have to remember that? But it had to be what was behind it—the need to show the world, the court and her father, that Alexei was the one with the power. That he was totally in control.

Here she was, with the whole court hanging on her every word, with her parents looking on. The freedom—temporary, surely—her father was enjoying hit home to her how easily Alexei could change everything, order everything with a flick of his head just as he had silenced the orchestra just moments before.

He had presented her with an ultimatum. Accept his proposal, here in the most public place possible, or everything he held over her would fall into place in the most appalling way.

She had thought that she couldn't face a future without him in it. But how could she ever have a future with a man who would force her hand in this way? Who would go to these lengths to emphasise the power he had over her?

'I can't!' she gasped, tasting the salt of her own tears sliding into her mouth as she flung the words into the silence, not daring to look into Alexei's face to see the effect they had as they landed. 'I won't marry you! And you can't make me!'

CHAPTER FOURTEEN

I won't marry you!

The words seared through Alexei's thoughts, burning an agonising trail behind them.

I won't marry you! And you can't make me!

'Make you?'

Alexei got slowly to his feet, his eyes still fixed on her indignant face, the way that her proud head was held so high, the green eyes flashing wild defiance into his. The stunned silence around him reflected his own shock and confusion, taking it and multiplying it inside his head.

He had been so sure. So convinced that at last he was on the right track with Ria. He knew he had pushed too hard, forced her into the position as his fiancée because he wanted her so much. And as a result she had felt bullied, trapped.

So he had come up with what had seemed like the perfect plan. To let her go, set her free. He had even arranged for her father to be liberated as a symbol of everything he wanted for her. But at the last minute he had known he couldn't go through with it. And something about her tonight, a new delicacy, a touch of melancholy, had given him a foolish, wild hope. He had known that he had to try.

He'd hoped a fresh proposal—one at the event that she had always longed to attend—might have some magic in it. But, if the truth were told, it had had the exact opposite effect of the one he had been looking for.

She had frozen, all colour leaching from her face, staring at him as if he had suddenly turned into a hissing, spitting poisonous snake right before her eyes.

'How the hell…?' he began but she shook her head wildly, loosening the elegant hair style so that locks of it tumbled down around her face. He could see how her eyes shone, the quiver of her lips that seemed to speak of some powerful emotion only just held in check, but every inch of her slender body was tight with defiance—and rejection.

'You may be king,' she declared, focussing on him so tightly that it seemed as if there was no one in the room but the two of them. 'And perhaps you can order people around—order their lives around for the fun of it! But you can't control people's hearts. You can't dictate the way I think—the way I feel! You can't force me to—'

But that was too much to take.

'Force? What force have I used?'

But she wasn't listening, launched on her stream of thoughts, flinging her fury into his face without a hint of restraint or hesitation.

'You might be able to command that I do as you say and I will have to obey you with a "yes, Your Royal Highness. Anything you say, Your Majesty".'

Her elegant frame dipped in the most flawless—and most sarcastic—curtsey ever delivered. That was, unless you remembered the one she had given him on the night she had come to his room, when the blue silk nightgown had billowed out at her feet, forming a perfect pool of silk on the floor around her. Alexei's groin tightened at the memory of where that had led but he had to fight the impulse, knowing that it would distract him too much.

And he didn't need any distractions, not if he was to work out just where everything had gone wrong—and think of some way to put it right.

'You can even make me marry you—but you can't command my heart. You can't force me to love you!'

Love.

Things might have moved rather faster than he had intended, the careful plan he'd decided on rushed and confused at the last moment, but he could swear that he had never said anything about… Why would she mention love? Why would it even be in her thoughts unless…?

'Who the hell said anything about love?'

Her only response was a swift, startled widening of her eyes, the sudden sharp biting down of her teeth onto the softness of her bottom lip in a way that made him wince in instinctive sympathy.

They couldn't talk like this, not with every ear in the place tuned to what they were saying, hanging on to every word. For a second he considered grabbing hold of Ria's hand, taking her out of here—on to the terrace, into the garden—but one glance into her face had him reconsidering. She would fight him all the way, he knew that, and they had already created enough of a fever of interest to be the talk of the country for several years or more.

'Everyone out of here.' His hand came up to brush off the murmurs of concern. 'Now.'

He might get used to this king business after all, Alexei reflected as everyone obeyed his order, moving out of the room at his command. Even though they all hurried to obey him, it still took far longer than he had anticipated to empty the room and shut the doors behind them. It seemed an age before he was alone with Ria, and she was itching to get out of here; he could see that in her eyes, in the uneasy way she moved from one foot to another, nervous as a restive horse.

But she had stayed, and he had to pin his hopes on that.

What the devil was he going to say that didn't make her throw up her head and run? There was only one place to start. One word that was fixed inside his head, immovable and clear.

'Love?' he said, still unable to believe that he had heard her right. 'Did you say love?'

Had she? Oh dear heaven had she actually made the biggest mistake ever and come out with it just like that—in front of everyone here? Ria could feel the colour flood up into her face, sweeping under her mask, and then swiftly ebb away again as she heard her own voice sounding inside her head.

'You can't make me love you!' She flashed it at him in desperate defiance, fearful that he might take advantage of it, use it against her.

But somehow he didn't look quite how she expected. There was none of the anger, none of the coldness of rejection, nothing of the withdrawal she had thought she would see in his face if she ever admitted to the way she was feeling.

'I wouldn't even try,' he said and his voice was strangely low, almost soft. 'You're right, love can't be forced. It can only be given.'

Was she supposed to find an answer to that? She tried, she really did, but nothing came to mind. Her brain was just great, big empty space, with no thoughts forming anywhere.

'But you did try to force it.'

'Is that what you thought I was doing?'

He raked both hands through his hair, pushing it into appealing disorder. The movement knocked the mask sideways slightly. And, as he had done earlier in her room, he snatched it off and tossed it to the ground.

'I thought I was proposing. Let's face it, I never really *asked* you to marry me—we just agreed on terms.'

We didn't exactly agree, Ria was about to say, but something caught on her tongue, stopping her from getting the words out. She was looking again at that shockingly unexpected proposal. The sudden silence, the gaping crowds, and Alexei on his knee before her.

The man who had been so convinced that Mecjoria wouldn't want him, that the nobility would reject him as they had once done ten years before, had taken the risk of proposing all over again, of opening himself up in front of everyone here tonight. He'd risked his image, his pride, his dignity—and what had she done? She had thrown the proposal right back in his face.

'I tried to set you free tonight. I knew I couldn't tie you to a marriage to me in the way that it was going to be. I couldn't trap you like that, cage you—force you into sacrificing yourself for the country. I had to let you go, no matter how much I wanted you to stay. I had no right to impose those terms—any terms on you at all.'

'But you reinforced those terms so clearly here tonight.'

'Did I?' Alexei questioned softly. His eyes were deep pools in his drawn face. She couldn't look away if she tried. But she didn't want to try.

'My father...'

'Your father was here tonight as a free man. Did you see any chains?' he questioned sharply. 'Any armed escort?'

'No.' She had to acknowledge that. 'Then why?'

'I wanted to give your family back to you. I know what it feels like to be without a family.'

It had happened to him twice, Ria remembered. When

he had been brought to Mecjoria, supposedly to spend the rest of his life with his father and mother reunited at last, only to have his father die suddenly and shockingly and then to have his parents' marriage thrown into question so that he was rejected by the rest of the royal family. Again when he had had his own family, with Mariette and baby Belle. That too had ended in tragedy.

But he had talked of setting her free, and he'd wanted to give her family back to her. None of this meant what she had believed at first.

'I'm not sure that my father deserves your clemency,' she said carefully. 'He has schemed against you—plotted…'

'Oh, I'll be keeping a very close eye on him from now on,' Alexei assured her. 'For one thing I never want you to have to deal with him again. If he tries to interfere in your life then he will have to answer to me. Though I know you'll be able to stand up to him for yourself from now on. And I think the fear that he might have lost your mother will be punishment enough. Love can do that to you.'

Love? That word again.

'I should know,' Alexei went on.

I loved once—adored her… Lost her.

'Belle…'

Alexei nodded sombrely, his eyes still fixed on her face so that she could read his feelings in his expression. And those thoughts made her heart contract on a wave of painful hope. Because the look on his face now as he looked at her was the same as when he had stared down at the little snapshot of Belle, the person he had loved most in all the world.

'It broke my heart to lose her. I never thought I'd feel that way again—about anyone. But this morning when you said that I'd trapped you, I knew I was risking losing you when I forced you into marriage.'

'For the good of the country and because you wanted me.'

She could risk saying that much. Did she dare to take it any further? He had wanted to set her free. Surely that was the act of a man who...

'And I wanted you every bit as much.' Her voice jumped and cracked as she forced herself to add more. 'I always have. I still do.'

Alexei lifted his hands, cupping her face in both of them, his lips just a breath away from hers.

'Forgive me for tonight. I tried to let you go, but I couldn't. But I thought it was worth one last try to show you that I love you and to...'

'Alexei.' Ria's hand came up to press against his mouth, stilling the rest of his words. She didn't need to hear any more. 'You love me?'

He nodded his dark head, his intent gaze never leaving hers.

'I love you. With all my heart—the heart I thought was dead when I lost little Belle. But you've brought it back to life again. You've brought me back to life. But I don't want to trap you. I don't want you here if it's not where you want to be. I'll set you free if that's what you truly want but—'

Once more she stopped his words, but this time with a wildly joyful kiss that crushed them back inside his mouth.

'That's not what I want,' she whispered against his lips. 'What I want—all I want—is right here, right now. In you.'

He closed his eyes in response to her words and she felt him draw in a deep, deep breath of release and acceptance.

'I love you,' she told him, needing to say the words, glorying in the freedom of being able to speak them out loud at last.

'And I love you. More than I can say.'

She didn't doubt it. She couldn't. She could hear it reverberate in his deep tones, in the faint tremble of the hands that held her face. It was there in his eyes, in the set of his mouth, etched into every strong muscle of his face. This was the only truth, the absolute truth. And it made her heart sing in pure joy.

'Can we start again, please?' she whispered, making each word into a kiss against his mouth. 'And if that proposal is still open…'

'It is.' It was just a sigh.

'Then I accept—freely and gladly—and lovingly. I'd be so happy to marry you and stay with you for the rest of my life.'

She was gathered up into his arms, clamped so close against his chest that she could hear the heavy, hungry pounding of his heart and knew it was beating for her. The kiss he gave her made her senses swim, her legs lose all strength so that she clung to him urgently, needing him, loving him, and knowing deep in her soul that he would always be there for her now and in the future.

It was some time before a noise from outside reminded them that everyone who had come here to attend the ball was still waiting. A thousand people, waiting to discover just what her reply had been to his proposal. Glancing towards the door, Alexei looked deep into her face and smiled rather ruefully.

'Our guests are getting impatient. We should let them in again. Let them share in our celebrations.

'But,' he added as Ria nodded her agreement, 'This will be the official celebration. The time for our private celebration will come later. I promise you that I'll make it very, very special.'

And the depth of his tone, the way he still held her close, reluctant to let go even for a moment, told Ria that it was a promise not just for tonight but for the rest of their lives together.

* * * * *

'I'm trying to be serious, Kayla.'

'Why?' she breathed against the velvety texture of his skin, delighting in the way his breathing was growing more and more ragged from her kisses.

But as her fingers trailed teasingly along the inside of one powerful thigh Leonidas suddenly clamped his hand down on hers, resisting the temptation to let it wander.

'Because I don't believe you're the type of girl who does this without knowing what sort of man she's getting herself involved with and without demanding some degree of emotional commitment.'

And he wasn't offering any. She couldn't understand why telling herself that caused her spirits to plummet the way they did.

'I'm not demanding anything,' she uttered, knowing that the only way to save face was to get the hell out of there.

Scrambling out of bed, managing to shrug off the hand that tried to restrain her, she heard his urgent, 'Kayla! Kayla, come back here!'

Elizabeth Power wanted to be a writer from a very early age, but it wasn't until she was nearly thirty that she took to writing seriously. Writing is now her life. Travelling ranks very highly among her pleasures, and so many places she has visited have been recreated in her books. Living in England's West Country, Elizabeth likes nothing better than taking walks with her husband along the coast or in the adjoining woods, and enjoying all the wonders that nature has to offer.

Recent titles by the same author:

A DELICIOUS DECEPTION
BACK IN THE LION'S DEN
SINS OF THE PAST
FOR REVENGE OR REDEMPTIONN

Did you know these are also available as eBooks?
Visit www.millsandboon.co.uk

A GREEK ESCAPE

BY
ELIZABETH POWER

MILLS & BOON

First published in Great Britain 2013
by Mills & Boon, an imprint of Harlequin (UK) Limited.
Harlequin (UK) Limited, Eton House, 18-24 Paradise Road,
Richmond, Surrey TW9 1SR

© Elizabeth Power 2013

ISBN: 978 0 263 90017 0

Harlequin (UK) policy is to use papers that are natural, renewable and recyclable products and made from wood grown in sustainable forests. The logging and manufacturing process conform to the legal environmental regulations of the country of origin.

Printed and bound in Spain
by Blackprint CPI, Barcelona

A GREEK ESCAPE

For Alan—
and all those wonderful sandwiches that kept me going!

CHAPTER ONE

'THAT'S IT! THAT'S the one we want! Stop wasting time, you idiot, and take it!' The camera clicked the second before the bird took off from its rock and flapped away over the crystalline water. 'Didn't think I'd let you get away, did you?'

From her vantage point on the rocky hillside overlooking the shingle beach Kayla Young swung round with a swish of long blonde hair, embarrassed that someone might have overheard her. There was nothing but a warm wind, however, passing over the craggy scrubland, and the relentless sun beating down from a vividly azure sky, and Kayla's shoulders drooped in relief.

She wasn't sure when she had first started talking to herself. Perhaps coming away all by herself to this lovely island wasn't doing much for her sanity, she thought, grimacing. Or perhaps it was a defence mechanism against the knowledge that today, back in England, the man she had thought she'd be spending her life with was an hour away from marrying someone else.

The wounds of betrayal were no longer so raw but the scars remained, and in defiance of them Kayla brought the SLR's viewfinder to eye level again. Only her clamped jaw revealed the tension in her as, silently now, she appraised the beauty around her.

Misty blue mountains. Translucently clear water. Surprisingly hunky Greek…

She'd been following a line inland, coming across the deserted beach, but now Kayla brought her viewfinder back to the shoreline in a swift doubletake.

Bringing her camera down, she could see him clearly without the aid of the zoom lens, and she found herself homing in on him with her naked eyes.

Black wavy hair—which would have been way past his collar had he been wearing one—fell wildly against the hard bronze of his neck. In a black T-shirt and pale blue jeans he was pulling fishing tackle from the wooden boat he had recently beached, and from the contoured muscles of his arms, and the way the dark cotton strained across his wide muscular chest, Kayla instantly marked him as a man who worked with his hands. A battered old truck was parked close to her rock, on the road just above the beach, and as the man started walking towards it—towards *her*—Kayla couldn't take her eyes off him.

For some reason she couldn't quite fathom she lifted her camera to zoom in on him again, and felt an absurd and reckless excitement in her secret survey. A few days' growth of stubble gave a striking cast to an already strong jaw, mirroring the strength in his rugged features. They were the features of a man toughened by life—a man who looked as fit as he was hard. A man not much more than thirty, who would probably demand his own way and get it—because there was determination in that face, Kayla recognised, as well as pride and arrogance in the way he carried himself, in the straight, purposeful stride of those long legs.

A man one definitely wouldn't want to mess with, she decided, with a curious little tingle down her spine.

She could see it all in every solid inch of him—in the curve

20% OFF*

with code
THANKSJUN

Visit www.millsandboon.co.uk
today to get this exclusive offer!

Ordering online is easy:

* 1000s of stories converted to eBook
* Big savings on titles you may have missed in store

Visit today and enter the code **THANKSJUN** at the checkout today to receive **20% OFF** your next purchase of books and eBooks*. You could be settling down with your favourite authors in no time!

MILLS
BOON

JUN13

of his tanned forehead and those thick winged brows that were drawing together now in a scowl because...

Dear heaven! he was looking up! He had seen her! Seen her pointing the camera straight at him!

As her agitated finger accidentally clicked the shutter closed she realised the camera had caught him—and, as he shouted something out, she realised that he was aware of it too.

She stood stock-still for a second as he quickened his stride; saw him moving determinedly in her direction.

Oh, my goodness! Suddenly she was pivoting away with the stark realisation that he was giving chase.

Why she was running, Kayla didn't know. Surely, she thought, it would have been better to stand her ground and brazen it out? Except that she hadn't felt like brazening anything out with a man who looked so angry. And anyway, what could she have said? *You caught my eye as I was sizing up the view and I couldn't stop looking at you.*

That would really have been asking for trouble, she assured herself, with her blood pounding in her ears and her legs feeling heavy. She darted an anxious glance back over her shoulder and saw the man was gaining on her now, along the stony uphill path that led to the safety of the villa.

And why had she been looking at him anyway? she reprimanded herself. She had had enough of men to last her a lifetime! It could only have been because he had an interesting face; that was all. Apart from that she wouldn't have looked twice at him if he had rowed across that water accompanied by a fanfare. She had learned the hard way that men were just lying, cheating opportunists—

'Oooh!'

Tripping over a stone, she struggled to keep herself upright, hearing her pursuer's footsteps bearing down on her.

Too late, though. She came a cropper on the hard and dusty

path and lay there for a few moments, winded and despairing, but surprisingly unharmed.

She heard the pound of his footsteps and suddenly he was there, standing above her. He was breathing hard, and his tone was rough as he tossed some words at her in his own language.

Utterly awestruck by the speed at which he must have run to have caught up with her, Kayla raised herself up on her elbows, her hair falling like pale rivers of silk over her shoulders.

Having little more than a few words of Greek to get by with, she quavered, 'I don't understand you.' Like him, she was breathless, and shaken by his anger as much as her fall.

He said something else that she couldn't comprehend, while a firm hand on her shoulder—bare save for the white strap of her sun top—pulled her round to face him.

Up close, his features were even more arresting than she'd first imagined. His cheekbones were high and well-defined under dark olive skin. Thick ebony lashes framed eyes that were as black as jet, and his brooding mouth was wide and firm.

'Are you hurt?' His question, delivered roughly in English this time, surprised her, as did that small element of concern.

'No. No thanks to you,' she accused, sitting upright and brushing dust off her shorts, trying to appear less intimidated than she was feeling.

'Then I will ask you again. What do you think you were doing?'

'I was taking photographs.'

'Of me?'

Kayla swallowed, fixing him with wary blue eyes. 'No, of a bird. I snapped you by accident.'

'Accident?' From the way one very masculine eyebrow lifted it was clear that he didn't believe her. His hostile gaze raked over her the pale oval of her face. 'What is this...*accident?*' he emphasised pointedly.

His anger hadn't cooled. Kayla could feel it bubbling just beneath the surface. Despite that, though, his voice had a deep, rich resonance, and although his English was heavily accented his command of her language was obvious as he demanded, 'Exactly how many did you take?'

'Only the one,' she admitted, her breathing still laboured from that chase up the hillside. 'I told you. It was an accident.'

'Well, as far as I'm concerned, young woman, it was one accident too many. Exactly who are you? And what are you doing here?'

'Nothing. I mean, I'm on holiday—that's all.'

'And does the normal course of your holiday usually include sticking your nose into other people's business? Spying on people?'

'I wasn't *spying* on you!' From the way those accusing ebony eyes were studying her, and from the suspicion in his voice, Kayla began to experience real fear. Perhaps he was on the run! Wanted by the police! That would go some way to explaining his anger over being photographed. 'My camera…?' Trying to hide her misgivings, she glanced anxiously around and spotted the expensive piece of equipment lying in the scrub nearby.

Stretching out in a bid to reach it, she was dismayed when the man leaped forward, snatching it up before she could.

'Don't damage it!'

He looked angry enough, she thought. But her camera was something she treasured. A gift to herself to replace her old one after she had discovered Craig was having an affair. Some women comfort-ate. She went out with her camera and snapped anything and everything as a form of therapy, and over the past three months she had needed all the therapy she could get!

'Give me one good reason why I shouldn't?'

Because it was expensive! she wanted to fling back. And

because it's got every photograph I've taken since I got here yesterday. But that would probably only make him more inclined to wreck it, if his mood was anything to go by.

'Perhaps I should simply keep it,' he contemplated aloud, his gaze sweeping over her still pale shoulders and modest breasts with unashamed insolence.

'If it makes you happy,' she snapped, needled by the way he was looking at her. But there was something about that gaze moving over her exposed flesh that produced a rush of heat along with a cautioning tingle through her blood. After all, she didn't have a clue who he was, did she? Supposing he really was wanted by the police?

A bird swooped low out of the pine forest above them, its frenzied shriek making her jump before it screeched away, protesting at the human intrusion.

For the first time Kayla realised just how isolated the hillside was. Apart from a cluster of whitewashed fishermen's houses, huddled above the beach at the foot of the mountain road, there was no other sign of human habitation, while the nearest village with its shop and taverna was nearly three miles away.

As she was scrambling to her feet a masculine arm shot out to assist her.

The sudden act of gallantry was so unexpected after all his hostility that Kayla automatically took the hand he was offering. It felt strong and slightly callused as he pulled her upright, bringing her close to his dominating masculinity. Disconcertingly close.

Her senses awakened to the outdoor freshness of him, to the aura of pulsing energy that seemed to surround him, and to an underlying masculine scent that was all his own.

Swallowing and bringing her head up—in her flat-heeled pumps, she still only reached his shoulder—she took a step back and said in a voice that cracked with an unwelcome tug of unmistakable chemistry, 'I'm not afraid of you.'

'Good.' His tone was terse, and still decidedly unfriendly. 'In that case you won't mind me telling you that I don't like interfering young women depriving me of my privacy. So if you want to enjoy your so-called "holiday",' he emphasised scornfully, dumping the offending camera into her startled hands, 'you'll stay out of my way! Is that clear?'

'Perfectly! And I can assure you, Mr... Mr...No-name,' she went on when he didn't have the decency to tell her. 'I've certainly got no wish to deprive you of anything. Least of all your privacy!' Deciding now that he was probably nothing more dangerous than a bad-tempered local, she pressed on, 'In fact you have my solemn promise that I'll do everything I can while I'm here to see that you maintain it.'

'Thank you!'

Kayla bit back indignation as he swung unceremoniously away, striding back down the path without so much as a glance back.

A few minutes later, coming up through the scrub below the modern white villa where she was staying, she heard the distant sound of a vehicle starting up, and guessed from the roughness of its engine that it was the truck she had seen parked at the head of the beach.

Kayla was still smarting from the encounter as she fixed herself a microwave meal that evening in the villa's well-equipped kitchen. With open-plan floors, exposed roof rafters above its galleried landing and spectacular views over the rolling countryside, the villa belonged to her friends, Lorna and Josh. Knowing how much she needed a break, they had offered Kayla the chance to get away for a couple of weeks.

She had barely met a soul since the taxi driver had dropped

her off here yesterday, so why did the first person she bumped into have to be so downright rude?

Slipping the dish into the microwave oven, she stabbed out the settings on the control panel, her agitated movements reflecting her mood.

Still, better that he was rude than charming and lying through his teeth, she thought bitterly, her thoughts straying to Craig Lymington.

How easily she had fallen for his empty promises. She had believed and trusted him when he'd professed to want to be with her for life.

'He'll break your heart. You mark my words,' her mother had advised unkindly when Kayla had enthused over how the most up-and-coming executive at her company, Cartwright Consolidated, had asked her to marry him.

They had been engaged for two months, and Kayla had been deliriously happy, until that night when she'd discovered those messages on his cell phone and realised that she wasn't the only woman to whom he'd whispered such hollow and meaningless words...

'All men are the same, and the high-flying company type are the worst of the lot!' her mother had warned her often enough.

But Kayla hadn't listened. She'd believed her mother was simply embittered and scarred by her own unfortunate experience. After all, hadn't her own husband—Kayla's father—been a company executive? And hadn't he deserted her in exactly the same fashion fifteen years ago, when Kayla had been just eight years old?

Because of that and her mother's warnings she had grown up determined that the man she eventually decided to settle down with would never treat her in such an abominable way.

But he had, Kayla thought. And she had been rudely awakened and forced to admit—to herself at least—that her mother was right. They *were* the worst of the lot! It was a realisation doubly enforced when she had had to suffer the demeaning overtures of one or two other male members of management who had tried to capitalise on her broken engagement.

After leaving the company where she'd worked with Craig, trying to put the pain and humiliation of what he had done behind her, she might have been able to pick up the pieces of her life if she had been allowed to. But her mother's condescending and self-satisfied attitude—particularly when she'd heard that Craig really was getting married—had made everything far, far worse.

Consequently when Lorna had offered her the chance of escaping to her isolated Grecian retreat for a couple of weeks Kayla had jumped at the chance. It had seemed like the answer to a prayer. A place to start rebuilding her sense of self-worth.

But now, as she took her supper from the bleeping microwave and prodded the rather unpalatable-looking lasagne with a fork, it wasn't thoughts of Craig Lymington that troubled her and upset her determined attempts to restore her equilibrium. It was the face of that churlish stranger she'd been unfortunate enough to cross this morning, and her shocking awareness of him when he'd pulled her to her feet and she'd felt the impact of his disturbing proximity.

Leonidas Vassalio was fixing a loose shutter on one of the ground-floor windows, his features as hard as the stones that made up the ancient farmhouse and as darkly intense as the gathering clouds that were closing in over the mountains, warning of an impending storm.

The house would fall down if he didn't take some urgent steps to get it repaired, he realised, glancing up at the sad state of its terracotta roof and the peeling green paint around its doors and windows. The muscles in his powerful arms flexed as he twisted a screw in place.

It was hard to imagine that this place had once been his

home. This modest, isolated farmhouse, reached only by a zig-zagging dirt road. Yet this island, with its rocky coast, its azure waters and barren mountains, was as familiar to him as his own being, and a far cry from the world he inhabited now.

The rain had started to fall. Cold, heavy drops that splashed his face and neck as he worked and reflected on the whole complicated mess his life had become.

To the outsider his privileged lifestyle was one to be envied, but personally he was tired of sycophants, superficial women and the intrusion of the paparazzi. Like that interfering slip of a girl he'd caught photographing him on the beach this morning, he thought grimly, ready to bet money that she was one of them. For what other reason would she have been there if she wasn't from some newspaper? He had had enough of reporters to last him a lifetime, and they had been particularly savaging of late.

He had always shunned publicity. Always managed to keep a low media profile. Anyone outside of Greece might not instantly have recognised him, even though they would most certainly have recognised the Vassalio name. It was his brief involvement with Esmeralda Leigh that had thrust him so starkly into the public eye recently.

Nor had it helped when a couple of the high-ranking executives he had trusted to run one of his UK subsidiaries, along with an unscrupulous lawyer, had reneged on a verbal promise over a development deal and given the Vassalio Group bad press—which in turn had brought his own ethics into question. After all, as chairman, Leonidas thought introspectively, the buck stopped with him. But he had been too tied up at the time to be aware of what was going on.

That ordinary people had been lied to and were having their homes bulldozed from under them didn't sit comfortably on his conscience. Nor did being accused of riding roughshod over people without giving a thought to their needs, breaking up communities so as to profit from multi-million-pound sports arenas and retail/leisure complexes and expand on Vassalio's ever-increasing assets. The fact that everyone affected had been compensated—and very well—had been consigned only to the back pages of the tabloids.

He had needed to get away. To forget Leonidas Vassalio, billionaire and successful businessman, for a while and sort out what was important to him. And to do that he had needed to get back to his roots. To enjoy the bliss of virtual anonymity that coming here would offer him. Because only one other person knew he was here. But now it looked as though even that might have been too much to expect, if that nosy little blonde he'd caught snooping around today had lied about why she was here.

And if she hadn't, and she really had been photographing birds, why had she been standing there taking a picture of him? Had she just fancied snapping a bit of local colour? One of the peasants going about his daily business? Or could it be that she'd just happened to like the look of him? he thought, with his mouth twisting cynically. In other circumstances he would have admitted unreservedly to himself that he hadn't exactly been put off by the look of *her*. Especially when he'd noted that she'd been wearing no ring.

But bedding nubile young women wasn't on his agenda right now. Heaven only knew the physical attributes he'd been endowed with acted like a magnet on the opposite sex, and he'd never met one yet that he'd wanted to bed who hadn't been willing, but, no, he determined as he oiled a hinge. Whatever her motives were, and no matter how affected she'd been by that spark of something that had leaped between them and made her pull back from him as though she'd been scorched when he'd pulled her to her feet, that girl certainly hadn't had bedroom games in mind.

She had to be staying in one of those modern villas that

had sprung up further down the hillside. That was the direction she had been heading in when he'd caught up with her. He wondered if there was anyone with her, or if she was staying there alone. If she was, he deliberated with his hackles rising, then she had to be here for a reason. And if that reason was to intrude on his peace and solitude...

Finishing what he was doing, annoyed at how much thought he was giving to her, he rushed inside, out of the rain.

She was going to find out the hard way that she couldn't mess with *him!*

CHAPTER TWO

THE THREE-MILE drive to the main village to get provisions had seemed like an easy enough mission, particularly when last night's storm had caused a power cut and made her fridge stop working.

Unless the thing had broken before then, Kayla thought exasperated, having come downstairs this morning to a cabinet of decidedly warm and smelly food.

But the polished voice of the car's satellite navigation system had let her down badly when it had guided her along this track. And now, having parked the car in order to consult the map and try and work out where she was, the little hatchback that her friends kept here for whenever they visited the island refused to start.

She tried again, her teeth clenched with tension.

'Come on,' she appealed desperately to the engine. 'Please.'

It was no good, she realised, slumping back on her seat. It had well and truly packed up.

Lorna had given her the name of someone she could call in an emergency who spoke relatively good English, Kayla remembered, fishing in the glove compartment for the man's number. But when she took her cell phone out of her bag she discovered that she didn't have a signal.

Despairingly tossing the phone onto the passenger seat, she looked around at a Grecian panorama of sea and mountains and, closer to hand, pine woods and stony slopes leading down to this track.

Beyond the open windows of the car the chirruping of crickets in the scrub and the lonely tugging of the wind only seemed to emphasise her isolation. She didn't have a clue where she was.

Glancing back over her shoulder, she recognised way below the group of rocks that ran seaward from the beach where she had seen that surly local yesterday, and that smaller island in the distance, clear as a bell today beneath the canopy of a rain-washed vividly azure sky.

With the sun beating relentlessly down upon her, with an unusable phone and only a broken-down car for company, Kayla glanced wistfully towards what looked like a deserted farmhouse, with a roof that had seen better days peeping above the trees at the end of the track.

Fat chance she had of making a call from there!

Or did she?

Sticking her head out of the window and inhaling deeply, she caught the distinct smell of woodsmoke drifting towards her on the scented air.

With her spirits soaring, she leaped out of the car, grabbed her precious camera and set off at a pace, her zipped-back sandals kicking up dust along the sun-baked track.

It was the truck she recognised as she came, breathless, into a paved area at the front of the house. A familiar yellow truck that had her stopping in her tracks even before she recognised its owner.

Wild black hair. Wild eyes. Wild expression.

Oh, no!

Coming from around the side of the house, the surly Greek was looking as annoyed as he looked untamed.

And justifiably so, Kayla decided, swallowing. She had invaded his territory again—unintentionally though it was—

and she would have run like the wind if she had realised it a second sooner. As it was, she was riveted to the spot by the sheer dynamism of the man.

In blue denim cut-offs and nothing else but a dark tan leather waistcoat, exposing his chest and muscular arms, he exuded strength and raw, virile masculinity.

'I thought I told you to stay away from me,' he called out angrily to her, his long, purposeful strides closing the distance between them. 'What do you want?' As if he didn't know! Leonidas thought, his scowling gaze dropping to the camera clutched tightly against her ribcage. 'Didn't you get enough photographs yesterday?'

He looked bigger and distinctly more threatening than he had the previous day, Kayla decided, unnerved. If that were possible!

'I...I just want to use your phone,' she informed him, ignoring his accusation and annoyed with herself for sounding so defensive, for allowing him to intimidate her in such a way.

'My phone?'

She could feel her body tingling beneath the penetrative heat of his gaze. Her T-shirt and shorts felt much too inadequate beside such potent masculinity.

'You *do* have one?' she asked pointedly, trying not to let his unfriendliness get to her. From the way he'd queried her request she might have been asking him to give her a mortgage on Crete! 'My car...' She hated having to tell him as she sent a glance back over her shoulder. 'It's broken down.'

He peered in the direction she'd indicated. But of course he couldn't see it, she realised, because it was way down the track, hidden by trees and scrub. And all she could focus on right then was the undulating muscles of his smooth and powerful chest, which was glistening bronze—slick with sweat.

'Really? And what seems to be the trouble?' he enquired with the sceptical lifting of an eyebrow. He looked at her with such disturbing intensity that Kayla felt as if her strength was being sapped right out of her.

Beneath the thick sweep of his lashes his eyes were amazingly dark, she noticed reluctantly. His nose was proud, his cheekbones high and hard, his mouth firm and well-defined above the dark, virile shadow around his jaw. As for his body...

She wanted to look at him and keep looking at him. *All* of him, she realised, shocked. She was even more shocked to realise that she had never been so aware of a man's sensuality before. Not even Craig's. But he had asked her a question, and all she was doing was standing here wondering how spectacular he would look naked.

Trying to keep her eyes off that very masculine chest, she uttered with deliberate vagueness, 'It won't go.'

That glorious chest lifted as he inhaled deeply. 'Won't move or won't start?' he demanded to know.

Entertaining a half-crazed desire to needle him, Kayla answered with mock innocence, 'It's the same thing, isn't it?'

Now, as those glinting dark eyes pierced the rebellious depths of hers, she realised that this man would know when he was being taken for a fool, and warned herself against the inadvisability of antagonising him.

'Does the engine fire when you turn the ignition key?' he asked, his sweat-slicked chest lifting again with rising impatience.

'No. Nothing happens at all,' she told him, frankly this time. 'So if you could just let me use your phone—if you have a signal—or if you don't...if you have a landline...' A dubious glance up at the house had her wondering if it had fallen into the state it was in long before telephones had been invented.

'It's Sunday,' he reminded her succinctly. 'Who are you going to call?'

She shrugged. 'The nearest garage?' she suggested flippantly, hoping the man whose name she had been given for emergencies would be at home. In fact Lorna had said to call *her* if she needed any help or advice, and right now Kayla felt she'd get more help from her friend back in England than the capable-looking hunk standing just a metre away.

Suddenly, without another word, he was walking past her.

'Show me,' he said over his leather-clad shoulder, much to her surprise.

She virtually had to run to keep up with him.

When they reached the car he held out a hand for the key and Kayla dropped it onto his tanned palm, noticing the cool economy with which he moved as he opened the driver's door and leaned inside to start the ignition.

It fired first time.

'I don't understand...' She turned from the traitorous little vehicle to face the man who had now straightened and was standing there looking tall and imposing and so self-satisfied that she could have kicked him—or the car. Or both! 'I tried and tried,' she stressed, with all the conviction she could muster, because scepticism was stamped on every plane and angle of his hard, handsome face.

He reached into the car again, switched off the engine and, dangling the key in front of her, said in his heavily accented voice, 'Perhaps you would care to try again?'

She jumped into the car, keeping her defiant gaze level with his, almost willing the little hatchback to refuse to start for her. Because how on earth was he going to believe her if it did?

It did.

She flopped back against the headrest, her eyes closing with a mixture of relief and rising frustration.

'There, you see. It's simple when you know how.'

There was no mistaking the cool derision that drifted down to her through the open door, and suddenly Kayla's control snapped.

'It wouldn't start! I couldn't make it! And if you think I

made it all up for some warped reason, just to come here and annoy you, then, believe me, I've got far more important things to do with my time! My phone won't work! My sat-nav's up the creek! And Lorna's fridge has broken down and ruined all the food I bought. And all you can do is stand there and accuse me of lying! Well, I can assure you, Mr… Mr…'

'Leon.'

She looked up at him askance, her blue eyes glistening with angry tears. 'What?'

'My name is Leon,' he repeated. 'And who is this Lorna you mention? Your travelling companion?'

'No. I'm here on my own,' Kayla blurted out without even thinking. A totally frustrating morning had finally taken its toll. 'Lorna owns the villa where I'm staying.' Lorna who— with her husband Josh—had miraculously come to her rescue by offering her a post in their interior design company after Kayla had found it too distressing to stay on at her old job.

'And you say the fridge has broken down?'

'Big-time!' What was he going to do? Drive down and check that she wasn't lying about that as well?

'Have you eaten?'

'What?'

His hand came to rest on the roof of the car as he stooped to address her through the open door. 'I know I'm Greek and you're English, but you seem to be having great difficulty in understanding me. I said, have you eaten?'

'No.'

'Then drive up to the house,' he instructed. 'I'll be along directly.'

What? Kayla nearly said it again, only just stopping herself in time.

He was offering her hospitality? Surely not, she thought, amazed. He was hard, unfriendly, and a perfect stranger to boot.

Well, not perfect, she decided grudgingly. Only in appearance, she found herself silently admitting. Whatever else he was, he was lethally attractive. But some masochistic and warped urge to know more about him—along with the thought of all that festering food she was going to have to throw away—motivated her, against her better judgement, into doing what he had suggested.

He had almost reached the paved yard by the time Kayla put her camera in the boot, out of the sun, having decided it was for the best since it seemed to offend him so much. Involuntarily, her gaze was drawn to his approach.

Unconsciously her eyes savoured the whole sensational length and breadth of him, from those wide shoulders and muscular arms to that glistening bronze chest and tightly muscled waist, right down to his narrow denim-clad hips. Very masculine legs ended in a pair of leather sandals, dusty from his trek along the track.

There was a humourless curl to his mouth, she noticed as he drew nearer, as though he were fully aware of her reluctant interest in him.

'Around the back,' he advised with a toss of his chin, and waited for her to go ahead of him.

That small act of courtesy seemed oddly at variance with his manners on the whole, she decided, preceding him around the side of the rambling old farmhouse.

Don't talk to any strange men. Never take sweets from a stranger.

Wondering what she was doing, ignoring all those clichéd warnings, Kayla realised her mother would have a fit if she could see her now.

'So…are you going to tell me something about yourself?' Leon whoever-he-was enquired deeply from just behind her.

'Like what?' she responded, still walking on ahead.

'Your name would be a good start,' he suggested incisively.

They had come around to the rear of the house, where weed-strewn shady terraces gave onto an equally overgrown garden.

'It's Kayla,' she told him, following his example and deciding that last names were superfluous.

'Kayla?'

Despite his overall unfriendliness, the way he repeated her name was like the warm Ionian wind that blew up from the sea, rippling through the tufted grass on the arid hills. An unexpected little sensation quivered through her. Or was it the sun that seemed to be burning her cheeks? The warm breeze that was lifting the almost imperceptibly fine hairs on her arms?

'Come.' He gestured to a rustic bench under a canopy of vines. Nearby were some smouldering logs within a purpose-built circle of bricks. Resting on a stone beside it was a grid containing several small plump, freshly prepared fish, their scales gleaming silver in the late morning sun.

'Did you catch those yourself?' She'd noticed a rod and fishing tackle in the back of his truck, and wondered if he went out every day to fish from the boat she'd seen him unloading the previous day.

'Yes, about an hour ago.' He was squatting down, repositioning a log on the fire. 'What's wrong?' he enquired, looking up at her when she still stood there, saying nothing. 'Are you vegetarian?'

She had been silently marvelling at how only this morning those fish had been in the sea—how he had already been down there, brought them back and prepared them for his lunch—but there was no way she was going to tell him that.

'No,' she replied, watching him place the grid on the bricks over the glimmering logs.

'Then sit down,' he commanded, before he turned and strode back into the house.

Left alone, Kayla took a few moments to study its sadly neglected exterior. With its ramshackle appearance, and the odd wild creeper growing out of its walls, it seemed almost to have become part of the hillside that rose steeply above it on one side. She wondered if it might just be a place he had found where it was convenient for him to shack up, and then looked quickly away as he emerged from inside with plates and cutlery and several different kinds of bread in a hand-painted bowl.

'Do I take it that you don't want any?' he called out, noticing that she was still standing where he had left her.

The fish were starting to cook, skins bubbling, their aroma drifting up to her with the woodsmoke, tantalising and sweet.

'No,' she refuted quickly, sitting down on the bench, and earned herself the twitch of a smile from that mocking, masculine mouth as he set the plates and cutlery down on a small, intricately wrought iron table that looked as though it had seen every winter for decades. 'So, why are you asking me to lunch if you want to be left alone?'

'Good question,' he responded without looking at her. He was using a fish slice to turn their lunch. Spitting oil splashed onto the glowing logs, making them sizzle. 'Perhaps it's the best way of keeping an eye on you,' he said when he had finished.

'Why?' She fixed him directly with eyes that were as vivid as cornflowers. 'Why are you so worried about my bothering you? Why do you think I need keeping an eye on?' she queried, frowning. 'Unless…'

'Unless what?' he urged, calmly setting the fish slice aside.

Her heart was beating unusually fast. 'You have something to hide.'

Squatting there, with his hands splayed on his bunched and powerful thighs, he was studying her face with such unsettling intensity that for a few moments Kayla wondered if her original supposition about him was right. He really was on the run from the law. Why else would he object so strongly to being photographed?

Leonidas made a half-amused sound down his nostrils. 'Don't we all?' he suggested through the charm of a feigned smile, and thought, *Particularly you, my scandal-mongering little kitten.*

For a moment he saw tension mark the flawless oval of her face. What was it? he wondered. Excitement? Anticipation? The thrill of getting some juicy snippet about him to pad out some gossip column she couldn't fill with the misfortunes of some other unsuspecting fool?

'Does valuing my personal space necessarily mean I have to be hiding something?' he put to her, a little more roughly, and saw her mouth pull down as she contemplated his question.

It didn't. Of course it didn't, Kayla thought in an attempt to allay her suspicions about him.

'No,' she responded, pushing her hair back behind one ear, wondering why she was finding it so easy to let herself be persuaded.

Disconcertingly, those midnight-black eyes followed her agitated movement before he swung away from the fire, went back into the house.

'What about you?' he quizzed, after he'd returned with a couple of chunky glasses, which he also set down on the table before returning to the makeshift barbecue.

'What *about* me?' Kayla enquired, noticing how the muscles bunched in his powerful legs as he dropped down on his haunches. Her mouth felt unusually dry.

'You're here on your own,' he remarked. 'Which can mean only one of two things.'

'Which are?' she prompted cautiously, watching him wield the fish slice and slide some fish onto one of the earthenware plates he had brought from the house. He handed it to her, before dishing out another portion for himself.

'You're either running away…' He put his own plate down on an upturned fruit crate opposite the bench and retrieved the rustic bowl from the table.

'Or…?' she pressed, swallowing, feeling his eyes watching her far too intently as she took a chunk of the wholesome-looking bread he was offering her.

'Or…you're chasing something.'

'Like what?' she invited, frowning, feeling as though those keen dark eyes were suddenly giving her a mental frisking. She had the feeling that behind that casual manner of his lurked a blade-sharp brain that was assessing her every reaction, and that every word and response from her was being systematically weighed and measured.

Leonidas's mouth compressed. 'Dreams. A good time.' He moved a shoulder in a deceptively nonchalant way. *Another sensation-charged story to smear the Vassalio name.* 'So which is it for you, lovely Kayla?'

With her pulse doing an unexpected leap at the way he had addressed her, Kayla viewed him with mascara-touched lashes half-shielding her eyes.

How could he be so perceptive? So shrewd? He was living here like a gypsy. Whether he was alone or with someone she couldn't tell—although from what he had said she would have put money on it that there wasn't anyone else in residence. A man close to nature, who wasn't afraid of hard work, yet with a keen mind behind all that physical strength and potent energy. And a comprehension of human nature that even Craig with his university degree and his boardroom ambitions hadn't possessed.

She had no intention, however, of telling this unsettling hunk that his first assumption was right. That she *was* running away, and that she hadn't fully realised it until now. Her broken engagement and her recently bruised heart weren't things she wanted to discuss with anyone—least of all a man she had only just met, who didn't really want her there…even if he obviously felt obliged to share his lunch with her.

Looking down at her plate, and the mouth-watering meal she was tucking in to, she shrugged and said, 'I've been doing some temporary work since leaving a job I'd been in for five years. I thought it would be a good idea to come somewhere quiet and have a think about what I want to do if I have to move on.' *If Lorna's company folds and I have to apply for something more permanent,* she thought, and prayed for Lorna and Josh's sake that it wouldn't come to that. Though they *had* been facing a lot of problems recently.

He nodded, whether in approval or simply in response to what she had said she wasn't sure. Positioning himself on the crate from which he had retrieved his plate, he said, 'You mean you're…what is it you call it…?' He pretended to search for the word. 'Freelance?'

Brows drawn together, Kayla said hesitantly, 'Loosely speaking.' Filling in for Josh and Lorna when she'd been at her worst, after their bookkeeper had suddenly taken off with someone she'd met on the internet, was simply helping two people she cared about a great deal.

Leonidas reached around him for a stoneware vessel that was standing on an old tree stump beside him, hooking his thumb through the handle and bringing it over his shoulder like some ancient warrior at a feast before offering some to Kayla.

A hunter, she ruminated. Like those warring Greeks who had fought to keep their lands from invading Romans. Clever. Living by his wits. Untamed.

'It's homemade and non-alcoholic. Try it,' he invited smoothly, thinking that if 'loosely speaking' meant skirting around the truth then the local wine would have been much better at loosening her tongue to his advantage. However, she was driving, and he had to maintain some responsibility for that. 'What were you doing in your job?' he persevered after she'd nodded her assent, reining in the desire to curb the small talk and cut straight to the chase.

'Accounts. I'm a qualified bookkeeper,' she answered, taking the glass he had filled for her and trying a sip. It tasted zesty and refreshing, with lime and other citrus juices blended with something that made it fizz. 'Why are you smiling like that?' If one could call that curious twist to his mouth a *smile,* Kayla thought.

Because that's about as unlikely as my being a nightclub singer, Leonidas considered, amazed and amused by what he decided must be barefaced lies.

'You don't *look* like a bookkeeper,' he remarked, studying her unashamedly in view of the yarn she was spinning him. Beautiful long hair and captivating features. Elegant swan-like neck, small but alluring figure. What he didn't expect was the hard desire that kicked through his body, mocking his efforts to remain in command even as he acknowledged her reaction in the colour that stole across her fine translucent skin.

'What's a bookkeeper supposed to look like?' she queried with a betraying little wobble in her voice, feeling his gaze like a hot brand over her scantily clad body and bare legs.

'Not blonde, beautiful and way too intrusive for her own good.'

She laughed nervously at his double-edged compliment, feeling a stirring in her blood that had nothing to do with the zesty punch, the good food, or the way the warm wind was sighing through the silver leaves of an olive tree that stood at the edge of the shady terrace above the overgrown garden.

'What about you?' she asked quickly, to try and stem the ridiculous heat that was pulsing through her veins. 'I thought this place was derelict. How long have you lived here?' She glanced up at the house, which she had believed was uninhabited. Most of it was in a serious state of disrepair, but one wing of the old building looked as if it had been renovated in recent years. 'I take it you *do* live here?'

'For the time being,' he said uncommunicatively, adding after a moment or two, 'I thought it would be as good a place as any to…what is the expression…? Bed down for a while.'

'You mean…you're just bumming around?'

Leonidas laughed, showing strong white teeth, and through the thick fringes of his lashes he surveyed the young woman sitting opposite him with guarded circumspection, wondering how far she was planning to carry this little charade. Yesterday she had displayed all the characteristics of an opportunity-grabbing undercover reporter, and again this morning, when she had wandered in here with that infernal camera—even if she *had* seemed genuinely distressed when she'd leaped into that hot, angry tirade about her phone, her fridge and her supposedly broken-down car. But if his suspicions about her were right—and he had little reason to doubt that they were—then from the questions she was asking and her response to the answers he was giving he had to admit that she was one hell of a good actress.

'I prefer to call it opting out,' he stated laconically.

'So…do you work?' Kayla enquired.

'When I need to.' Which was twenty-four-seven a lot of the time, he thought grimly. If she was here intent on making a killing out of the Vassalio name, then she would know that already.

And if she wasn't…

If she wasn't, he thought, irritated, refusing to give any credence to that possibility, then she shouldn't have inflicted herself upon him in the way she had.

'And what do you do? For a living, I mean?'

She was still treading cautiously, still playing the innocent.

If she'd been trying for an Oscar, Leonidas thought, she would have won it hands-down.

'I'm in construction.' *As you probably well know,* he tagged on silently.

'A builder!' Kayla interpreted, realising her assessment of him was right. He *was* a man who worked with his hands.

'Loosely speaking.' Deliberately Leonidas lobbed her own phrase back at her. Playing along with her whatever her game was, he thought with increasing annoyance. And suddenly he was fed-up with pussyfooting around.

Slinging his plate onto the table, he stood up, thrusting his hands into his pockets, intimidation in his stance and every hard inch of him as he said grimly and with lethal softness, 'OK, Kayla. This has gone far enough.'

'What has?'

He had to hand it to her. She looked and sounded perplexed. He might even have said shocked.

'The charade is over, sweet girl.'

'What charade?' Kayla didn't have a clue what he was talking about. 'I don't understand…'

'Don't you?' He laughed rather harshly. 'Do you think I don't know what your little game is? Don't know why you're here?'

'No.' She had leaped to her feet and stood facing him now with her hands on her hips, her eyes wide and contesting. 'You've obviously got me mixed up with somebody else! I don't know who you think I am, but whoever it is I'm not the person you were expecting.'

'I was hardly *expecting* anyone—least of all another blood-sucking female with her own self-motivated agenda! Unless you're going to tell me you've come all this way by yourself to slap a petition on me as well!'

'No, I haven't!' Kayla riposted, wondering what the hell he was talking about. 'And whatever your problem is—whoever it is you've come here to escape from—I'd appreciate it if you didn't take it out on *me!*'

She was gone before he could utter another word.

CHAPTER THREE

IT WAS THE crash that woke her.

Or had it been the rain and thunder? Kayla wondered, scrambling, terrified, out of bed. She had been tossing and turning in a kind of half-sleep for what seemed like hours, although it might only have been minutes since the storm began.

Now, as she pulled open her bedroom door, the full force of the gale made her cry out when it almost blew her back into the room. In the darkness she could see an ominous shape lying diagonally across the landing and a gash in the sloping roof, which was now open to the wind and the driving rain.

Kayla gasped as lightning ripped across the sky, so close that the almost instantaneous crash of thunder that followed seemed to rock the foundations of the house.

Fumbling to turn on the light switch, she groaned when nothing happened.

'Oh, great!'

Finding the chair where she had folded the jeans and shirt she had travelled in two days ago, with trembling hands she hastily pulled them on over her flimsy pyjamas, and then groped around for her bag and the small torch she always carried on her keyring.

Debris was everywhere as she moved cautiously under the fallen tree-trunk. Twisted branches, leaves, twigs and pieces of broken masonry and plaster scrunched underfoot as she picked her way carefully downstairs.

It was as if the whole outdoors had broken in, she thought with a startled cry as another flash of lightning streaked across the sky. The crash that followed it seemed to rock the villa, causing her to panic at the torrent of rain that was coming in on the raging wind.

And then she heard another sound, like a loud hammering on the external door to the villa, and mercifully a voice, its deep tone muffled, yet still breaking through to her through the tearing gale and the rain.

'Kayla! Kayla? Answer me! Are you in there? Kayla! Are you all right?'

The banging persisted until she thought the door was caving in.

Reaching it and tugging it open, she almost cried with relief when she saw the formidable figure of Leon standing there, his fists clenched as though to knock the door down if it wasn't opened. Rain was running down his face and his strong bronzed throat in rivulets.

It took all her will-power not to sink against him as he caught her arm and shouted something urgently in his own language.

'Get out of here! Quickly!' he ordered, reverting to English. 'There's been a landslide further up the mountain. This house might not be safe to stay in.' And as she hesitated, casting an anxious glance at her belongings, 'We'll come back for your things in the morning!' he shouted above the wind and the lashing rain. 'You're coming with me!'

Petrified, rooted to the spot by the sound of splitting timber somewhere close by on the riven hillside, Kayla felt herself suddenly being whipped off her feet. She was only pacified by the realisation that she was in a pair of strong, powerful arms, being held against Leon's sodden warmth as he ran with her to the waiting truck.

He had left the vehicle's lights on, and after he had set her quickly down on the passenger seat Kayla saw him race around the bonnet with his head bent against the storm, his purposeful physique only just discernible through the rain-washed windscreen.

He opened the driver's door, his long hair dripping, and as he climbed into the cab beside her and slammed the door against the wind she noticed that his shirt, which was unbuttoned and hanging loose, like his jeans, was soaked through and clinging to his powerful torso.

'Thank you! Oh, thank you!' Dropping her head into her hands as the truck started rumbling away, Kayla couldn't think of anything else to say. 'I didn't know what was happening!' she blurted out when she had recovered herself enough to sit up straight and turn towards him. 'I woke up and thought the world was coming to an end!'

'It would have been for you,' Leonidas stated with grim truthfulness, 'if that tree had fallen on you.'

But it hadn't, she thought gratefully. Nor was she now exposed to the damage it had caused. Thanks to *him,* she realised, and wondered how she would have coped if he hadn't been passing right at that moment.

'What happened?' she queried, baffled, as she began to gather her wits about her. 'Did you just happen to come by?'

'Something like that,' he intoned, without taking his attention from the zig-zagging mountain road. The truck's wiper blades were barely able to cope even at double-speed with the torrential rain.

At half-past one in the morning?

For the first time noticing the clock on the dashboard, Kayla realised exactly what the time was. Had he been out late, seen what had happened as he had driven past? Or had he been in bed? Had he heard the landslide and driven down especially?

Of course not, she thought, dismissing that last possible scenario. No man she knew of would be so gallant as to risk his own safety for a girl he didn't even know let alone like. And it was patently obvious from her two previous meetings with him that he clearly didn't like her. Or *any* of her sex, if it came to that!

'Why are you doing this if you think I'm someone who's out to make trouble for you?' she enquired pointedly, her hair falling, damp and dishevelled, around her shoulders.

'What would you have preferred me to do?' Every ounce of his concentration was still riveted on the windscreen. 'Leave you there to swim? Or worse?'

Kayla shuddered as she interpreted what 'worse' might easily have meant.

'Is it always like this on these islands?' she queried worriedly, staring out at the truck's powerful headlights cutting through the sheets of rain.

'If you come here in the spring it's a chance you take,' he returned succinctly.

Which she had, Kayla thought, deciding that he probably thought her stupid on top of everything else.

'What's likely to happen to the villa?' she asked anxiously, watching the gleaming water cascading off the hills and filling every crack and crevice on the rugged road. 'That tree came right through onto the landing.'

'We'll go down and inspect the damage in the morning.'

'But the furniture and furnishings. And my things,' she remembered as an afterthought. 'Everything's going to get wet.'

'Only to be expected,' he answered prosaically, changing gear to take a particularly sharp bend. 'With a hole in the roof.'

A hysterical little laugh bubbled up inside of her. Nerves, she decided. And shock. Because there was certainly nothing funny about the havoc this storm had wreaked upon the little Grecian retreat her friends had worked so hard for.

'What am I going to say to Lorna?' She was worrying about how she was going to break the news to her, thinking aloud. 'She and Josh have got enough problems as it is.' And then it dawned on her. 'Oh, heavens!' she breathed, still shaking inside from her ordeal. 'Where on earth am I going to stay? Tonight? Tomorrow? At all?'

'Well, tonight you're going to stay with me,' he told her in a tone that was settled, decisive. 'And tomorrow, when you've telephoned your friend to let her know what has happened, we'll think of something else.'

We, he'd said, as though they were in this thing together. Which they weren't, Kayla thought. Yet strangely she gleaned some comfort from it—along with a contradictory feeling of being indebted to him, too.

'Like what?' She didn't know where to begin, or even if the island had any other suitable or affordable accommodation. Lorna had offered to let her stay in the villa rent-free, and although Kayla had insisted on paying her, it was still only a nominal amount. The alternative was that she could fly home...

'There are three hotels on this side of the island. One of them—the largest—is closed for refurbishment,' Leon was telling her, 'but I'm sure as it's out of season one of the other two will be able to accommodate you.'

'I can't stay with you tonight,' she informed him. 'It's such an imposition, for one thing.' She didn't even *know* him! And from what she had seen of him over the past couple of days neither did she want to. 'You said yourself you wanted to be left alone.'

'Which you've failed to acknowledge since the day you arrived,' he told her dryly. 'So why break with tradition?'

'I'm sorry.' Now she felt even worse. 'You don't have to do this. I'm only making a nuisance of myself…'

'What would you prefer me to do?' he asked. 'Put you out into the storm?' He laughed when he saw the anxiety creasing her forehead. 'Relax,' he advised. 'You're coming back with me. So, no more arguments to the contrary—and definitely no more apologies. Understood?'

Uneasily, Kayla nodded.

'I didn't hear you,' he stated over the rumble of the engine and the jaunty rhythm of the wiper blades trying to keep pace with the interminable rain.

'Understood!' she shouted back, and kept her gaze on the windscreen and her hands in her lap until he brought them safely off the road and onto the paved area of the old farmhouse.

The part of the house he led her into was remarkably clean and tidy. It was surprisingly well-furnished too, even though most of the furniture looked worn and in need of replacing, and the tapestries on two of the walls, like the once colourfully striped throws over the easy chairs, were faded from the sunlight and with age. But with its whitewashed walls and cool stone floors it had an overall rustic charm that offered more comfort than she had imagined from the outside.

She was too tired and weary from her experiences to take too much interest in how he was living, and said only after a cursory glance around her, 'I'm really not happy about this.'

She didn't know anything about him, for a start, even if he *had* just rescued her from a house that might possibly be unsafe. He was still a stranger, and up until now a decidedly hostile one.

'I'm afraid you've no choice,' he told her, opening a cupboard and pulling out towels and spare bedlinen, 'because I've no intention of trying to find you a hotel tonight. No hotelier would welcome you turning up at this hour—even if it were safe enough to do so. And if you really don't profess to know me—' He broke off, his speculative gaze raking over her as if, by some miracle, he was at last beginning to believe her. 'I'm not a criminal,' he stated. 'Unless, of course, the police want to charge me with some driving offence I don't yet know about.'

Kayla smiled, relaxing a little, as he had intended her to.

Clever, she thought. Clever and probably very manipulative, she decided, but was too tired to worry about that tonight.

After she had declined his offer of any refreshment, and the room he showed her into was rustic but practical, with the same weary air about its furnishings. Like downstairs, the walls looked as though they hadn't been whitewashed in a long time. A big wooden bed took pride of place, and from the few masculine possessions scattered around the room she gathered that *he* had been using it up until now.

'I'm afraid it isn't five-star, but it's warm and dry and the sheets are clean.' They looked it too. Crisp and white, if a little rumpled, and there was a definite indentation in the plump and inviting-looking pillow. 'Well, I was only in them for half an hour,' he enlightened her, with his mouth tugging down at one side.

So he had been to bed and got up again—which could only have meant that he must have driven down in the storm especially.

'Think nothing of it,' he advised dismissively as their eyes clashed.

Kayla wanted to say something, to thank him at the very least for deserting his bed in the middle of the night to come and see if she was all right. But his manner and all that had gone before kept her mute.

'What will *you* do?' she enquired, glancing down at the bed he'd given up for her. Suddenly worried that she might have given him the wrong idea, quickly she tagged on, 'That wasn't meant to sound like…'

'It didn't,' he said, although the way his gaze moved disconcertingly over her body did nothing to put her at ease. 'Don't worry about me.' He'd started moving away. 'There's a perfectly adequate sofa in the living room.'

Adequate, but not comfortable. Not for his manly size. She had noticed it on the way through and thought now that it wouldn't in any way compensate for losing the roomy-looking bed he'd imagined he would be occupying.

'I really feel awful about this.'

'Don't,' he replied. 'I'm sure you're used to better. As I said, it isn't five-star.' His tone, however, was more cynical than apologetic, and a little dart of rebellion ran through her as their eyes met and locked.

She didn't tell him that she had had a taste of luxurious living and it wasn't something she was keen to get back to. Not when it had meant accompanying Craig to company dinners and luxury conference weekends where she had watched her ex paying homage, she realised now, to people he merely wanted to impress—people he knew could further his corporate ambitions—without really liking them at all.

'I'm more than grateful for—' A sudden vivid flash, accompanied by a deafening crack, had her cutting her sentence short with a startled cry.

'It's all right,' he said. His voice came softly from somewhere close behind her as the thunder seemed to reverberate off the very walls. 'This house might look as though it's seen better days, but I can assure you, Kayla, the roof is sound. No tree is going to fall in on us, I promise you.'

Her visible fear had brought him over to her. She only realised it as she felt his hands on her shoulders through the thin fabric of her shirt, warm and strong and surprisingly reassuring in view of his previous attitude towards her.

'I'm all right.' She took a step back and his hands fell away from her. She wondered what was most unsettling. The storm—or the touch of this stranger whose bedroom she was unbelievably standing in.

'Of course you are,' he said. 'But get out of those damp clothes. And get a good night's rest,' he advocated, before leaving her to it.

He was right about her clothes being damp, she realised with a little shiver after he had gone. Just the short journey from the villa to the truck and then from the truck to this house had been enough to soak her shirt and jeans. She was grateful to peel them off.

There were a few moments in the king-sized bed when she wondered what she was doing there, unable to keep her thoughts from the man who must have been lying there not more than an hour before. Had he been lying here naked? She felt a sensual little tingle, and her nostrils grasped the trace of a masculine shower gel beneath the scent of fresh linen. But it was only for a few moments, because when she opened her eyes again the tearing winds and driving rain had ceased and a fine blade of sunlight was piercing the dimly shaded room through a slit in the shutters.

Scrambling out of bed, Kayla went over and flung them back, feeling the heat of the sun on her scantily clothed body as it streamed in through windows that were already open to the glittering blue of the sky.

The bedroom overlooked the front yard, the dirt track and the rolling hillside that descended so sharply, with the mountain road, to the blue and silver of the shimmering sea.

She could see the truck parked there on the flagstones, where Leon had left it in the early hours.

A surge of heat coursed through her as she thought about how he had come to her rescue last night, and how helpless she had felt in those hostile yet powerful arms as they had carried her to that truck when she had been too shocked and too bewildered to move.

'So you're awake.' A familiar deep voice overlaid with mockery called out to her as if from nowhere.

Startled, Kayla realised that he had been doing something to his truck. She hadn't noticed until he had pulled himself up from under it.

Uncertainly she lifted a hand, mesmerised for a moment by the shattering impact of his hard, untrammelled masculinity.

With his hair wild as a gypsy's, and in a black vest top and cut off jeans, he looked like a man totally uninhibited by convention. Self-sufficient and self-ruling. A man who would probably shun the constraints that Craig and his company cronies adhered to.

But this man was looking at her with such unveiled interest that her stomach took a steep dive as she realised why.

She was wearing nothing but her coffee and cream lace-edged baby doll pyjamas and, utterly self-conscious, she swiftly withdrew from the window, certain she wasn't imagining the deep laugh that emanated from the yard as she hastily pulled the shutters together again.

The bathroom was, as she'd discovered last night, clean and adequately equipped. Some time this morning a toothbrush, still in its packaging, had been placed upon two folded and surprisingly good-quality burgundy towels on a wooden cabinet beside the washstand. Impressed, silently Kayla thanked him for that.

Fortunately her hairbrush had been in her bag when she had made her hasty exit from the villa last night, along with a spare tube of the soft brown mascara she had remembered to buy before leaving London.

Never one to wear much make-up, she had nonetheless always felt undressed without her mascara. A combination of pale hair and pale eyelashes made her look washed-out, she had always thought, and Craig had agreed.

A sharp, unexpected little stab of something under her ribcage had her catching her breath as she thought about Craig, but surprisingly it didn't hurt as she reminded herself that what Craig Lymington thought wasn't important any more.

Leon was in the large sitting room off the hall, locking something away in a drawer, when Kayla came down feeling fresh and none the worse for her experiences of the previous night.

He was superb, she thought reluctantly from the doorway, noticing how at close quarters the black vest top emphasised his muscular torso, how perfectly smooth and contoured were his arms, their hair-darkened skin like bronze satin sheathing steel. She was pleased she'd put mascara on, and that when she'd brushed her hair forward and then tossed it back, as she always did, it had looked particularly full and shiny this morning.

He looked up and his gaze moved over her. He was clearly remembering what she had looked like at the window earlier.

'I've been trying to ring Lorna but I can't get a signal,' she said quickly, hoping he hadn't noticed the way she'd been ogling him. 'Is it all right if I use your landline?'

'You could—if it was connected,' he returned. He took his own cell phone out of his pocket and handed it to her as she came into the room. It felt smooth and warmed by his body heat, reminding her far too easily of how *she* had felt being held against his hard warmth the previous night.

'As soon as it's a respectable enough time,' she began, while trying to deal with how ridiculously she was allowing him to affect her, 'and after you've dropped me off at the villa, do you think you could point me in the direction of the nearest hotel?'

'One thing at a time,' he advised her. 'The first thing is not to plan anything on an empty stomach.'

'Is that your philosophy on life?' She struggled to speak lightly, which was difficult when there was so much tension in her voice.

'One of them,' he answered, with his mouth tugging down at one corner.

She wondered what the others were, but decided against asking. For all the hospitality this man had shown her, he didn't welcome too much intrusion into his personal life, and Kayla certainly felt as though she had intruded enough.

Surprisingly, she got through to Lorna's office on the first try. Gently, Kayla broke the news to her about the storm and the tree coming down, wanting to spare her friend as much distress as she could. Lorna and Josh had been trying for a baby for quite some time, and Lorna had had two miscarriages in the past two years. Now she was well into the second trimester of another pregnancy, and Kayla regretted having to cause her any more stress as she concluded, 'I haven't had a chance to look at it in daylight, but we're going down after breakfast to assess the damage.'

'We?' Lorna echoed inquisitively, so that Kayla was forced to gather her wits together in order to avoid any awkward questions.

'Someone from a neighbouring property. They took me in for the night,' she explained, taking care not to even suggest that 'they' was really 'he'. She wasn't ready to be bracketed with another man in her life just yet.

'Then tell them that I can't thank them enough for taking care of my friend.' True to character, Lorna seemed more concerned about Kayla than about the tree crashing down on her precious villa. 'I'm so glad there was someone else there! What would you have done otherwise?'

My thoughts exactly, Kayla mused, unable to keep her eyes from straying to Leon's superbly broad back as he moved lithely out of the room while her friend made plans for what she intended to do.

'Lorna's parents are going to come over and sort out what needs doing,' Kayla reported to him a few minutes later, having found him in the huge and very outdated farmhouse kitchen at the end of the hall. It contained a dresser and a huge wood-burning stove over which Leon was busily wielding a frying pan. A large pine table stood in the centre of the room, already laid for one. Two large-paned windows faced the front of the house, offering stupendous views of the distant sea, while two more on the other side of the room looked out onto the terraced gardens. 'Lorna and Josh have their own business and don't have much free time,' she explained, handing him back his phone, which he casually slipped into the back pocket of his jeans.

Unlike you, Kayla thought, and for a moment found herself envying his flexible lifestyle. His free spirit and total autonomy. The complete lack of binding responsibility.

'Have you always been so self-sufficient?' she asked, watching him cutting melon, which he put on the table beside a plate of fresh pineapple slices. She wondered if he had already eaten or just wasn't bothering.

'I like to think so,' he responded, without looking at her. 'I've always believed—' and found out the hard way, Leonidas thought, his features hardening '—that if you want something done properly there's no surer way but to do it yourself.'

'Another of your philosophies?' Kayla enquired, her hand coming to rest on the back of one the pine chairs and her head tilted as she waited for an answer, which never came.

No man was an island, so the saying went. But Kayla had the distinct impression that this man was—emotionally, at any rate. He seemed more detached and aloof from the rat race and the big wide world than anyone she had ever met. Uncommunicative. Guarding his privacy like a precious jewel.

'Who did you think I was when you accused me of playing some game with you yesterday?'

'It isn't important,' he intoned, moving back to the stove.

'It seemed to be very important at the time,' Kayla commented, still put out by the names he had called her. 'The things you said to me weren't very nice.'

'Yes, well…we can all make mistakes,' Leonidas admitted, adding freshly chopped herbs to the sizzling frying pan and beginning to accept that he might have made a gross error of judgement in treating her so unjustly. 'I came here to relax. I didn't expect some uninvited young woman with a camera to be taking secretive photographs of me. When you realised I'd seen you on the rocks and you ran from me I decided that you must definitely be up to no good.'

So he had charged at her like an angry bull, Kayla thought, wondering what he'd thought she was hiding that had incensed him so much.

'Yesterday,' he went on, 'when I invited you to lunch, it was to try to find out why.'

'You accused me of spying on you,' she reminded him, folding her arms in a suddenly defensive pose as she bit back the urge to remind him that she hadn't been trying to photograph him on that beach. 'What did you imagine? That I was some sort of secret agent or something?' she suggested with an ironic little laugh. 'Or a private investigator, hired by a jealous wife—?' She broke off as a more plausible possibility struck her. 'A wife who's taken you to the cleaners and who's still hoping to uncover the hidden millions you haven't told her about that you've got stashed away somewhere? Gosh! Is that it?' she exclaimed, when she saw the way his dark lashes came down over his unfathomable eyes, wondering if she'd hit the nail on the head. 'Not about the millions. I mean…'

'About the wife?'

She nodded. Why else would he have referred to her as a blood-sucking female yesterday? He must be licking his wounds after a very nasty divorce.

'Nice try,' he said dryly, the muscles in his wonderfully masculine back moving as he worked. 'I'm sorry to have to shoot down such a colourful and imaginative story, but I'm not married. And since when did a man simply wanting to protect his privacy mean there's an avaricious and avenging wife in tow?'

'It doesn't,' Kayla answered, wondering why the discovery of his marital status should leave her feeling far more pleased than it should have. 'It just seemed a little bit of an overreaction, that's all,' she murmured, feeling her temperature rising from the way he was looking at her—as though he knew what baffling and unsettling thoughts were going through her head.

'So how did you know about this house?' she asked, since it was apparent now that it wasn't just a deserted building he'd happened to stumble across.

'I was born on this island,' he said, in a cool, clipped voice. 'I have the use of this place when I want it.'

'Who owns it?' she enquired, looking around.

'Someone who is too busy to take much interest in it,' he answered flatly, suddenly sounding bored.

'What a pity,' Kayla expressed, looking around her at the sad peeling walls. 'It could be nice if it was renovated. Someone must have treasured it once.'

Once, Leonidas thought, when its warm, welcoming walls had rung with his mother's beautiful singing. When he hadn't been able to sleep for excitement because his grandfather was taking him fishing the following day...

'Obviously the current owner doesn't share your sentimentality about it,' he remarked, and found it a struggle to keep the bitterness out of his voice.

'You said you were born on this island?' Kayla reminded him, feeling as though she was being intrusive again, yet unable to stop herself. Even less could she envisage him as a helpless, squalling infant. 'It's idyllic. What made you leave?'

His features looked set in stone as he tossed two slices of bubbling halloumi cheese onto slices of fresh bread, topping them with rich red sun-dried tomatoes before he answered, 'I believed there was a better life out there.'

'And was there?'

Again he didn't answer.

But what sort of satisfaction was there in never settling anywhere? Kayla wondered now. In just drifting around from place to place?

'Eat your breakfast,' he ordered, putting the meal on the table in front of her. 'And then we'll go down and inspect the storm damage.'

CHAPTER FOUR

THE STRUCTURE OF the villa had sustained less damage than Kayla had feared. However, after Leon had helped her to clear up the debris and mess caused by the falling tree, it was still a far cry from what it had been when she had arrived.

'I'll have to look for somewhere else,' she accepted defeatedly, trying to sound braver and less anxious than she was feeling as she dropped the last packet of ruined food into a refuse bag.

'My very next step,' Leonidas assured her, taking his phone out of his pocket.

He had changed into a pale blue shirt and jeans before leaving the farmhouse earlier and, looking up from the bag she was tying, Kayla noticed how his rolled-up sleeves emphasised the dark olive of his skin and the virility of his strong arms.

'I think you've done quite enough already,' she reminded him. Not only had he rescued her from a terrifying situation last night, he had given her food and shelter, driven her back here, and then refused to leave when it came to the clean-up operation. 'I'm indebted enough to you as it is!'

'If that's all that's worrying you—forget it,' he drawled. 'I'm not likely to be extracting payment any time soon.'

'That's not funny,' she scolded, still unhappy about being in his debt. Or was it that mocking glint in his eyes that affected her more than his hostility?

Whatever it was, she thought, he unsettled her as no man had ever unsettled her in her life. Not to this degree anyway, she realised. And there was more to it than just the danger of getting too involved with a man whom, until the day before yesterday, she had never even met. It was the potent attraction this man held for her, purely physical in its nature and stronger than any she had felt before. Which was illogical, she decided, when she had been engaged to Craig and fully intending to spend the rest of her life with *him*.

But Leon was already taking the necessary steps to get her fixed up with an alternative place to stay.

Listening to that deep voice speaking in Greek to some hotelier on the other end of the line, Kayla realised how much more difficult it would have been for her if she had been left to find accommodation herself. There would have been the language barrier to overcome for a start.

Now, though, as he came off the phone, Kayla saw him shaking his head. 'I'm afraid they're fully booked for the next three weeks.'

There were three hotels on the island, he had informed her, one closed for refurbishing, and he was now ringing the second one on his list. But again he was shaking his head as he finished speaking to their last possible hope. 'They said they would have had a room if you had telephoned yesterday, but they've had to close this morning because of flooding in part of the hotel last night.'

She could tell that he was almost as dumbfounded as she was.

'Well, that's that, then,' she said, swinging the bin bag up off the tiled floor. 'I'll just have to make the best of it here until Lorna's parents arrive tomorrow.' And after that… She gave a mental shrug as she crossed the tiny kitchen. Who knew?

Watching the determined squaring of her shoulders as he

tried to relieve her of the bag, Leonidas felt his heart going out to her.

'Don't be ridiculous,' he said as she opened the door to the garden. 'You can't stay here.' The tree was leaning across the landing at a precarious enough angle to be a safety hazard. Also, because of the galleried landing, the ground floor was open to the elements, as well as to any more debris from the fallen tree.

'No?' Kayla said, coming in from dumping the bag outside. 'And I suppose you can come up with a better idea?'

'Yes, I can,' he stated pragmatically. 'You will stay with me.'

Not can. *Will,* Kayla noted, which marked him as a man who usually got his own way.

'With you?' He was leaning against the sink with his thumbs hooked into his waistband, looking very determined, and a little bubble of humourless laughter escaped her. 'Now look who's being ridiculous,' she accused.

'If you think I'm leaving you here, with that tree likely to come down on you at any moment,' he said, with an upward toss of his chin, 'you can think again.'

'I'm not your responsibility or your problem, Leon,' she stressed trenchantly. 'Anyway, I came here to be alone.'

'Why, exactly?' Leonidas was regarding her with hard speculation. 'What is a girl like you doing on her own in a quiet and remote place like this when you could be enjoying the company of other people your age and living it up somewhere like Crete or Corfu? And don't tell me that you are simply soaking up the sun while considering your next career move, because you could have gone anywhere to do that.'

'Perhaps I don't want to be "living it up",' Kayla replied, feeling pressured by his unwavering determination. 'I came here for peace and quiet. Not to share with anyone else.'

'So did I,' he reminded her, in a way that suggested that the best-laid plans didn't always turn out as one would expect.

'Exactly! And the last thing you want is a...what did you call me? Oh, yes—a "blood-sucking female with her own self-motivated agenda" dumped on you!' she quoted fiercely, with both hands planted on her denim-clad hips. 'Well, believe me, this *isn't* on my agenda!'

'All right. So we didn't get off to a very good start. I shouldn't have said those things to you,' he admitted, coming away from the sink. It seemed to constitute some sort of apology. 'But the fact remains that as things stand this place is a potential hazard, and—my responsibility or not—if you think I am going to stand by and let you risk your safety just because of a few ripe phrases on my part yesterday, then you still have a long way to go in assessing my character. I carried you out of here last night and I'll do it again if I have to.' His features were set with indomitable purpose. 'So, are you going to be sensible and swallow your pride and accept that there isn't an alternative?' he asked grimly.

'There's always an alternative,' Kayla said quickly, refusing to accept otherwise—although the thought of him man-handling her out of there when she wasn't being distracted by falling trees and a possible landslide was far too disturbing even to contemplate.

'Like running away?'

Those jet-black eyes seemed to be penetrating her soul, probing down into her heart and digging over her darkest and most painful secrets.

What right did he have to accuse her of running away? Even if she was, it was none of his business! Yet suddenly everything she had suffered over the past weeks, and everything that had gone wrong since she had been here, finally proved too much.

'Who says I'm running away?' she flung at him grievously. 'And if you think that just because I chose to come on holiday by myself, then I could just as easily wonder the same thing about you! And those weren't just a few ripe phrases you used. You were taking out all your woman problems—whatever they are—on *me!* Do you want to know why I'm here on my own? Then put this in your pipe and smoke it! Saturday was supposed to be my wedding day—only the groom decided he'd rather marry somebody else instead! He just kept the same date and the same time at the same church with the same photographer for *convenience*.' She couldn't keep the bitterness out of her voice.

'Because he wanted to marry her in a hurry, although he *did* have the decency to let me know she was pregnant before I broke off our engagement three months ago. And if that wasn't enough we all worked at the same company, which is why I had to leave. I live in a small community, so the whole neighbourhood knew about it as well, and I just couldn't stay there and face the humiliation. So if running away because I'm not thick-skinned enough to stand there and throw confetti over my ex-fiancé and his pregnant secretary is wrong, then I'm sorry!' She uttered a facetious little laugh. 'I'll just have to toughen up in future.'

'Forgive me.'

Leonidas's face was dark with contrition. And shock too, Kayla decided, almost triumphantly.

'The man's a...' He called him something in his own language which she knew wasn't very complimentary. 'I spoke without knowing the facts.'

'Yes, you did.' Now she had got it all off her chest she was beginning to feel a little calmer. 'Anyway, it's all history. Water under the bridge. I'm over him now.'

'Are you?'

'Yes, I am,' she asserted, her mouth firming resolutely. 'He kept to everything we'd planned for us—for our day...'

Strangely, that was what had hurt the most in the end. 'Even down to the guest list,' she uttered with another brittle little laugh. 'Well, most of it anyway,' she said. 'It's funny how when you're a couple you seem to have a lot of friends. Then when you break up you realise that they weren't really your friends at all. Most of them were Craig's. Acquaintances, really. He didn't have any real friends. They were all company people. People he'd met through his job. Sales reps. Customers. His management team and their wives. The office hierarchy that he liked us to socialise with.'

'You don't sound very enamoured,' Leonidas remarked.

Kayla glanced up to where he was standing with his hands thrust into his pockets, listening with single-minded concentration to all she was saying. 'I'm just angry with myself for not knowing better.'

'How could you?' Those masculine brows came together in a frown. 'How could anyone prepare for something like that happening?'

'Oh, I had a good tutor, believe me. Dad did the very same thing to Mum—ran off with his secretary. So it wasn't as though I wasn't forewarned. I just wouldn't listen. I thought it could never happen to me. But now I know never to get mixed up with that type of man again.'

'And what type is that?'

'The type with a nicely pressed suit and a spare clean shirt in the office closet. The type who's always late home because his workload's so heavy. The type who thinks every reasonably attractive female colleague is only there to boost his ego.'

Leonidas's dark lashes came down over his eyes, but all he said was, 'I thought that kind of male chauvinism went out with the nineteen-seventies.'

'Oh don't you believe it!' Kayla returned censoriously. She was mopping water from the fridge with all the venom she felt towards Craig Lymington and his kind. 'There's something that happens to a man when he gets behind a desk, gets himself a secretary and has his name on the door. Something he thinks sets him outside the boundaries of accepted moral behaviour. But I'm not going to bore you with that. It's my problem and I should have known better. I didn't want to know and I paid for it. End of story.'

Leonidas doubted somehow that it *was* the end of the story, and reminded himself never to tell her what he really did for a living.

'You've had a tough time,' he accepted, deciding that this damsel in distress who had been so badly treated by her fiancé would probably feel nothing but contempt for him if she knew more about him.

She would instantly bracket him with the type of man she despised. And if for one moment he did let on who he was, he had learned enough about her already to know that she would want nothing to do with him. She would refuse his help—no matter how desperately she needed it—which would do nothing to get her out of the predicament she was in now.

'However,' he continued, 'the most pressing problem you have right now is where you're going to sleep tonight. As I've already said, I wouldn't dream of allowing you to talk yourself into thinking it's all right to stay here…' No matter how far outside the boundaries of morality she might think he was if she knew about his desk and his secretary and the spare shirts he kept in his Athens and London offices. 'Which means you either sleep out in the open or you come back with me. Unless, of course, you're thinking of returning home?'

Almost imperceptibly Kayla flinched. With the villa unusable and nowhere else to stay, it did seem the most feasible thing to do. But if she did, what would she be going back to? Her mother's smugness over having been right about Craig? The neighbourhood's silent sympathies? The whispered comments behind her back? What would everyone say if they realised that not only had her proposed wedding turned out to be non-existent but also that the holiday she had been determined to take on her own had turned into a disaster as well?

'If it's your modesty you are worrying about, and you're thinking I might try and—what is the phrase you English use?—"take advantage" of you,' Leon said, remembering, 'then I must assure you that I wouldn't contemplate trying to seduce a girl who is on the rebound.'

'I'm *not* on the rebound,' Kayla denied hotly. But then, realising that he might take that to mean she wanted him to take advantage of her, she added quickly, 'I mean…' And then ran out of words because she didn't know how to phrase what she was trying to convey.

'I know what you mean,' he said, making it easy for her, although there was a sensual mockery on that devastating mouth of his that had her wondering just how pleasurable his taking advantage of her might be, if she were so inclined to let him.

'So what's it to be, Kayla?'

Her name dripped from his lips like ambrosia from the lips of Eros, although she doubted that even the Greek god of love could have harboured the degree of sensuality this man possessed.

She didn't want to go home, that was for sure. Yet neither did she want to be indebted to a total stranger—even if he did look like the answer to every woman's darkest fantasy! That didn't alter the fact that he was a stranger, and no woman in her right mind would agree to stay with a man she didn't even know. So where did that leave her? she asked herself. On the ground outside?

Very quietly, Leonidas said, 'Pack a bag and come with me.'

'You know I can't stay with you.'

'I'm not going to try and talk you into it. Pack a bag,' he

instructed again, without offering her any idea of what his plans were. 'I'll finish mopping up here.'

Leon had asked her to follow him in the car. The little hatchback coughed a few times when Kayla tried to start it, which brought him over from the cab of his truck to investigate.

The engine fired into life just as he was approaching the bonnet.

Looking up at him through the car's open window with a self-satisfied glint in her eyes, Kayla asked, 'Do you believe me now?'

That masculine mouth pulled to one side, although he made no verbal response. Perhaps he was a man who didn't like being reminded of his mistakes too often, Kayla thought, unable to help feeling smug.

'It needs a good run,' he said, speaking with some authority. 'It's probably been standing idle for too long, which isn't good for any car.'

Following his truck down the zig-zag of a mountain road, Kayla was tempted to stop and take in the breathtaking views of the sea and the sun-drenched hillsides. But she kept close behind Leon's truck, envying his knowledge of every sharp bend, admiring the confidence and safety with which he negotiated them.

After guiding her down past a cluster of whitewashed cottages, he pulled up outside another, with blue shutters and, like the rest, pots of gaily coloured flowers on its veranda.

'Since you refuse to stay with me, I will have to leave you in the capable hands of Philomena,' Leon told her, having come around the truck to where Kayla was just getting out of the car.

'Philomena?'

'A friend of mine,' he stated, moving past her. 'There is one small snag, however,' he went on to inform her as he swung her small single suitcase out of the boot.

'Oh?' Kayla looked up at him enquiringly as he slammed the lid closed.

'She doesn't speak any English,' he said.

'So why would she want me staying with her?' Kayla practically had to run after him. It was obvious that he wasn't going to allow that rather large drawback—to Kayla's mind, at any rate—to interfere with his plans.

'Her family have all grown up and moved away,' he tossed back over his shoulder. 'Trust me. She will be very glad of the company of someone else—especially another woman.'

'But have you asked her?' Kayla wasn't sure that anyone—no matter how lonely they might be—would welcome a guest turning up unexpectedly on their doorstep.

'Leave the worrying to me,' he advised, and uneasily Kayla did.

He had said Philomena was a friend, but as he brought Kayla through to the homely sitting room of the little fisherman's cottage without even needing to knock, she calculated that the woman in dark clothes who greeted them with twinkling brown eyes and a strong, character-lined face was old enough to be his grandmother.

Her affection for·Leon was clear from the start, but suddenly as they were speaking the woman burst into what to Kayla's ears sounded like a fierce outpouring of objection. The woman was waving her hands in typically European fashion and sending more than a few less than approving glances Kayla's way.

'She isn't happy about my staying here and why should she be?' Kayla challenged, taking in the abundance of framed family photographs and brightly painted pottery and feeling as much mortified as she felt sympathetic towards the elderly woman.

'She's happy, Kayla,' Leonidas told her, breaking off from a run of incomprehensible Greek. He started speaking very quickly in his own language again, which brought forth another bout of scolding and arm-waving from a clearly none-too-pleased Philomena.

'I'm sorry,' Kayla apologised through the commotion, hoping the woman would understand as she picked up her suitcase and starting weaving through the rustic furniture towards the door.

'No, no! No, no!' A lightly restraining hand came over Kayla's arm. 'You stay. Stay Philomena, eh?' The look she sent Leonidas shot daggers in his direction. Her voice, though, as she turned back to Kayla, was softer and more encouraging, her returning smile no less than sympathetic as a work-worn, sun-dappled hand gently palmed Kayla's cheek. 'You come. Stay.'

A good deal of gesticulation with a far warmer flow of baffling Greek seemed to express the woman's pleasure in having Kayla as her guest.

'You see,' Leonidas remarked, looking pleased with himself as Philomena drew her gently away from the door. 'I said she would want you to stay.'

The appreciative look Kayla gave her hostess turned challenging as she faced the man who had brought her there. 'Then what were you arguing about?' she quizzed.

'Philomena has no one to scold nowadays, so she likes to scold me.' His mouth as he directed a look towards their hostess was pulling wryly. 'Philomena bore seven children, but her one claim to fame, as she likes to call it, is that she delivered me. I'm eternally grateful to her for introducing me to this universe,' he expressed with smiling affection at Philomena, 'but she does tend to imagine that that gives her licence to upbraid me at every given opportunity.'

'For what?' Kayla was puzzled, still not convinced.

One of those impressive shoulders lifted as he contemplated this. 'For leaving the island. For coming back. For not coming back.'

Kayla noted the curious inflexion in his voice as he made that last statement. Her smile wavered. 'And what about just now?'

'Just now?'

Leonidas looked at the woman who had pulled him screaming into the world. She had been there—never far away—throughout his childhood. A comfort from his father's strict and sometimes brutal regime of discipline, his rock when his mother had died.

'I don't think she's happy with the way I've turned out,' he commented dryly to Kayla, and thought that if it were true he wouldn't blame Philomena. There were times lately, he was surprised to find himself thinking, when he had been far, far from happy with himself.

'Oh?' Kayla clearly wanted to know more, but he had nothing more to offer her.

Gratefully he expressed his thanks to Philomena, adding something else, which brought Kayla's cornflower-blue eyes curiously to his as he started moving away.

'I've told her to take care of you,' he translated, with a blazing smile that made Kayla's stomach muscles curl in on themselves. And that was that. He had gone before she could utter another word.

Kayla settled in to her new accommodation with remarkable ease, and as she had suspected, despite the language barrier, she found Philomena Sarantos to be a warm and generous hostess.

She wondered what Leon had meant about Philomena being unhappy with the way he had turned out. Had he meant because of his lifestyle? Not having a steady job? Because he seemed content to drift from place to place?

Two days passed and she saw nothing of him. But then, what had she expected? Kayla meditated. Hadn't he made it clear from the beginning that he didn't welcome intrusion into his life? And, although he had invited her to stay with him at the farmhouse the morning after that tree had come down, she wondered if it hadn't been merely a hollow gesture on his part. He'd known she would refuse, so he'd been perfectly safe in offering her his roof over her head.

What did it matter? she decided now. She'd had enough to occupy her time without bothering herself about Leon over the past couple of days.

The previous day she had driven up to the villa after Lorna's parents had texted her with the estimated time they would be arriving. They had brought some local men with them who were arranging for the removal of the tree, and someone else who, having inspected the building, pronounced the place off-limits for the time being.

After arranging with the men for the necessary works to be carried out, her friend's parents had been extremely concerned as to where Kayla would stay. But having satisfied them— just as she had done with Lorna, over the phone the previous day—that she had found suitable alternative accommodation, she had seen the couple off to spend a few days on Corfu and—in their own words—'make the whole trip worthwhile'.

Now, with the sun having just risen and another glorious day yawning before her, Kayla traversed the dusty path that led from Philomena's cottage and gasped with delight when it brought her down onto the sun-washed shingle of a secluded cove.

Striding down through the scrub, Leonidas came to where the beach opened out before him and stopped dead in his tracks.

Kayla was wading, shin-deep, in the translucent blue water,

moving shorewards. She was looking down into the water and hadn't spotted him yet.

He would have considered the fine white cotton dress she was wearing with its sheer long sleeves and modest yoke demure in any other circumstances, because it made her look almost angelic with her loose blonde hair moving in the breeze. But she had evidently—perhaps unintentionally—allowed the sea to lap too high to preserve her modesty, for now the garment clung wetly to her body, so that the gold of her skin and her small naked breasts were clearly visible beneath.

As she waded forward the sun struck gold from her hair, illuminating the lustrous gold of lashes that lay against her cheeks as her interest never wavered from the water.

Transfixed by her beauty, he noticed the grace of her movements, the way her progress changed the light, making her breasts appear indistinct one moment and then tantalisingly defined the next. A virginal siren, tantalising enough to set his masculine hormones ablaze as his gaze swept the length of her tunic, which only reached the tops of her slender thighs.

She looked up—and when she saw him she put her hand to her mouth in shock. Then her bare feet were running lightly over the shingle towards the white floppy hat he had only just noticed lying discarded nearby.

'I didn't see you,' she called out, snatching up the hat that had been covering her ever-present camera and the rest of her things lying there on the shingle.

'Evidently not.' He couldn't contain the slow smile that played across his mouth as he noted the purposeful way she covered her wet top with the hat, her own smile feigning nonchalance, as though she didn't care.

'Have you been standing there long?'

Not nearly long enough, Leonidas thought, struggling to keep control of his unleashed hormones and the effect she was having on him. He was glad he hadn't simply worn bathing shorts, as he'd been tempted to do, and instead had donned linen trousers with a loose, casual shirt.

She had probably had enough of men lusting after her for their own primeval satisfaction—including that fiancé of hers—without having to endure the same kind of treatment from him.

'You shouldn't go bathing like that without a chaperone,' he chided softly, the dark lenses of his sunglasses revealing nothing of his thoughts.

'I didn't mean to.' Beneath the pale swathe of her hair a modestly clad shoulder lifted almost imperceptibly. 'The sea was beckoning me while I was paddling and I just got carried away.'

'It has a way of doing that, and before you know it—' He made a gesture with his hand like a fish taking a dive. 'It's nature drawing us back to itself.'

He saw her golden head tilt and was struck by the vivid clarity of those cornflower-blue eyes as she surveyed him. 'What a beautiful thing to say.'

Leonidas laughed. 'Was it?' He found himself swallowing and his throat felt dry. He had been accused of expressing himself in many ways in his time, he recalled, but beautifully had never been one of them.

She had turned round to gather her things and was starting to pull on white cropped leggings.

'How are you getting on with Philomena?' he asked.

Thrusting her feet into flip-flops, Kayla retrieved the hat she had momentarily discarded and turned back to face him, keeping its wide brim strategically in place across her breasts.

'She's great.' Her face lit up with genuine warmth. 'She reminds me of my gran.'

'That's good.' He knew he was looking self-satisfied as he flipped open the notebook he'd taken out of the back pocket of his trousers. 'And what does your grandmother think of your being here alone?' He was in danger of sounding distracted, but it was vital he got something down. Something he'd forget if he didn't consign it to paper this very instant. 'Isn't she afraid you'll fall prey to some licentious stranger?'

'No.' Picking up her camera and sunglasses, which she slid onto her head, Kayla pushed a swathe of golden silk back off her shoulder with the aid of the sunscreen bottle she was holding. 'She died. A few months ago.'

The sadness in her voice required nothing less than Leonidas's full attention. 'I'm sorry.'

'Yes. So am I,' Kayla responded, reaffirming his suspicion that she had cared a great deal for her elderly relative.

'You were close?' He didn't even need to ask.

She nodded. 'Mum and I never really were. And after Dad left he was never the loving father type whenever I got to see him, so we just drifted apart over the years. But Gran—Mum's mum—she filled the void in every way she could.'

She was looking over her shoulder out to sea but Leonidas knew that she wasn't seeing the white-crested waves and the indigo blue water. She was hiding emotion—nothing more—because she was embarrassed by it.

'So you lost your fiancé on top of losing a grandmother?' he commented, with a depth of feeling he wasn't used to. 'That's rough.'

She shrugged. 'At least I had Lorna,' she told him with a ruminative smile. 'On both counts she was there for me. She helped me through.'

'Tell me about her,' he said somewhat distractedly Kayla thought as she started walking casually a step or two ahead of him, because he was busy scribbling in a notebook.

But she told him anyway, about the friend she had known from her first day at school who had come to mean as much as a sister to her. About the interior design work that Lorna and her husband were involved in, and how brilliant they were at what they did, but how, with the state of the market and then losing their biggest customer, things had become extremely difficult for them recently. She even went on to tell him how she might find herself looking for another job if things didn't improve.

He wasn't really listening, she decided, relieved, feeling that she had gabbled on too much.

'What are you writing?' She stopped on the shingle, turning to him with her chin almost resting on the hat she was still clutching to her beneath her folded arms.

'Just jotting down a few things I don't want to forget.' He had snapped the notebook closed and was stuffing it into his back pocket.

'You were sketching.' Suddenly it dawned. 'You were sketching *me*.'

'Leave it, Kayla.' His words were laced with a warning not to pursue it.

'You were sketching me. Oh, no!' Kayla hid her face in the wide brim of her hat. How could he? With the ends of her hair all lank and dripping, and she wasn't even wearing any mascara, let alone a bra! 'I look like a drowned and lashless rat!'

'You look like an angel,' Leonidas told her, voicing his earlier thoughts.

'You can't be serious!' Kayla protested, bringing her head up, clinging to her crushed hat as her only defence against those shaded yet all-seeing eyes.

'I never joke about beauty. Particularly the beauty of a woman,' he said, in a voice that seemed to trickle with pure honey.

And you would have known scores of those! Known just what to say to make them feel like you're making me feel now, Kayla thought hectically. Weak-kneed and breathless and wanting so much to believe that all he was saying was true!

She pulled a face, and in spite of everything managed to say with a tremulous little laugh, 'Does that line usually work?'

The firm masculine mouth compressed, and she couldn't seem to drag her gaze from it as he prompted, 'Does it work in what way?' Now that mouth took on a mocking curve. 'In getting you into my bed?'

Kayla felt heated colour steal into her cheeks. Which was ridiculous, she thought. She was hardly a novice to male attention. She'd been planning a wedding, for heaven's sake! Yet there was something about this man that was more exciting and more dangerous to her than any other man she had ever met.

'Isn't it customary?' she returned somewhat breathlessly in answer to his reference to getting her into bed.

'Possibly,' he acceded, 'but not in this case. And not with someone who has been made to feel so unsure of herself that she blushes at the mere mention of a man and woman finding pleasure in each other. Or a man taking any interest in her. There's really no need to hide from me, Kayla.'

Perhaps there wasn't. But when he took the hat she was clutching to her like a shield and his hand accidentally brushed the sensitised flesh above her modest neckline she realised that it was herself that she was afraid of. Of feelings that were too reckless and wild to think about. Purely physical feelings that had surfaced the moment she had first seen him standing on that other beach a few days ago.

Now, with her wet top doing nothing to protect her from his gaze, she could feel her blood starting to surge and the peaks of her breasts tightening in response to his hot regard, so that all she could think about was that hard masculine body locked in torrid sensual pleasure on some bed. And not just any bed. On hers!

'Are you saying that your interest is purely aesthetic?' she queried, her voice croaking from her shaming thoughts and the knowledge of how her rapidly rising breasts were betraying her to him.

'No.' He had removed his sunglasses and was hooking them onto the waistband of his trousers. Now she could see his eyes clearly.

They were dark and heavy-lidded beneath the thick swathe of his lashes, and glittering with such intensity of purpose that her every nerve went into red alert as he closed the screaming distance between them.

CHAPTER FIVE

HIS MOUTH OVER hers was like an Olympic torch blazing into life, setting her insides on fire and sending molten sensations of light searing through her blood.

His kiss was passionate, yet tender. Dominant, yet testing. And the mind-blowing expertise with which he lured her mouth to widen for him was the technique of a man who had studied and understood women—a far cry from a man who had such a laid-back attitude to life. A wanderer. A drifter. Without purpose or design.

He smelled of the earth and of the pines that clad the higher slopes of the hillsides. He was burning with everything wild and unfettered, unrestrained. And yet she felt his restraint— a purposeful holding back—as he held her loosely within the exciting circle of his arms.

That was until the hands that were still clutching her camera and the sunscreen bottle against his wide, cushioning shoulders suddenly slid around his neck. Then, with a groan of defeat, his restraint fell away, leaving only raw passion in its wake as he tossed her hat aside and pulled her hard against him.

Kayla heard a gushing in her ears and wasn't sure whether it was the heavy pounding of her blood or whether she was being captured and submerged beneath the relentless power of the sea.

She could feel the whole hard length of his body—every last inch of it—and she could feel her own responding to the drugging hunger of his mouth.

His back was firm and muscled, and she wished she wasn't encumbered by her possessions so that she could slide her eager hands across it. There was no such encumbrance though in the way her body locked with his. His chest was a wall of thunder, crushing her aching breasts, while the potent evidence of his hard virility was making her pulse with need.

When he put her from him, holding her at arm's length, she uttered a strangled murmur of breathless shock and disappointment.

'Why did you do that?' she quavered. Why had he kissed her when he had just claimed he had no intention of trying to get her into bed?

He was breathing as heavily as she was, and a deep flush was staining the olive skin across the strong, hard structure of his cheeks.

'Because you were wondering what it would be like if I did.'

Still trembling, and perturbed by how easily he could not only read her mind but also by how easily he could bend her to his will, she challenged brittly, 'So why did you stop?'

'Because, as I told you before, I have no intention of taking advantage of a woman on the rebound,' he reminded her, even though his breathing was still laboured and his strong face racked from the passion he was struggling to keep in check.

'And—as I told *you* before—I'm not on the rebound,' Kayla protested adamantly, shamed by her response when he was showing such self-control, and when she seemed to have relinquished all of hers in one experimental kiss!

'Aren't you?' he disputed, although there was a wry smile tugging at one corner of his mouth that softened his challenging remark, before he went on to add, 'You had a relationship with him, didn't you?'

'Well, of course I did,' Kayla returned. 'Of sorts.'

'Of sorts?' He tilted his head, his brows drawing quizzically together. 'How am I supposed to interpret *that?*'

'Any way you like!' Kayla tossed back at him, too embarrassed to tell him that Craig's enthusiasm for her had seemed to go off the boil for several weeks before their break-up, and that she was ashamed of herself now for not suspecting the truth. She had believed him when he had blamed work overload for his not showing enough interest in her. When he'd assured her that things would be different when they were married. When he had got the precious promotion he'd spent all his time working for.

'Were you living with him?'

'No.'

'Why not? If I ever set my mind on a woman I want to become my wife, then she will be firmly in my life—and my bed—before I even ask her.'

'I didn't want us to move in together. Not until we were married,' Kayla emphasised. 'And Craig was in full agreement with that.'

'Really?' Mocking scepticism marked that hard masculine face. 'You could do without each other *that* much?'

'Not that it's any concern of yours,' Kayla pointed out, hating having her relationship with her ex scrutinised so closely by this man she scarcely knew, 'but we wanted to start married life properly. In a place that was our own. I didn't want to just move into his flat. Anyway, there's more to a relationship than jumping into bed with each other at every given opportunity,' she stressed, unconsciously wiping her mouth with the back of her hand. Her lips still felt bruised and swollen and, like her susceptible body, burning from Leon's wholly primal, earth-shattering kiss.

'Is there?' he asked, and she could feel those perspicacious eyes following her involuntary action, mocking her, disconcertingly aware.

'Yes!' She was trembling, knowing that the way she had just behaved with him made nonsense of everything she was saying. And the worst thing was he knew it too. 'The type of man I let myself get involved with doesn't just give in to basic animal lust.'

He chuckled under his breath. 'Is that what I was doing? Then you must forgive me if I fail to live up to the constraints of the type of man you are obviously used to. Although I *could* hazard a guess that your relationship was sadly lacking in what was required to make a lifetime commitment, and that the lack of passion between you could have been why he was getting his satisfaction elsewhere.'

The reminder hurt, stinging her pride and giving rise to that same feeling of inadequacy she had felt after she'd got over the initial blow of Craig's betrayal—especially coming from someone who oozed the sort of sexual potency that this man did.

'I'm sorry,' he murmured, surprising her suddenly. 'I didn't mean to rub it in.'

'Didn't you?' she accused, hiding her hurt pride and dignity beneath the burnished gold of her lowered lashes.

'Well, all right.' A self-effacing smile touched that mouth that had the power to drug her. 'I did. But until it stops hurting, Kayla, you aren't ready for an involvement with any other man. And even if you were, the last thing a sensitive girl like you would want is an involvement with a man like me.'

Why not? Crazily, she heard the mortifying question spring to her lips and was half-afraid that she had actually spoken it. Wasn't he just the type of man she needed right now to drive the bitter after-taste of Craig and all his shallow-minded smart set out of her mind?

'Believe it or not, I'm not looking for one,' she responded, to assure herself as much as Leon. Well, she wasn't, was she? Wasn't she better off—as her mother had always claimed to be—on her own?

'Sensible girl,' Leonidas drawled and, stooping to pick up her hat, deposited it gently and unceremoniously on her head.

'Thanks.' Kayla pulled a wry face. 'Perhaps you'd like to sketch me like this?' she challenged broodingly, relieved, nevertheless, that the disconcerting subject of her love-life had finally been swept aside.

What wasn't so easy to sweep aside, however, was the memory of what had transpired between them a few moments ago. Why had she responded to him so shamelessly if, as he'd suggested, she was still affected by what Craig had done? Was she so wanton? So desperate for a man? Any man? she wondered. Might she have let this virtual stranger take her here on the shingle without a thought for how it might leave her feeling afterwards?

'I won't be sketching you at all,' he said dismissively. 'For the simple reason that you are wrong. I'm no artist. But if I were, and if I had to keep looking at you looking like this...' His gaze slid over her tantalisingly wet top, making her quiver inside from the powerful impulses generated by the naked need in his eyes, 'then—old boyfriend or no old boyfriend— I definitely would wind up taking you to bed.'

The climb up through the scrub to Philomena's cottage was hot and hilly, and Leonidas walked ahead of Kayla, protecting her from the dense and thorny vegetation that was encroaching on the narrow path, thriving in the rough terrain.

He had had an exacting morning, sorting out a problem that had arisen back in his London office—a case of divided opinion between a couple of members of his board, which his second-in-command had apologised for bringing to his attention.

They said it was tough at the top, he reminded himself

with a grimace. And they could say it again, because no matter how much he needed to escape the rigours of the office for a while, he still needed to keep his finger on the pulsing heart of his business.

Shopping malls, leisure complexes and housing developments didn't build themselves, and after the flak he had taken from the press over the neglect of local residents with last year's bitter fiasco he needed to ensure that no loopholes were left for mercenary lawyers and unprincipled members of his team to make unscrupulous deals over.

Being labelled 'ruthless', 'unscrupulous' and 'a profiteer' by the media wasn't something he wanted repeated any more than he wanted further episodes like the one with his publicity-hungry bed-partner Esmeralda Leigh. He had a reputation to uphold—one that he valued—both in his corporate and his private life, and he would protect and defend it with every shred of his power and his unwavering principles. But he hadn't got where he was today without treading a path that had made him tough, hard-nosed and uncompromising, and he had no intention of wavering from that path. Of allowing himself or anyone else to imagine for one moment that he was going soft. Not even this infernally beautiful girl...

Hearing her breath coming shallowly some way behind him, he stopped and waited for her to catch up. She was clutching her bottle of sunscreen lotion, the bulky camera dangled around her neck, and with her white leggings, her tunic top and that huge floppy hat she looked like an overgrown child who had just raided her great-grandmother's attic. He was happy to notice—for his own sake—that her top had nearly dried.

'Here. Let me carry that.' He could see her cheeks were flushed and that she was finding it a struggle keeping up with him, and he held out his hand for the camera, which she happily relinquished. Silently he extended his other hand.

Realising his intention, Kayla hesitated briefly, and saw a mocking smile touch his sensational mouth.

'It's all right. It doesn't constitute a tacit agreement to let me into your bed,' he advised her dryly.

Of course it didn't, she thought. But an impulse of something so powerfully electric seemed to pass between them when she took his hand that it certainly felt like it.

'Thanks,' she uttered tremulously, hoping that he would think it was the uphill climb in the heat over the rough ground that was making her sound so breathless. Not that every cell was leaping in response to her physical awareness of him just as it had when he had kissed her down there on the beach.

'Where did you learn to speak English so proficiently?' she asked, needing to say something—although she *was* genuinely interested to know.

'When I work, I work mainly in the UK,' he informed her. 'And my grandmother was English, so I had a head start while I was still knee-high to a cricket.'

'Grasshopper.'

'What?' The way he was looking down at her, with such charismatically dark eyes, sent a sensually charged little tingle along Kayla's spine.

'It's knee-high to a grasshopper,' she corrected him, contemplating how well the backdrop of the rugged coast and the meandering hillsides served to strengthen the ruggedness of this man who had been born part of them. But she'd picked up on what he'd just said about *when* he worked. So his employment definitely wasn't regular, she thought, reminded of the recent slump in the building trade and how difficult it had made things for a lot of its workers. Perhaps that was why he'd chosen to 'opt out', as he'd put it, for a while.

'How old were you when you left the island?' She found herself wanting to know much more about him.

'Fifteen.'

She remembered him saying that he'd left to find a better life. 'On your own?' she queried. 'Did you leave to go to college?' she asked, when he didn't answer her question. What else could possibly have taken him away at such a young age?

He laughed at that—a sound without humour. 'No college. No university. I did have hopes of furthering my education, but my father wouldn't hear of it.'

'Why not?' Kayla asked, amazed.

'He wanted me to get out into the world, like he had, and "do an honest job" as he called it.'

'Really?' Kayla sympathised. 'And what did *he* do?'

'He eked a living out of this land,' he told her, with an edge to his voice that had her looking at her curiously.

'And where are they now? Your parents?' She couldn't believe they could still be living on the island, otherwise why would he be staying here alone in some absentee owner's sadly neglected house?

'My parents are dead,' he told her as he walked half a stride ahead of her. There was no emotion now beside that surprisingly hard cast to his mouth.

'I'm sorry,' Kayla murmured. She had discovered during a conversation in the villa with him the other day that he, like Kayla, was an only child.

'One learns to get over these things,' he replied.

From the harshness of his tone, however, she wondered if he had. Or was there some other reason, she pondered, for that inexorable grimness to his features?

'Still…you have Philomena,' she said brightly, hoping to lighten the mood. She couldn't understand why down there on the beach he had behaved like an exciting lover and yet now seemed as uncommunicative as ever.

Was it by chance that he had just happened to come across her down there? Or had he come looking for her especially?

A sharp little thrill ran through her at the possibility that he had.

'Did she tell you where I was?'

His disconcerting glance at her took in what she knew was her thoroughly dishevelled appearance, and a lazy smile curved his mouth, instantly transforming his features.

'Are you suggesting I asked her?'

Mortified that he would even think she might have wanted him to, Kayla tried to tug her hand out of his, and sucked in a breath when he refused to let it go.

'Yes, I did,' he admitted easily, without any of the embarrassment that was burning Kayla's cheeks. 'I came down to Philomena's to check on you. You've had a bad experience. I didn't like to think of it ruining your holiday.'

He actually cared?

Well, of course he was concerned for her, she thought, mindful of the lengths he had gone to in rescuing her the other night, and then not only helping her to clean up the villa afterwards but also bringing her to Philomena's as well.

'It hasn't. Thanks,' she offered, grateful to him, and was warmed by a flash of something closely resembling admiration in his eyes.

She wondered if he had a girlfriend or a partner. It certainly seemed he'd had a stormy affair, judging by the way he had referred to her when he had been generalising about her sex the other day.

'Why were you so unfriendly to me when we met those first couple of times?' she queried, suddenly needing to know. 'You still haven't told me.'

She started as he suddenly stopped dead, pulling her round to face him on the path.

'Do you *never* stop asking questions?' he demanded, his face a curious blend of impatience and amusement.

'No.' She gave him a sheepish little look and shrugged her

shoulders. 'I'm afraid it's a fault of mine. Apparently, according to my star sign, I was born on "the Day of Curiosity",' she quoted with a little giggle.

'And do you really believe all that stuff?'

Seeing the scepticism marking the strong and perfectly sculpted features, she laughed and said, 'No. But they've got that part of me right!'

'You can say that again,' he remarked dryly. 'And as a matter of interest exactly when *is* this illustrious day?' He made a half-amused sound down his nostrils when she told him. 'So you've just had a birthday?' he observed. 'And how old are you, Kayla?'

'Twenty-three.'

'Old enough to know when a man doesn't welcome any more probing into his private life.'

And that told her, Kayla thought, feeling suitably chastised. This time when she tried to pull her hand away she was even more disconcerted when he allowed her to do so.

They had reached the top of the path that ran up alongside Philomena's cottage. There was an area at the back, with a lime tree and a couple of orange trees, where Philomena also grew aubergines and sweet peppers, and where chickens foraged freely in the open scrub.

'How's the car going?' Leon asked, noticing it parked against the side wall of the cottage.

Still feeling put down, but relieved to be speaking on a much less personal level with him, Kayla murmured, 'Fine.' And suddenly, with tension causing a little bubble of laughter to burst from her, she proclaimed, 'Which is more than can be said for yours!'

His truck was parked on the edge of the dirt road just behind the little hatchback, and she could see that one of its tyres was completely flat.

'Oh, dear!' She tried not to giggle again as he thrust the

camera at her and, swearing quietly under his breath in his own language, went to deal with changing the wheel.

Leaving him to it, Kayla wandered into the garden, where Philomena was pegging out some washing, sending a couple of chickens scrambling, clucking noisily.

'A flat tyre.' Kayla made a gesture to indicate what she meant and Philomena nodded, rolling her eyes.

Which meant what? Kayla wondered, curious. Had Philomena hoped that the boy she had brought into the world thirty-odd years ago might be doing better for himself by now? Was that what Leon had meant when he'd said she wasn't happy with the way he had turned out?

Dismissing it from her mind, she moved to help Philomena, but her hostess waved her aside with a warm but incomprehensible protest, pointing to the reclining seats in the welcoming shade of a sun umbrella. Not wishing to offend, Kayla went inside and donned a bikini with matching red and white wrap, which she tied, sarong-style, just above her breasts, before coming back outside into the now deserted garden.

A short time later Philomena emerged from the house with two glasses of something cool and refreshing—juice for her, Kayla realised gratefully, and something a little stronger for Leon.

'I'll take it out to him,' she volunteered, putting her glass down on a nearby table and leaving a thankful Philomena hurrying back inside, because the telephone had started ringing inside the house.

Her discarded wrap had fallen down behind the chair, and wasn't very easy to reach, so with a little sliver of excitement Kayla left it where it was and proceeded to take the glass to Leon as she was.

For the last twenty-minutes or so her ears had been tuned to every sound coming from the dirt road—from the slamming down of a boot to the chink of metal being laid down on sun-baked stones. Now, as she rounded the corner of the house, Kayla's heart kicked into overdrive.

With his shirt removed, and faded blue jeans having replaced his linen trousers, Leon was crouched down, securing a nut on the spare wheel, and for a few moments Kayla could only stand there, watching him unobserved.

His body was beautiful. The bronzed skin sheathed muscles that were flexing as he worked, revealing the tension in his straining biceps and across his wide shoulders, in the tapering structure of his strong and sinewy back.

'Philomena thought you'd like something to drink,' Kayla told him, dry-mouthed, noticing before he turned around how his hair waved below the nape of his neck like jet against burnished bronze.

He dropped the spanner he was using and stood up, his movements cool and easy. That knowing curve to his mouth suggested that he was well aware of her reluctance to let him think that it was entirely her idea.

'That's very good of her.' His answer and his lopsided smile assured her that two could play at that game. His eyes, however, were tugging over her scantily clothed body in a way that was making her feel naked.

'You've been a long time. You should have let me help you,' Kayla remarked, handing him the glass. The accidental touch of his fingers against hers sent a sharp little frisson through her.

'And do you think I would have achieved much with you looking like that?'

Kayla swallowed, watching him drink, trying not to make it too obvious that she was having difficulty staying unaffected by *his* state of undress.

In fact she was finding it impossible not to allow her gaze free rein over his superb body—from the contoured strength of his smooth chest, with its taut muscles and flat dark nipples, to the black line of hair that started just above his navel and ran down inside the waistband of the denim that encased his flat stomach and narrow hips.

He was like a beautiful sleek stallion. All leanness and rippling muscle, with the power to dominate and excite, to control and to conquer using the pulsing energies and surging potency of his body.

'Do you see what I mean?' he taunted softly.

Yes, she did, and she could feel those energies transmitting their sensual messages along her nerve-endings, tugging shameless responses from every erogenous zone in her body.

Beneath the satiny white cups of her bikini her burgeoning breasts throbbed, sending a piercing arrow of need to the heart of her loins.

He was so raw, so masculine, and so shamelessly virile. She wanted to know what it was like to have a man like him filling her, taking her to the wildest edges of the universe with him while she lay beneath him, sobbing her pleasure, in glorious abandon to his thrilling and governing hands.

Shocked by her thoughts, she tried to shake them away, feigning an interest in his truck to try and restore some sense of propriety in herself, grappling for equilibrium.

'Did this thing come with the house?' she queried in a tight, strained voice, slapping the grimy, battered bonnet. 'Or did you have to buy it?'

'It's mine,' Leonidas answered, taking a breath from quenching his thirst and watching her from under the thickness of his dark lashes.

'Perhaps it's time you bought a new one,' she suggested cheekily, amused, deciding that it wasn't only the tyre that needed changing. The bodywork looked as if it wouldn't object to a lick of fresh paint either.

'Perhaps it's time you stopped having a laugh at my expense.'

Was that what she was doing? 'I'm sorry.' Seeing his eyes darkening, quickly Kayla strove to suppress her mocking banter. After all, he probably couldn't afford anything better, she thought. Not like Craig, with his company Jaguar and his inflated expense account. This man would have no such perks. 'I didn't mean to laugh about it—honest.'

'Didn't you?' He had emptied his glass with one final long draught. Setting it aside, he came to where Kayla stood with her hand resting on the top of the radiator grid, as though in apology to the vehicle itself. 'I suppose you measure a man's status by the type of car he drives, huh?'

'No.'

'What would you prefer? A Porsche? Or a Mercedes?' he asked roughly.

'Well, both would be nice…' Her voice tailed off when she noticed how forbidding he looked, and she realised that she wasn't just imagining that hardening in his voice. 'I wasn't making fun of you. Not really,' she tagged on, suddenly afraid that he might think less of her if he thought she had been. 'I suppose I was just getting my own back.'

'For what?'

'For embarrassing me earlier. Making me feel awkward. When you said I was being too inquisitive about your private life.'

He laughed very softly then, his strong implacable features suddenly losing some of their austerity. His eyes, however, were disturbingly reflective as they rested on her face.

'And I thought you were doing it just to prompt some reaction from me,' he murmured silkily, with no apology for silencing her earlier.

'Prompt some reaction from you?' Kayla's throat contracted with heightening sexual tension. 'Why would I want to do that?'

'Because I'm probably one of the only men you've met who

isn't instantly falling over himself to respond to your temptingly sexy signals.'

'I'm not giving off *any* signals!' Kayla breathed, mortified. 'And I'm certainly not trying to get your attention.'

'Aren't you?' Those shrewd eyes tugged over her flushed, indignant features, regarding, assessing and stripping her of her deepest and hottest secrets. 'You wouldn't have come out here looking like this...' an all-encompassing glance took in breasts thrust tantalisingly upwards by the shaping of the cups and skimpy briefs barely skimming her abdomen '...if you weren't.'

Shamefully, she wished she had bothered to retrieve her cover-up before flaunting herself in front of him like this. Because that *was* what she had been doing, she admitted silently. Flaunting herself.

She wanted to say something to redeem herself. Or simply to run away. Anything but stay there and face him like this.

She wished she had run when he suddenly reached up and cupped her cheek, his broad thumb playing across the softness of her pouting lips.

'If I made love to you, Kayla,' he said huskily, 'it would be a fleeting moment's pleasure. That's all. No commitment. No strings. And I don't think you came here to let some man with his own issues to sort out use you like that. A girl like you needs something more than anything I could offer you. Something more meaningful. Not a brief fling to try and forget the man who cheated on you with a few hours of what I can't deny would be sensational pleasure.'

He was deadly serious, but even his words were exciting her. Or was it his thumb, tracing the curve of her plump lower lip, forcing her to close her eyes against the reckless desire to taste him? To inhale his musky animal scent mingling with the smell of grease and metal and everything that made this man exciting to her?

'Who said I want you to make love to me?' she murmured in pointless protest, her eyes inky beneath lashes still half-lowered against his gaze.

'You're inviting it with every denial you utter,' he breathed hoarsely, his voice overlaid with desire. 'And you're not so naïve as not to realise that you're making me as hard as a rock.'

'You're wrong!' she argued breathlessly, and in the only way she knew of saving face she pulled away from him, almost tripping over her own feet in her flip-flops as she virtually ran back to the house.

Upstairs, away from Philomena's shrewd eyes, she went into the shower-room and peeled off the bikini that seemed to be sticking to her.

Why on earth was she so attracted to him? she berated herself under the cool jets of the shower, trying to lather away the sensual heat from her body and that elusive scent of him that still clung to her skin where he had briefly touched her.

He had admitted himself that he was a man with issues.

Woman issues! Which was why he had shut her up, coming back from the beach today.

Well, what did she care? His business was his business. As far as she was concerned, he was simply a man who had helped her out of a difficult situation. Nothing more. It was just that she couldn't seem to stop making a fool of herself when she was with him, let alone concentrate on anything but him when she wasn't!

She tried to think about the past couple of months. Her ex. What had driven her here. Tried to stir up some other emotions to blot out the crazy, reckless feelings she was experiencing for Leon.

But, try though she did, feeling bitter suddenly seemed like a wasted emotion—because Craig and what he had done didn't seem to matter so much any more.

CHAPTER SIX

KAYLA DIDN'T SEE Leon the next day, or the day after that, and when he did come down to the cottage again, looking stupendous in a white T-shirt and light, hip-hugging trousers, it was only to deliver logs to Philomena.

'So you're still roadworthy, then?' Kayla remarked, almost coyly, when he came into the sitting room after offloading and stacking the logs beside the huge indoor oven, still embarrassingly mindful of their conversation the last time they had met.

'Just about,' Leonidas reassured her with a self-effacing grimace. 'And I see that you're just about as cheeky as ever.'

'No, I'm not,' Kayla asserted, thrilled nevertheless by the sensual gleam in those midnight-black eyes that seemed to promise some delightful retribution if she didn't stop. Wildly she wondered if he had been right the other day, and she *had* been taunting him solely for his attention. Because despite all he had said about no attachments and no strings, she wanted that attention now—like crazy! 'We were wondering why we hadn't seen you,' she said, as nonchalantly as she could.

'We?' He picked up on her deliberate choice of pronoun—and on the little tremor she couldn't keep out of her voice. Obviously, from the way his mouth compressed in mild amusement. 'Are you saying you missed me?'

'No.' Kayla was glad that Philomena had left the room—though not before she'd noticed how the woman had laid a grateful hand on Leon's arm for the work he had just done. The unspoken affection the two of them shared touched Kayla immensely.

Yet she *had* missed him, she thought, and Leon knew it too—evidently from the way he laughed in response.

'In that case you won't object to spending the day with me,' he said, deliberately misinterpreting what she had said. 'Philomena told me you were asking one of her neighbours about the little island the other day—about if you could book a trip across there.'

He meant that dark mass of land she could see jutting out of the sea from practically every aspect of this hillside.

'She also mentioned that you spend far too much time worrying that you aren't doing enough to help her around the place. She wants you to enjoy your holiday—so do I—and as there are no organised trips to that island I'll be happy to take you over there myself.'

Even as he was suggesting it Leonidas told himself that he was being unwise. He had assured Kayla—as well as himself—that he wasn't prepared to have any sort of relationship with her, but try as he might he just couldn't keep away. Yet if he spent time with her, he warned himself, he would be deceiving her with every word he uttered. And if he didn't…?

If he didn't then he'd go mad thinking about her, he admitted silently, feeling the thrust of his scorching libido flaring into life just from sparring with her, not to mention from the scent of her, which was acting on his senses as powerfully as if he'd just opened the door on some willing wanton's boudoir.

Her appearance wasn't helping his control. She was wearing white shorts, which showed off far too much of those deliciously creamy legs, and a sleeveless lemon blouse tied under her breasts. It revealed just enough of her shallow cleavage to make him want to see more, and left her gradually tanning slender midriff delightfully bare.

'Thanks, but I think I'll give it a miss today,' she said, disappointing him.

'Suit yourself,' he muttered, turning away. He was relieved that the decision had been made—especially since he had been entertaining the strongest desire to tug open that tantalising little blouse and mould her sensitive breasts to his palms until she sobbed with the pleasure.

'Well…'

Her sudden hesitancy stopped him in his tracks. Battling to control his raging anatomy, he didn't turn around, his breath locking in his lungs as he heard her tentative little suggestion behind him.

'If you could just give me a minute…?'

He swung round then, his desire veiled by his immense powers of self-control. His eyes, as they clashed with hers, were smouldering with a dark intensity and he saw an answering response in the darkening blue of hers that was as hungry as it was guarded.

Almost cleverly guarded, he thought, but not quite enough. She was as on fire for him as he was for her, he recognised, regardless of any feelings she might still be harbouring over that louse who had let her down.

Kayla, as she stood there, captured by the powerful hold of his gaze, felt a skein of excitement unravelling inside her and knew that a watershed had been reached. That with one look and one inconsequential unfinished sentence a silent understanding had somehow passed between them. She had crossed a bridge that was already burning behind her and she knew there could be no turning back.

'No rowing boat today?' Kayla remarked, surprised when, after driving them to a beach further along the coast, Leon guided her towards a small motor boat moored alongside a wooden jetty. 'I didn't think you'd be seen dead in anything less than fifty years old!' she said laughingly.

'Didn't you?' he drawled, with a challenging and deliciously sensual gleam in his eyes as he handed her into the boat. 'Contrary to your thinking, *hrisi mou,* I can…' he hesitated, thinking of the words '…come good when circumstances demand.'

'And *do* circumstances demand?' she enquired airily, in spite of her pulse, which was racing from his nearness and his softly spoken endearment.

'Oh, yes,' he breathed with barely veiled meaning. 'I think they do.'

It was a day of delight and surprises.

With effortless dexterity Leonidas steered the boat through the sparkling blue water, following the rocky coast of his own island to begin with, and pointing out coves and deserted beaches only accessible from the sea.

Having a field-day with her camera, Kayla lapped up the magic of her surroundings whilst using every opportunity to grab secretive and not so secretive shots of this dynamic man she was with: at the wheel, in profile, with his brow furrowed in concentration, or turning to talk to her with that sexy, sidelong pull of his mouth that never failed to do funny things to her stomach. She captured him looking out over the dark body of water they were cutting through, his T-shirt pulled taut across his broad muscular back, his black hair as windswept as hers from the exhilarating speed at which they were travelling.

She'd need to remember, she realised almost desperately, wondering why it was so important to her to capture everything about this holiday. This island. These precious few hours. This man.

Suddenly aware, he glanced over his shoulder and, easing back on the throttle, said challengingly, 'Don't you think you've taken enough?' She was about to make some quip about it being her 'fix', but he cut across her before she could with, 'What are you going to do? Put them on the internet?'

With a questioning look at him, not sure how to take what he'd said, she pretended to be considering it, and with a half-tantalising, half-nervous little giggle, answered, 'I might.'

'You do that and our association ends right now.' His contesting tone and manner caused her to flinch.

'If you're that concerned, then keep it,' she invited, holding the camera out to him. She hadn't forgotten what a private person he was. 'I promise I'm not going to publish them on the web, but take it if you don't trust me not to.'

For a moment her candour made Leonidas hold back. How could he demand or even expect integrity from her when he wasn't being straight himself?

Briefly he felt like flinging caution to the winds and telling her the truth. Only the thought of the repercussions that could follow stopped him.

She would be angry, that was certain. But he had come here seeking respite from all the glamour and superficiality that went hand in hand with who he really was, and he wasn't ready yet to relinquish his precious anonymity. It didn't help reminding himself that it was primarily because of trusting a woman that he had felt driven to take some time out. Because of being too careless and believing that a casual but willing bed partner would share the same ethics as he.

Not that this girl was in any way like the mercenary vamp with whom he had unwisely shared the weekend that had proved so costly to his pride and reputation. But his billionaire status and lifestyle still generated interest, despite his best attempts to keep it low-key—and never more so since his unfortunate affair with the media-hungry Esmeralda—and Kayla was only human after all. What a boost it would be to her bruised ego after being ditched so cruelly by her fiancé for news of her liaison with a man whose corporate achieve-ments weren't entirely unknown to filter back to the world press. One text home to this Lorna might be all it would take to bring the paparazzi here in their droves.

'It's stolen enough of your time from me for one day,' he said, smiling. Yet he still took the camera she was offering and stowed it away in a recess beneath the wheel.

They had lunch on the boat—a feast of lobster and cheeses, fresh bread and a blend of freshly squeezed juice. Afterwards there were delicate pastries filled with fruit and walnuts, and others creamy with the tangy freshness of lime.

Kayla savoured it all as she'd never savoured a meal be-fore, and there was wonder mixed in with her appreciation.

'This must have set you back a fortune,' she couldn't help remarking when she had finished.

'Let me worry about that,' he told her unassumingly.

'But to hire a boat like this doesn't come cheap…' Even if only for a day, she thought. 'And as for that lunch…' She wondered if he would have eaten as well had he been alone and decided that he wouldn't, guessing that he must have been counting on her being unable to resist coming with him today.

'What are you concerned about, Kayla?' he asked softly, closing the cool box that had contained their picnic before stowing it away. 'That I might have spent more than you think I can justifiably afford? Or is it finding yourself in my debt that's making you uneasy?'

'A bit of both, I suppose,' she admitted truthfully. After all, she'd always been used to paying her way when she was with a man, to never taking more out of a relationship than she was prepared to put in. Emotionally as well as financially, she thought with a little stab of self-derision as she remem-bered how with Craig she had wound up giving everything and receiving nothing, coming out a first-rate fool in the end.

'Don't worry about it,' Leonidas advised. 'I promise you

I'm not likely to starve for the rest of my holiday. As for the boat, I hired it to take myself off exploring today. Your coming with me is just a bonus, so there's no need to feel awkward or indebted in any way. If you want to contribute something, then your enjoyment will suffice,' he assured her, and refrained from adding that most women he'd known would have taken his generosity as their due.

The island, when they came ashore, was beautiful. Lonely and uninhabited, it was merely a haven for wildlife, with only numerous birds and insects making their voices heard above the warm wind and the wash of the sea in the cove where they had left the boat.

There was no distinct path, and the climb through the surprisingly green vegetation was hot and steep, but the feeling of freedom at the top was worth a thousand climbs.

It was like standing in their own uninhabited world. In every direction the deep blue of the sky met the deeper blue of the sea. Looking back across the distance they had covered, Kayla saw the hulk of mountainous land they had left with its forests and its craggy coastline slumbering in a haze of heat.

There were huge stones amongst the grass—sculpted stones of an ancient ruin, overgrown with scrub and wild flowers, a sad and silent testimony to the beliefs of some long-lost civilisation.

'You said you came to sort out some issues?' Kayla reminded him, venturing to broach what she had been dying to ask him since they had left that morning. 'What sort of issues?' she pressed, looking seawards at the waves creaming onto a distant beach and wondering if it was the one where she had first seen him over a week ago. 'Woman issues?' she enquired, more tentatively now.

He was standing with his foot on one of the stones that had once formed part of the ancient temple, with one hand resting on his knee. The wind was lifting his hair, sweeping it back off features suddenly so uncompromising that he looked like a marauding mythical god, surveying all he intended to conquer.

'Among other things,' he said, but he didn't enlarge on the women in his life or tell her what those 'other things' were.

Kayla moved away from him, pulling a brightly flowering weed from a crack in what had formed part of a wall. She was getting used to his uncommunicative ways.

She was surprised, therefore, when he suddenly said, 'I used to dream of owning this island when I was a boy. I used to sit on that hillside...' he pointed to a distant spot across the water, indiscernible through the heat haze '...and imagine all I was going to do with it. The big house. The swimming pool. The riding stables.'

'And dogs?' Kayla inserted, her eyes gleaming, following him into a make-believe world of her own.

'Yes, lots of dogs.'

So he liked animals, she realised, deriving warm pleasure from the knowledge. Contrarily, though, she wrinkled her nose. 'Too costly to feed.' Laughingly she pretended to discount that idea. 'And too much heartache if they get sick or run away.'

'They couldn't run away,' Leonidas reminded her. 'Not unless they were proficient swimmers.'

'Haven't you ever heard of the doggy paddle?' She giggled, enjoying playing this little game with him. Her eyes were bright and her cheeks were glowing from an exhilaration that had nothing to do with their climb. 'So you were going to build a house with a swimming pool? And have horses? Racehorses, of course.'

He shot her a sceptical glance. 'Now you're wandering into the realms of fantasy,' he chided, amused.

'Well, if you can own the island and have a house with lots of dogs, I can have racehorses,' Kayla insisted light-heartedly.

'They'd fall off the edge before they'd covered a mile,' he

commented dryly. 'I was talking about what seemed totally realistic to a twelve-year-old boy.'

Tugging her windswept hair out of her eyes, Kayla pulled a face. 'But then you grew up?'

'Yes,' he said heavily. 'I grew up.' And all he had wanted to do was run as far away from these islands and everything he had called home as he could possibly get.

'What happened?' Kayla asked, frowning. She couldn't help but notice the tension clenching his mouth and the hard line of his jaw.

'My mother died when I was fourteen, then my grandfather shortly afterwards. My father and I didn't see eye to eye,' he enlightened her.

'Why not?'

'Why do we not get on with some people and yet gel so perfectly with others? Especially those who are supposed to be closest to us?' He shrugged, his strong features softening a little. 'Differing opinions? A clash of personalities? Maybe even because we are too much alike. Why aren't *you* close to your mother?' he outlined as an example.

Watching a lizard dart along the jagged edge of the wall and disappear over the side, Kayla considered his question. 'I suppose all those things,' she admitted, rather ruefully. And then, keen to shrug off the serious turn the conversation had taken, she said, 'So, are you going to sketch me a picture of this house?'

'No.'

'Why not?' She had seen him scribbling in his notepad again, when he had been waiting for her in the truck outside Philomena's, and wondered what he could possibly have been doing if he *hadn't* been sketching. He'd also been speaking to somebody on his cell phone at the same time, Kayla remembered, but had cut the call short, leaning across to open the passenger door for her when he had seen her coming. She'd wondered if he'd been speaking to a woman and, if he had, whether it was the woman at the heart of his 'issues'.

'It isn't what I do,' Leonidas said.

'No son of mine is going to disgrace the Vassalio name by painting for a living!'

Leonidas could still hear his father's bellowing as he ridiculed his talent, his love of perspective and light and colour, beating it out of him—sometimes literally—as he destroyed the results of his teenage son's labours and with them all the creativity in his soul. Art was a feeling and feelings were weakness, his father had drummed into him. And no Vassalio male had ever been weak.

So he had channelled his driving energies into creating new worlds out of blocks of clay and concrete, in innovative designs that had leaped off the paper and formed the basis of his own developments. Developments that had made him rich beyond his wildest dreams. And with the money it had all come tumbling into his lap. Influence. Respect. Women. So many women that he could have had his pick of any of them. Yet he hadn't found one who was more disposed to him personally than she was to the state of his bank balance. Not beyond the pleasures of the bedroom at any rate, he thought with a self-deprecating mental grimace. In that it seemed he was never able to fail.

'So what about you, Kayla? Didn't you have any aspirations?'

'I suppose I did but not like yours,' she said, twirling the stalk of a pink flower in her fingers. 'I think I was always practical and realistic. Besides, I was brought up with the understanding that if you don't expect you can't be disappointed.'

'And because of that you never allowed yourself to dream?'

He was sitting on one of the larger stones, one leg bent, the other stretched out in front of him, and Kayla tried to avoid noticing how the cloth of his trousers pulled tautly over one muscular thigh.

'Of course I did,' she uttered, wondering why she suddenly felt as if she needed to defend herself. 'But I've never been one for mooning over things I can't have. Especially things which are totally out of my reach.'

He leaned back and crossed his arms, his muscles bunching, emphasising their latent strength. 'And you don't believe that everything is within your reach if you jump high enough?'

He made it sound almost credible, which seemed quite out of kilter, Kayla thought, with his laid-back attitude to life.

'If you jump too high you usually fall flat on your face. Anyway, you're one to talk,' she commented, still hurt over his refusal to give her a glimpse into even the smallest area of his life. 'You don't even have a steady job.'

'I get by.'

'But nothing that offers real security or fulfils your potential?'

'And why is it so important to fulfil my "potential"?' he quoted. His eyes were dark and inscrutable, giving nothing of his thoughts away.

'Because everybody needs a purpose. Some sort of goal in life,' Kayla stressed.

'And what is your goal, *glykia mou?*'

The sensuality with which he spoke suddenly seemed to emphasise the isolation of their surroundings, and with it the fundamental objective of each other's existence.

'To be happy.'

'And that's it? Just to be happy?' He looked both surprised and mildly amused. 'And how do you propose to achieve this happiness?'

Cynicism had replaced the mocking amusement of a moment ago. She could see it in the curling of his firm, rather cruel-looking mouth—a mouth she was aching to feel covering hers again.

'By staying grounded and true to myself, and not ever attempting to be something I'm not,' she uttered—croakily, because of where her thoughts had taken her. Afraid that she was in danger of sounding a little bit self-righteous, she added, 'By appreciating nature. Things like this.' She cast a glance around her at the wilderness of the island. At everything that was timeless. Untrammelled and free. 'By creating a happy home. Having children one day. And animals. Lots of animals.'

'And that's all it's going to take?' Again he looked marginally surprised. 'Setting up home and having babies?'

'It's better than being a drifter,' she remarked, knowing she was overstepping the mark yet unable to stop herself, 'without any ambition whatsoever.'

'You think I don't have ambition?'

'Well, *do* you?' she challenged, aware that she had no right to, as she pulled her hair out of her eyes again, yet driven by the feeling that he was mocking her values and finding them wanting.

'You'd be surprised. But just for argument's sake, what do you see me doing?' How would *you* have me realise this ambition?'

'You're good with cars,' Kayla remarked, ignoring the mockery infiltrating his question. 'You could be a mechanic. You could even start your own business. With the prices they charge for servicing and repairs these days you could make a comfortable living.'

'If I were a mechanic I wouldn't be able to take time off to come to places like this for weeks at a time.' His mouth compressed in exasperating dismissal. 'And I certainly wouldn't have met you.'

It was there in his eyes—raw, pure hunger. The same hunger that had been eating away at her ever since they had met and which now was taking every ounce of her will-power not to acknowledge.

'You could save enough to be able to buy your own garage,' she went on in a huskier voice. 'Put a manager in. Then you could take time off once in a while.'

'You think it's that simple? A steady job? A mortgage on a business and—hey! You're rich! That isn't how it works, Kayla.'

'How do you know if you don't try? Anyway, it was only a suggestion,' she reminded him, noticing how snugly his T-shirt moulded itself to the contours of his chest, the way his whole body seemed to pulse with unimpeded virility. 'You have to have drive and determination too.'

He laughed. 'And in that you think I'm sadly lacking?'

'You said that, not me,' she reminded him sombrely. 'I was only trying to help.'

'For which I'm very grateful,' he said, with that familiar mocking curl to his lips. 'But that sort of help I'm really able to do without.'

'Suit yourself,' she uttered, moving away from the ruin and gasping at the speed with which he leaped up and joined her as she came onto a plain of shorter grasses, interspersed with tall ferns and flowering shrubs.

'And now you're looking and feeling thoroughly chastened,' he remarked laughingly, catching her hand in his while his fervid gaze played with dark intensity over her small fine features, coming to rest on the pouting fullness of her mouth.

'You're very perceptive,' she breathed, hardly able to speak because of the wild responses leaping through her from his dangerous and electrifying nearness. 'And for a man without ambition you certainly believe in getting what you want.'

'You'd better believe it,' he asserted softly.

Even in a whisper his voice conveyed a determination of purpose that none of the self-important types she had known had ever possessed, and it sent little skeins of excitement unravelling through Kayla's insides.

'As for my lack of ambition… As I said, you'd be surprised. But what might *not* surprise you right now is to know that my most burning ambition is to feel you lying beneath me and to taste those sweet lips again, *agape mou*. To make love to you slowly and thoroughly until you're crying out for my length inside you. And I think at this moment you want the same thing—regardless of how unfulfilled or goalless you think I am.'

She wanted to protest but it would have been pointless, Kayla realised. She was already melting the moment his mouth came down over hers. She responded to it hungrily—greedily—her arms going around his neck, pulling him down to her as if she could never have enough.

Their kissing was hot and impassioned—a passion demanding only to be fed as, mouths fused, they sank together onto the sun-warmed grass. And Leonidas did as he'd wanted to do since he had arrived at Philomena's house that morning: tugged firmly on the ties of Kayla's blouse.

He gave a sigh of satisfaction when it fell open, revealing the pale lace and satin of her bra.

Slipping a finger inside, he revelled in the warmth of her soft skin before he pulled down the lace, releasing one modest-sized breast from its restraining cup.

Small, he measured, moulding the soft pale mound to his work-roughened palm, yet perfectly in proportion to the rest of her and more than satisfyingly sensitive, he realised as he caressed the pale pink areola into burgeoning arousal.

She moaned softly from the excitement of what he was doing to her. She arched her back, aching for his mouth over the swollen nipple, and almost hit the roof when he suddenly dipped his head and granted her wish.

There was no one and nothing around them. Nothing except

the wash of the waves on the beach below them and the wind that was teasing her hair into the finest strands of spun gold, inviting him to touch it, caress it, lose himself in the perfume that was all woman, all her own.

His lips were burning kisses over her breasts, her throat, the tender line of her jaw, finding and capturing her mouth again with the dominant pressure of his.

'Leon...'

She breathed his name into his mouth, saying it as no one had said it in a long, long time. No one called him Leon these days. Only Philomena...

Far away from this idyll, back in London, in Athens and on the corporate world stage, he was known only as Leonidas. Leonidas Vassalio. Hard-headed businessman. Decisive. Practical. Ruthless...

The reminder almost dragged him back to his senses, but not quite.

Her hands had ripped open his shirt, and he gave a deep guttural groan at their caressing warmth over his bared chest, but they were travelling downwards—down and down—in a quest to drive him wild, break his control.

He sucked in his breath, every nerve flexing like tautened wire, until finally, when she touched that most intimate part of him, even through his clothes, he was lost.

He wanted to stop this madness. Come clean about who he was. Because how could he justifiably do this with her if he didn't?

But as if sensing his reticent moment she was begging him not to stop, and her whimpers of need were all it took to bring about his final undoing.

If he told her who he was now he would be inviting her anger, and he couldn't face that, he realised in meagre justification. Couldn't ruin the mood and her artless belief in him no matter how much he knew he should.

It took little effort to remove her shorts, with her lace-edged briefs following them to where he'd cast them aside.

She was beautiful. A natural blonde, he noted with a soft smile of satisfaction as her legs parted before him and she lifted her body in a sobbing invitation for him to claim his prize.

It would be so easy, Leonidas thought, to remove his own clothes and take all that she was offering, assuage the fire that was burning in his groin. Just one thrust could take him to paradise...

He was hotter and harder than he had ever been in his life just from thinking about such damning pleasure, but through the torment of his stimulating thoughts a shred of sanity—of principle—remained.

He couldn't do it. Couldn't abuse her trust like that. Not while he still felt it necessary to deceive her. And yet she was slick with wanting, sobbing her need and her craving for release from this passion he had aroused.

She was lying with her face turned to one side and her arms above her head in a gesture of pure surrender. An angel, he thought, inviting him to share heaven with her. Or Eve, tempting him among the grasses of her sensuous Eden.

With torturous restraint he dipped his head and pressed his lips to the heated satin of her pulsing ribcage, his mouth moving with calculated precision over her slender waist to the flat plane of her abdomen and beyond. Very gently he parted her legs wider and slipped his arms beneath her splayed thighs.

Feeling his mouth against that most intimate part of her drew a shuddering gasp from Kayla. That dark hair brushing the sensitive flesh of her inner thigh was a stimulation she couldn't even have imagined.

It was the most erotic experience of her life. She had been intimate with a man before, but it had never felt like this. This abandoning of herself so completely to a pleasure that promised to drive her wild.

He knew just how to tease and titillate, just where and how to touch, employing his lips and the heat of his tongue to start a fire building in her as he tasted the honeyed sweetness of her body.

She thought she would die from the pleasure of it, and her body tautened in breathless expectation as flames of sensation licked along her nerve-endings and produced a burning tingle along her thighs.

Her juices flowed from her body, mingling with the moistness of his, anointing his roughened jaw with everything she was—until the mind-blowing sensation proved too much and she cried out as the fire consumed her in an orgasm of pulsating, interminable throbs.

Her sensitivity increased until she couldn't take any more pleasure, and she clamped her thighs around him, trapping him there, holding him to her in a sobbing ecstatic agony of release until the last embers of the fire he had ignited finally died away.

After a while, Kayla looked up at him where he lay beside her, propped up on an elbow. 'Why didn't you…?' Crazily, even after the intimacy they had shared she was too embarrassed to say it.

'Why didn't I what?' Leonidas leaned across her, tracing the curve of her cheek before picking a small windblown flower out of her hair. 'Take what I wanted?' he supplied, helping her.

She nodded, closing her eyes against the exquisite tenderness of his touch.

'Because I don't think you're a girl who indulges in casual sex, and you wouldn't have thanked me for it tomorrow.'

'Because you think I'm on the rebound?' Suddenly self-conscious of her nakedness, when he hadn't even undressed beyond his gaping shirt, she sat up to retrieve her clothes. 'I'm not—I promise you,' she said resolutely, wriggling into her panties.

She was well and truly over Craig now. But perhaps there were other reasons for Leon not taking their lovemaking the whole way. Perhaps he was remaining faithful to someone, she thought uneasily. Someone who moved him to anger and roused his passions in a way she might never be able to do...

'Did you bring *her* here?' She couldn't look at him as she started fastening her blouse.

'Who?'

'The woman you won't talk about?' she said grievously.

He laughed—a deep, warm sound on the scented air, mingling with the drone of insects and the mellifluous birdsong. 'You really are a very imaginative little lady.'

'Not as imaginative as you, with your island mansion and your racehorses,' she accused, kneeling up to tug her shorts on.

'Uh-uh,' he denied. 'The racehorses were your idea,' he reminded her with a hint of humour in his eyes, although the slashes of colour across his cheeks were evidence of the passion that still rode him. 'And now I really think it's time that we started back.'

'I'm being serious,' she stressed, wishing he wouldn't continue to evade the issue, wondering if he was only doing it because there really was someone else.

'So am I,' he breathed heavily, getting up and pulling her with him, and this time his determination brooked no resistance.

CHAPTER SEVEN

LOOKING BACK, LEONIDAS wasn't sure how he had managed to stop himself making love to Kayla that afternoon. Heaven knew he had wanted to. A fact not made any easier by the knowledge of how much she had wanted him, too. But there were ethics to be observed, and there was no way that he could have taken all she had been offering when he wasn't being straight with her. It had all boiled down to guilt, he decided shamefully. Guilt because he wasn't telling her the truth.

But the truth was that he had come here to be alone. Not to indulge in any social or sexual entanglements with a girl who could carry him along with her ridiculous yet infectious sense of make-believe. Well, make-believe to *her,* at any rate. Because he could afford that island, had it been for sale—and a dozen like it, did she but know it. But it seemed like a life-time since he had indulged in that childish game, and he had found it oddly refreshing.

In the world he moved in there was no room for fantasising or dreaming. Only for cold hard facts and figures. Securing deals. That was living the dream. Or so he had thought.

Until now, though, he hadn't begun to realise how deeply and for how long his dreams had been buried. Firstly by his father, and then more recently beneath the weight of his own responsibilities. He had been so busy making money—reaping the benefits of all he had worked for during the past decade or more—that he hadn't taken the time even to question where those dreams had gone. And now this little nobody had come along, making him question his values. He was annoyed with himself for allowing her to get under his skin to such a degree. But that didn't change the fact that he wanted her more than he had wanted any woman in a long time—much less one who would have been in her own marriage bed right now if things had worked out as they should have.

A hard possessiveness kicked in as he imagined her naked with the faceless, double-crossing character who had betrayed her—he could only temper his indignation at the thought of the two of them together by imagining himself in Kayla's bed. And that brought other problems as his body hardened in response to imagining her sobs of pure pleasure directed at him and him alone as he made himself master of her body.

But things couldn't go on as they were. He was either going to have to come clean at some stage, he decided grimly, or end their relationship before it went any further. Neither prospect filled him with any pleasure.

He knew exactly what she thought about company men, and after the experience she had had with that lowest of the low fiancé of hers—not to mention her father—she'd be blameless for thinking he was no better. Yet staying away from her wasn't an option he welcomed either. He was just relieved that his secretary had e-mailed him with some plans that needed his urgent attention, so that for today at least he didn't have to think about how he could come clean with Kayla. However he chose to tell her, he knew she wasn't going to welcome finding out...

When Leon didn't put in an appearance that day, and didn't come down the next morning, Kayla jumped at Philomena's suggestion that she drive up to the farmhouse with some bread Philomena had just baked.

She'd scarcely given a thought to her ex since Leon had taken her over to that island, she realised, noticing how it seemed to shimmer in the morning sun. She couldn't help marvelling at the difference between the two men and wondering what she had ever seen in Craig.

Had her love for him been so shallow that the first man who came along could make her forget him and the hurt he had caused her so completely? But then Leon wasn't just any man, she reminded herself, with a sudden tightening of her breasts and that familiar stirring of heat at the very heart of her femininity. He made her feel like no other man had ever made her feel.

A throbbing excitement leaped along her veins at the memory of their afternoon on that islet, when he had driven her crazy for him, playing with her like a love-toy, winding her up only to let her run wild with delirious sensation as he had taken her to heights her mental and physical being had never scaled before.

She had wanted him so much! And it had been patently obvious that he wanted her. So why hadn't he taken their lovemaking to its ultimate conclusion? Was it because there was someone else? But he had called her imaginative when she had broached the subject with him, so perhaps it was simply that he didn't think she was ready to embark on a relationship with him—in which case, she decided with a delicious little shiver, it was up to her to show him that she was.

When she arrived at the farmhouse her heart gave a little leap when she saw the truck parked outside.

So he was in! She wondered if she was being too presumptuous in coming. Supposing he didn't want to see her? Or she'd disappointed him in some way?

Feeling queasy in the stomach just from entertaining that possibility, she tripped lightly round to the glass-paned peeling doors at the back of the house. One creaked open at her less than confident knock.

When she called out there was no reply, and so gingerly she moved inside, still calling his name. He wasn't in the sitting room, and nor did he emerge from the kitchen when she moved enquiringly towards it.

Perhaps he'd gone for a walk, she mused, standing there in the hall, wondering what to do.

About to take a look outside, she heard a sudden thud on the boarded floor above. She dumped her carrier bag with the bread she'd brought on an old pine chest just inside the door.

'Leon?' she called out, and when there was still no response, unthinkingly she raced up the stairs.

His bedroom was in shadow, with semi-closed shutters, but a quick glance towards the bed revealed him lying there on his back, still drugged from sleep, groping blindly for something on the floor on the other side of the bed.

Kayla moved over and, picking up a chunky little clock, replaced it on the cabinet beside the bedside lamp.

'Are you all right?' she asked, knowing what an early bird he usually was. It was already after ten and she'd obviously woken him, she realised, guessing he'd reached for the clock and knocked it over when he'd heard her calling him.

'I must have crashed out,' he mumbled, drawing an arm across his forehead. His eyes were heavy with sleep and his hair was dishevelled and, like his unshaven jaw, satanically dark. 'What are you doing here?'

'I brought you some bread. I thought you were out, but the door was open,' Kayla responded with a nervous gesture of her hand. She was aware that she was gabbling, but it was difficult to do anything else when faced with the sight of his bronzed body, naked save for the fine sheet that barely covered his hips and certainly left nothing to the imagination. 'Aren't you pleased to see me?'

'What do you think?' he drawled, in a voice thickened by sleep and by the involuntary response of his anatomy.

Heated colour touched Kayla's cheeks and yet she couldn't keep her gaze from straying to his potent virility. Driven by something more powerful than her own reasoning, she dropped down onto the bed.

'I think you must be overjoyed,' she whispered, touching kisses to the warm, undulating muscles of his chest, using the pale, sensuous fountain of her hair to caress him as her lips moved over the tautened flesh of his tight lean waist and her hands dealt tremblingly with the sheet.

He let out a deep shuddering gasp of anticipation. 'Why did you come?' he asked heavily.

'I just thought that one good turn deserved another,' Kayla whispered, feathering kisses over his tightly muscled abdomen. She didn't know where she was finding the courage to seduce him like this. She only knew by instinct alone that he was a man who liked his women confident and worldly, not wimpish and nursing the old wounds of a previous relationship.

'Close your eyes,' she ordered softly, getting up.

Leonidas's heart seemed to stop, and then thundered into life when she came back to the bed and straddled him. She was wearing a white top with a little red skirt that swirled about her thighs, and his mind whirled in a vortex of conflicting thoughts as he realised that she had obviously removed what she had been wearing underneath.

'Kayla. Stop this...' He wasn't sure whether he'd spoken the words or whether they were just buzzing feverishly through his brain.

'Why? Is it too early for you?' Kayla teased, excitement driving her even as her mind raced with interminable doubts.

Was she carrying things too far? Didn't he like a woman taking the initiative? He was more down to earth and unfettered by convention than any man she had ever met. He didn't want a woman who was anything but what *he* was. Not someone weighed down with emotional baggage; someone who didn't know her own mind.

Beneath her Leonidas shivered as he felt her sliding down his body, the moist heat of her searing his skin like a molten poultice.

'Dear—!' He swallowed the profanity, his breathing laboured, his body on fire. He had to stop this! But as her soft mouth took possession of him his senses spun into chaos.

He had never felt so powerless, and yet at the same time so shamelessly empowered. His body was a temple of pleasure at which this amazing woman was worshipping.

He felt his size increase and harden like burning, quivering steel. His body was taut as a bow, holding back the flaming arrow it needed to release before it consumed him in its raging inferno.

He fought to contain it, the struggle almost overwhelming him. And just when he thought he had won the battle she slid along his length, positioning herself above him to take him into her.

He tried to pull back, but he was powerless to do anything but push against her slick hot wetness, groaning in defeat as he allowed himself the freedom to let her do whatever she would.

Looking down at him, Kayla registered the rapturous agony on his face, that line of pained pleasure between his closed lids. It lent him a vulnerability she hadn't seen before—one that called to everything in her that was soft and feminine and tender—and yet she felt powerful too. She was in control and glorying in it, dominating the pace and the depth and the rhythm. That was until she heard the guttural masculine groan when he suddenly clamped his hands over her hips and pushed harder and more determinedly into her.

The depth of penetration dragged a small cry of ecstasy

from her lips. She felt the explosion of his seed deep within her and started to climax almost instantaneously.

It was the most fulfilling experience of her life.

They were both breathing heavily when she collapsed, wet and gasping, against the warm damp cushion of his chest, and then he was rolling her round so that she was lying pressed close to his side.

'What was all that about?' he quizzed, as soon as he could speak again. His breathing was still heavy and laboured.

Kayla wasn't sure whether there was disapproval in his husky tones. 'Didn't you like it?' she enquired, almost diffidently.

'Of *course* I liked it!' he shot back, his voice incredulous. 'But right now I'm not sure whether to applaud you for your resourcefulness or to paddle that pretty bare bottom of yours and send you packing back to Philomena's.'

'Why?' An uneasy line pleated Kayla's brows as she lay facing him with her hair wildly dishevelled. 'Do Greek men always have to be the dominant partner?' She was beginning to feel hurt and embarrassed.

'No. But whoever chooses to be should take responsibility for what they're doing. Is there any chance that you could be pregnant after that delightful little escapade?'

'Of course not! I'm not that stupid!' she snapped, trying to sit up and failing when he kept her anchored to his side. She didn't feel it was necessary to add that she was taking the pill. She had tried to come off it after her break-up with Craig, but her periods had gone so haywire that her doctor had suggested it might be best for her to keep taking it until her emotions were on a more even keel.

'So what happens now?' Leonidas asked, his breath seeming to shiver through his lungs.

'What do you mean?' Blue eyes searched the midnight-darkness of his for some sign of tenderness—the tenderness that had been stirred in her by seeing him so vulnerable while she had been making love to him—but there was none.

'We've just become lovers and you don't even know who I am.' Something he was going to have to rectify—and as soon as possible, he realised, floundering. It was a feeling that was alien to Leonidas Vassalio.

'Yes, I do. Or as much as I need to,' she murmured, feeling his powerful body tense as she applied a trail of butterfly kisses over the slick warmth of his heavily contoured chest.

'I'm trying to be serious, Kayla.'

'Why?' she breathed against the velvety texture of his skin, delighting in the way his breathing was growing more and more ragged from her kisses.

But as her fingers trailed teasingly along the inside of one powerful thigh his hand suddenly clamped down on hers, resisting the temptation to let it wander.

'Because I don't believe you're the type of girl who does this without knowing what sort of man she's getting herself involved with and without demanding some degree of emotional commitment.'

And he wasn't offering any. She couldn't understand why telling herself that caused her spirits to plummet the way they did.

'I'm not demanding anything,' she uttered, knowing that the only way to save face was to get the hell out of there. 'And I'm sorry if I offended you!'

Scrambling out of bed, managing to shrug off the hand that tried to restrain her, she heard his urgent, 'Kayla! Kayla, come back here!'

She didn't, though. Her wounded pride propelled her into the adjoining bathroom, her mind focussed only on tidying herself up and getting out.

Stung with regret for upsetting her, momentarily Leonidas flopped back against the pillows. He hadn't intended her to take what he had said in the way she had. He had been trying to explain, in a roundabout way, what he should have told her long before, but procrastinating had only made an awkward situation far more difficult. After what had just happened he didn't know how or where to begin. He only knew that he couldn't let it happen again before he told her the truth—and all he'd managed to do was let her believe she'd offended him…

Offended him! He couldn't stop a lazy smile from touching his mouth.

She'd blown his mind, he thought, when she'd woken him up from a deep, deep sleep and dragged him straight into a cauldron of sizzling pleasure. He hadn't had time to catch his breath—let alone think! And he wouldn't have been caught so off-guard, still in bed, if he hadn't been up practically all night trying to get round one last hitch with those amended plans…

The plans!

He shot up in bed just as Kayla was emerging from the bathroom.

He'd left all his paperwork spread out over the kitchen table with his laptop—incriminating evidence of who he was! It had been late, and he'd obviously crashed out on the bed after he'd come up here and showered!

'Kayla, come here!'

The authority in his voice would have stopped a lesser mortal, but she ignored it as she moved around the bed, frowning, tugging at the draping folds of the bedlinen.

'Are you looking for something?' he asked, knowing he had to act quickly.

Kayla made a grab for the red briefs he was holding up, which only succeeded in bringing her across the bed and against his disturbingly masculine body as he withheld them, effectively securing what he wanted.

'You haven't offended me. You were wonderful,' he murmured, his warm breath a delicious sensuality against her hairline. 'Now, come back to bed. I want to talk to you,' he said, and just as an incentive slipped his hand under the tantalising little skirt and let his fingers play along the outer curve of one taut, silky buttock.

Kayla groaned, weakening beneath his mind-boggling powers of persuasion. She felt vulnerable and incredibly sexy with no panties on, but she despaired at herself too, at how easily and effortlessly he could bend her to his will.

Whatever he had to say, she had the strongest suspicion that she wasn't going to like it. He didn't want commitment. Of course he didn't. And anyway she wasn't ready for another serious relationship yet. Yet neither was she ready to let him have it all his own way.

Catching him in an unguarded moment, reaching round to adjust the pillows behind them, she managed to wriggle out of his arms and snatch her underwear from his grasp, saying, 'I can talk better over a cup of coffee,' as she ran giggling out of the room.

'Kayla, come here!'

She was in the hall, pulling her panties back on, when he raced down the stairs, still fastening his robe, but darted off again laughingly as soon as she saw him coming.

'Will you just stand still and let me talk to you?' he called after her as she grabbed the carrier bag she'd left on the chest and headed for the kitchen. He had to break it to her gently. She'd be angry, it was true, but not as angry as she would be finding it out for herself.

'Go and sit down,' he commanded softly when she turned around. He was pointing to the sitting room. 'I will make the coffee.'

'Fine,' she agreed airily, pivoting away again, 'but I'll keep you company while you're doing it.'

'In the sitting room,' he breathed, in one last attempt to prevent her from seeing all his papers.

She turned in the kitchen doorway, her chin lifting in playful challenge. 'And since when did you suddenly start issuing so many orders?'

'Since I thought you were running out on me without finishing what you started.' One purposeful stride brought him over to her, his mouth a sensuous curve. But inside he was a heaving mass of turmoil.

He had to keep her out of the kitchen—stop her going in there before he had a chance to explain. He cast a surreptitious glance over her shoulder at the table in the centre of the room, heaving with incriminating evidence. He should have told her before. Should have kept her in bed...

'Kayla...'

The way he spoke her name never failed to turn Kayla's bones to jelly.

'Say it again,' she murmured huskily.

'What?' He looked tense, she thought, and mystified too.

'The way you say my name.'

'Kay-lah.'

She groaned her satisfaction and nestled against his chest above the gaping V of his dark satin robe. His skin smelled of the lingering traces of shower gel overlaid with a sensual musk.

'It should be censored—or at least X-rated,' she purred, with her tongue coming out in a provocative caress of that bared skin. It felt silky and tasted slightly salty...

Dear heaven!

Leonidas dragged in a breath, at a loss for the words he needed to say. He didn't know what powers this girl used to bewitch him, but even as he struggled to engage his normally incisive brain his body was responding with an urgent message of its own. It was taking all the mental strength he possessed not to rip down her panties, lay her down right here on the marble floor and enjoy the pleasure of having her beneath him, with himself in the driving seat this time. But he *had* to get her out of this room!

Swiftly his mouth swooped down over hers in a bid to distract her enough to manoeuvre her back into the hall. But he hadn't reckoned on how distracting her soft mouth would be to him.

Feeling her warm body against his, he could only respond to it in a kiss that went on and on, until they both came up for air and her head dropped back against his shoulder.

A few moments later, lifting her head, she murmured, 'What is that?'

Leonidas's spine pulled into a tight, tense rod. All he had succeeded in doing was turning her round, so that their positions were reversed, and she was now looking at the plans he'd set up on an easel. Allowing her to pull out of his arms, he felt the slaying blow of defeat.

Stepping down into the kitchen and dumping the bread bag on the table, bewildered, Kayla couldn't take it in. There were papers. Lots of papers. A laptop and a memo pad. And what she had thought were sketches looked like some sort of plan…

'What is it?' Her eyes skittered from the easel to the table and then the briefcase standing open on the floor. 'Is it something you're working on? Some building work…?'

Leonidas took a step towards her. 'Kayla, I can explain.'

'Explain?' She looked at him with confusion in her questioning blue eyes. 'Explain what?'

What was he doing with what looked like a whole set of plans for some development scheme? And a big, *big* development scheme by the look of it, she realised, when her gaze swept back over the table. Something proposed by the Vassalio Group—a big, *big* developer. She knew that much as her eyes took in the recognisable black and gold logo at the top of the plan she was staring at.

'I don't understand…' Why had his cosy farmhouse kitchen taken on the look of some executive's pad? Why was he looking so serious?

At that moment his cell phone rang from somewhere, shrilling across the sudden pregnant silence.

He pulled it out of the pocket of his robe, his eyes never leaving hers as he intoned incisively, 'Vassalio.' And then the penny dropped.

It was like an unashamed declaration directed specifically at her, Kayla thought, realising she had started to tremble.

Vassalio. Leon. Leonidas Vassalio. She knew the name. Of course she did! She'd heard it often enough in the media, seen the company logo on billboards and advertising for commercial developments, but she'd never taken much notice of it until now.

'You lied to me,' she accused in a virtual whisper when he cut the call short, feeling so shocked and betrayed that it was almost painful to breathe. 'You've lied to me ever since I got here!'

'Misled,' he corrected as he dropped his phone back into his pocket.

As if it made a difference!

'Most of it was what you assumed.'

'Hah! Like I assumed I knew who you were when we were doing what we were doing just now?'

Leonidas Vassalio. The man she had just taken advantage of—and who had let her!

'How could you do it?' She was referring to the sex, shame creeping over her, scorching her already flushed cheeks. What a laugh he must have been having—and at her expense!

'You didn't give me much choice,' he reminded her dryly.

'You could have stopped me any time you wanted to!'

'Really?' A sceptical eyebrow arched sharply. 'You think I'm that superhuman?' His mouth twisted in hard self-derision. 'Show me any red-blooded man you think would be capable of resisting being dragged out of sleep by a sex-goddess with no panties on.'

He made her feel cheap, and she wished fervently that she could turn back the clock instead of just standing there, hating herself for feeling the burn of desire stir deep down inside her where she was still moist and slightly tender from their spontaneous and unrestrained coming together.

'If it makes you feel any better,' he said, running fingers through his long dishevelled hair, 'I didn't intend for things to go as far as they did.'

'Oh, really?' she shot back, her features distorted with self-disgust. 'What a bonus it must have been for you when they did!'

'It wasn't like that.' He sounded defensive, exasperated—angry, almost. 'Why the hell do you think I didn't take things to their natural conclusion the other day on that island?'

'Because it was more fun stringing me along.'

'That isn't true.'

'Isn't it? And what about just now? You wouldn't have thought twice about doing it again.'

'That wasn't my motive,' he stated decisively. 'I was trying to coax you into the sitting room so that I could break it to you gently who I am without it flaring up into the mess we find ourselves in now.'

'You mean instead of me finding out for myself what a rotten lying cheat you really are?'

'If that's what you want to believe,' he rasped, grim-mouthed. 'But it was never my intention to deceive you.'

'Why?' It was a small cry from somewhere deep down inside of her. 'Why should I believe anything you say?'

'All right. I deserve that,' he accepted with no loss of dig-

nity. He clearly wasn't a man to grovel or to eat humble pie.
'Look, I apologise for not telling you before now,' he continued. 'But I didn't know who you were when you first arrived.
For all I knew you were a snooping journalist on a mission for
a story, and I came here for some privacy. To get away from
all the media attention and publicity that's been dogging me
over this past year. I wasn't going to risk losing all that for a
girl I didn't even know. Apart from which, I found it rather
refreshing being with someone who wasn't playing up to me
because of the size of my bank balance.'

'So you used me!' Kayla breathed. 'Just for your own
amusement.'

'That isn't what I'm saying. But if you want to think that,
then there's nothing I can do to stop you.'

'You could have trusted me enough to tell me the truth!'

He made a self-deprecating sound down his nostrils. 'A
man in my position can't afford to trust.'

'Which just goes to show the type of people you mix with,'
she tossed back, refusing to give any quarter. He had lied to
her. Deceived her. And, though it was killing her to acknowledge it, that made him no better than Craig.

'I can't argue with that,' Leonidas conceded. 'But I don't
suppose it would make any difference to tell you that you don't
fall into their category.'

'You mean because none of the others have been such a
push-over as I've been?' Near to tears, it came out almost on
a sob, but there was no way in a million years that she was
going to let him see that. Forcing aggression into her voice,
she uttered, 'A builder. Hah! You must have been laughing up
your exclusive designer sleeve!'

Ignoring that last remark, he said, 'That was your interpretation when I said I was in construction—which, as you
can see…' he gestured to the plans on the easel, the others on
the table '…I *am*.'

'And you let me think it! That's worse than lying! That's…'

'Kayla, stop it!' He made a calming gesture with his hands. 'I can understand how you must feel.'

'Can you?' Her eyes were dark and tortured, and her mouth was twisted in wounded accusation. No wonder he'd got nasty about her taking photographs of him in the beginning!

'I've said I'm sorry, haven't I?'

'And you think that makes it all right? An apology from the great Leonidas Vassalio!' Her bitter little laugh made him visibly wince.

'No, it doesn't make it all right.' Beneath the robe his tanned chest fell in hopeless frustration. He hadn't intended it to sound as dismissive as it had come out. 'I was constantly aware that I was going to have to tell you sooner or later.'

'Oh, really?' Kayla shot him a look of pure incredulity. 'Like when, exactly? After we'd had sex again?'

'Kayla, stop it!' He was moving towards her, but she backed away.

'So how did you imagine I'd respond?' She'd come up against a chair, the one where she'd sat that morning after he'd rescued her from the villa, but she didn't want to think about that now. 'By being grateful to you?'

'Which is exactly why I've never said anything,' Leonidas admitted raggedly.

'Because it would have spoilt your fun!'

'Because I didn't want to hurt you.'

'Oh, you wouldn't have hurt me, Leon!' Hadn't she been hardened by Craig? And before that her father? she reflected bitterly, before tagging on with painful cynicism, 'I'm sorry. *Is* it Leon? Or should that be Leonidas now?'

The emphatic distaste she placed on the name everyone knew him by made him flinch. But he couldn't blame her, he thought. He had misled her, and then been stupid enough to imagine he might be let off lightly when he came clean and admitted it. But she had been hurt too deeply before and he should have known better, he realised. It was crass of him to have thought she would be anything but angry and bitter, especially after finding out in the way she had.

'You wouldn't have hurt me, Leonidas,' she reiterated, in an attempt to ease the pain of another betrayal—and by a man she had believed was different from men like Craig and her father and all the others. A construction worker who'd come here to fish and sketch and live rough for a while because he valued his solitude and his privacy. Except all the time she'd been naïve enough to imagine he'd been sketching he'd been controlling his multi-billion-pound empire! 'I just wouldn't have touched you with a bargepole.'

But she had, she thought bitterly, remembering just how eagerly she had touched him—with her mouth and her hands and her whole reckless and stupidly trusting body. Tears stung her eyes as she thanked her lucky stars that she hadn't quite succeeded in giving him her heart as well.

'Kayla...' He made another move towards her, but she backed away again, knocking the chair into the table this time and pushing some of his papers askew. 'I'm still the same person I was when you were driving me wild for you upstairs.'

'No, you're not! You're as bad as every other *company man*—' she breathed it with venom '—I've ever met. Only worse. Because you've arrived! And to think I was trying to suggest things you could do to make life better for yourself!' She couldn't believe she could have been so stupid. Such an unbelievable fool!

'Which I found very endearing,' he added earnestly.

'Don't touch me!' She made a small panicked sound as he took another step towards her, the thought of what his lips and hands could do to her exciting her in a way that made her feel sick with herself. 'You know exactly what I think about men like you!'

'Then we've both been misguided,' he concluded, his shoulders drooping, suddenly seeming to give up trying to placate her. 'You for taking everything at face value, and I for imagining I could get away with letting you. I just wanted to believe that for a while at least my name and my money weren't the most important things about me.'

There was something in his voice that had her silently querying the inscrutable emotion in that strong, rugged face. 'Is that supposed to make me feel bad?' she challenged. 'Because it doesn't.'

'No. I've already told you,' he persisted. 'It wasn't my intention to hurt you, or to let things go as far as they did.'

'And what about Philomena?' Her gaze had fallen to the bag with the loaf the woman had lovingly baked for him. 'Does *she* know?' she threw at him, hurting, remembering how eagerly she had driven up here to see him, with nothing but making him want her on her mind. 'Does she know what a fool you've been taking me for? Or didn't you risk telling her?'

Thick black lashes came down over his incredibly dark eyes. 'I've never taken you for a fool,' he stated, exhaling deeply. 'As for Philomena...she knows I had my reasons.'

'And she went along with them?' She couldn't believe that of the gentle yet down-to-earth Philomena.

'What do you think?' he said.

She remembered the argument that had ensued the day he'd first taken her down to the cottage, the remonstrations by Philomena since, which seemed to leave him no more than mildly amused.

'You're despicable,' she breathed, as a fragment of memory tugged at her consciousness in relation to something he had said about having had a trying year.

Unscrupulous. Ruthless. Riding roughshod over people. Those were words she had heard in connection with the name Leonidas Vassalio. And then she remembered. It was that stun-

ning American model turned actress—Esmeralda Leigh. She'd
publicly named him as having fathered her child. It was she
who had called him unscrupulous, when he had challenged
the proof of his paternity—though there had been no close-
up photograph of him in the article Kayla remembered reading. Just a long shot of him leaving his office, looking rather
different from how he looked now, which had been inset in a
full-colour spread of Esmeralda lounging in the drawing room
of her exquisitely and expensively furnished Mayfair home.

'Esmeralda was right. You *are* unscrupulous!'

'And if you had read the outcome of that fiasco you would
have the sense to realise that anything the woman says is fab-
ricated. Her claims were proven to be totally untrue.'

'Well, she wasn't the only one who was good at lying, was
she?' Kayla reminded him grievously, realising now what he'd
meant that day when he'd referred to a petition being slapped
on him. 'Was it because of her that you decided to get your
own back when you met me? Were you afraid if I knew who
you were I might try and get pregnant so I could use you as
a ticket to an easy life? Well, stuff your money! And stuff
you! Not everyone puts as much value on money as on truth
and integrity! I might not be in your league when it comes to
material wealth, but at least I can hold my head up and know
that what you see is what you get. That everything about me is
real. You wouldn't understand that if it was scrawled all over
one of your concrete eyesores, and as far as I'm concerned,
Mr Vassalio, I never want to see you again!'

CHAPTER EIGHT

'I HAD HOPED your time in Greece would make you feel better,' remarked Yasmin Young, an abrupt and artificially blonde forty-five-year-old to Kayla, who had just come downstairs and declined her mother's offer to cook her breakfast. 'But ever since you've been back you haven't eaten properly. You're too thin. And you've been going around like someone who's lost a shilling and found sixpence. I was right when I said you were unwise, cutting your holiday short like that. I've told you before,' she reiterated, going over what seemed to Kayla like a mantra from her mother these days. 'He isn't worth wasting any more time over, you know. None of them are.'

She was talking about Craig. Kayla hadn't told her mother anything about meeting anyone while she had been away. But the maternal advice applied equally to how she was feeling about Leonidas—and had been ever since she'd returned to the UK on that wet and windy mid-May morning, hurting and feeling so gullible and betrayed. And all because she had been stupid enough to get herself emotionally involved with a man right out of the same mould as Craig, her father and all the others. Because she *had*, Kayla thought, berating herself—even if she had only realised it when it was too late.

'I know,' she responded now, even managing to feign a smile as she poured herself a hasty cup of coffee. She shook her head at her mother's concerned suggestion that she should at least try and eat some toast.

'I'd better go or I'll be late,' she said, rushing out of the door without bothering to finish her coffee.

At least she wasn't out of work and dependent upon her mother to help support her, she thought in an attempt to brighten herself up as she sat in heavy traffic on her way to work. At least she still had a job. And it promised to be a potentially permanent one if Josh and Lorna managed to land the huge contract they had been hoping to secure for the past few weeks.

It would be the break they needed and they were both beside themselves with excitement —particularly as their potential client was Havens Exclusive, a company that provided luxury homes and apartments for the higher end of the market. Kayla was keeping her fingers crossed for them both.

Without her having to worry about things like whether Kendon Interiors would still be trading this time next year, Lorna might have a chance with her pregnancy this time, she thought, hoping fervently that her friend would be able to carry this baby to full term. And being busy again could only be good for *her* too, Kayla decided, because apart from the satisfaction of being able to stay in a job she enjoyed, it helped keep her mind off Leonidas.

She hadn't heard from him since that morning she had stormed out of the farmhouse. Not that she'd wanted to, or even imagined that she would. He didn't know where to find her, for a start.

She'd wasted no time in leaving the island after driving back to Philomena's that last morning, having discovered that there was a ferry leaving that day.

'Leon…he good man,' Philomena, having guessed what had happened, had tried to tell her gently. He could act stupidly sometimes. Like most men! At least that was what the woman had seemed to be saying with her gestures and a world-weary rolling of her eyes.

Well, he hadn't shown any evidence of his virtuous qualities with *her!* Kayla seethed, still hurting from the way he had deceived her, even though it was more than six weeks on. She tried not to think about how he had rescued her that night in the storm and helped her with the clean-up operation the following day. Nor did she want to think about the affection he'd shown towards Philomena. Remembering just filled her with longing, and with such an aching regret that things couldn't have been different that at times it almost took her breath away. He was a rat when all was said and done. She didn't need him or want him! And she certainly never intended to be so taken in by anyone again! So why did she spend every waking moment trying not to think about him? Why did the thought of never seeing him again leave her feeling so down and depressed?

Fortunately the buzz around the office kept any further disturbing introspection at bay, since one of Havens' senior management team was coming in to meet with Josh and Lorna the following day.

'They've already been through our history and our previous trading figures, and now I think they just want to give us the once-over,' Lorna remarked anxiously. Her mid-length bobbed hair was coming out of the clips she had tried to fasten it with as she despaired of her devoted but untidy husband's muddle of an office. Like Kayla, she was blonde and petite—apart from her burgeoning middle—which was why they had often been taken for sisters, Kayla reflected fondly, knowing she couldn't have cared more for Lorna if she *had* been her sibling.

Consequently, having worked late to help tidy up Josh's office and prepare the conference room for what they hoped

would be the final meeting, Kayla was getting ready to go
home when the telephone rang in her office.

'Hello, Kayla.'

She almost froze, recognising Leonidas Vassalio's deeply
accented voice at the other end of the line.

'How did you find me?' Stupid question. A man with his
money and influence would have ways and means, she realised, her pulses leaping. Or had she told him where she
worked? She couldn't even think clearly enough to remember.

'How have you been?'

She didn't answer but, aware that Josh and Lorna were still
around somewhere in the building, moved over and closed
the door. She'd been too hurt and ashamed of herself even to
tell them that she had met someone in Greece, and she didn't
want them finding out about it now.

'What do you want?'

'I'd like to see you.'

'Why?' she asked, breathless from the dark and sick responses suddenly surging through her.

'I would have thought that was obvious after the way you
ran out on me that day,' he remarked dryly. 'So suddenly.
Without a word.'

'What did you expect me to do?' she asked pithily, in spite
of the way her heart was thudding. 'Stick around so you could
make an even bigger fool of me?'

'It was never my intention to make a fool of you.' His voice
had dropped a semi-tone to become almost caressing, reminding her of how treacherously it had excited her when she'd been
deceived into believing he was someone else.

'No?' It came out sounding more wounded than she'd intended. 'I'd like to know what you'd have done if you'd really
been trying.'

'Yes, well…'

His words tailed away on a heavily drawn breath while

Kayla pictured him, wherever he was, his hair wild and un-tamed, looking as casual as he sounded in his automatic as-sumption that she would even consider seeing him again.

'I know you're still angry....'

'Whatever gave you that idea?' It came out on a shrill lit-tle laugh.

'Have dinner with me,' he suggested, amazing Kayla with his unerring confidence.

Even so, her heart leaped traitorously in response.

'Why?'

In the moment's silence that followed she imagined a mas-culine eyebrow tweaking at her challenging response.

With more composure than she was managing to retain, he answered, 'Because we have things to discuss.'

'Oh, really? Like what?' She could hear Lorna and Josh still working in the conference room above—moving chairs, closing windows for the night—as she pushed her loose hair behind an ear with a shaky hand. 'Like why you made a com-plete idiot out of me in Greece? Like why you pretended to be somebody you weren't when I was in trouble and needed help? And why you kept pretending even when I was taken in by you and offered you suggestions of what you could do with your life to improve your lot? Or is it the other thing you want to apologise for? For having sex with me when you were lying through your teeth and thinking I'd simply forgive you if I found out? Because *you're* the idiot if you think I'd go anywhere and discuss anything with you after what you did.'

'And that's all you have to say?' His voice was toneless now, devoid of any emotion.

'Why? Do you really want to hear some more?' She could feel the bite of tears behind her eyes but she willed them back. She couldn't cry. Couldn't let him hear how brutally he had hurt her and make an even bigger fool of herself into the bar-gain. 'Because there's a whole barrelful where that came from!' Resentment defended her from the pain he had inflicted upon her, the hurt to her pride, her trust and her emotions.

'I think I get the message,' he rasped under his breath. 'As the saying goes, see you around.'

He had rung off before she could even regain her wits.

Kayla was at the office early the following morning, to prepare the conference room for the important meeting. She had slept very little for thinking about Leonidas, but she hid her tiredness behind a bright façade as she put out pens and paper, tumblers and a jug of water, arranged fresh flowers for the centre of the long table and generally helped Lorna to stay calm.

Her friend was flitting around in a state of anxious excitement. Worried for her, Kayla insisted that she sat down and took a few deep breaths before the man from Havens arrived.

'Supposing after all this they don't think we're solid enough and change their mind about giving us their business?' Lorna said worriedly. 'Or they think we don't have enough expertise and decide to go with a company that's bigger and better?'

'Bigger, maybe—but not better,' Kayla assured her, meaning it. 'Anyway, you said yourself the contract's as good as in the bag. This meeting's only a formality, so stop worrying,' she advised gently. But secretly she *was* concerned.

Lorna was nearly six months pregnant now, and Kayla knew how much this coming baby meant to her and Josh. Lorna had to stay free from stress if this pregnancy wasn't to end in the same traumatic way as her previous two pregnancies had, and getting overwrought about anything was bad news.

Havens had said that they might require some extra financial information, and Kayla was pleased, therefore, that as their bookkeeper she had been asked to attend the meeting. It would help take the pressure off Lorna.

'You'll also serve as our charm offensive,' Josh had joked. Consequently, when he rang down to her office at ten o'clock sharp and asked her to join them, Kayla slipped her charcoal-grey tailored suit jacket on over her sleeveless blue blouse and, checking the French pleat she'd carefully styled her hair in that morning, took the lift to the first floor, prepared to charm the Havens man for all she was worth.

'Come in, Kayla.' A quiet-voiced Josh—mousy beard neatly trimmed and looking unusually smart today in a jacket and tie—was standing at the top of the table. Lorna was sitting on his right. But it was the man who had been sitting opposite her and was now getting to his feet that made Kayla feel she'd suddenly been gripped by some hideous hallucination. Until Josh said, 'Kayla, this is Mr Vassalio. Mr Vassalio, this is our invaluable bookkeeper, Kayla Young.'

She wasn't sure how she managed to walk around the table to take the hand Leonidas was holding out to her. She felt stiff-backed and winded, and in the four-inch heels she hadn't given a second thought to wearing that morning, suddenly in danger of over-balancing.

'Miss Young.'

She didn't know what automatic response gave her the emotional strength to take his hand in the outward appearance of a formal handshake, or whether he could feel the way her fingers were trembling as he held them in his warm palm a fraction of a second too long.

'Mr Vassalio.' It came out as a croak from between lips that felt as dry as kindling, while flames seemed to be leaping through her blood—not just from the shock of his being there, but from his devastating appearance too.

Since she had last seen him he seemed to have changed his whole persona. The designer stubble was gone, as was the long, unruly hair. Now expertly cut, the jet-black layers waved thickly against a pristine white collar, although the mid-grey suit he wore, with its fine tailoring, could do nothing to tame the restless animal energy of the man beneath.

Clean-shaven, he looked harder—and even more dynamic, if that were possible. The evidence of the high-octane lifestyle he had disguised so well on the island was emblazoned on every hand-sewn stitch of his designer clothes. She had often thought him totally out of place in the run-down environs of the farmhouse. Today he was exactly where he belonged. Here, in the halls of business, he cut a figure of formidable power in his dress, his manner, and in the overwhelming authority he exuded.

Kayla couldn't think, paralysed by the dark penetration of his gaze and the mockery touching his stupendous mouth. When she did eventually manage to drag her gaze from his it was with a confused look at Josh, and she blurted out the first thing that came into her head.

'Not Mr Woods…?'

It was the wrong thing to say, and she realised it when she saw the dismayed look on Lorna's tense and nervous features. But it was with a Mr Woods that the appointment had been made.

'Woods couldn't make it.'

Leonidas's response drifted down to Kayla as though through a thick fog. She was hot and perspiring. Her clothes, so fresh and cool only minutes before, now seemed to be sticking to her.

'Mr Vassalio's the main man. Havens Exclusive is one of the companies within his group. He wanted to see us for himself,' Lorna told her. 'Isn't that right, Mr Vassalio?'

'Leonidas, please.' The smile he gave Lorna could have melted a polar ice-cap, and Kayla saw her friend visibly relax.

'Leonidas.' Smiling up into the perfect symmetry of his dark masculine features, Lorna repeated the name as if it was some sort of coveted trophy. She was positively glowing in the man's effortless charm, Kayla realised, wondering what her friend would say if she told her what a cheat he was. What a liar!

'Perhaps Miss Young would sit here...' he was already pulling out the chair beside his '...and fill me in on anything I might need to know.'

It was all purely a formality. Like his handshake, Kayla thought with a little shiver. She knew he would already have had Havens suss out their financial credibility and their ability to meet their commitments before he'd let one of his companies consider investing a penny.

But was this just a bizarre coincidence? Or had he specifically arranged for Havens to take advantage of Josh and Lorna's expertise, armed with the knowledge that she, Kayla, worked at Kendon Interiors? Had he known when he'd telephoned her last night that he'd be coming here today? If so, why hadn't he said so? Or had his intention been to give her the shock of her life? To get his own back for refusing to have dinner with him? Because if it had, he had succeeded. And how!

She couldn't stop her eyes from straying to him as he began talking business with Josh and Lorna. She couldn't help noticing how richly his hair gleamed in the light of the window behind him. Nor could she keep her ears from tuning in to the resonant tones of his voice, any more than she could stop the subtle spice of his aftershave lotion acting on her nostrils like some exotic aphrodisiac.

His hands were a magnet for her guarded yet brooding gaze—long, tapered hands that had made her cry out with their tender and manipulative skill. The dark silky hairs that peeped out from under an immaculate shirt cuff were an all too painful reminder of his dark and dangerous virility.

He had been stupendous before. Now he was no less than sensational! A man who would turn heads with his dynamism and that air of unspoken authority. A man who was wealthy and ruthless and powerful. She'd known that before she'd left the island. But this man she didn't know at all.

Seeing him in full corporate action, power-dressed and dominating everyone else in the room, she couldn't believe that this was the man she had taken the initiative with and pleasured so uninhibitedly that last morning, and it left her feeling as mortified as if she had tied him up first and chained him to the bed.

Except that this man could never be chained or dominated...

Heat suffusing her body, she looked up and met his eyes just as he was finishing saying something to Josh about the FT Index. From the smouldering burn of his gaze as it dropped to her fine blouse she knew he had guessed what she was remembering, and from the discreet curve of his mouth she knew, with shaming certainty, that he was remembering it too.

She was glad when the meeting was over, the terms of the contract finalised, and he was preparing to leave. Being polite and courteous for Josh and Lorna's sakes was beginning to tell on her nerves.

At least he would go now, she thought. And hopefully after today, after he gave Havens the go-ahead to start the process for the contract rolling, she would never have to see him again. She didn't know why that prospect failed to satisfy her as it should. In fact it left her surprisingly down-spirited.

She just wanted to get back to her office. Get stuck into spreadsheets and invoices and try to forget that Leonidas Vassalio had ever existed.

He was talking to Lorna about the baby, asking her when it was due. Seeing she was no longer needed, Kayla seized the opportunity to excuse herself, and was heading for the door when she heard deep Greek tones request, 'Could I presume upon you, Josh, to spare your Miss Young for a little while longer? There are one or two things I need to run through with her, if she'll be good enough to walk with me back to my car.'

Go to hell! Kayla wanted to toss back as she pivoted round. But of course she had to be on her best behaviour for her friends' sake. There was no way she was going to let them down.

'Take all the time you need,' she heard Josh saying amiably, unaware of the conflict going on inside her.

Leonidas was holding the door wide for her, his arm outstretched so that she had to duck underneath it, and her startling response to his raw and overpowering masculinity made her voice falter even as she sniped in a hostile whisper, 'Does everybody *always* jump over themselves to please you?' She was breathing shallowly, trying to shrug off her involuntary reaction to him, how the heady, tantalising scent of him affected her.

'Not everybody.' Amusement laced his tones, but there was something about the look he gave her which excited her even as she rebelled against the way it seemed to promise, *but you will*.

'Why didn't you tell me yesterday?' she remonstrated as soon as they were in the corridor of the modern office unit, keeping her attention on a large potted fern that was benefiting from the light from the wide windows.

'Tell you what?'

As if he didn't know!

'That you were coming here today.' She was acutely aware of him walking beside her.

'You didn't give me the chance.'

'Really?' Her head swivelled round from the view across the landscaped business park. 'I don't seem to recall you trying to bring it into the conversation.'

'For what other reason were you imagining I wanted to take you to dinner?'

Colour burned her cheeks at the hard edge to his voice. He was an executive now, Kendon Interiors' biggest client—or would be when that contract was signed—and with that remark he was reminding her of it in no uncertain terms.

'Then you should have made your motives more obvious.'

'Like you're doing now, in bringing me along here instead of using the lift?'

'I always prefer to use the stairs.'

'As you did on your way up?'

Of course, Kayla thought, realising that she had walked right into that one. She should have known that his keen brain would have been attuned to every sound that had heralded her approach. He would have heard the ping of the lift and the door gliding open only seconds before she had come into the room.

'What's wrong, Miss Young?' His deliberate use of her surname seemed mockingly incongruous with the electricity that was crackling between them. Even the light click of her heels against the comparatively sturdy tap of his over the polished floor seemed to stress the glaring differences in their sexualities. 'Don't you want to chance the two of us being alone together in a lift?'

Kayla's heart seemed to stop when he opened the glass fire door onto the next level and her jacket brushed his sleeve as he let her through.

'Why are you flattering yourself that I'd let that bother me?'

'Because if you could read my mind, Miss Young, you'd know that I have the strongest urge right now to rip that prim little suit off your body, followed by your blouse and then your—'

'Do you mind?' Her heels clicked more agitatedly at all he was suggesting as they came down onto the ground floor. From behind her desk the young receptionist smiled at them as they passed, her eyes feasting appreciatively on Leonidas.

'Modesty, Miss Young?' Though his mouth was twitching

at the corners, he kept his eyes on the external glass doors, which slid open to admit them into the morning sunshine. 'I hadn't noticed any of that when you were bouncing up and down on my bed.'

'Stop it!'

'Why? Can you dismiss it that easily?' he tossed at her, sounding more impatient now. 'Because I can't. Or are you saying you've forgotten just how much pleasure we gave each other?'

'I thought there was something you particularly wanted to discuss with me?' she parried huskily as her memory banks seemed to burst with erotic images of their time together before she'd found out who he was, that he had lied. 'If there isn't, then I'll get back to my office. I do have things to do, you know.'

'So do I.' His words came out on a harsh whisper.

They had reached his car: a sleek dark monster of a thing that put every other vehicle in the car park into the shade. This statement of his wealth and importance was something Kayla should have expected. Nevertheless, it still managed to knock her metaphorically sideways.

Stupidly, when he had phoned her last night, she had half envisaged him calling from his truck. But the truck belonged to Leon. Leon the drifter, who chopped logs and caught his own lunch and made sketches of her on a whim like some carefree, exciting bohemian. Or pretended to, she remembered, hurting. But this piece of expensive machinery belonged to Leonidas, Chief Executive of the Vassalio Group. International tycoon. The grandest player in the company man's arena.

'You look pale,' he commented in a surprisingly soft voice, his eyes tugging over features she knew looked sallow beneath her tan, taking in the dark smudges under her eyes. 'And thinner. Have you been overworking?'

'Not particularly,' she answered, and felt his dark scrutiny reawakening every aching hormone in her body. *I've just been lying awake at night, wondering how I'm ever going to forget you!*

His gaze had dropped to her middle and a cleft appeared between his eyes. 'You aren't…?' His meaning was obvious.

'Pregnant?' Kayla quipped curtly.

A furore of emotions seemed to cross his strong features and for one crazy moment she wished she could tell him that she was. Not because she wanted his baby. Or did she? The thought came like a bolt out of the blue. Surely she couldn't…?

She pushed the notion aside, refusing even to go there.

No. She would have just liked to see him rocked off his axis. Taken down a few degrees from his arrogant assumption that he could come here and—what? Take up from where they had left off? But she couldn't lie, couldn't deceive or hurt anyone the way he had deceived and hurt her.

'No, I'm not. Foolish though you might have thought me, I wasn't *that* foolish. Or mercenary,' she tagged on after a moment, thinking of the adverse publicity he had been subjected to by the famous Esmeralda. And to what end? To try and hang on to a man she couldn't bear to let go?

Was that relief in those spectacular eyes of his? She couldn't be sure. Nor could she understand why she felt such a bone-deep emptiness inside as she watched him open the passenger door of the car with one inconsequential movement of the remote control mechanism.

'Get in,' he commanded softly.

'No.' She was trembling from his nearness and everything his determination implied. But he was standing between her and the door he had just opened, and with the car in the next bay effectively blocking her route she couldn't escape without causing a scene.

'I said get in,' he rasped. 'Or, so help me, I'll start ripping off those clothes of yours here and now and make love to you in front of this whole blasted building! So what is it to be, Miss Young?'

She wanted to call his bluff. To resist getting into his car and falling victim to her own weakness for him, which would leave her hating herself for letting him use her as Craig had used her, for continuing to let him take her for a fool. She had a worrying suspicion, though, that if she did he would be quite capable of carrying out his threat. And so, reluctantly, with her heart beating wildly, she complied.

CHAPTER NINE

As Leonidas got in and started the car Kayla's nerves were stretched to breaking point.

Where was he taking her? As he put the car in motion she was so dangerously drawn to his dark magnetic presence that she didn't know how she would respond if he intended to do all he had threatened.

There were trees and bushes throughout the business park, separating units identical to the one that Kendon Interiors occupied. Kayla shot an anxiously challenging look at Leonidas as he brought the car around the trees to the last unit, which was still unoccupied, and cut the engine, leaving her tense and rigid at their screaming privacy.

'Tell me this is just some bizarre coincidence,' she implored him, her voice shaking. 'Your coming here today.'

'If you're asking if your friends approached my company with their business, then I'd like to say yes. But as it was my not being entirely honest with you that created a situation where I've had to virtually kidnap you to get you to talk to me, then I have to tell you that we brought our business to them. When you unintentionally made me aware of what Kendon Interiors were about it interested me, and I wanted to find out more. The company whose custom they lost because of the economic downturn are an old established company and well-known to me, and I knew they wouldn't have been dealing with your friends' business if what they had to offer wasn't a cut above the average in their field. Havens needed a new design company, and having had Kendon Interiors vetted over the past few weeks I liked what I saw and recommended them to my directors at Havens.'

'And you knew I'd still be working for them, of course?'

'With what amounted to a virtual rescue package in the shape of a potential and very valuable client on the table, your redundancy seemed pretty unlikely,' he drawled.

So he *had* been listening to her that day on that beach when he'd seemed preoccupied with what he had been scribbling in his notebook—and had acted on it! Nothing would escape this man.

'So you used what I told you about Josh and Lorna's difficulties and deliberately set out to get them on your books just so you could get to me? That's stalking!' she accused heatedly.

'I prefer to call it a good corporate move,' he corrected. 'And while you drove me nearly insane in the bedroom, Kayla, I think you should be aware right here and now that I never let passion of any kind rule my head. Do you really think I'd let a company of mine waste money on a product they didn't need? A product that wasn't going to be of enormous benefit to me financially? I'm a businessman, Kayla, first and foremost. And while I can't deny that advising Havens to use Kendon Interiors' skill and expertise does generate some secondary benefits, my corporate interests are what concern me over and above anything else.'

'If by "secondary benefits" you mean getting me back into bed, forget it!' Kayla retorted, with her pulses racing.

'I was referring to the benefits to Kendon Interiors,' he returned phlegmatically.

Why did she have to open her mouth and put her foot in it again?

Abashed, Kayla sank back against the cushioning black

leather with her eyes pressed closed, her hair a pale contrast against the headrest.

'You never cease trying to make me feel uncomfortable, do you?' she expressed in a censuring whisper.

'Quite unintentionally, believe me,' he answered, almost as softly. 'I think it's this unnatural denial by you of everything there is between us that is responsible for it.'

'There's *nothing* between us,' she refuted, knowing that in doing so she was guilty of doing exactly what he was accusing her of. Everything that was feminine in her was craving those strong arms around her again.

'No?' he queried, with such a wealth of meaning that her eyes flew open in guarded challenge.

He was looking at her without restraint, his eyes glittering with dark desire as they touched on the fullness of her trembling mouth. She felt her breathing grow shallow, felt an excruciating need at the very core of her as his heated gaze slid down to the silvery blue of her blouse, and her breasts rose and fell sharply in traitorous betrayal of her emotions.

'Leonidas…'

It was the first time she had spoken his full name without penetrating sarcasm. It was a breakthrough, he thought, even if she did sound like an accused prisoner who had just realised that any further denial of her crime was useless. Or perhaps she couldn't fight this thing that was making her so tense and cagey, that was driving him almost insane with the need to have her.

Scarcely daring to trust himself, he trailed a finger lightly along the silky texture of her jaw and heard her breath shudder brokenly through her lungs.

'Is that a plea?' he enquired huskily, feeling the ache in his body intensify in throbbing response.

No, it isn't! Kayla wanted to cry out in protest—except

that the feelings he was arousing were preventing her from saying a thing.

'What do you want?' she asked falteringly at length, not daring to look at him. If she did then she'd be lost, she realised, despairing at herself. And she couldn't lose herself to him again—not after the last time. Not after the way he had treated her.

'I want us to finish what we started,' he said, amazing her with his arrogance and yet making her go weak in spite of everything. But at least he wasn't touching her any more.

'Why? Did you fall madly in love with me in Greece and realise you can't live without me?' she suggested with bitter poignancy.

There was a far too lengthy pause before he answered.

'Only fools and adolescents fall madly in love,' he responded dismissively, and his cynicism was stinging even though it was no less than she would have expected from him. 'But I have to admit to having acted entirely out of character with you. You think you know me, but you don't, and I intend to show you exactly who Leonidas Vassalio is.'

'And how do you propose to do that?'

'By asking you to stay with me under my roof for a few weeks. In fact I'm insisting upon it.'

'Insisting?' He sounded so sure of himself, as though he wouldn't take no for an answer, that Kayla viewed him with a guarded question in her eyes. 'You're joking, surely?'

'On the contrary,' he said. 'I've never been more serious in my life. I think it would be a good idea if you move in tomorrow.'

'And if I don't?' It was a breathless little challenge, and one that he didn't take up immediately.

He didn't know why it was so imperative to keep this girl in his life—only that he had to. And if bending her to his will was the only way to do it, then so be it, he determined grimly.

'It would be a pity,' he expressed now. 'Especially as Josh and Lorna imagined we were all getting on so well. But starting a partnership of any kind without total harmony all round doesn't augur very well for future business.'

What was he saying? She wasn't sure, but she had a very good idea.

Though he wasn't actually telling her to her face, she felt sure that he would use Josh and Lorna's difficulties as a lever. The contract wasn't signed yet, and he could use his influence on Havens to get them to withdraw from supplying Kendon Interiors with their greatly anticipated custom. And if that happened...

Mortified, she breathed, 'You'd rescind that contract and see a business go down the drain if I don't do exactly what you're asking?' For what other reason would he have so miraculously sought Josh and Lorna out—regardless of what he'd said—if it wasn't to use their company's problems to his advantage?

His eyes, as she finished speaking, were darkly reflective, giving nothing away.

'Well, since you seem to know me so well...'

He didn't finish. He didn't have to, Kayla thought bitterly, staring with hurt, disbelieving eyes across a patch of manicured lawn to the vacant unit in front of which they were parked. A 'TO LET' sign was pinned to its rendered fascia. The place looked dark. Empty. Soulless.

Like he was, she thought achingly, and knew she had fallen in love with him back there on that island. In love with a man she hadn't even known...

A bell rang in her mind, reminding her of something he had said that last day after they had made love, but she pushed the memory aside. She didn't need anything that threatened to topple the barrier she had been forced to erect against him. Yet when he caught her chin between his thumb and forefinger and turned her head to look at him just the touch of that broad thumb sliding sensuously across her mouth almost broke her trembling resolve.

'Open your eyes,' he commanded softly.

When she did she saw something in his face that for a moment seemed to mirror her anguish—some emotion that burned with a dark and almost painful intensity. But then it was gone, like the extinguishing of a light, and his features seemed only to harden as he leaned forward, tilting her chin higher until there was just a hair's breadth between his mouth and hers.

His scent and his nearness were killing her. She wanted…

Oh, dear heaven! She wanted him! Even knowing what he was like. Even after the way he had deceived her! All she could think about was being naked in his arms and making love with him until…

She pressed her eyes closed to try and blot him out. A traitorous sensual tension gripped her. His breath was warm against her mouth, and the heady spice of his shaven jaw was acting like a powerful drug, stripping her of her will and her power to resist, until without even being aware of it she was leaning into him, her lips parting involuntarily to receive his kiss.

'No.' In an instant he was pulling back. 'Now isn't the time—and this certainly isn't the place.' His breathing came raggedly through his lungs. 'There will be ample opportunity in the future, I promise you. But in the meantime, if you're going to get to know me, *hrisi mou,* somehow I don't think we're going to achieve it like this.'

The sensual snub left her bruised and angry with herself—for feeling such bitter disappointment as well as for allowing him to see how much she still wanted him physically. It just showed him, once again, how he had the power to humiliate her just by turning her into a yearning, quivering wreck.

'I don't need to get to know you, Leonidas Vassalio. I know exactly what you are. You're playing games with me for your own amusement! And you're using my friends to exploit the situation, no matter how you might try to dress it up! All right. I'll go along with your little game.'

If she didn't, and Havens withdrew their offer, Kendon Interiors would be plunged straight back into the difficulties they'd been facing before. And if that happened, if Lorna was subjected to more stress during her pregnancy... Kayla shivered, unable to bear thinking that the safety of a baby's little life might easily be in her own hands.

'I'll move in with you,' she conceded, in a voice clogged with emotion, 'but I'm not sleeping with you, if that's what you're imagining. I'm only doing it for Josh and Lorna's sake, so don't you ever forget that—and don't imagine for one moment that I'm going to enjoy it.'

'I wouldn't be so presumptuous,' he assured her with mockery in his eyes. 'And now I'm going to take you back. Your firm has a proposed contract to fulfil...'

The sudden seriousness of his tone served to remind her of exactly what he was—a typical high-flying executive, ruthless and manipulative, like all the rest she'd known.

'And they're not going to fulfil it if one of their principal staff is out testing her luck by antagonising their biggest client.'

Of course. He had the upper hand and he knew it, Kayla thought, shooting back nevertheless, 'Is that a threat?'

'Why not go the whole hog and call it blackmail?' he suggested smoothly. 'I'm sure you'd prefer to.' When she didn't answer, 'Tomorrow,' he reminded her, as he brought his powerful car around to the front entrance of Kendon Interiors. 'I'll pick you up at eight.'

The pool threw back reflections of the dazzling white mansion. A modern house, built to Georgian design, Leonidas's principal UK home was a breathtaking showcase of large airy rooms, all exquisitely furnished, combining modern with Regency and luxury with unfaltering good taste. A rich man's castle, presided over by a resident staff who catered for this king of enterprise with unstinting respect and affability, as if he was more to them than just the man who paid their wages.

Now, lying beside the luxurious pool in equally luxurious grounds before it was time to get ready for the company dinner to which he was taking her tonight, Kayla was forced to accept, from what she'd observed over her first couple of days in his spectacular house, that the respect shown between Leonidas Vassalio and his staff was entirely mutual.

'Are you ready?' he asked two hours later, as she emerged from the suite of rooms he had assigned to her. It comprised a bedroom with floor-to-ceiling wardrobes, a four-poster bed and a carpet thick enough to drown in, a separate dressing room and a bathroom with a huge sunken tub within a setting of honeyed marble.

'I don't know,' Kayla responded, trying hard not to reveal how just the sight of him standing there at the top of the stairs in a dark evening suit and exquisitely fine shirt was making her blood sing with need. 'I'm your puppet. You tell me.'

He moved towards her like a dark panther, his equally dark eyes taking in every detail of her appearance.

She was wearing a strapless dress with a pale blue bodice that ran into a darker blue, the colour continuing down into purple and then burgundy as it swirled around her ankles. Silver high-heeled sandals gave him a glimpse of burgundy-tipped toes.

She'd twisted her hair up into a knot, leaving a few tendrils to fall softly around her face. Her only concession to cosmetics was a smudge of smoky-blue shading on her eyelids and a burgundy gloss enhancing her lips. Her long lustrous lashes, he was pleased to notice, she'd left naturally gold. Delicate spirals of silver hung from the lobes of her ears, matching the delicately twisted necklace that lay against her softly-tanned skin.

'You look beautiful.' For a moment it was all Leonidas could say. 'And you're not my puppet,' he countered when he had found his voice again. 'You're an independent-minded if not stubborn young woman whom I'm delighted to be accompanying tonight. If I'd wanted a puppet I wouldn't have had to travel too far to find myself a dozen of those.'

No, because every woman he knew would probably leap at the chance to do his bidding, Kayla thought. Whereas *she* was a woman who had walked away from him—said no to him when it had mattered—and that surely had to prove too much of a challenge for a man like Leonidas.

'Then you should have found yourself a dozen, shouldn't you?' she said, smiling brightly for the benefit of a manservant who was passing as they started down the magnificent staircase.

'Perhaps I should have,' he agreed, sounding mildly amused.

From the magnificent staircase to his magnificent car, to dinner in the ballroom of an equally magnificent hotel, Kayla was entranced but at the same time overwhelmed by the world he moved in. It was poles apart from that of the man he had purported to be—a man who had 'opted out', driven a wreck of a truck and bedded down in the run-down environs of a Greek farmhouse.

Here she saw a man at the very pinnacle of his prosperity. A man who lived and travelled in style and circulated with some of the most influential names in society. A man eloquent enough to hold an audience of over three hundred captive as he delivered an after-dinner talk on human complacency towards the state of the planet, leaving his peers congratulating him after a standing ovation that left him remarkably unfazed.

'You were brilliant,' Kayla remarked, unable to resist saying it as the tables were being cleared and couples were beginning to wander onto the dance floor to enjoy the middle-of-the-road music provided by a professional live band. She hadn't had a chance to speak to him since before he'd given the talk, and he'd been surrounded by many guests wanting to speak to him ever since.

'I was just stating fact and emphasising the responsibility that we as professional bodies should engage for the sake of our children and our children's children. We're only custodians of this earth. We don't own it,' he said. 'But am I to assume that I've hit on one topic that you're not going to flay me over tonight?'

With a change of tone he had wiped away her attempt to strike an equal balance with him if only for a few hours. Retaliation was futile, she decided. And anyway a smiling brunette, very glamorous and sophisticated, came up to him at that moment to thank him effusively, ogling him with such a blatant come-on in her sultry green eyes that there was no room for doubt as to exactly what she wanted from him.

'He's so eloquent!' she enthused to Kayla, daring to touch red-tipped fingers to his dark sleeve. 'He made my flesh go all goosebumpy just listening to him!'

'Really?' Kayla responded, trying to look impressed. 'Well, if that makes you goosebumpy then you should take a look at his sketches!' She felt the bunch of muscle in his powerful arm as she slipped hers through it in a gesture of pure possession. 'Of course he's very modest about them, but I'm sure he'd show them to you if you asked him nicely.'

Smiling uncertainly, the woman uttered something that Kayla didn't catch and, realising she was intruding, moved hastily away.

'I know you've got your grievances,' Leonidas rasped, as soon as his admirer was out of earshot, 'but do you have to air them in public? And what was *that* display of play-acting all about?' he queried, locking her arm against the sensuous fabric of his jacket as she would have pulled it away.

'I thought I was supposed to act as though I was enjoying being with you?' she murmured, with a bright smile for anyone who might be watching them.

He made a disapproving sound down his nostrils. 'You're behaving like every woman I went to Greece to get away from.'

Which was why he had been so careful not to tell you who he was, her inner little voice piped up to remind her. But she didn't want reminding, and silenced the voice with the flash of another smile and a clipped, 'How do you *want* me to behave?'

'As Kayla Young. Guileless. Easy to like. And infernally inquisitive.'

'A fool,' she tagged on, all falseness gone. She was only aware then that he was leading her onto the dance floor. 'Guileless. Easy to like. And an infernally inquisitive, easy-to-fool fool!'

'How can I forget it?' he murmured, slipping those strong arms around her. 'You aren't prepared to let me.'

'Any more than I'm prepared to let you forget that I'm here under protest.'

'No, you aren't,' he purred silkily, drawing her close, sending Kayla's senses reeling in shaming response. 'I don't think "protest" can in any way account for the way we're both feeling now.'

This close to him she could feel every steel-hard muscle of his body—in the whipcord strength of his back and shoulders, in his hard hips and powerful thighs, and in the stirring evidence of his arousal. It made her want to press herself against him, and it took every shred of will-power she possessed not to do it.

'You aren't feeling anything. Just a bruised ego and severely dented pride because you can't bear a woman ever saying no to you.'

He laughed very softly, and with his cheek against hers whispered in her ear, 'Not a woman whom I know wants me as much as I want her—no.'

Even his breath was a turn-on against her treacherously pulsing flesh, without the stimulus of his stunning appearance and the way he'd had everyone there tonight eating out of his hand. It made her wish that they didn't have the baggage of the past hanging over them and that she was somewhere else, alone with him, not moving like this under an exquisite chandelier, with three hundred other people in the room.

'In fact, do you want to know what I think you are thinking now?'

The lights spun gold from Kayla's hair as she lifted her head in challenge. 'No,' she dismissed with a saccharine-sweet smile. 'But no doubt you're going to tell me anyway.'

'Well, let's see if I'm right,' he suggested. He was looking down at her and emulating her smile in a way that to anyone watching would have marked them undoubtedly as lovers— hungry for each other, wanting only the privacy of their bedroom. 'I think that right now you would prefer to be back at the house and for me to be slowly undressing you with some soft music playing. And I think you'd like me to remain clothed while I carry you naked up to my bed. There's nothing like the sensuality of cloth to add zest to lovemaking, is there, Kayla? Particularly when the man wearing it doesn't give a fig for how you might abuse it, just so long as he can gratify your desires and make you sob with pleasure.'

It was so close to what she had been thinking that Kayla could scarcely breathe. She could feel her cheeks burning from the shaming imagery. 'You're just indulging in your own un-inhibited fantasies.' she croaked, her throat as arid as a Grecian hillside, and she felt those dark masculine eyes appraising the results of what his mind-blowing words had produced.

'Am I?' he challenged softly, with a knowing smile.

She wasn't even aware that the music had stopped until his arms fell away from her, and then she could see one of the older male guests to whom she'd been introduced earlier beckoning him from the bar.

'I'll be a few minutes,' Leonidas apologised, and left her to flee to the mercifully deserted sanctuary of the powder room.

A flushed-faced, bright-eyed creature stared back at her from the mirror above the luxuriously equipped basins. She felt as though she had just been aroused to fever-pitch only to be left abandoned and wanting. Wanting *him,* she acknowledged painfully, wondering how she still could.

How could she stay under his roof when every time he touched her it was like dropping a firework into a powder keg? When her common sense went up in smoke just at a look from him, even without the X-rated things he'd been saying to her just now?

And yet he hadn't attempted to touch her intimately since he'd brought her to his house—had merely treated her with a detached respect that had kept her awake over the past two nights wondering why he hadn't. Had he finally accepted that he had treated her unfairly and was now doing his best to make it up to her? Or was his plan to wear her down with the sort of earth-shattering sensuality he'd used just now until she was begging for him to make love to her?

She hadn't met a company man yet whose motives weren't entirely self-centred, so why should Leonidas Vassalio be any different? She rebuked herself for her moment of weakness in even daring to hope that he might be. Wasn't he using the plight of two people she cared about purely to satisfy his own selfish demands? And he'd already lived up to the type of man he really was in the way he had lied to her in Greece.

Even so, it was with a sick and building excitement that a little later she sat in the shadowy intimacy of his car, acutely aware of him sitting there beside her, changing gear with an immaculately cuffed wrist as he took a bend, driving them home, his jacket discarded in the back...

Only the hall light was burning on a dimmer switch as they came through the electronically operated gates and he admitted them into his magnificent house. Having watched the way he'd used his security card to open the impressively carved door, Kayla couldn't help comparing this man, with his millions and his discreet surveillance staff and his stringently guarded home, with the one who had slept with his doors unlocked—open to the world—alone on a lonely Greek hillside.

'Thanks. I think I'll go straight up,' she murmured, breathless with anticipation. She wasn't sure how she was managing to drag herself away from him as she started towards the wide sweeping stairs.

'Kayla...'

His soft command stopped her in her tracks, her heart beating a frenzied tattoo. If he touched her...

Dear heaven! She *wanted* him to touch her! To take the decision away from her, carry her up these stairs and drive her wild in the sumptuous luxury of his bed!

She turned round, her legs threatening to buckle under her. 'What?'

'You dropped your wrap,' he said, in a voice that was screamingly intimate.

Even the purposefulness of his tread on the pale marble was a sensuality that made her tense and yearning body throb.

Very softly he moved over and placed the blue and silver sequinned stole which she hadn't even realised had slipped off lightly over her bare shoulders. Then, with heart-stopping gentleness, he turned her round to face him.

He had retrieved his jacket since stepping out of the car,

and the dark cloth now spanning his shoulders was a sensuality she wanted to touch.

It was a replay of all he had tormented her with earlier, and she caught her breath, held in thrall by the scent and warmth and power of him as he stooped and pressed his lips against her forehead.

'You look tired,' he remarked, gazing down with some dark, unfathomable emotion at the naked hunger in her eyes. 'Get some rest,' he advised softly, leaving her excruciatingly lost and aching for him. 'We've got another busy day tomorrow.'

CHAPTER TEN

'WHY DIDN'T YOU tell me you were seeing him?' Lorna gasped, amazed, after Leonidas had telephoned Kayla in the office on Monday morning. 'And don't tell me you aren't, because that phone call certainly wasn't about trading figures! You're going out with him, aren't you?'

Imperceptibly, Kayla tensed. She hadn't told anyone that she was staying with Leonidas. All she had told her mother was that she was spending a couple of weeks with Lorna, and as Leonidas lived within a reasonable driving distance of Kendon Interiors, which meant that she could still come into the office, she had decided not to involve her friend in the lie.

'Don't spread it about,' she implored, reluctant to reveal her secret or to face the awkward questions that people would ask if she did.

What could she tell them, anyway? That she was only with Leonidas because he had made it impossible for her to refuse? That he was as good as blackmailing her to get her to comply with his wishes, and that she didn't intend staying in his house a second longer than after that contract was signed?

'If the paparazzi get wind of it they could turn his life into a circus,' she tagged on as casually as she was able to, although she was aware, from things Leonidas had already mentioned in passing, that they really could do just that.

'I won't. Well, only to Josh, of course,' Lorna stated unnecessarily. 'But how did you manage it? No, scrub that,' she put in hastily. 'You're smart and you're beautiful—he wouldn't have been worth his salt if he hadn't noticed you the moment you walked into the conference room last week. Wow! Won't that be one in the eye for Craig!' she continued, clearly flabbergasted. 'Honestly, Kayla! Do you *know* how rich he is?'

Rich and manipulative and using his power to get exactly what he wants, Kayla thought desolately. Because what he wanted was her, back in his bed. She was certain of that, despite the fact that he was making no advances to her in that respect, and regardless of how much he had hurt her—was still hurting her with his calculated plan to use her friends' precarious position as a lever to get her to fall in with him.

It was for that reason that she still couldn't bring herself to tell Lorna about meeting him in Greece. Lorna, who always thought the best of people, would instantly imagine that he had cast his company's business their way because Kayla had recommended them. She might even think he was doing it as a favour to her, Kayla, and she couldn't bear her friend to be deceived by him as she had, when nothing could be further from the truth.

'His money doesn't interest me,' Kayla tried to say nonchalantly, which produced a knowing little laugh from her friend.

'Well, no. I can see that there's far more that would interest you before you even got to his wallet! Gosh! If I wasn't married—and pregnant...'

'Which you are,' Kayla emphasised, managing a smile, knowing that her friend was only jesting. Lorna adored Josh, and her one desire in life was to give birth to their healthy baby. Dropping an almost envying glance to her dearest friend's burgeoning middle, Kayla decided right there and then that whatever it took to help Lorna fulfil that desire she would do, regardless of the cost to her own emotions.

* * *

During that week Leonidas went away on some unexpected business, returning a couple of days later to steal Kayla away early from the office and take her to a charity auction, where canapés were handed round on silver dishes and champagne flowed like water from a spring.

It was an event where the proceeds from the various items on offer went to a tsunami relief fund, and it soon became clear to Kayla that it was because of Leonidas's attendance and his company's support of the event that so many people had got involved.

'Did you enjoy that?' he asked her afterwards, when they were in the car, pulling away. 'As far as you were able to, of course, bearing in mind that your enjoyment level was probably stuck on zero in view of who you were with.'

Like her, he had refused the champagne after the first half-glass, and she was beginning to discover that his driving standards—as with most of what he did—were impeccable.

'Very amusing,' she remarked dryly, turning to look out of the window, secretly admiring the gardens surrounding the grand English country manor his company had hired to host the event. 'What was the object of the exercise in bringing me here today? To show me how charitable you can be?' She'd been surprised when he had paid over the odds for a small and not particularly well done watercolour of one of the local landmarks. 'There are those who might say you can afford to be.'

'You would be one of them, I take it?' When she didn't answer, already wishing she hadn't been so quick to snipe at him like that, he went on, 'It isn't about affording it, Kayla. It's about having enough clout to make others aware of the importance of events like this and bringing everyone together to contribute.'

Which he had done—and very successfully, she accepted, secretly impressed. Although she couldn't bring herself to admit it aloud, privately she couldn't deny that she had enjoyed herself—very much.

Hé took her to a West End show one evening—one she had wanted to see and for which she had been unable to get tickets. Afterwards, coming out of the exclusive restaurant where he had taken her for a late dinner, they were leapt on by photographers who almost succeeded in trampling her to death before Leonidas got her into the waiting limousine he'd had one of his aides bring to whisk them away.

'How do you cope with all this?' Kayla challenged, and he could tell from the all-encompassing gesture of her small chin that she meant the security and the car and the public demands his billionaire status made upon him, and not just the frightening intrusion of the paparazzi.

'One learns to live with it,' he said in a matter-of-fact voice, and then, more solicitously, asked, 'Are you all right?'

She nodded, but he could see that she wasn't. That anxious line between her eyes assured him that she was anything but happy being there with him. Also, being jostled by those photographers had caused the fine white silk of her dress to tear, and her beautiful hair, which she had styled so elegantly before they had left the house, was coming out of its combs. She looked as if she had been out in a gale—or with a far too impassioned lover.

The thought made him hard, but he steeled himself against it. She wasn't ready to accept him back into her bed just yet.

Consequently, when they reached the house he left her to go to bed alone and went straight to his study, where he spent hours catching up on some pressing paperwork in an endeavour not to give in to the almost overwhelming urge to mount the stairs two at time, rip back her bedcovers and watch her hollow protests dissolve beneath the surging demands of their entwined bodies.

The photographs were emblazoned across the tabloids the

next day, with Kayla caught looking surprised and dishevelled and Leonidas urging her determinedly into the car.

'Have you seen them?' she wailed, ringing him on his mobile, having already spent half an hour on the phone, dodging awkward questions from her mother. She wasn't sure where he was, but her call had been diverted to his secretary first, who had obviously been asked to field his calls.

'Yes, I did, and I'm sorry,' he expressed, sounding annoyed over the publicity.

She was beginning to appreciate why he'd gone off to that island to escape it all for a while. Why he had been so angry when he had caught her supposedly taking photographs of him that first day.

'Say nothing,' he recommended, when she told him that someone from the press had found out where she worked and had been ringing the office to try and get her to talk to them. 'Throw them a crumb and they'll knead it into a whole loaf. If you say nothing it will blow over within a week.' He apologised again before ringing off.

A couple of hours later a large bunch of red roses was delivered to the office as added consolation from Leonidas, much to the excitement of everyone at Kendon Interiors—particularly the female contingent, who had already seen the article and were still drooling over the hard and exciting image of the high-powered tycoon.

As arranged, he picked Kayla up himself from the office that evening, using his car's superior power to roar out of the business park before one lurking newspaperman and a couple of young girls from the office who had rushed out to get a glimpse of him knew what had happened.

'Thank you.' Kayla looked gratefully across at him as he brought the powerful car into the early rush-hour traffic. 'For getting me out of there so fast—and for the roses.' Remembering her telephone call to him earlier, however, and the manner in which she had finally got to speak to him, she asked, before she could stop herself, 'Did you get your secretary to send them for you?'

Wasn't that what company men did? she reflected bitterly, remembering other roses. Before turning their focus on their adoring secretaries themselves?

'I'm not your father, Kayla,' he answered grimly, without taking his eyes off the rear window of the car in front of them, uncannily reading her mind. 'Nor am I your ex-fiancé. When I send flowers I never do it without choosing exactly what I want myself.'

Which put her in her place, good and proper! She didn't doubt that in this instance at least he was telling her the truth.

He was due to fly to the Channel Islands for a conference that weekend. Expressing concern, however, at Kayla being left to the mercies of the press for a couple of days, he instructed her not to stray beyond the boundaries of his home, and made sure she complied by instructing one strong-armed member of his security staff to keep his eye on her.

'What are you imagining I'll do if I go out?' she quipped as he was leaving for the helicopter that was standing, its blades whirring, on the landing pad in front of the house. 'Find some man to impregnate me so I can tell everybody it's yours?'

She regretted it almost as soon as she'd said it.

'You aren't a prisoner, Kayla,' he said, all emotion veiled by the dark fringes of his lashes. 'I'm only thinking of your privacy and your safety.'

And he was gone, leaving her with only the briefest touch of his lips branding her cheek.

As it was a good weekend she swam in the pool and sunbathed on the terrace, catching up with some reading and watching a couple of adventure movies in the mansion's impressive professionally equipped cinema room.

Nothing, though, could compare to her traitorous excitement at hearing Leonidas's helicopter returning on Sunday evening after she had gone to bed—deliberately early so that she wouldn't have to see him. Wouldn't have to battle with this underlying sexual tension that was building in her daily with a terrifying intensity, and which was becoming almost impossible to keep from him whenever he touched her—however casually. And she *had* to keep it from him, she thought, harrowed and racked with frustration. Because wasn't this part of his ploy? To wear her down with wanting him? Just to redeem his indomitable masculine pride? And if she did ever succumb again to her own foolish and weak-willed desire for him, what then?

No, she had to be strong, she determined. Had to resist him at all costs. Just until that contract was signed.

When Leonidas picked her up from the office the following evening it was to take her for an early dinner in a favoured bistro he knew and then, much to her surprise, on to a photography exhibition.

'I thought as you're so attached to that camera of yours,' he said, pulling up outside the small but well-attended little gallery, 'you might appreciate seeing what the professionals have to offer. Of course if you'd rather not...'

'No. No I'd like to,' Kayla put in quickly when he looked in two minds about whether to park or drive away. Craig had hated anything like this, and even Josh and Lorna couldn't understand what Craig had used to call her 'camera fetish'. Just the chance to be among like-minded people for a change was something she didn't want to pass up.

The exhibition, by private invitation only, was being hosted by an acquaintance of Leonidas's, and Kayla could tell as soon as they were inside that he and the gentle grey-haired man were true friends. There was none of the deference or playing up to Leonidas that she had seen among some of the people at the functions she'd attended with him, until she'd wondered how he could ever tell who was really sincere.

'Leonidas tells me that you're quite the enthusiast,' the man said to her, smiling. Leonidas—still dressed, as she was, in a dark business suit—was, with the rest of the twenty or so guests, browsing some of the artwork around the gallery. 'If ever you feel you have something to offer, then you know where to come.'

'It's just a hobby!' Kayla laughed warmly, wondering what Leonidas had been saying to his friend about her. That he had said anything at all gave her a decidedly warm feeling inside.

'So what do you think?' Suddenly he was there beside her, sharing her interest in a waterfall scene with some interesting use of light.

'It's good,' she expressed, enervated by his dark executive image. 'But if it had been mine I'd have toned the light down a little.' She was finding it hard to concentrate when she could feel the power of his virility emanating from him, and her nostrils were straining for every greedy breath of his cologne. 'It isn't subtle enough for me.'

'And you like subtlety?'

Dry-mouthed, Kayla touched her tongue to her top lip and saw the way his eyes followed the nervous little action. 'Every time.' She even managed to smile, but her lips felt stretched and burning.

'Perhaps this will be more to your taste.' They had moved on and he was referring to a landscape captured beneath an angry sky.

'Much too wild,' she dismissed laughingly, and saw the sexy elevation of a dark eyebrow.

'Are you saying you prefer something more…tamed?'

There was sensuality in the way he said it, in that momentary hesitation. Or was she imagining it? she wondered, her heart still racing when he immediately invited her opinion on the technicalities of the photograph—its depth of field, how it captured the eye.

He knew a lot about the subject, and she was impressed.

'I've studied a bit,' he said modestly, when she told him so. 'Unlike you. You're a natural,' he commented, making her glow inside. 'So, what about this one?'

'Too much Photoshop,' she quipped, wrinkling her nose, and he laughed.

For a moment it felt as it had that day he had taken her to that little island and she'd been insisting on racehorses on a piece of land not a mile wide. Indulging in make-believe. Playing games with him. Except that it was different tonight. Tonight the very air around them was pulsating with a dangerous chemistry, and she wasn't with Leon, the man she'd believed to be open and carefree with scarcely two pennies to his name. She was with Leonidas Vassalio, hardened billionaire, powerful magnate and the man who had hurt her—was still hurting her just by being the type of man he was. The type who would use her concern for her friends to get what he wanted.

'My Gran used to say that the camera doesn't lie. But it does,' she accepted, suddenly feeling low-spirited. 'Maybe not in her day,' she went on, 'but in this day and age the emphasis seems to be on how much you can artificially enhance or embellish, and on what you put in or take out. You can't really tell what's real any more and what isn't. There's so much that isn't as it seems.' *Including you,* she thought achingly, and had to glance away, pretending to be temporarily distracted by the other guests milling around them so that he wouldn't see the emotion scoring her face.

'And that means so much to you?'

'Yes, it does,' she said. 'I like the camera to capture things as they really are.' She turned back to him now, her feelings brought under control. 'Men and women. Places. Things. I like them portrayed "warts and all", as the saying goes. I'm not a fan of illusion. Being fooled into seeing something that isn't really there.'

He tilted his head, the movement so slight that she wasn't sure whether she had imagined it or not. His eyes were dark pools of inscrutable emotion and she wondered what he was thinking. That he had done just that with her when he hadn't told her who he was?

'Let's go home,' he said.

He spoke very little to her on the relatively short journey back, while the car ate up the miles in the gathering dusk.

There had been a sporadic press presence at the main gates of the house over the past few days, and Leonidas wasn't taking any chances when they arrived home.

'We'll take the east entrance,' he told Kayla as he turned the car down a quiet lane that stretched for a couple of miles and which, from the manicured trees above the high wall that soon came into view, obviously skirted his property.

Another pair of electronically opened gates brought them past a small lodge and into his home through a smaller and more secluded side entrance.

'Why isn't this part of the house used?' Kayla whispered as they came out of rooms covered in dustsheets which Leonidas had had to unlock to allow them into the main body of the house. She felt like a child creeping around when she should have been in bed. Or a guilty mistress sneaking away from the ecstasies of her lover's bed...

'I had this part converted for my father, but he never came here,' he said, his voice taking on a curiously jagged edge.

'Why not?' Kayla asked, thinking how thick and black his hair was as he stopped to lock the door behind him. It made her want to rake her fingers through it, twist the strong tufts around them as she lay beneath him, crying out from the terrifying pleasure he was withholding from her.

'I believe I told you before. We were never able to get on. I wanted us to try and establish some sort of rapport as he was getting older.' They were moving along a softly lit carpeted passage now. 'To try and forge some sort of bond with him.'

He was so close behind her that if she stopped he would collide with her, Kayla thought hectically, craving the feel of his warmth through her prim little jacket and tight pencil skirt.

'And did you?'

'No. There was too much between us—far too much to even imagine we could repair it. He didn't want to share in my good fortune or the things I could give him. He didn't want anything from me,' he concluded, with something in his voice that she might have mistaken for pain if she hadn't known better.

'Why not? Wasn't he proud of you?' she queried, feeling for him in spite of herself as they came through an archway into the main hall alongside the sweeping staircase. She couldn't believe that any parent with a son like Leonidas—driven, enterprising, so overwhelmingly successful—could possibly be anything else.

'Oh, I think he was satisfied that I'd turned out to be the man he had been determined to mould me into,' he accepted harshly.

Kayla glanced back over her shoulder and saw the rigidity of his features, the hard cynicism touching his mouth. 'And what type is that?'

'The type who understands that sentiment and idealism are for fools and that common sense and practicality are the only two reliable bedfellows.'

'Do you really believe that?' she murmured, with wounded incredulity in her eyes as she stopped, as he had, at the foot of the stairs.

'What does it matter what I believe?' he said.

He meant to her. And yet it did matter, she realised—far too much—and she had to sink her nails into her clenched palms to keep herself from blurting it out.

He was hard and ruthless. She'd realised that even before she'd left Greece. Although she hadn't known how hard and how calculating he could be until she'd seen him in full corporate action, which was how he had managed to climb to the very top of the executive ladder while still only thirty-one. Yet there was an altruistic side to his nature too, reined in beneath that cold and ruthless streak, which could have had her eating out of his hand if she had been weak enough to let it. But she wasn't, she thought turbulently as she found herself battling against a surge of responses to that dark and raw sensuality that transcended everything else about him.

'Thank you for taking me to the exhibition,' she said, in a husky voice that didn't sound like hers. 'It was thoughtful of you. I think I'll go straight up. Goodnight.'

If she had thought he would let her go then she had been fooling herself, she realised too late, when his firm, determined fingers closed around her wrist.

'You might not like the man you think I am—or what I stand for—but it excites you, Kayla.'

How right he was! She felt panicked as he drew her towards him and brought the fingers of his other hand to play along the pulsing sensitivity of her throat.

'*This* excites you.'

'No, don't—please...' It was a hopeless little sound. The sound of one who knew her cause was lost.

'Why? Are you afraid that if for one minute you let your guard down you might just have to acknowledge how much you want me?'

'I don't want you.' Rebellion warred with the dark desire in her eyes. Futile rebellion, she realised when she saw him smile.

'No?'

He was barely touching her, yet every feminine cell was screaming out to the steel-hard strength and warmth and power he exuded. She could feel her breasts straining against her blouse, could feel the moist heat of her desire against the flimsy film of her string.

'You want me and it's driving you mad. It's driving us both mad,' he admitted, and his scent and his nearness and that iron control were electrifying as he tilted her chin with a forefinger—all that was touching her now. 'You want me,' he said huskily, his dark eyes raking over her upturned mouth. 'Say it.'

It was a soft command, breathed against her lips, and it was that excruciating denial of the kiss she was craving, which finally broke her resolve.

'I want you! I want you! I want—!'

His mouth over hers silenced her wild admission in the same moment that she twined her arms around his neck to pull him down to her.

He caught her to him, those strong arms tightening around her.

Kayla wriggled against him, seeking even closer contact with his body, her own a mass of desperate wanting as their mouths fused, broke contact, devoured in a hunger of frenzied need.

He was tugging off her jacket, letting it lie where it fell, ripping buttons in his urgency to get her out of her clothes. But when her hands slid under his jacket and it fell away from those broad shoulders he suddenly swept her up off her feet and mounted the stairs with her as effortlessly as if she were a rag doll.

Of course. The staff.

The thought penetrated her consciousness, but only for a second, because all that mattered was that she was with this man, destined for his bed, and she was going to know the full meaning of his loving her.

In the physical sense…

She shook that thought away, because all she wanted was to have him inside her—anyhow, anywhere and any way it came.

He set her down on her feet before they had even reached his room, pressing her against the wall of the carpeted landing, as hungry for her mouth as she was for the pleasuring mastery of his hands on her body.

He surfaced only to tug off her gaping blouse, pulling her against his hard hips so that he could deal with the back zipper of her skirt.

It slipped to the floor and she was standing there in nothing but a white lacy bra and string and black high-heeled sandals, revelling in his groan of satisfaction as he caught her to him again.

His tongue burned an urgent trail along the shallow valley between her breasts and, clutching his shoulders, she arched against him as his mouth moved ravishingly over a lacy cup.

The fine silk of his shirt was a sensual turn-on under her urgently groping hands, the fabric of his immaculately pressed trousers heightening her pleasure as he suddenly cupped her buttocks and lifted her up and her legs went around him, her fingers tangling wildly in his thick black hair.

It was the culmination of everything he had promised and everything she had dared to imagine, she realised as they finally made it to his room and he dropped her down onto the yielding sensuality of his big bed.

They had been lovers in the spring, but it hadn't been like this, she thought as he came down to her, still fully clothed, and removed the last scraps of her underwear with swift and amazing dexterity. Perhaps he had been right when he'd suggested that his power and influence excited her. Perhaps she was no different from all those other women she'd seen visually devouring him, she thought. Because she had no control over the desires he aroused in her.

Naked, she writhed beneath him, wanting him naked too, wanting the hands that were reclaiming her body never to stop—because she had been made for them. For this…

When he moved away to hastily shed his clothes, she watched with her hair spread like wild silk over the darker sheen of his pillow, her arms arched above her head in wanton abandon to the thrilling anticipation of what was to come.

'I called you an angel once,' he said hoarsely, looking down at her from where he was standing, unashamed and magnificent in his glorious nakedness. 'But I was wrong. You're a she-devil.' It was said with a curious tremor in his voice.

'And you…' she whispered, her body pulsing as he finished sheathing himself—not taking any chances this time—and came back to join her '…are the devil incarnate.'

'Yes,' he murmured, his voice humorously soft against her lips.

But she didn't care, because she was on fire for him, burning up in a conflagration of need and wanting and desire.

Skilfully and with controlled deliberation he slid down her body, anointing her skin with kisses, although his body was taut with his own need and his breathing was as ragged as hers.

Their hunger was too demanding for much foreplay. As he moved above her, positioning himself to take her, Kayla welcomed his hard invasion, her legs opening for him like silken wings for the sun.

His sliding into her was an ecstasy she couldn't have imagined and she lifted her hips to accommodate him, a small cry spilling from her lips.

His penetration was deep, with each successive thrust taking him deeper, until he was filling her, stretching her, turning her into a being of mindless, unparalleled sensation where nothing else mattered but the union of their two bodies.

She was riding with him, being taken to a place where only the two of them existed—a rapturous world of feeling and sharpening senses that grew into a mountain of exquisitely unbearable pleasure, urging her upwards to its summit. And suddenly as she reached the top the mountain started to ex-

plode, and she cried out from the pleasure that was bursting
all around her. She was falling, tumbling in a freefall of interminable sensation, clinging to the man she never wanted to let
out of her arms, part of him, belonging to him, as he tumbled
with her through the sensational universe.

When she came back to earth she was sobbing uncontrollably, all her pent-up feelings for him released by the shattering throbs of her orgasm.

Some time afterwards, when her sobs had subsided, Leonidas asked, 'Are you all right?'

She was lying in the crook of his arm and the warm velvet
of his chest was damp from her tears.

'Yes, I'm fine,' Kayla murmured, and rolled away from
him, unable to tell him why she had wept. If she did, then
he would know, and she didn't want to admit it to herself. So
she stayed where she was, on her side, with her legs drawn
up, not wanting to face the truth or the reality of what had
just happened.

Leonidas woke shortly before dawn.

Kayla was still lying with her back to him, as far over on
her side of the bed as it was possible to get. With a crease between his eyes, Leonidas slipped quietly out of bed, so as not
to disturb her, and went to take a shower.

When he returned, wearing a dark robe, she was still sleeping, but now lying on her back. What little make-up she'd been
wearing last night was smudged—either from his over-zeal-
ous treatment of her or from crying, he remembered uneasily—and her hair was alluringly tousled from making love.

Unable to help himself, he stooped to press his lips lightly
to her forehead. She stirred slightly, her brow furrowing as
though her dreams were troubled.

'Leon…'

He wasn't sure, from her soft murmur, whether that was

what she'd said, but if it was it wasn't meant for the man who had made love to her last night. Not Leonidas Vassalio, corporate chairman and billionaire. Not after the way she had cried after they had made love.

She didn't trust him or even like him, and she despised herself for wanting him. Why else would she have shed tears of such bitter regret when she'd been overtaken—as he had—by their mutual passion last night?

It was his fault for thinking in the beginning that he could have a casual fling with a girl like her and that keeping the truth from her wouldn't matter. Nor had he been right in thinking he could bend her to his will in making her come here to try and get her to want him as she had in Greece. She was never likely to. She was hurting, and he had never intended that.

What was that old adage? he pondered distractedly, moving away from the bed. If you loved something, you had to let it go. If it came back to you, it was yours. If it didn't, it never would be.

But what he felt for this beautiful, bewitching girl wasn't *love,* he thought, steeling himself against any emotion. Not as she deserved it. And she certainly wasn't his. So wasn't it time to let her go?

Wearing a silver-grey suit, white shirt and silver tie, Leonidas was perched on one of the high stools, browsing through a newspaper, when Kayla came into the huge, sterile-looking kitchen an hour or so later. Behind him the sky was overcast beyond the panoramic window, and even a myriad lights in the halogen-studded ceiling couldn't detract from the dreariness of what should have been a bright summer day.

'Good morning.' He scarcely glanced up from whatever he was reading in the *Financial Times,* although just that briefest glance from him set her insides aflame as she thought about how intimately and passionately he had pleasured her last night.

After a moment he cast the newspaper aside on the kitchen counter beside him. 'Kayla, we have to talk,' he stated without any preamble, angling his long, lean body to face her on the stool.

'About what?' she queried, with sudden queasiness in her stomach. What was he going to say that lent such a serious tone to his voice?

'I've been a moron,' he told her. 'If that's the correct expression. You were right. I have been trying to keep you in my life for the sake of my own pride—my ego, if you like—because I didn't like my ethics being brought into question in anyone's mind. Particularly the mind of a girl who was very sweet and trusting and whom I treated very unfairly when I was with her in Greece and I needed to put that right.'

'What are you saying?' Kayla queried in a small, broken voice.

'That I've been very selfish and inconsiderate and that you don't need to pander to my fragile ego any longer. Your friends' contract is assured, if that's what you've been worrying about, so you're free to cast me off…if that's what you wish,' he added with some hesitancy, and as though he was picking his words very carefully. 'Whenever you like.'

If it was what she wished?

Pain speared through her so acutely it felt like a knife slicing through the life-force of her very being. She'd never been let down and effectively rejected in such a considerately phrased manner before. But he'd got what he wanted, she thought wretchedly, trying to concentrate on her breathing. It was her total capitulation that he had needed to redeem his pride, and now she had given him that he needed nothing more.

He was just like all the others—right out of the same mould. The type of man she'd vowed never to be attracted to again.

Except that this man was different. This man wasn't even capable of feeling. Not love, she accepted, anguished. He'd practically admitted that to her himself last night. Loving was a weakness—something only fools entertained—and Leonidas Vassalio was anything but weak, and certainly no fool.

'Well…' Her smile felt stretched as she tried to put on a brave face, and she wondered if she was visibly shaking as much as she was trembling inside. It occurred to her then why he'd wanted her kept out of the way of the press while he'd been away last weekend. Because he didn't want anyone thinking she was a permanent fixture in his life. 'I'd better go and start packing,' she said as tonelessly as she was able, and wondered at the unfathomable emotion that turned his eyes almost inky black.

'I have to fly to Athens,' he informed her, consulting his watch, his tone similarly flat.

It was a trip, she'd discovered, which he took on a regular basis, often going back and forth between London and his Greek office. 'If you're keen to go today, I obviously won't try and stop you, but I shan't be able to take you myself. I can, however, arrange for a car to be put at your disposal whenever you wish to leave.'

'That won't be necessary,' Kayla murmured, wanting to get out of there—and quickly—before the tears that were burning the backs of her eyes overflowed and gave her away.

He nodded as though he understood, and somehow she managed to drag herself from the room with her pride intact, safe in the knowledge that he would never know the truth. A truth she only admitted to herself now, as she stumbled over the stairs up which he had carried her so purposefully last night. That she was deeply and hopelessly in love with Leonidas Vassalio.

CHAPTER ELEVEN

MOVING LEADENLY THROUGH the silent cottage, Leonidas was checking each familiar room. He had promised Philomena's daughter he would do that for her, and that he would take anything he wanted. Anything that meant something to him, she had said.

Coming back through the kitchen, he let his glance touch painfully on a cherished oil-lamp, some sprigs of dried herbs, the stack of unused logs beside the huge stove, and his nostrils dilated from a host of evocative scents—rosemary, sage and pinewood, trapped there by shutters which remained reverently closed against the intrusion of the outside world.

There was nothing for him here. He had everything he wanted in the memory of Philomena's presence, her warmth and her voice, often scolding but always wise, and he wished fervently that she was there now, with her affectionate scolding and her wisdom.

He could hear her still, when he had run down here on countless occasions to escape his father's bellowing and his character-moulding brutality.

Be true to yourself, Leon.

But he hadn't been, had he? Not in his hopes and aspirations. In everything he hadn't been able to feel. Not since he'd been a child, or maybe a young adolescent, but certainly not as a man.

Since his mother had died and his father had blamed him for it he had built a hard, impervious shell around himself. A shell that no one, not even he himself, could crack. Only once had he ever—

He slammed the brakes on his errant thinking.

No, he hadn't been true to himself, he realised grimly. But that, like everything about this house, was now part of the past.

Grabbing one final look around filled him with such an ache of grief in his chest that he had to take a minute to steel himself before stepping outside into the bright sunlight and closing the door for the last time.

'I was just going to ring you,' Kayla said brightly as Lorna came through on her cell phone. 'The men have done a great job! The builder's been paid—in fact he's only just left—and the villa looks as good as new!'

She was standing looking up at the rafters above the galleried landing, and at the freshly rendered walls, which now bore no sign of the damage they had sustained earlier in the year. She tried not to think about how Leonidas—or Leon, she amended painfully—had rescued her that night, risking his own life in coming down here and carrying her out to the truck. She wasn't going to think about that. Or anything else about him, she decided achingly, just as she had promised herself she wouldn't when she had stepped off the ferry the previous day.

Josh hadn't been able to leave the business, and as his in-laws were away on an anniversary cruise Lorna had been fully intending to come here and do the inspection herself. But that had been before her doctor had strongly advised that she was in no condition to travel, so Kayla had immediately allayed her friend's anxieties by offering to come instead.

What she hadn't anticipated was how unbearably being here would affect her. She had known it would be painful, but just how excruciating she hadn't been prepared for. All she wanted to do now was lock up the villa, drive down and see Philomena, and then get the hell off this island before the last ferry left that day.

Now, to try and take her mind off the memories that were killing her, in a voice thickened by emotion she asked, 'Is there any news yet on that contract?'

The business that Havens Exclusive were giving them had all been agreed in principle, but the company seemed to be dragging its heels, and the paperwork that would secure it still hadn't come through. Josh and Lorna were on a knife-edge, waiting for the contract to arrive, and Kayla was secretly worried that it never would.

'That's why I'm ringing.'

The anxious note in Lorna's voice told Kayla that it still hadn't arrived.

'I rang Havens yesterday, and they seemed to think it was sent to us two weeks ago. Then today someone else said they didn't think it had been. I tried to ring Leonidas, to see if he knew anything about it, but his office said he was in Greece this week. I know you're not seeing him any more, but as you're already in the country, and as you said things between you only sort of…fizzled out…'

It had been the only way Kayla could describe her break-up with Leonidas to her friend without falling apart emotionally. 'I was wondering…is there anything you can do to get hold of him from your end? To see if you can find out what's happening?'

Lorna sounded in such a state that, although her nerves were already stretched to breaking point at the thought of calling him, Kayla agreed to help.

She knew he made regular trips between the UK and Greece, and with her heart thumping a few minutes later she got through to his Athens office.

'I'm afraid Mr Vassalio isn't here this week,' a thickly accented female voice informed her in nonetheless perfect English. 'You should be able to contact him on his mobile.'

'Thanks,' Kayla said, feeling deflated after it had taken so much courage to call in the first place.

It seemed too personal, ringing his cell phone number. Far, far too intimate… After a few moments, though, for Lorna's sake, she forced herself to do it.

'You have reached the voicemail of Leonidas Vassalio…'

Just hearing his deep tones sent fire tingling through her veins, but with her heart beating like crazy Kayla cut them off in mid-sentence. There was no way she could leave a message without her voice shaking uncontrollably. And then he'd know, wouldn't he?

She'd try him again later, she decided, breathing deeply to steady her pulse-rate. In the meantime she would do what she'd planned to do before Lorna had rung and pop down to see Philomena.

The shutters were closed when Kayla pulled up alongside the cottage, which wasn't that surprising as the late summer sun still burned fiercely here at this time of day, she thought. Even so, the flowers outside in their pots looked neglected and wilting, and there was an ominous air of emptiness about the place.

The door leading from the yard where she had sunbathed in the May sunshine looked securely closed, which was unusual, she realised, and there was no bread baking in the old clay oven, or any spotlessly clean washing hanging on the line.

As she came around the house, looking up at the shuttered windows, a man loading a cart called to her from a little way down the lane. He tilted his head, his weathered face sympathetic, and the expressive little gesture of his hands assured Kayla of what she dreaded most.

Oh, no!

As she wandered numbly around the side one solitary chicken ran clucking across the yard, and the sound only seemed to emphasise its screaming loneliness.

Her heart heavy with grief, Kayla got into the car, fighting back the emotion she could barely contain. But she knew she had to, because if she let it out for just a moment then she'd be swamped by it, she thought. By memories that were so much a part of this place. And Leonidas...

Her cell phone was sticking out of the bag she'd tossed onto the passenger seat, jolting her into remembering that she was supposed to try and contact him again.

Did he know? About Philomena? And then she realised that of course he would know. He would be heartbroken, she thought. In which case how could she ring him and ask him about something so trivial as a contract? She couldn't. Anyway, his office had told her that he hadn't come to Athens. And yet his London office had stated categorically that he had...

Of course!

Her gaze lifted swiftly to the hillside and the invisible ribbon of road that wound up above Lorna's villa. He would have been told about Philomena and he would have come here to be with her family. Because she was *his* family. Or the only person worth calling 'family' that Leonidas Vassalio had. In which case he would be here! Not in Athens! Here! At the farmhouse! Where else would he stay?

She didn't know if the little hatchback would stand up to the punishing drive as she tore out of the lane and took the zig-zagging road up to the familiar dirt track. She only knew she had to see him. She prayed to heaven that he would be there, and that he wouldn't send her away.

The farmhouse looked the same as she swung into the paved yard. Pale stone walls. Green peeling shutters. Its rickety terracotta roof seeming to grow out of the hillside rising sharply above it. The truck was still there too, looking as dusty and as sorry for itself as it ever had.

No one answered when she knocked at the flaking door.

Coming around the back, she noticed how baked everything looked from the hot, Ionian summer, remembering with a sharp shaft of pain how she had sat there on the terrace under that vine-covered canopy, enjoying the fish Leonidas had cooked for her the first time she had come here.

Again, there was no response to her knock, and after several attempts to make him hear she tried the doors. They were locked, just as Philomena's had been.

Everything was the same, but nothing was, she thought achingly, peering through one of the half-open shutters. Supposing he had gone? Supposing he hadn't been here at all? She couldn't bear it if he wasn't. She didn't think she'd ever find the courage to face him again.

She could see papers lying all over the kitchen table, just as there had been on that dreadful morning when she'd seduced him so shamelessly before discovering who he really was. And there was his pinboard with his plans on, propped up against the easel.

So he was immersing himself in work. Was that how he was dealing with his grief? Carrying on regardless with that formidable strength of character? That indomitable will that was such an integral part of the man she had so desperately fallen in love with?

A sound like a twig snapping behind her had her whirling round, her pulses missing a beat and then leaping into overdrive when she saw him striding up through the overgrown garden.

'What are you doing here?' He spoke in such a low whisper that she couldn't tell whether he welcomed seeing her, but his eyes were penetrating and his features were scored with shock.

'I came to check the villa. For the builder. I mean for Lorna.'

She was waffling, but she couldn't help it. Just the sight of him, in a loose-fitting, long-sleeved white shirt tucked into black denim jeans seemed to be turning her insides to mush.

He looked like the old Leon, with his chest half-bared and that thickening shadow around his mouth and chin. But his hair—only slightly longer than when she had seen him last—was still immaculately groomed, and with that air of power that Kayla could never detach from him now he was still very much Leonidas—the billionaire. He looked leaner, though, she decided, and his eyes were heavy, and she remembered in that moment that he was in mourning.

'I—I heard about Philomena.' She made a helpless little gesture. 'Just now. I went down there. I'm so…so sorry—' Tears threatened and she broke off, unable to keep the emotion out of her voice.

He merely dipped his head in acknowledgment. Perhaps he didn't trust himself to speak, Kayla thought.

'I thought you were gone. I wasn't sure if you'd even been here, and I wanted to see you. To tell you.' She was prattling on again, but she didn't know what else to say to him. He wasn't making it particularly easy for her.

As he crossed the flagstones, taking his key out of his trouser pocket, she was struck, as she always was, by the grace and litheness with which he moved, and by his sheer, uncompromising masculinity.

'Is that why you came?' He glanced over his shoulder as he stooped to unlock the door.

'Yes,' she answered, because it *was* the only reason. She would never have had the courage to seek him out over anything less.

'And who told you I was here?' He pushed open the door, gestured for her to go inside.

'No one. I just put two and two together,' she said, moving

past him with every cell responding to the aching familiarity of him beneath her flimsy feminine tunic and leggings.

'And came up with four?' He sounded impressed as he followed her in. 'What made you so sure I was in the country?'

'I'd been trying to ring you,' she admitted, and then felt like biting off her tongue. But the atmosphere of the ancient farmhouse, with its familiar rusticity and evocative scents, was so overwhelming that she hadn't stopped to think.

'Oh?' His tone demanded more as he guided her into the sitting room. It looked the same, with its jaded walls and tapestries and its faded striped throws over the easy chairs. 'What about?' He gestured for her to sit down.

'Lorna's been getting worried,' she said, subsiding onto the sofa. 'I'm sorry,' she murmured, seeing the grooves already etched around his eyes and mouth deepening. 'I didn't want to mention it. Not right now.'

'The world has to keep turning,' he said, sounding resigned. 'Do you want some coffee?'

'Something cold,' she appealed, thinking that nothing seemed so cold and detached from her as he did right then. She wondered if she should have come; wondered painfully if he was annoyed with her because she had.

He returned minutes later with two tall frosted glasses of an iced citrus drink.

'So Lorna's worried?' he reminded her as she sipped the liquid gratefully. It was sharp and very refreshing. 'What about?'

'They haven't received the contract that Havens were supposed to be supplying.'

'Supposed to be?' His eyes were darkly penetrative as he set his own glass down on a side table.

'I was just worried that…'

'Yes?'

Why was he looking at her like that? Kayla wondered. As though he wanted to plunder her very soul?

'…that you might have changed your mind. About giving them that order.'

There. She had said it. So why didn't she feel any relief? And why was he looking at her with his mouth turning down in distaste, as though she was something that had just crawled out from one of the cracks in the walls outside?

'So you still think I'd do that? You are still so shot through with doubt and suspicion over what your father and your fiancé did to you that you think every man who carries a briefcase and has a secretary can't be anything but an unscrupulous bastard?'

'That's not true!'

'Isn't it?' he shot back. 'We're a type. Isn't that what you said?'

He was standing above her, hands on hips, his legs planted firmly apart. It was such a dominant pose that her gaze faltered beneath his. With heart-quickening dismay she realised she had let it fall to somewhere below his tight lean waist—which was worse.

'Well, it's true, isn't it?' she said, hurting, feeling her body's response to his hard virility even as he stood there actively judging her. 'You lied to me about everything! Every single thing! And when I didn't like it you used my friends to blackmail me into living with you until…'

'Until what?' he pressed, relentless.

'Until you'd got what you wanted.'

'And what was that?' His eyes were shielded by the thick ebony of his lashes and his question was an almost ragged demand.

'You know very well.'

'No, I don't. I'm afraid you're going to have to spell it out for me.'

'Until you'd got me to go to bed with you.' There were flags of pink across her cheekbones, lending some colour to her pale skin beneath the summer-bleached gold of her loose hair. 'Wasn't that the whole idea of having me move in with you?' she said wretchedly. 'To salvage your pride and your ego? Wasn't it enough that you made a complete fool out of me without robbing me of my dignity and my self-respect as well?'

'Is that what I did?' His eyes as they met hers held some dark, unfathomable emotion. 'I really didn't realise that in making love with me you were sacrificing all that.'

The raw note in his voice had her searching his face with painful intensity, but his features were shuttered and unreadable.

Her fingers were icy around the glass, but she couldn't seem to feel them. She couldn't feel anything except her aching love for him and the raw agony of seeing him again when he didn't share her feelings, when he had admitted to being incapable of love—virtually ridiculing it—that night he had carried her to his bed.

'I just wasn't happy being another notch on your bedpost,' she murmured, looking down at the striped fabric covering the sofa and wondering what had happened in his life to make him so hard-bitten as she plucked absently at a loose strand of the faded weave.

'Neither was I. That was why I let you go.'

'That was very magnanimous of you.' Her throat was clogged with emotion. Pray heaven that he didn't guess just how much he had hurt her!

'Just as well I did—in the circumstances,' he said. 'I wouldn't have been able to keep my hands off you if you had stayed.'

The 'circumstances' meaning the loss of her dignity and self-respect, Kayla realised painfully, wanting to tell him that making love with him had been the most intense and pleasurable experience of her life.

'Well, you can tell Lorna that she doesn't need to worry...'

Suddenly he was talking about business, dismissing what had happened between them as easily and as ruthlessly as he had dismissed her from his life. 'That contract should have been with Kendon Interiors over two weeks ago. I'll get on to Havens right away and your friends will have it within the next forty-eight hours.'

So he hadn't been withholding it, Kayla thought. She had satisfied his requirements and he was upholding his part of the bargain. She just wished it hadn't cost her so much to make it possible. But it had. And it hurt—like hell.

'What's wrong?'

Through the crushing emotion that seemed to be weighing her down she caught his hard yet strangely husky enquiry. His eyes were narrowed, probing, digging down into her soul again, and Kayla sucked in a panicky breath as he moved closer. He'd claimed her body as his own, and she would bear the brand of his consummate lovemaking for the rest of her life, but she wasn't going to let him know that he had branded her heart as well!

'I'd better go.' She leaped up, spilling some of the juice she had scarcely touched over her clothes and over the flags. 'Oh, no…'

'I'll get you a towel.' The glass was retrieved from her shaking hand.

'I can do it myself,' she told him, her voice cracking.

'Kayla!'

There was a thread of urgency in his voice but she took no heed of it as she stumbled along to the kitchen. The pain of loving him was like a knife piercing her heart.

It would be so easy to break down. To let him see how much she cared. But if she did that then she would only be inviting more humiliation—and ultimately more pain. He would use her again, solely in the name of pleasure. And she would let him, she thought wildly, knowing she had to clean herself up

as quickly as she could and get as far away from this place—
from him—as was humanly possible.

She'd been a fool to come, she realised, grabbing several
sheets of kitchen paper from the roll that hung next to the sink
and starting to dab it hastily over her wet tunic. She should
have telephoned him. E-mailed. Anything but risk coming
here and putting herself through this. But she'd wanted to see
him. Speak to him. What kind of a first-rate fool did that make
her? She was a glutton for punishment if she'd imagined that
coming here—even if it was purely to offer him her sympathies over Philomena—would leave her unaffected and un-
scathed. And if she'd been hoping, even subconsciously, that
seeing him again might change the status quo between them,
then she'd forgotten—or was choosing to ignore—every lesson
she'd thought she had learned. For all his good points—and
there were a lot of them—he was still a ruthless businessman.
A self-confessed, hard-headed realist, who believed that love
and sentimentality were for fools.

Well, she'd leave him to his laptop and his papers and his…
Plans?

The word died from her consciousness as she swung painfully round to face them, having tossed the damp, scrunched-
up kitchen roll into the bin. The easel was angled towards the
front window, which was why she hadn't seen it when she'd
peered through the back shutters earlier. But the pinboard was
a canvas, and what she'd thought were plans was…

A full-length painting of *her!*

He had captured her as she must have looked that day coming out of the sea, wearing only her white smock-top and bikini
briefs. Her hair was blowing loose and she was looking down
at something in the water, her golden lashes accentuated with
a sensuality she had never attributed to them before. What she
was wearing was sheer, yet her body was indistinct through
the folds of virginal gossamer. It was a work of bold strokes.

Movement. But above all else of the soul. Only a man could have painted her with such intrinsic sensuality, she thought. A man who loved his subject. Who knew her inside and out...

She put her hand up as though to touch it and as quickly retracted it, her fingers curling into a tight ball which she pressed to her mouth as tears started to fall.

They had changed to racking sobs in the time it took Leonidas to cross from the doorway and reach her.

'Kayla...' The depth of her emotion tore at him and she put up no resistance as he pulled her into his arms.

She was crying for Philomena. He wasn't blind enough not to know that. She was remembering where she had come from that day and who she had been staying with...

'Oh, my darling beautiful girl, don't cry.'

He'd intended to say it in Greek, and only realised when she lifted her head and looked at him with soul-searching intensity that he had said it in English—and that it was too late.

'Why didn't you tell me?' she breathed in a shocked little whisper.

'About the painting?' His voice trembled with emotion as he used his thumb to wipe away her tears. 'Or about being in love with you?'

There. It was out now, he thought, and he would have to bear the consequences of baring his soul.

'What?' Kayla couldn't believe that she was hearing properly. 'About the painting...' She shook her head as though to clear it—uttered a little laugh through her tears. 'Both!' Was he really saying this? Hectically, her eyes searched his face.

'Why do you think I wanted you with me?' he uttered deeply, on a shuddering note, hardly daring to believe that she wasn't ridiculing him.

'To salvage your pride.' Pain lined her forehead as she remembered that last morning. 'You said so yourself.'

'Well, there was a bit of that, I'll admit.' He pulled a self-deprecating face. 'But mainly it was because I wanted to get you to trust me again. There was no other way I could think of that would break through the barriers you'd erected against me—and not just because I hadn't been straight with you in the beginning, but because you believed I was the type of man who had hurt you so badly before—the type you so clearly despised. I was hoping you would look beyond the outer shell and see that I was different from those other men you'd known. Yet I only compounded my mistakes by browbeating you into staying with me. I would never have gone back on my word over that contract. But when I realised that you really believed I was manipulative enough to be using your friends to get to you—was actually capable of destroying everything they had if you didn't do exactly what I wanted—I guess it was more than a crushing blow to my pride. I decided I didn't have anything to lose. I needed to earn your respect. That's why I wanted to take things slowly for a while and not complicate matters by taking you to bed, though it was torture having to exercise enough restraint not to do so. When we did make love and you cried I knew it was because your heart didn't want it, even though physically you couldn't resist this thing we have between us any more than I could.'

'That isn't true,' Kayla denied emphatically, knowing she had to tell him now. 'I was crying because I love you—because the whole experience for me had been so…so amazingly incredible. And because I knew—thought—you didn't feel anything for me and that sooner or later you'd want me to go. And you did,' she reminded him, with all the agony of the past few weeks rising up to torment her again. 'Why? If you feel the same way I do?'

'Because I didn't fully realise it—or want to acknowledge it—until after you'd gone,' he admitted, his chest lifting heavily, 'and I didn't want to hurt you any more than I knew I already had.'

'And all the time you've been doing this…' She pulled back from him slightly to gaze awestruck at the painting. 'Wow! Do I really look like that?'

'You'd better believe it,' he said, with a sexy sidelong grin.

'It's brilliant. You're a genius,' she praised, and he laughed. 'No, I'm serious,' she breathed, meaning it. She couldn't understand why, with so much talent, he hadn't made art his career.

He made a self-deprecating sound down his nostrils when she asked him. 'There were reasons,' he divulged almost brokenly.

'What reasons?' she pressed gently, realising that it was stirring up some deeply buried pain for him to talk about it.

'My father had other ideas for me,' he said. 'He wouldn't countenance having a son who painted for a living. He thought it less than manly. We argued about it—and never stopped arguing about it.' And now he had started pouring out his most agonising secret he couldn't stop. 'We were arguing about it in the car the night my mother died. If I hadn't been determined to oppose his will he wouldn't have kept turning round to shout at me and we would never have had the accident that killed her. I wouldn't let up when I knew I should have, and it was my mother who ultimately paid the price. After that even the thought of painting was abominable to me. How could it be anything else?' he suggested, his strong features ravaged by the pain he had carried all these years. 'Knowing that she'd died because of it. Because of *me!*'

'You didn't kill her!' Kayla exhaled, understanding now what devils had been driving him all his life to make him so hard-headed and single-mindedly determined—understanding a lot of things now. 'You were—what? Fourteen? Fifteen? Barely more than a child! Your father was the driver. He was also an adult. It was up to him to exercise restraint until he'd stopped the car.'

'My father didn't see it like that,' he relayed. Yet for the first time he found himself taking some solace from the tender arms that went around him, from the gentle yet determined reasoning in her words.

Art was feeling and feelings were weakness. His father had indoctrinated that into him. But the feelings he had for this beautiful woman—which were being unbelievably reciprocated—made him feel stronger than he had ever felt in his life.

'This house…it's yours, isn't it?' Kayla murmured, with her head against his shoulder. 'This is where you lived when you were a boy.'

Locked in his arms, she felt the briefest movement of his strong body as he nodded. 'It was the first time I'd been able to bring myself back here since my father died last year. The first time I'd been back—apart from visits to Philomena—in over fifteen years.'

His voice cracked as he mentioned the grandmother figure who had filled the void when he had been left motherless and without the nucleus of a loving family. Understanding, Kayla held him closer. Hadn't she lost a grandmother too?

'I love you,' she whispered. It was the only thing it felt right to say just then.

He smiled down at her and her heart missed a beat when she recognised the sultry, satisfied response of the man she had fallen in love with. 'I love you too—very much, *psihi mou*. We may not have got off to a very good start, but knowing you has made me see that there are more important things in life than everything I've been pursuing. Oh, money and position are wonderful to have, but they're nothing without the most precious things in life—like a caring partner and a family. Without love,' he murmured against her lips, acknowledging it indisputably now. 'Do you think you would find it too much of a punishment to marry a company man with a briefcase and a secretary—who, incidentally, is fifty-three years

old and worth her weight in gold? A man who—also incidentally—*does* own an island and builds eyesores for a living?
Though not literally. He leaves the spade and shovel work to
his minions nowadays.'

He was joking about the minions. She could hear it in his
voice. But she couldn't believe he was actually asking her to
be his wife.

'Of course if you don't want to…' He was looking so uncertain, so vulnerable, that she reached up and brought his
head down to hers.

'Leonidas Vassalio, of course I'll marry you,' she whispered smilingly, before she kissed him and felt the surge of
power that trembled through his body as he caught her to
him. 'Leon…'

That's better, his eyes said approvingly when he lifted his
head, and the gleam in their dark depths promised everything
that was joyous and exciting. 'And now…' suddenly he was
sweeping her up into his arms '…I believe we have some unfinished business upstairs.'

Much later, after he'd gone to make some coffee, Kayla was
surprised when he returned almost immediately.

'Your cell phone is bleeping,' he told her, handing over
her bag, and she was alarmed to see the display on her phone
showing half a dozen missed calls—all from Josh.

'Lorna's in hospital,' she told Leonidas when she'd finished speaking to her friend's husband. 'She was rushed in
for a Caesarean section this afternoon but everything's OK.'
She was laughing and crying as she added, 'Both mother and
daughter are doing well!'

'Thank heaven for that!' he expressed, with his hand against
his robed chest, looking as thrilled and almost as relieved as
Kayla felt. 'This means we have to get a move on if we want
to catch up with Josh and Lorna—particularly if you're going

to fill my island with dogs and horses and babies, Mrs Vassalio. It's in the Bahamas, by the way. And at this exact moment I can't do too much to fulfil your dreams with the first two things on your wish-list, but I can certainly do something right now about fulfilling the last!'

Later, lying in his arms, Kayla stirred and stretched contentedly.

He's a good man, Philomena had tried to tell her, and Kayla knew that now. She also knew that as men came—company or otherwise—they didn't come any better.

* * * * *

A sneaky peek at next month...

MODERN™

INTERNATIONAL AFFAIRS, SEDUCTION & PASSION GUARANTEED

My wish list for next month's titles...

In stores from 21st June 2013:

☐ His Most Exquisite Conquest – Emma Darcy
☐ His Brand of Passion – Kate Hewitt
☐ The Couple who Fooled the World – Maisey Yates
☐ Proof of Their Sin – Dani Collins
☐ In Petrakis's Power – Maggie Cox

In stores from 5th July 2013:

☐ One Night Heir – Lucy Monroe
☐ The Return of Her Past – Lindsay Armstrong
☐ Gilded Secrets – Maureen Child
☐ Once is Never Enough – Mira Lyn Kelly

Available at WHSmith, Tesco, Asda, Eason, Amazon and Apple

Just can't wait?

0613/01

Join the Mills & Boon Book Club

Want to read more **Modern**™ books?
We're offering you **2 more** absolutely **FREE!**

We'll also treat you to these fabulous extras:

- **Exclusive offers and much more!**

- **FREE home delivery**

- **FREE books and gifts with our special rewards scheme**

Get your free books now!

visit **www.millsandboon.co.uk/bookclub**
or call Customer Relations on **020 8288 2888**

FREE BOOK OFFER TERMS & CONDITIONS
Accepting your free books places you under no obligation to buy anything and you may cancel at any time. If we do not hear from you we will send you 4 stories a month which you may purchase or return to us—the choice is yours. Offer valid in the UK only and is not available to current Mills & Boon subscribers to this series. We reserve the right to refuse an application and applicants must be aged 18 years or over. Only one application per household. Terms and prices are subject to change without notice. As a result of this application you may receive further offers from other carefully selected companies. If you do not wish to share in this opportunity please write to the Data Manager at PO BOX 676, Richmond, TW9 1WU.

The World of Mills & Boon®

There's a Mills & Boon® series that's perfect for you. We publish ten series and, with new titles every month, you never have to wait long for your favourite to come along.

Blaze®
Scorching hot, sexy reads
4 new stories every month

By Request
Relive the romance with the best of the best
9 new stories every month

Cherish™
Romance to melt the heart every time
12 new stories every month

Desire™
Passionate and dramatic love stories
8 new stories every month